RISING
STØRM

THE
RISING
STORM

CERI A. LOWE

bookouture

Published by Bookouture in 2018

Previously published in 2014 as *Paradigm*

An imprint of StoryFire Ltd.

Carmelite House
50 Victoria Embankment
London EC4Y 0DZ

www.bookouture.com

ISBN: 978-1-78681-460-9
eBook ISBN: 978-1-78681-459-3

Prologue

Carter

Present Day

'You have five minutes of this life left.'

As the words that came through the speaker finished, a wretched wailing sound broke out from the cell next door. Carter focused on breathing deeply and tried to ignore the awful noise. If *he* could keep himself together, then surely the old-timers should be able to manage it. It just confirmed everything they said about anyone over the age of thirty.

The screaming started again, up and down like a Storm Siren. Carter sat on the fold-down bed and pushed his back against the hard, cold wall, waiting as the screams diminished to sobs, concentrating on counting down in time with the clock, in a mixture of excitement and anticipation. He would be brave; he would make his parents and his professor proud. He would be the best leader the Industry could ever imagine. He would change everything, like he'd promised.

The voice came again: 'Four minutes remaining.'

There was the occasional thump of a fist against the wall of the chamber next door and then the sound of crying from somewhere else, further down into the Catacombs. But otherwise, there was silence. He hugged his knees to his chest, the hairs on his arms prickling. A sliver of concern worked its way up his spine. This was the start of the most important journey of his life. He pushed all thoughts of Isabella from his mind and waited.

The process of travelling down into the depths of the Catacombs had taken longer than he'd expected, and thinking back he realised he couldn't really remember all of it. The drugs he'd been given when they'd come to collect him that morning had begun to blur his memory straight away.

As the group of men, women and children had walked across Unity Square, the sun was just an arc of beautiful red in the distance. But when they reached the entrance to the Catacombs, one of the men begun to sob loudly behind him.

'Shut up,' Carter whispered. 'They'll hear you.'

'I miss my wife,' the man choked, 'and my daughter.'

Carter looked at him with pity; he was a wreck.

'What's your name?' he quietly asked.

'Pablo,' the man replied, sniffling.

'Well, Pablo,' Carter said, calmly, 'you had five years with them and those are the rules.'

'But it's not enough,' Pablo cried. 'I want my little girl.'

Having a child – or even one confirmed to be on the way – allowed you at least five years above ground for a first child, sometimes more. Five years was the minimum mandated time together as a family. But the older you got, the harder it was. And now it was his turn to contribute to society. Although it would be hardly surprising if old

Pablo were never woken up; at somewhere in his early forties, he would struggle to readjust. Carter had seen it happen before, many times.

'They'll be fine,' Carter told him, not meeting the man's eyes. 'And they'll be waiting for you up top like nothing ever happened. They're your family, right? And you'll be back before you know it.'

'What if I never get woken up?'

Carter patted his arm. 'Of course you will,' he said, with strong reassurance. 'And they'll be right there when you come back.'

Pablo nodded miserably and fell silent. Carter reminded himself that once the needle went into his arm, even the biggest of lies could be forgotten underground – especially for someone like Pablo. But at least, for now, he was quiet. And every second that passed was one second closer to Carter becoming Controller General. He moved away from the group and pushed his way ahead to the front.

Until they reached the core of the Industry Headquarters, the journey was dim and quiet. The long line of those who had been selected trudged through the electronic walkways and tunnels down into the depths of the Catacombs on the traditional last walk. It had been that way ever since the early days. As the covered paths became wider and opened out into the last of the long, straight stretches of underground passage, the guards stopped and a door in the wall, placed slightly higher than the level of the tunnel, slid open. A young man with black eyes stepped out onto a dark ledge in front of them and addressed the group.

Carter knew who it was straight away – the current Controller General, Bobbie Alderney. Alderney only had a couple of years of his tenure as the leader of the Community remaining.

'I won't keep you long,' he said coolly, 'but I wanted to thank you for your co-operation today. As you know, making yourselves available for use in the future is both an honour and a duty. The Industry thanks each and every one of you.'

From halfway down the line, Pablo sniffed loudly. Carter shot him a warning glance, but it was too late.

'Controller General,' Pablo called out, 'I'd like to make a request.' The line fell silent and Alderney snapped his neck to look in the man's direction.

'And what,' he asked slowly, 'might that be?'

'I'd like to go back, Controller,' Pablo replied. 'I have a family.'

There was a ripple of anger and disbelief through the crowd. Alderney watched with a curled smile on his face.

'That's against the rules,' a woman at the back shouted angrily.

'What makes you so special?' spat another.

'You're a disgrace.'

Pablo looked distraught. 'I don't belong here,' he said. 'I belong up there with my daughter.'

There was a surge of jostling and pushing as people at the back made their way to the front to see what was happening. A grumbling rose from the crowd. Alderney was still silent, observing the group. Carter watched as his eyes flicked from one individual to another and then back to Pablo.

'Please,' begged Pablo. 'I'm just one man – there are plenty more here. Just one won't make any difference.'

'One man can make all the difference,' said Carter, hauling himself up onto the ledge next to Alderney. He glanced across at the Controller General, who tightened his lips and nodded for him to proceed.

'Pablo,' Carter continued, 'what's the most important thing in your world?

'My family,' said Pablo, irritated. 'That's obvious.'

'Is it?' said Carter. 'You're not acting that way. What happens to the family of a dissenter?'

'I'm not a dissenter; I just want to be with them.'

Carter looked at Alderney and then back at Pablo. 'But if you refuse to be frozen, you *are* a dissenter,' he said. 'Look at these people – all dedicating their lives, like so many others have before them. You're saying to them that they don't matter, that you're more important than them and their families. Do you see that?'

Pablo shook his head. 'I'm just one person,' he said earnestly. 'It won't make any difference.'

'But it will,' said Carter. 'It will make all the difference. Do you see that you need to be brave now, that you need to make your family proud? It's what we all have to do.' Carter's tone was firm, almost threatening. He could feel his heart pounding.

There were nods from the crowd and Pablo opened his mouth to speak, before closing it again.

'I'm sorry,' he said. The crowd turned away from him and the grumbling slowly died down.

'Walk on,' said Alderney and nodded at Carter. 'Good work, Warren,' he continued. 'All I've heard about you must be true. You saved that man's life there.'

And with that, he folded himself back into the door and disappeared.

After that, few people spoke until they reached their cells, exhausted. Pablo kept his head firmly fixed on the floor and held his own hands tightly together.

'It will be OK,' whispered Carter. And then nothing more was said.

'Three minutes remaining.'

The liquid light in the chamber turned to a clock and began to count down. Carter watched the soft rhythm of the numbers as their calmness slowed his heartbeat to a steady pulse. The chamber was perfectly square and there was little furniture – just the light, a squat table and the raised bed he was sat on, attached to the wall. It was perfect.

The voice sounded through the speaker.

'Your time has now ended. Please remove your clothes and place them on the floor. Put on your sleep case. Your duration in the Catacombs will begin in exactly one minute. The Industry thanks you for your immediate co-operation.'

There was a desperate whimper and then a thump on the wall from the chamber next door. Carter squeezed himself into the sleep case and lay on the bed with fifteen seconds to go. It was icy cold and he shivered. His assistant appeared as the clock turned over to zero.

'Carter Fordham Warren. Fifteen years and thirty-five days old. No viruses or contaminations. Certified capable to breed. Vital organs guaranteed for donation—' she ticked a form on her slate and smiled '—should anything go wrong.'

Carter smiled back at her nervously as she kept talking.

'Sign here please, Carter Warren, and we'll see you some time in the next twenty years. The exact time will, of course, depend on when the Model decides that you are needed again.'

He tweaked a smile. 'Any chance you can be a bit more precise?'

'Nothing is ever guaranteed,' she said, searching his forearm for a vein. When she found it she stopped, the needle lingering over his skin before she pierced his skin. 'One other thing,' she whispered, her face gleaming. 'I hear there's a chance you're going to become a father. We need to get conclusive tests done, but they believe there's a real chance!'

Carter's mouth dropped open but no words came out. They knew already. If the Industry found out that there was a chance of him being a father, they would send him back. It would mean being above ground for five years to take care of it, and definitely giving up his chance at becoming Controller General. No one with young children had ever been allowed to be Controller General. It was against the rules. He tried to speak again but the injection had already started to take effect.

'If it turns out to be true, then Mendoza's plan has worked,' said his assistant, trying to contain her excitement, 'and with only one attempt too.' She spoke gently. 'When you come back you'll have the best chance to be Controller General, Carter. Even better than before.'

The assistant continued with her work and whispered in his ear. 'Go to sleep now, we'll see you in a few years. Sweet dreams.'

Carter desperately tried to force words out, but the serum was too powerful. He blinked helplessly at her.

'Sssh…' said the assistant, calmly. 'Don't worry, I won't tell anyone. It will be our secret.'

As his eyes closed, the anaesthetic coursed into his bloodstream and the numbness spread slowly through his body.

When he opened his eyes again she was there, in front of him. Not the assistant, but the girl from the ceremony the night before. He remembered what the assistant had said and he tried to sit up. The girl stood still, her head down.

'Why aren't they sending you back to me?' she asked, sullenly. 'They told me we'd get married and have a baby.'

'I can't,' Carter tried to say, but realised the words were just inside his head. He tried again, desperate to add: 'I don't want to come back yet, I can't…' There was a fizzing noise and the girl disappeared.

Carter's assistant zipped up the sleep case and nodded to the security porter standing in the doorway.

'He's under,' she said. 'Move him to the shelves.'

And with that there was darkness, and he could feel and hear nothing more.

When the shrill, ugly alarm sounded fifteen years later, Carter was still numb. He tried to move, but nothing worked. In the darkness he began to count and, although he thought he had reached one thousand, he wasn't sure where he had started from. Slowly, he blinked his eyes and, almost without realising it, he was fully awake. Then the voice came again.

'Your time has now come to leave. Your clothes and a brief cleansing will be provided. An assistant will be with you shortly.'

Other than squirt a hose directly into his mouth and then all over his body, the assistant did very little assisting. His clothes – the ones he had been wearing when he had entered the chamber fifteen years before – were wrapped in a waterproof packet on the same low table that had been in the room previously. The only thing that was different was the assistant. She handed him a pill and a glass of thick syrupy liquid.

'Drink it,' she instructed.

Carter knocked back the glass.

'I'm back already? What year is it? The assistant before said that I…' Carter's first words were stilted and came out in a choked, gruff growl punctuated by coughs. But the relief to be awake and alive was overwhelming.

The assistant ignored him.

'You have five minutes to prepare before you permanently leave this accommodation. Please ensure you are dressed and ready to go. The Industry thanks you for your co-operation.'

As the words ended, the bed snapped back against the wall, throwing Carter onto the floor. The numbers of the electronic clock began to count down. Hoses in the ceiling came on automatically and showered him again, before blasting hot air, which dried him almost instantly. Exhausted, he'd just managed to slide into his trousers when the clock reached zero. His assistant handed him his personal information card and a sick bag, then ushered him out into the long hallway.

Boxy chambers ran the length of the corridor on both sides and all the doors were open. He remembered it like it was yesterday. For him, it almost was. The floor, a thick black conveyor belt, wobbled ever so slightly as Carter stepped out onto it. The man in the chamber opposite still had his trousers around his ankles when the final alarm sounded and he moved onto the belt.

Carter tried to act normal. As normally as he could for someone who had been woken up after fifteen years of cryonic sleep with no idea whether Mendoza's plan for his return had really worked.

The floor shook for a second; the assistants stepped back into the rooms and then a belt carried the rest of them off towards the Control Room. The man from the chamber opposite who hadn't managed to dress himself properly was drenched in a slime that could have come from himself or the girl next to him who was also being sick at each gap in the conversation.

'Different to the way down, eh, kid?' said the man, smiling weakly, before quickly reaching for his chuck bag. The girl nodded and looked away. Her tunic was on back to front and her hair was matted. Carter turned away from them in an attempt to separate himself, but he could still hear their chatter.

'How long have we been here?' the girl asked.

The man with his trousers in his hand looked embarrassed and confused.

'No idea.' He shrugged. 'Different for all of us, isn't it?' There was the sound of retching and the chug-chug of the travelator. At least there was no screaming on the way back up.

'I had an escapee on my downward,' the girl was saying to the man who seemed to be interested.

'Yeah?' he said. 'He got back in line though, right? Nobody would be that stupid.'

The girl nodded.

'Of course.' She wiped her mouth with her sleeve. 'He got pretty far – almost back to the lifts. I don't see him here though. He's probably…'

Her voice trailed off as the travellator jerked forwards slowly, past a service area carved into the rock wall. There was a bin for old bags and a rack with fresh ones and some towels. Carter squared up his empty chuck bag and dropped it into the trench without it touching the sides.

'It wouldn't have mattered anyway. Lifts only go one way on that side of the Catacombs,' said Carter. 'Everyone gets caught.'

He remembered watching a couple of the older children attempting to walk backwards against the flow of traffic and how skilfully they were redirected back into line by the security officers. One boy had cried noiselessly, tears streaming down his face in rivulets smudged with a dirty sleeve as he wiped them away. Others had skipped ahead, weaving in between the legs of the adults. Carter was thankful when he'd finally been pushed into a chamber on his own, away from everyone else. Especially Pablo, crying for his wife and daughter.

'Good system,' said the girl. 'You can't have people deciding it's not their time. Nothing would work if we were all allowed to just run around, doing what we wanted. It would be like the old days.'

'Yeah,' said the man, looking around at the cameras overhead. He'd managed to put his clothes on during the conversation. 'And who wants that?' Then they both laughed weakly and the girl attempted to pull back her matted hair into a ponytail.

The travelators took them to the edges of a round room with a stage in the centre where the current Controller General stood, speaking through an amplifier.

Her hair was thin and wavy, the colour of tree bark, and her eyes were bright blue and sharp. She didn't look familiar – and she didn't look happy. She looked older than she should be – perhaps even over thirty, although that would be against the rules. Carter could not imagine that it would be too long before the Contendership for her post would begin and that made him excited. He wondered how long it had been since Alderney had gone. There were more people in the gathering crowd than he'd imagined there would be. He looked around for anyone who might be like him, in line for the job. The woman addressed the crowd.

'Good evening. Many of you will have been underground for the duration of my tenure so far, so let me introduce myself. My name is Anaya Chess and I am the Controller General. You will each have received your cards from the assistant on duty in your chamber. Anyone who has not received their card should raise their hand now.'

'Don't feel quite right,' whispered the pale girl with ratty hair to no one in particular. She sat herself on the ground and everyone around ignored her. She lay there for a while as the crowd milled past her and then she stood again weakly, wobbling from side to side.

Carter edged in front of her to get a better view of Chess as she spoke again. This time, even the girl looked up.

'As Controller General, I am responsible for ensuring that you all make your way back to the Community safely. Firstly, for those of you still feeling a little unwell, please be assured that this is completely normal. Your bodies will need time to adjust and some of you will still be feeling the side effects of the fluids we have been using to keep you safe. This will all wear off in a few days' time. Remember, each of you has been in a suspended state for between five and twenty years and, your muscles have been chemically maintained, so it will take some time, up to a week, to feel fully refreshed.

'Secondly, between now and then you may find you have some temporary loss of memory or feel different to the way you did before you came here. You may even experience short blackouts. That, also, is completely normal and will pass within a few days.

'Finally, you are re-entering our Community at a very special time. Since you have been away, some things have changed – you will discover these for yourselves when you make your way back. We are in a time of—' she stumbled over the word '—*exciting* transition, and amongst you this evening are the Contenders for the position of Controller General when I—' she faltered again '—step down from the position very soon.'

The crowd rearranged themselves and Carter felt his palms grow clammy. So the Contenders were here, in this room – that meant, almost certainly, that he was one of them. He looked around at the mass of faces as Chess continued.

'The announcements will be made shortly, but until then, may I be the first to say welcome back to you all. As you know, since the Storms, we have had to work hard together to ensure that we have a steady supply of people with the right skills to stabilise our environment. The small sacrifice most of us have to make at some point in our lives is what ensures our survival. You are all, in your own way, our heroes.'

There was a weak cheer from the crowd and Carter could see that two or three other people around him were now sitting down on the floor. One girl stood facing the front, eyes glued on Chess. Carter picked her out straight away – she was bound to be one of the Contenders; she looked alert, different to the others somehow. Anaya Chess allowed the applause to die down before continuing.

'Your card contains all the information you need about your new homes, families and places of work. And, of course, it has retained information from the time before you came here, including qualifications and personal data.'

A man at the front raised his hand.

'I had two children,' he said. 'Can you tell me where they are? Are they here or…?'

Chess turned to him, her voice calm and cool.

'I cannot answer any questions with regards to your individual circumstances. And, as you know, things and people move on. If your previous family are still alive, well, it's likely they will have made their own choices. Any information you need will be on your personal card. Swipe it at any FreeScreen and you will receive all the updates that you need.'

The man looked no more assured than when he had asked the question. He raised his hand with a follow-up but Anaya Chess ignored him. Carter watched as a guard infiltrated the crowd and beckoned the man to one side.

'As I was saying,' Chess continued, 'for those of you who have not already had the opportunity to do so, please scan your cards on any of the FreeScreen terminals around the edges of the room. There are four Transporters due to leave in the next fifteen minutes. Please exit through the tunnel that has the same colour as your card; this will ensure you take the Transporter with the drop-off point closest to your designated area of the Community. You will notice that there has been some expansion since you were here last.' She smiled – a smile that, to Carter, didn't carry the assurance he thought it should. Chess nodded to the crowd. 'The Industry thanks you for your co-operation. Welcome to your new lives.'

Those who had positioned themselves on the floor got up and others wandered over to the terminals in the walls. There were four tunnels, each leading out in a different direction: blue, red, yellow, green. Carter headed for the blue tunnel, quickly followed by around a hundred others. They jostled around at the terminals, muttering to themselves as they made their way out. As Carter leaned over to scan his card, a scrawny, smiley boy stepped aside to let him through.

'After you,' said the boy, who couldn't have been more than nine or ten. When he saw it was Carter, there was a flicker of recognition between them. Harrison Reynolds had lived three doors down from Carter as they were growing up and at one time, they'd been in the same year at the Academy – until Harrison had been selected for the Young Freezers Programme. Carter remembered because it had been less than six months after his own parents had been killed. It was rumoured that Harrison's father had died a few months later. There had been a lot of bad luck in the West Quarter that year.

'Harrison?' said Carter, but the boy was already turning to queue for another terminal. The last time he had seen the boy had been topside when the latest Freeze lists had been announced. Harrison had taken the news of entering the Young Freezers Programme with jubilation, running circles around Unity Square. Back then, Harrison had been the taller of the two.

Carter watched as the small boy looked at the screen and then sped off down an opposite tunnel. As the crowds swelled forward, Carter didn't bother scanning his card; he knew already where he was going – the West Quarter. The address had been printed on the wrapper of his clothes and on the inside of the paper bag, where he was guaranteed to see it. Clever, he thought – as long as you saw it before you threw up. The Industry at its best.

As they filed through into the blue tunnel, the juddering floor began to move beneath them, swirling them onwards. One boy of about twelve carried another, much younger, on his back. The younger one was howling for his mother who, from what Carter could make out, had died in the twenty years the boy had been underground. The same voice of the Controller played warnings and announcements, although this time her voice was recorded, and sounded younger and more sure of herself.

'Handrails are provided for your safety. Please do not push your fellow returners. Transporters will not leave until every returner has exited the building. Please scan all information cards as you leave. Handrails are provided for your safety. Please do not push your fellow returners…'

The voice reverberated around inside his head until Carter found himself reciting the words along with at least half of the others standing around him. He shook his head at himself and started reciting chemical formulae instead.

The moving corridor funnelled out into a series of platforms, each with a full-length Transporter waiting as crowds piled into the carriages.

Carter held back until everyone else had boarded and then slipped between the doors before they clipped shut. He pressed himself against the smooth wall while the engines started up, feeling the soft growl of machinery as the Transporter started at a slow glide. Across the carriage, he caught a glimpse of Harrison Reynolds, holding the hand of the smaller boy who had lost a parent in the years underground, and for a second his chest hurt. He smiled at them both but they ignored him, already wrapped up in each other's grief.

Within seconds and without warning, the speed of the Transporter accelerated, swaying the passengers across the carriage, and Carter grabbed onto a support rail above his head. There was a slithering sound that rose to a growl and then, together, the group of returners made their thundering way through the maze of underground Industry tunnels and up and out into the world above ground, a world that Carter, aged fifteen years and thirty-six days, had not seen in a long, long time.

Chapter One

The Storms

Alice

90 years earlier

On the day the Storms started, Alice Davenport watched the collapse of her world from nine floors above the city, through her living room window. She had stayed home from school because she was sick. Or at least that was what she decided she would tell her mother – but as a general rule, her mother didn't bother to ask much. Not since it had been just the two of them.

The real reason Alice stayed at home was Jake Anderson. In the last school it had been Ricky Thornton mocking Alice – about how her teeth stuck out and how her skinny, pale-brown arms were as thin as twigs.

Before Ricky, there had been a James, and before him, a Zak – each with their own particular flavour of unkindness.

In this version, Jake was making fun of Alice's mother, which was more difficult to deal with. He ridiculed her cheap, tatty clothes and the way she left a distinct smell of wine in the air when she staggered through the streets in the early morning sunlight as he was doing his paper round. Jake Anderson was a boy to be believed – because Jake had been in the depths of the city with his parents during Hurricane Alison, when Tower Bridge had fallen. His parents had been crushed but he had survived. His teasing got worse after that.

By the time Jake had started needling her about her mother, Alice Davenport was fed up of the pattern. There was always a 'Jake'. And the worst part was that there was always some truth to their cruelty.

On the morning that the Storms started, Alice's mother had wandered into the flat just after 5.30 a.m. – and fifteen minutes later was asleep, mouth open and eyes shut on the sagging mattress next to Alice. Outside, the gulls squawked with their bleak, morning calls. Alice thought her mother looked peaceful as she slept; the tough lines on her face had relaxed and she looked younger, though never as young as before.

It was the familiar click and close of the front door and the padding of her mother's footsteps on the old stairs that had woken her. Still half in the clutches of a dream, Alice had curled up tight inside the sleeping bag on the mattress and waited. Like most mornings, her mother had stumbled into her room, lifted up the mattress and stuffed a ball of notes underneath. Then, as always, her mother had settled herself down on the mattress next to Alice and passed out.

Her mother's wet, slicked-back hair leaked thin beads of water across Alice's side of the pillow, the fronds of her fringe like curled-up water snakes. Alice pulled herself further down the pillow, away from the dampness until she was alongside her mother's belly. It was an ugly, grey colour, different to her face that was always smeared with fake tan and pink blusher accompanied by a ribbon of red lipstick. The gash of pillar-box was still there, even now, smudged a little at the corners but wildly bright against the drabness of the mattress, slung on the floor in the corner of the dingy hole they both called a bedroom.

The bedroom was one of two in the apartment stacked neatly on the top floor of a block of flats, ten layers high above the city. The wallpaper was old and peeled off the walls in places revealing layers of different-coloured patterns, like the skins of a decaying onion. It was a medium-sized authority-owned flat, set over two floors with a tiny staircase inside that wound upwards to the two bedrooms and a green porcelain bathroom that always smelled of cheap bleach.

Alice and her mother slept in the room with the door that hung lazily off the hinges. Not like the door to the spare bedroom – the only room with a bed – that was always closed tight.

'You mustn't ever go in there,' her mother had said soon after they had moved in. 'Not ever.'

'Why can't it be my bedroom?'

'Because it's a bad room. And even when I'm in there, you can't even be outside the door. Do you hear me?'

Alice heard her – she never went in there and neither of them used the bed to sleep in. Each night, they stayed on the mattress together. When her mother finally got in from work, that was.

Whenever anyone came up to the bedrooms, the staircase creaked. And that was often. On the wall there was a crinkled map of the globe. It had once hung inside a crystal glass frame in her father's study in the days before, but now it had to make do with a rusty nail in each corner, pegging it in place. Alice had put it there herself when she and her mother had first moved in, balancing precariously on a chair with a claw hammer in one hand and a scratch of rusty pin tacks in the other. The glass frame that had protected it was long gone. It had been destroyed, like many other things, in the move to the city. On the evenings when her mother left her alone, Alice would sit on the stairs and look at the map, thinking about the different countries she wanted to visit when she was older. She imagined the crimson and yellow sunsets of Africa and the peanut- and saffron-infused scents of the Far East, and beaches where they would dance in the ice-blue waves of Thai oceans, teaching multi-coloured birds to talk.

When the realisation had sunk in that these dreams would never come true, Alice instead had started to spend her evenings climbing another set of stairs, these ones made of ugly metal that led sharply upwards to the roof of Prospect House. In the twilight, before the teenagers gathered there, she would look out across the flatness of the city that spread out for miles beneath her like a mechanical meadow filled with insects. If there was no work, her mother would sometimes join her there.

'This place is only a stop gap,' she had said as they'd gazed across the spires and towers in the first week that they'd moved in. She'd lit a cigarette and the smoke had lingered across the horizon. 'Don't worry – we'll be out of here soon. We just have to save some money and we'll be gone. We'll be where we are supposed to be.'

'Where are we supposed to be?' Alice had asked.

'I don't know yet,' her mother had replied, her voice sounding weary.

'But why do we have to stay here?' Alice had asked. 'Why couldn't we just stay in our old house?' Alice's mother had bit her lip so hard that a tiny drop of blood had leaked from the corner of her mouth. 'Because sometimes things have to get worse before they get better,' she'd answered, and sucked at the trail of blood on her lip. And there'd been nothing much else to say after that.

As much as Alice hated their new home, there were days that were brighter than others. Sometimes she would stand on her balcony at the back of the flat, watching the pigeons dive at the fragments of stale bread that she dropped from a bag in the evening sunlight. She wondered who would feed them if she wasn't there and decided that probably nobody would. It was her duty.

Other times, Alice would peak on tiptoe across at Mr Hutchinson, the next-door neighbour, who would always stand on his back balcony smoking a pipe. She watched as he drew in hard on his pipe and sucked big lungfuls of smoke inwards, only to heave them out in dirty great 'O's across the city. Once he'd caught her looking, but he'd just smiled and kept hacking out the big puffy circles that floated out over the balcony. Alice watched until they disappeared into the nothingness of the clouds and sometimes she imagined she was bound up in the smoke rings and floating high above everything else, even higher than the flats. Watching the smoke was one of the things Alice loved most.

On the day the Storms started, there was a lot of smoke – but Alice saw none of it. That morning, as her mother curled into a ball of sleep next to her, Alice heard the first echoes of rain on the window; they were only slightly louder than the grumbling in her stomach. She stretched, got herself out of bed, and headed towards the kitchen. The flat was cold with patches of dampness flowering in the corners, and the cupboards were empty except for some stale biscuits. She stuffed them into her mouth and washed them down with a glass of pale orange squash. A white sun eked through the gap in the curtains and threw a sliver of light onto the carpet, barely reaching in from the balcony outside.

While her mother was still dozing, Alice wormed her hand underneath the mattress and felt for the wad of notes, a little tacky to the touch. She drew them out carefully and stuffed them into her pocket. On good days when she could sneak some cash from underneath the mattress, Alice would buy herself a hot dog from the man who stood outside the tube station. But if her mother was still at work when she left for school, Alice took the longer route through Frederick Street market and picked up whatever she could while the stallholders were distracted. She knew the scarves that Jade at school liked – Jade's mother always packed pastries for lunch. And Harry's father ran a crisp factory so sometimes he would pass Alice a few bags of salt and vinegar if she could lift the football stickers he collected.

'I'll go shopping later on,' her mother groaned from the floor as Alice was leaving.

'I'm hungry now,' said Alice under her breath and slipped on a T-shirt before tiptoeing down the stairs and out of the front door. Shivering in the cold, she felt the world slide sideways and rock her back and forth like a golf ball on a ship deck. Bright lights dazzled her eyes as she made her way towards the lifts. Everything smelled of rotting fruit, even the cold, wet air. Alice was beginning to think that maybe she really was ill after all.

Usually she enjoyed hanging over the edges of the balcony, picking at the peeling paint and watching the city, but that morning the swirl of the wind and pattering of the rain made her feel sick. Something just did not feel quite right.

Inside the supermarket shop at the bottom of the plaza that folded into the shadow of Prospect House, Mr Shah was packing things into boxes. He looked her up and down suspiciously. Alice held up the wad of cash and he smiled.

'You shouldn't be out on your own,' he scolded her. 'The riots have started again and police are shooting. People are shooting people.

Shooting just for standing on the street, can you believe it? I am closing up tonight. No more Shah's Market. We're going back up North. Back to where people are not mad as bats. London is for fools. You should stay inside or else the police will get you and that mother of yours. Scoop you up like sh—' Shah's words seemed to hit Alice like a round of bullets, short and painful, before he noticed her shivering.

'I just need some food,' said Alice in a whisper. 'I don't care about the police.'

'You look cold,' he said. 'You should have put a jumper on – it's very cold outside today. Cold. Cold. And the rains are coming. There's another hurricane on the way. This one's going to be bigger than Hurricane Alison, you know.'

Alice grabbed a small trolley and started throwing cans into the basket. Tomatoes, tinned meat, dried goods – things for a storm. Cheap things. Things she could reheat. She looked at her arms, covered in goosebumps, as she pushed the trolley and she realised she was shaking. Using the trolley as support, she went up and down each aisle in a methodical, quiet daze.

'River is up again,' called Mr Shah down the aisle. 'Going to flood the whole city if this rain carries on. I'll be gone, long gone.'

Mr Shah ran everything through the scanner at double speed and Alice packed the food into thin plastic bags, matching his dexterity. By the time she had finished there were eight sagging bags of food bulging from the web of plastic. Mr Shah looked at Alice and then at the pile of shopping as she handed over the cash.

'You want to leave some here and come back for them? Maybe you want to fetch your mother to help?'

'No,' she said. 'I'll manage.' She pulled the thin rings of plastic high up her arms, handles biting into her skin in raised pink circles. Four bags per arm, Alice hooked her hands together at her skinny waist and shuffled her body forward. She inched towards the flats, eyes fixed on the bottle-green door and teeth clenched together, bone-hard and determined. It was just as she got inside the sheltered porch that the real rain started.

It was 8.35 a.m. on 17th September 2018.

From the porch, it took two runs to get all of the shopping back into the flat. A tall man, hands covered in oil and smelling of smoke, got into the lift with her and stood very close as the doors pulled together. Alice pushed the shopping forward with her legs, forming a barrier between them. The man grinned, gappy-toothed, and as the doors opened at his floor, he bent down and fished into one of the shopping bags. He picked out a bar of chocolate.

'Cheers,' he said and slipped onto the sixth floor, flashing broken teeth in a sneered black smile as he went. Alice shivered and pulled the shopping close to her as the lift creaked upwards.

When she got back to the flat, Alice found her mother sitting on the stained sofa, looking out at the rain.

'Why aren't you at school?' her mother asked, turning around. Her skin looked worn and sleepy and above her eye was the metallic shine of a new bruise.

Alice felt a pain hit her somewhere in the chest. 'I don't feel well,' she said. 'It's the rain.' Her mother held out her hand and Alice went over to her. Thick wheals lashed her arms where she'd been carrying the bags. The sick feeling came lurching back.

'Did you take my money?' her mother asked. 'That's my money.'

Alice hesitated then nodded, pushing her hands into her pockets.

'I did the shopping, Ma, all of it,' she said. 'We don't need to go out today; you can rest. Get some sleep.' Alice's mother looked more relieved than annoyed and she put her arms around Alice.

'Don't take my money without asking – I told you. Some of that was for the electric people.' The rain drummed heavily on the window outside and they sat there together, watching as it came down in torrents. It beat harder and faster until the window front was a stream of water and they couldn't see anything more than the slight outline of the barrier on the balcony. The rhythmic chord strummed with enough regularity that eventually they both fell asleep on the sofa.

As she drifted in and out of consciousness, Alice heard the pattering of rain and her mother moving around the flat, lifting and carrying things. She dreamed of waterfalls and swimming pools and being deep inside a submarine watching fish writhe past in cloudy portholes in giant tidal streams. She wanted to get up and help her mother but each time she opened her eyes, the sickness rose up from her stomach. She turned over and looked at the swirls in the carpet but that made her feel even worse. She closed her eyes again and put a cool palm on her own forehead that seethed red and angry. Through the red-blackness of her eyelids she could see shapes and crowds of people dancing across the wall, through their front room and out towards the balcony. Outside there were lights and bangs like fireworks.

'What's going on?' said Alice, as shapes danced across the wall. She tried to lift her hand up to point at the wall, but it continued to hang limply by her side.

'It's the rain,' said her mother. 'It's making people crazy.'

When Alice awoke, the sky was dark and the banging of the rain had eased into a soft patter against the window. She propped herself up against the pillows and stretched her legs out flat. They ached and her head was sore, but she didn't feel sick any longer. As she blinked her eyes open, her mother was standing above her with a cup of tea. The steam twisted in circles dizzying upwards towards the ceiling.

'How are you feeling?' she said and crouched down next to Alice.

'Tired – how long did I sleep for?' Her voice came out as a whisper, raspy and hoarse.

'It's five o'clock in the evening. I think you had a fever.'

Alice looked out at the thick black clouds in the sky, drowning the stars.

'It's so dark,' she said.

Her mother gently brushed her fringe away from her eyes. The bruise was a deep violet.

'Yes, it's very dark. Most of the street lights are out.'

'But you're not going out are you? Please?'

Alice's mother looked out of the window at the driving rain. 'It still hasn't stopped,' she said. 'We have electricity on and off, but the phone line isn't working. I have to go out tonight, Alice. People need someone like me…' Her voice disappeared into the pitter-patter of the rain.

'Can't you stay home?' pleaded Alice. 'Please?'

Her mother looked at Alice and then back out of the window. She hesitated for a while and Alice felt her lip quivering; she could see her mother's hands were shaking as she combed her hair over the blue-black flower that was spreading down her face: the bruise that was as almost as dark as the sky.

'I have to, Alice. I'm sorry. The punters won't wait because of the rain. The rain makes them impatient. And now there's less chance of police out there.' She handed Alice the tea and turned to leave, in a veil of perfume and a smudge of lipstick. She checked herself in a compact mirror.

'I'm scared,' said Alice, but it came out in a whisper.

'Don't answer the door to anyone,' called her mother, 'and keep the windows shut.' Then she slammed the door hard and left the echo reverberating through the room.

As the evening turned into night, Alice burrowed herself deeper into the sofa, unable to muster enough strength to get her aching limbs up the stairs. She crawled into the kitchen to get a drink and looked at the clock. It was four in the morning and her mother still wasn't home – but that wasn't too unusual. The luminous green second hand scratched around the dial to the rhythm of the rain. Alice gulped down two more glasses of water. She picked up the phone receiver but there was no sound.

Outside in the street there was the noise of car alarms and shouting. There were two gunshots and then a loud explosion followed by the shattering of glass. Step by step, she felt her way back to the sofa and laid her head back down on the pillow. Although the pounding heaviness in her limbs was still there, it was noticeably less than before – but something inside her still felt wrong. Very wrong.

Alice slept intermittently for hours and when she fully woke, it was way past the time when the sun would usually clamber its way over the spires of the city and hang nervously in the folds of the sky. The night was fractured by frightening noises – sometimes she woke to hear the tick-tick-tick of hail against the window and other times to heavy feet outside and the banging of a fist on her front door.

'Is there anyone in there? Come on, get out here, we're leaving!'

The shouting was frightening, desperate and not the voice of her mother. Alice wrapped herself tighter in the blankets and pulled the pillow over her head. She heard the same voices calling along the corridor, banging on each of the doors in turn. Even if she had wanted to, Alice couldn't move. Her legs felt glued together and full of cement.

'I'm fine,' she said in a voice so timid that she wasn't sure that she could even hear herself. 'I'm fine.' The sound of banging quietened into a dull thud and then into nothing, and all she could hear was the dripping of the rain.

On the third day after the Storms started, her mother still wasn't home. When Alice got up to refill her water jug, there was a hammering coming from somewhere in the building but she couldn't be sure where. Moments later she saw a white blaze that came from outside the window and lit up the whole of the sky with an iridescent flash, like slow-motion sheet lightning. She drank down the water quickly then ate some biscuits and mummified her body back inside the folds of the blankets. There was no sign that her mother had been back at all. Her eyes felt hot and fiery. All night she dreamed of explosions and furnaces and shooting flames that licked the inside of her brain until all her memories were burned and blackened.

Twice she woke up screaming empty words. Then there was silence and, through her dreams, Alice remembered being frightened. It was a cool, quiet type of frightened that didn't come from watching a scary movie or the barking of an angry dog. It was the type of terrified that bled out of the clouds slowly, dripping down onto the balcony where paint had been blistered by the sun and eked into the tenth-floor flat over several hours. It was the type of scared that came at the start of things, rather than at the end.

Finally, several mornings after the Storms had started, Alice awoke feeling almost normal – although she wasn't really sure what that felt like any more. She tested out her legs slowly on the carpet and tenderly limped into the kitchen. Each morning she checked the rooms carefully, peering in every corner for any trace that her mother had returned. But she hadn't. The green hands of the clock read ten minutes past ten. When she turned on the cold tap, a slushy grey-brown liquid dripped out, slumped into the sink and dried up into a pile of rusty sediment. The hot tap did exactly the same.

In the dim light that filtered in through the curtains, Alice could see that most of the shopping she had bought was still on the counter, including cartons of juice and crisps as well as biscuits, tins of soup and fruit. She pulled together a crisp sandwich breakfast, followed up with chocolate and washed down with apple juice. She wiggled her toes and flexed her legs, feeling a spurt of life force coursing through her bloodstream.

'Ma,' she called, as she did every morning, but there was nothing. Then Alice stretched her arms and her neck and shook herself all over. She took a deep breath and opened the curtains – but what she saw immediately terrified her.

Instead of the usual view of the diagonal cranes and the London Eye in the distance, the city below her was all but unrecognisable, covered in water. Fires burned in the windows of the houses of the street opposite. A man stood on the roof of his car as a swan sailed past him. A strong gust of wind blew him clean into the water and, as he flailed around, the swan took off into the air. In the flat, the balcony doors banged against their hinges and from upstairs there was a thump and then the crash of glass. Alice shook in fear, her heart beating fast inside her ribcage. She held her breath. There was silence, except for the pattering of rain on the window. A soft, regular pattering.

'Ma?' Alice's voice was tentative and quiet. From upstairs, Alice thought she could hear something, a soft, fluttering noise, the same kind that her mother made when she was brushing her hair, getting ready for work. She put one foot on the first of the creaky stairs. The countries of the crinkled map looked back at her.

'Ma?' she said again. 'Are you home? I can help you again. Look, I'm not sick.'

Alice stopped still and listened, but there was no sound coming from the bedroom any more. Her throat felt raspy from tiny pieces of crisp lodged in her throat. She took the stairs slowly, one at a time, her heart skipping a beat every time the creaks got louder. An icy draught gusted downwards from the landing and around the staircase. The sound of flapping started again.

'Ma?' Alice's voice was almost a whisper. As she got to the top of the stairs, she could see that the door to the spare bedroom was open, swishing backwards and forwards. She took one step closer.

The spare bedroom.

Alice could feel her entire body begin to shake. All the hairs on her body were upright, alert, terrified. The door banged shut and then yanked itself open again in the wind. She didn't care that her mother would shout at her for going in there.

'Ma?' she croaked. 'Did you come back for me?'

Alice picked her fingers over the peeling wallpaper of the landing: horrible brown flock wallpaper. Her mother had said they could change it when they had some money. Her mother had said a lot of things. Alice swallowed deeply and stepped into the spare bedroom, steeling herself for whatever was inside.

The room was painted red, pristine and clean with a cream-coloured border three quarters of the way up the wall. There were fresh flowers, now dead, in a vase on the bedside table. Apart from the bed, the table was the only furniture in the room and on it stood two bottles of cheap supermarket vodka. One had been opened and was half drunk. A freezing draught of ice-cold wind blew in through a partially smashed window and rain had already begun to seep down the walls forming small pools on the floor at the bottom of the soaked curtains. There were pictures of naked women on the walls, twisting over motorbikes.

The shock and disappointment was overwhelming. Alice took a deep intake of breath as a deft, quick movement caught her eye. Matching the border, the linen on the bed was cream and cool – except there was a deep crimson stain, bleeding out like a bruise with a dark grey creature moving at the centre of it. Alice exhaled and screamed all at once. The dove, partially decapitated, ruffled its wings when it saw Alice, and flapped its body back and forth on the bed.

She took another step towards the bird, its black bead of an eye following her movement. It raised a wing and let it fall.

'I thought you were my mother,' she said.

A trail of blood snaked from the jagged hole in the window across the room and onto the bed where the bird shook the last coughs of life from its beak. Alice watched as it snapped its neck backwards and forwards until the jumpy twisting finally stopped and the only sound was that of the wind whistling past the serrated edges of the broken window pane and Alice's own heart beating.

'Where are you, Mum?' she whispered. 'I'm scared.'

Chapter Two

The Academy
Carter

Carter was the last to step out into the cool night air. He'd been stuck at the back, standing on the panel that housed the throbbing, driverless engine for the entire journey and it had made him feel sicker than ever. The noise humming through his feet and the constant chatter of the crowd grated through his skin and sank into his bones. When the vehicle stopped and everyone bled out into the night, Carter could taste his own relief. Those first few seconds of calm were delicious.

As he stepped down onto the earth, the damp air soothed his skin and the smell of the moonlit night washed away some of the thick, cloying smell of the other passengers. There wasn't much at the stop; a small red-brick shelter with four backlit screens inside and, on the far edge where the dirt met the perimeter fence, a row of warning signs that rose like tombstones for as far as he could see. The signs were new.

DANGER OF DEATH
DO NOT APPROACH THE BARRICADES

A slow, thin mist floated over the foreboding boundary wall that separated the Community from the Deadlands. It loomed upwards like a range of glittering mountains, the mist shrouding the tops of the shredded metal. The Barricades looked higher than Carter remembered. Much higher. Instead of the old hopscotch of fence-work, they were sheet metal and stone, studded with sharp glass, and towered tall above his head. And there were cameras. Hundreds of them.

A clutch of scrawny birds hovered on the other side before vanishing into the whiteness. Then, with a sharp click that made his neck snap back to watch, the doors of the Transporter pulled shut and the empty carriages darted back along the invisible track towards the sealed underground tunnel.

'They're a wonder, those things,' said a man who'd stepped off the Transporter just before him. He was older, somewhere closer to twenty. He gestured towards the Transporter, the last of its carriages quickly being gobbled by the hole of the tunnel. It slipped into the darkness without a sound. The opening where the tunnel had been snapped shut.

'They've come a long way since I was last on one,' he said. 'They'd only just been invented then. Dirty, smelly things, they were. Can you believe they can go above ground, all the way around the Community? And no drivers; it's all mechanical magnets. Isn't it amazing?'

Carter nodded and looked up at the sky without replying. The space where the tunnel had been was gone, replaced by a skein of black trophene that covered the hole in the bank on top of which was the Barricade and beyond it, out of sight, the Black River. The spitting rain pinpricked his face and, as he opened and closed his eyes, he could feel the coolness underneath his eyelids. The ground felt refreshingly soft. Gradually the majority of the crowd that had disembarked began to peel off into groups and walk the rest of the way, but the man was still there, limpet-like at his side.

'My name is Osian,' he said. 'Osian Woolcroft. I'm a Descendant like you, as you've probably guessed. He flashed his card and, in the top right-hand corner, there was a blue circle, just like his own. 'Original Descendant, born from Original Scout blood.' He smiled. 'Jayden Woolcroft, I believe he was called. I've kept his name.'

Carter nodded. 'Yes.' he said shortly, his eyes fixed on the sky. He wished the man would leave him to it, there were so many things he needed to do.

'I'd pat that man on the back if he were still around,' Osian said, grinning. 'It's because of him I got to choose my lovely wife. A Descendant too, of course. I'd never have picked anyone else, but I guess I'm lucky we were both from good stock.' He guffawed loudly. 'I suppose if she'd been one of the First Generation, we'd have still been alright, but I just feel grateful every day that she wasn't one of the Lab Made, you know.'

Carter nodded again, irritated. He knew all too well how a match between a Descendent and a Lab Made could never work. Even relationships between First Gens and Descendants was discouraged. Not yet forbidden, but definitely discouraged. The man's voice was beginning to annoy him a little.

'It's more important now than ever,' Osian continued. 'To keep the lineage, I mean. It's OK to be friends with them, they're all great people and we're all equal and that but you want to know who's in your past – and their past – don't you?'

A thin wind whistled through the trees and out across the Barricade.

Osian cleared his throat. 'There's a lot of us been brought back – did you notice? Many of us from the Gilbert Pinkerton Era. Are you

Pinkerton? No, you look a little later than that – I'll bet you don't even remember when Pinkerton was Controller General, do you?'

Carter shook his head. Gilbert Pinkerton was more his parents' era – a strong but fair, rule-driven Controller General who had given the Community some great stability. It had been expected that Professor Mendoza would have continued in Pinkerton's footsteps in the following election until she was beaten by Alderney in the final selections. Carter remembered his father's disappointment at the results announcement.

'I guess they're preparing for the new Controller General,' said Carter, 'bringing in a supportive crowd. I don't mean to be rude but I have to…'

'I dare say,' said Osian, his eyes searching Carter's. 'In fact, I think it's going to be a young woman I met earlier. She's blue too, I believe, or maybe she was red, First Gen. Definitely a red but related to a blue, something like that. Elizabet, she said her name was. Very confident.'

'Possibly,' said Carter. 'I'm sure we'll find out soon.'

'I'm sure we will,' said Osian. 'I'm sure we will.' A layer of mist floated over the top of the Barricade and dispersed amongst the metal. The silence was almost awkward.

'Well, it was nice to meet you,' said Carter. 'Have a great return.'

As he waited for Osian to leave, a light pattering of rain hit the leaves at the side of the trackway.

'Let's go, let's go,' said the man, looking up at the sky. 'If we leave now, we'll make it before the downpour starts. Who knows, it might even be a big one?' The last of the stragglers swiped their cards at the FreeScreen terminals in the shelter and then started off down the track.

'I'll wait for a while,' said Carter, watching them blend shapeless into the darkness. 'I want to clear my head.' He was keen to find out if what the assistant had said to him about being a father was true – and he didn't want to do that in the presence of someone he had only just met. The fact that he was here, several years in the future, meant that what Mendoza had said to him that night must have been true. And that there was a real chance the Industry hadn't known he was going to be father until he had been frozen deep underground. If they'd made the girl take the test before the needle had entered his arm, they'd have stopped his freezing and he would have been forced to stay above ground. He shivered at the thought of what might have happened next. But then, if the plan had worked, there must have been a baby. It would be a child now. Not even a child, but almost the same age as him. A strange mixture of emotions flooded through him – the expected sadness and trepidation but, in and amongst that, a small tremor of excitement.

'You don't want to be alone on your first walk back,' said Osian. 'You heard what they said about the dizziness and the blackouts. Come on, we'll all go together. Rules are rules.' He waved at the last group who were about to leave and gestured for them to wait. Carter shook his head. He'd had enough of their company already. From the direction of the group a buzz of whooping and general excitement leaked out into the night and, more than anything else, he just wanted to be alone and get himself together. He resisted the temptation to put the man directly in his place and gestured towards the shelter.

'I'll be fine,' he said. 'I'm going to wait for a while.' He pointed to the FreeScreen terminal. 'I need to do some research – missed my chance while we were down there.'

The man opened his mouth to protest then closed it again.

'Have a good return,' said Carter, firmly.

'As you choose,' said Osian, nodding in an offhand manner and folding into the group that was beginning to leave. They half-skipped, half-ran together in the direction of the Community, whooping and cheering. From what Carter knew of where he was, the centre was about an hour's walk south.

He watched as the group split, joining together again in smaller clumps as their heads bobbed off into the distance. He could still hear their conversation, high-spirited and punctuated with chirrups of excitement, but it wasn't long before the chattering dissipated to a whisper in the moonlight. Within five minutes they were completely out of sight and all he could hear was silence. His relief was palpable.

As the clouds cleared, just for a moment, there was a moon. A papery globe that winked through the night air once before it disappeared again. In the darkness he didn't recognise the location of the drop-off point but it was just short of the central track – that much was obvious. The glow of the Community hummed gently to the southwest, the edges of the Barricade glinting with an edge of danger to the north.

The long, single main road that bisected the Community with its arterial spurs jutting sideways from the central track wound its way through to the Community like a ribbon. He checked through his pockets for his identity card and felt its pulse gently reverberating into life. It was slightly warm; hard plastic but warm, the blue circle shining brightly in the corner.

The light of an empty Transporter loomed in the distance. He checked the screen: one was due from the south to take any stragglers back with it into the safety of the Community and to their new homes.

His new home was probably less than a ten-minute walk from where he had lived before with his grandfather and fifteen minutes from the Community Academy. He wondered if his grandfather was still alive, still reachable. But more, he wondered about what his assistant had said before he'd slept. He had a regretful recollection of the night before he had left, but forced himself not to think about it. Then, through the darkness, a thick ball of ice from the sky caught the edge of his temple.

It was then that the rain and hail really started – great, heavy curtains of freezing water that cut through the night cloud. Pellets of hard ice interspersed with heavy, cold rain. He darted the few steps towards the safety of the shelter as the ice fell around him. And then suddenly, before he could scan the screen, through the rain, there was something else. The snap of a twig, the rustle of a branch – something that caught his attention so acutely, he was sure he could feel it breathing. There was someone watching him. Through the falling darkness he craned his eyes until he could see it through the torrents: a figure somewhere in the clump of trees on the other side of the road. It was small – a girl. And she was waving to him.

'Carter! Carter Warren! I need to talk to you.'

He blinked through the rain and squinted; it was definitely a young girl, with long silver-blonde hair. She lifted her arms, wildly flailing in Carter's direction from the other side of the track.

'Carter!'

He stared through the rain and sleet. Who was she? And how did she know who he was?

With the rain and the voice came dizziness, and two chunky ice balls to the cheek knocked him to the corner of the shelter.

'Carter!'

He looked up into the light. And then he watched as the girl ran towards him into the shelter. She stood over Carter, who was crouched in a heap on the floor, shivering. A scarf half-covered her face and she protected her head with her hands.

'You're the one,' she said, breathing heavily. 'I know who you are. You need to be the one who people look to, the person who saves us all. Find Isabella and go to the old Delaney House, near the Barricades in the south – you know where. We can't go together. They'll see us.' She flicked her hand in the direction of the cameras on the far side of the Barricades. Carter looked at her warily.

'I wanted us to go together, but we can't,' she continued, looking around nervously. 'I have to go. You mustn't let them win this time. They're coming for me. *And they might be listening.*' The last part came out as a whisper.

Carter looked at her, blinking in the light.

'Who might be listening?' he started.

'Shh!' said the girl, glancing up at the cameras again. 'They're coming for me. Don't let them know that you saw me. Make sure that you go to the Barricades. She'll show you. Isabella. When you find out the truth, you'll know why. I will be there waiting for you there and we can talk more. It's your time to change everything, like you promised. Don't tell them you saw me,' she said again. She held out her palm then rubbed it against Carter's.

Before he could ask any further questions, the girl put a finger to her lips.

'*Veritas liberabit vos,*' she said and there was silence for a second before she looked around and ran back out of the shelter and through the blinding lights of the oncoming Transporter. There was a piercing scream and Carter couldn't tell whether it came from the machine or the girl. He closed his eyes tightly. The driverless carriage stopped for a second, its motion camera flickering into the shelter, picking up everything except the curled-up Carter. After it sensed no passengers, it reversed back in the direction it had come from.

Carter kept his eyes closed tightly until there was silence. His mind raced with questions about the girl. How did she know Isabella and, most importantly, how could she possibly know him? He so desperately wanted to find Isabella, to see how she was, to see who she had become. The thought of her cut him like a knife.

He snapped open his eye, looking around for the girl. The air smelled dark and smoky, and both the mysterious girl and the Transporter had gone.

In the moonlight, after the hail, there was a flavour to the air that felt different. A warm blush of lavender and bracken wafted over him for a second before it disappeared, taking with it the strange words of the girl and the scent of summer evaporating into the night. That smell reminded him of something he desperately wanted to forget – but, however hard he tried, Carter couldn't quite get the sweet, delicate scent of lavender from his mind.

That worried him. His ability to focus on his work and push back unnecessary, upsetting distractions had become one of his greatest talents. It had needed to be. Although it wasn't his only strength. Before he'd gone into the Catacombs there was nothing he hadn't excelled at – in his Academy days he'd had an exemplary record in all subjects and had even been called to the Industry Headquarters on two occasions for work experience – an honour that was only afforded to the most diligent of students.

The first time, when he was eleven, he'd developed a new set of flavours for the synthetic food team that won him a whole box of fauclate. Then, when he was just turning fourteen, he identified and fixed a glitch in the Model – a problem that, if left untended, would have sent half the population of the Community underground. Not one of the senior analysts had even realised there was an issue.

'You've got the dynamics wrong,' Carter had said, switching seven different dials a fraction of a centimetre deftly while they'd watched in amazement.

'You can't touch that, kid,' the chief technician had told him, pushing Carter away, but the others had held him back.

'He knows what he's doing,' one of the analysts had observed. 'He can manage this thing with his eyes closed; he's a genius.'

After that, the Industry had sometimes called on Carter to make the occasional repair or tweak to the Model, which he'd done for no reward other than to be in the central control tower. He'd loved the buzz and whirr of the machinery and the soft click of his fingers on the panel buttons that spat out directions of who was to be frozen and who was to be returned. The pure mathematics of it had fascinated him. And his genius had fascinated all those around him. Whenever he was close to the Model, the deftness of his movements had been so captivating that people had felt compelled to watch as he'd pushed the straw-blonde hair away from his pale-blue eyes, and focused intently, until the task had been completed.

All that said, it would be his exemplary Academy record in Censomics and Synthetics, plus an outstanding Contribution to the Community, that would win the day. These things combined would most definitely make him the natural successor to the post of Controller General. The greatest gift that most people could expect to give to the Community was that of new, well-bred life. Carter had always said he would choose the ultimate position of Controller General over father-hood any day, but he had done what he needed to – what he had been *told* to. Becoming Controller General was the one thing he had been groomed for his whole life – the most important thing, above all else.

From his very first school lesson, Carter had been fascinated by everything, but it was Censomics that had interested him the most. The study of Population Control and Community Management was so much more important than the mythical history lessons that described an old world he could not understand. It was a place that his grandfather had known something of, but only from the stories that had been handed down to him by his father. As a direct descendant of an Original Scout, Carter's lineage had earned him enough credit to compete for the Controller General position.

Carter's parents, Nikolas and Jacinta Warren, had been involved in a terrible accident whilst on a scouting mission outside the Barricades. The rumour was that it had involved wolves.

'What sort of accident?' Carter had asked, distraught, when he'd heard. 'Have they been frozen? Will they be coming back?'

'No,' his grandfather, Milton, had told him. 'This is the sort of accident where you don't come back. Not ever.'

It was later that evening that the ten-year-old Carter had vowed to become Controller General.

'What makes you think you would be a good Controller?' his grandfather, serious, had asked. 'You know they're going to ask you that one day. You'll need to have an answer if you get invited to the final selection.'

'Because if I'm Controller General, I can do anything,' the boy had answered. 'I can change the world and make everyone happy.'

'Well, I don't think that's possible,' his grandfather had replied. 'Not even for the Controller General. But I'd be very proud of you if you were chosen.'

'Then I'll do it to prove that I can. And I'll show everyone I was right. I'll be the best son they could have asked for,' Carter had said in a sombre tone. And that was the decision made.

There weren't any further scouting missions after the one in which his parents disappeared. The Industry stopped asking for volunteers and the Scouting Programme was abandoned. On the very rare occasions when they needed waste to be deposited out in the Deadlands or for land surveys to be undertaken, it was done by machine. The dangers were reiterated daily on the FreeScreens. Carter thought it was a shame – if he hadn't been identified as a Contender, he'd have quite liked to have been a Scout.

'You will be better than them,' his grandfather had said curtly one night. 'They both would have wanted to become Controller General, although they were never even made Contender.'

'But why?' Carter had asked.

'They were bright,' his grandfather had told him, 'but not exceptional like you. Only those who are *real* Contenders get the chance to develop Contributions. The rest of us… well, we just do what needs to be done.'

Carter had shrugged. 'Mendoza says I'm doing fine without them. And anyway, my Contribution isn't going to be a stupid invention like Transporters. It's going to be an idea that changes the world.'

His grandfather had laughed and pointed towards the complex chemical equations on the slate that they had been working through.

'Well, unless you do well at Academy and do everything that Professor Mendoza says, you won't even make the Contender shortlist,' he'd said firmly, as they'd returned to the Synthetics homework that Carter had so swiftly diverted them from.

Each night, Carter would ask about the old world, about his great-grandfather Richard and what it was like when he'd lived there. He'd wanted to know everything: the difference between football and pinball, what had been the point of national anthems, and why animals were kept in zoos.

His grandfather had told him everything he knew: how football was a dangerous game played by kicking the bladder of an animal around a field for fun, and how it caused riots and many, many deaths. He'd told Carter how pinball was much smaller and played on a table for money by gamblers who were greedy and not happy with their lot. His grandfather had reminded him that anthems were chanted to tell people who you were. He'd never been sure about zoos and usually concluded that they were for disease research.

But one thing Milton Warren had been always clear about, was that these things, amongst others, had destroyed what it really meant to be human.

The sound of his grandfather's voice twirling around strange words that no longer existed had given Carter a sense of awkward longing for the things he had never experienced. His grandfather had seemed to talk about them with definite disdain, even though the stories were all second-hand, passed down from his own relatives decades earlier. Like most, his grandfather had despised any nostalgia for the old world.

'Seems stupid to me,' he'd said. 'It makes no sense at all.'

'It was dangerous,' his grandfather had replied. 'It sounds like a frightening place to be.'

Carter had shaken his head: 'Why was everything so complicated?'

His grandfather had shrugged and made his way out of Carter's room.

'Because they got it all wrong,' he'd muttered as Carter had settled himself to sleep, thoughts of the old world swirling around inside his head.

As Carter sat in the coldness of the shelter, the memory of his grandfather's voice echoed around in the wind. He wondered if he was still alive – he hoped he would be. The old man who had taken care of him throughout his teenage years and guided him towards his dream of being Controller General. Professor Mendoza too. Even now, Carter felt himself chill at the thought of his old mentor, the Censomics professor and most revered teacher in the Community. It was only those with a profound level of knowledge of Censomics who could become the Controller General – except Professor Mendoza had failed at the final assessment.

'You could just become a professor,' his grandfather had said as they'd talked through theories of population control. 'How about that?'

Carter had laughed.

'I am not going to end up like Professor Mendoza,' he'd said. 'I will be Controller General, or I will be nothing.'

His grandfather had smiled. 'I know you're determined,' he'd said. 'But whatever you choose, you should listen to the professor. She may not be Controller General, but she knows more than anyone else here. She will be the one to get you where you need to be. And stay away from that Lab Made girl. Nothing good ever came of anyone whose ancestors were grown in the Catacombs.'

Carter waited in the shelter in the near-darkness as his memories caught up with themselves. The Model called people back to the Community when they were needed. The fact that he was here must mean that it was finally his time to contend for the position of Controller General. If it was, at fifteen he would be one of the youngest to be considered. Then there was the strange girl with the bizarre message, who had then disappeared. She had talked about saving them all. It reminded him of something Mendoza had once said in one of his lessons.

'They didn't want to be saved,' the professor had begun. 'They had the technology to be able to control and manage their populations and resources, and could have anticipated what had happened if only they had not been preoccupied with nonsense.'

She'd cleared her throat and waited for the class to settle down. The quiet had been pristine, beautiful, and she'd smiled at the class. While Carter had admired her for her knowledge, there had been something imperfect... incomplete... about her. She hadn't made Controller, he'd thought. But *he* would.

There'd been nods throughout the room, especially from Isabella who had chosen to sit next to him. Isabella with the voice as velvety soft as moss, like the song of a nightjar. Isabella: the girl with the short blonde hair and deep-green eyes that sparkled in the sun. Isabella: the Lab manufactured, green-eyed, green card holder.

Carter had turned his head to catch another glimpse of her sweet, crooked smile.

Inquisitive, mischievous and daring, Isabella had been the first person to climb the tall oak on the west side of the Community to get a glimpse of the fallen city on the other side. She'd winked back at him as Mendoza had continued.

'We waged war on different sectors of our society, marginalised and side-lined until it was person against person, legitimised by the media. So much so that after the Storms we made no attempt to recreate the past. When something is broken—' she'd paused and looked around at the room '—we don't fix it. We reinvent it.'

From next to him, Carter had heard a voice cut through the quiet.

'So were the Storms a good thing?' It was her. His heart had raced, even though he'd known it shouldn't.

'Anticipating my homework once again, Isabella?' the professor had asked, sharply. 'As you have asked the question, I'll give you all a head start in your preparation. I would like you to pair up and, before the next session, debate whether the Storms were a good or a bad thing. Take whatever side you want to – there is no right answer. Because, in short, the Storms were what they were: a horrific and catastrophic disaster that destroyed the majority of human and animal life and created an almost impossible legacy. But what we have now – well, it's perfect, isn't it?'

Carter had turned his head again and Isabella had lifted her eyebrows at him.

'You can be my partner,' she'd mouthed. Carter had nodded in agreement with the air of someone who didn't care too much, but when he'd turned back to face the front of the room, his cheeks had burned flame red. He'd lost himself in the words of the professor as she'd continued and tried hard to ignore the aching desire to see if Isabella was looking at him. But even when he'd felt her eyes boring into him, he didn't move.

'Tomorrow we'll run the same exercise but discuss our cryonic freezing processes,' the professor had said, 'so you'll need to complete your homework this evening. But first, we're going to watch a short screening.'

When the picture had stated moving, Carter had alternated between looking at his slate and the main screen, listening to Professor Mendoza and trying hard to stop thinking about Isabella.

'There was simply nowhere above ground that was safe for a long time. The Storms, in one form or another, lasted for just over five years.' Professor Mendoza had paused for a few seconds as the camera had panned across expanses of black water, dotted with pale-coloured floating objects.

'For those who survived above ground after the first Storms hit – and there were very few – life was impossible. With no recourse to clean water, heat or food, most died within the first few days – others within weeks, and mostly from radiation poisoning. It was only those fortunate enough to have been rescued and brought to the Industry facilities who survived. You won't be surprised to know that a large number of those were under the age of eighteen. Children, it turned out, were a great deal more resourceful than adults.'

Carter hadn't been able to imagine it any other way. Controller Generals were always appointed before their eighteenth birthday. He'd planned it to be before his sixteenth, whatever era that happened to be in. Next to him, Isabella had raised her hand and he'd felt the rush of cool air as she'd moved.

'I have one more question,' she'd said. 'What is beyond the Dead-lands?' The room had gone very quiet and Carter had looked at the professor.

'Another good question, Isabella,' she'd said. 'Does anyone else know the answer to this?' A thick silence had fallen across the room.

'Monsters,' someone had shouted from the front, making the classroom burst into laughter.

'Thank you,' she'd said, 'but not exactly. We know that there are still areas that have been subject to significant contamination and there could be anything there. In the early days, when the next generation of Scouts went out into the Deadlands, we found out that the threats exist as far as the sea. But we were never able to get that far on foot – the terrain is extremely dangerous, which is why we keep our Community barricaded at all times. As you know—' she'd glanced briefly at Carter '—due to security issues we have currently suspended all research into those areas. All right, no more questions.'

The film had started with the usual broadcast warnings. The voice of one of the original Scouts had filtered through the speakers.

In the years since we have been underground, things have changed completely. Many of the buildings are gone, crushed under the forces of the water and withered to dust. The people are gone too – the only creatures I have seen so far are birds overhead flying west and some wolf-like creatures that have come from the north-east. The wolves are the most dangerous – they attack without provocation. We watch for the signs of when the rain is coming – it's all we can do.

There'd been some whispering in the background that Carter hadn't been able to quite distinguish before the narrator had moved on.

Plant life has flourished; there are trees that have grown through the concrete, and branches with diseased fruit. London is unrecognisable as the city it was before.
My name is Alice Davenport and this is the Deadlands.

As the reveries of his Academy days faded, Carter steadied himself against the edge of the shelter and stood upright. He rubbed the spot on his temple where the hailstones had hit him, but there was no blood. He swiped into the FreeScreen, watching the colours change and settle on his details. His name appeared on his home screen, along with his address and connection information. The words glowed brightly, making his head hurt and his heart beat faster.

Name: Carter F. Warren
Address: 47 Drummond Row, Unity Square District, West
           Quarter
Birth Status: Descendant

Cryonic Status: Released from Catacombs [15 year tenure]
Reproduction Status: Positive
Life Status: Active, Confirmed Contender
Industry Rank: Contender, Controller General Position
Industry Mentor: Lilith McDermott
Immediate Family: Parents (Nikolas & Jacinta Warren), deceased
                                  Brother (Silas Warren), unborn, deceased
                                  Grandfather (Milton Warren), deceased

As he stood there in the fading light, his eyes filled slowly with thick tears and his throat hurt. The one remaining thread of family he cared about was gone and he hadn't been able to come back soon enough to say goodbye. Carter swallowed hard to blink back the tears. The old man who had stayed up late at night helping him with homework, who had spent hours with Professor Mendoza planning his grandson's career and had arranged additional tuition, was gone.

Carter ran his finger gently over the old man's name on the terminal and held on tightly to the side of the shelter for support. As his finger traced through the letters, the screen scrolled upwards. What he saw next shocked him almost as much as his grandfather's death. His heart pounded and his legs shook. Underneath his grandfather's name there was one more line of text. He looked at the screen again. Then he swiped out of the terminal and back in again. So it was true. The assistant had been right and Mendoza's plan had worked. But there was something more. There were two of them. Twins.

Biological Children: Twins, Ariel & Lucia Warren-Davenport

Chapter Three

The Neighbour

Alice

In the cupboard under the stairs Alice found a claw hammer, an unopened packet of nails and an axe that was covered in tiny flecks of cobalt-blue paint. It was the same colour her father had painted the bathroom in their house back in the country.

She started with the table. She wasn't exactly sure why she was doing what she was doing, but it was something she had seen on television months before about preparing for a hurricane. There had been a lot of those programmes in the last year. Her mother had always turned the channel over.

'You don't want to watch things like that,' she'd said. 'This rubbish is too depressing.' And then, 'Get me a can of lager out of the fridge before the soaps start.'

When it came to storms, it was all, apparently, about the preparation.

'Board up the windows, close all the hatches,' Alice said to herself as she smacked the blade against the table. The axe wasn't heavy, but it was difficult to control. The first splinters of wood she managed to hack off the edges were as thin and useless as her arms felt.

Her cheeks turned crimson at the effort as she shaved sticks into small piles that grew slightly larger with practice. Next she moved on to the sideboard and then a desk until she had enough pieces of thin wood to board over the window in her mother's bedroom as well as the glass door that looked out onto the balcony. It took her until nightfall to cover over both, but it was the satisfying sound of the rain on wood that soothed her as she sucked on some biscuits and fell asleep in the sunken arms of the sofa.

The next morning, the rain had stilled to a thin mist. Alice thought it had stopped altogether until she got to the window. She pulled back the curtains, damp with water that had blown in through the cracked window and onto the wood. Fine droplets steamed downwards in filmy white sheets, but at least the wind was still. Alice crept out onto the balcony. The skies were the colour of weathered slate and slithered with showering rain that came from all directions.

Looking across the city, there was smoke – a lot of it – from small fires that burned in the upper floors of some of the higher buildings further out of town. Alice counted at least fifteen fires and watched as two smaller buildings collapsed at their knees, exhausted, as she stood there. It felt unreal; like television. The London Eye stood like a stopped clock in the distance, bent and broken.

The river that snaked through the centre of the city had burst its banks, flooding the streets with rancid, stinking tidewater that swirled over parked cars and street lights, and around trees and houses. It was deep now and the water had risen well above the windows of some of the houses opposite. The sharp summits of buildings stuck out like exclamation marks and others created even tables that protruded in miniature from the deep, swirling mass.

Alice couldn't work out how deep the water was, but on the higher ground she could see the very tops of traffic lights and the shiny cabs of trucks. There were lines of cars reflected in the depths of the water where the pavements used to be. She edged out closer to the balcony rail. In the pools, she could see things floating. Different-coloured things of different shapes and sizes. It didn't take her long to work out that they were the empty bodies of animals and people.

Through the tick-tick of the rain, there were other sounds; strange noises that didn't feel like they belonged in the city. There was a creak and then a bang as the red-brick railway arch collapsed. A boom that came from the far edges of the city shook the roots of the block, and the last of the faithful gulls, most of which had long left, skimmed over the winds peppered with leaves, and away towards the sea. Their departure seemed almost final and Alice waved sadly with both hands across the balcony.

Then, on the other side of the street, someone waved back. There was a man standing on the roof of one of the low-slung buildings. He shook a hand towards her and shouted something but she couldn't exactly hear what it was. He waved and called again.

'I can't hear you,' said Alice. 'I really can't.' She lifted her hand to the man and shook it slowly back and forth. The man called again. One of his arms was bleeding and, as he waved the other, she could see a pool of blood gathering around his feet. He kept talking, kept shouting, but Alice wasn't even sure he was calling out to her at all. His words, picked up by the wind, were blown across the city like shrapnel as he whirled around in a circle.

'Hello,' she called in a brittle voice, but the stick-like figure couldn't hear her.

She watched the man as he paced in lines on the very edge of the roof, sometimes gesturing and then other times veering in the wind as the lean of the breeze took him. And then, suddenly, his legs slipped from under him and he tipped awkwardly out into the water. For a while he floated around, before his body stopped. Alice imagined the lower half of him catching on the tops of trees and shop awnings that were hidden underneath the water. Then, as quickly as he'd fallen, he stopped moving and slid downwards in a graceful swirl under the water. There was the glug-glug of a plug being pulled out and then he was gone.

Everything inside Alice hurt.

After a lunch of cold soup and the rest of the apple juice, Alice lined up what food she had left. There were still two packets of biscuits, four cans of soup and some bananas, but she wasn't hungry. She was thirsty – thirsty for something that wasn't thick and gloopy.

'Water, water everywhere,' she said to herself and supped on a can of super-value chicken and lentil broth to quench the dryness in her throat. It was thick and messy and the bits of chicken kept getting stuck between her teeth. She thought about the man who'd been standing on the roof of the building and the blood dripping from his hand, pooling around his feet. She thought about the way he had stamped about in the puddles of rainwater that had gathered on the sticky waterproof tar. It was then that Alice got the idea.

She went to the kitchen, grabbed two saucepans by their worn handles, then headed out of the front door. She turned right towards the ladder to the roof with its spine-like black rungs that spiralled around and around towards the top. Before she climbed, Alice looked across at the other side of the city and breathed in the air. Acrid black smoke danced across the surface of the water and, like the balcony facing the opposite direction, there were buildings on fire in the distance. Apart from the calling of a pair of gulls, the scene was eerily silent. All the people had gone.

One of the birds twisted on the wind, diving headlong into the water below before pulling back up again, coasting the currents of air. There was all kinds of rubbish floating, gathering around the edges where the buildings and roofs met the water, swirling around like flies. She saw a pram, empty and turned on its side, being carried along through what used to be the streets with a white-and-brown cat clinging to the edges. In the distance, Alice thought she heard it meow. It held its head back, contorted against the water and dug its claws deep into the fabric as it sailed through the city.

'Hold on,' she whispered and a trickle of tears dribbled from her eyes. She bit her lip hard and headed along the balcony towards the staircase before she had to watch the cat slipping below into the darkness as its exhausted paws gave up hope.

The cold metal bit through her fingers as she clung to the railing of the stairs. It was dripping with water and she sucked on the cold iron, dragging as much water as she could with her tongue.

Water, water, everywhere.

Savouring the wetness, she moved her feet slowly, one over the other, listening to the dull clanking of her feet against the metal. She'd never been afraid of heights before, but there was something in the cold slap of the wind and the smell of the air that made her not want to look down.

When she got to the roof, the small paved area was empty, but she could feel the ugliness of the place, clammy on her skin. Empty cans of lager littered the floor, along with drug paraphernalia and junk. There was a small patio area with some bolted-down tables and chairs and a row of plastic bins around the outside. Plastic bins that were full of water.

Alice hauled herself up the last few steps and skidded across the lawn of plastic turf towards the bins. Her feet gave way under the slippery surface and she lost herself in the softness, grazing her knee on the coarse grass. She lay there for a second looking up at the inky grey sky that looked ready to explode its contents over her until her thirst picked her back up.

She checked the bins quickly and chose the one that looked the cleanest. She hesitated for a second and then plunged her head into the ice-cold water. It made the inside of her head tingle and her eyes hurt. At the bottom she could just make out blurred shapes: food cartons, cans and cigarette butts that had been ground into the bottom. Alice pulled her head out quickly and then set down the saucepans that she had brought with her.

'Rain, rain, go away; come back another day,' she said quietly.

Looking across the roof at the drowned city below, the tops of buildings stuck out like rotting teeth from the gums of a bad mouth. The hollow sun was paper yellow through the stringy clouds, dim light casting shadows onto the murky water. To Alice, it didn't seem like any particular time of day. It could have been dawn or dusk or both.

From the roof she had an almost panoramic view of the city, stretching out in an endless expanse of water punctuated only by the higher buildings and the tops of trees. The more that she looked at the water, the more she could see. Giant blue gunmetal shapes that twisted and formed into monsters and creatures that she couldn't quite describe. When she looked away, they disappeared and then reformed with long necks, huge snaking limbs and torsos of brick and steel like the fragments of a bad dream.

Slowly, she walked around the edge, breathing in hungry gulps of an air that smelled of firework nights and the rotting decay of autumn. Across to the north, another explosion sounded and she watched as a tower building melted downwards, taking the next one with it like balsa wood dominos. Then she left, sneaking down the stairs like a thief – a feeling with which she was not unfamiliar.

As the late afternoon crested into evening and Alice was drifting off to sleep, there was a sharp knocking on the front door. The sound of the banging caused her to jump off the sofa in fright and she landed on a glass that smashed into her knee. A triangular shard of clear glass stuck out sideways like the fin of a shark, reflecting the white light from the window. As she sat there, transfixed by the drips of blood that pooled in the carpet, there was another crash at the door, this time accompanied by a voice. The pain in her knee hadn't quite registered.

'Is there anyone in there? Mrs Davenport, is that you? I know there's someone in there. You must help me. I'm starving. Please.'

Alice stared at the blood running down her leg and then out past the kitchen towards the hallway. The thumping on the door boomed across the floor and pounded into her knee. She wasn't sure if it was the banging or just the pain from the glass triangle in her leg.

'Mrs Davenport, *please.*' The voice sounded desperate this time, whining almost. Alice bit down on her bottom lip and used two hands to pull the shard out of her leg. Immediately, a red river gushed down her shin and, at the sight of it, she let out a scream.

'I can hear you,' said the voice at the door that had changed from desperate to a pleading whimper. 'I know you're there. I heard you going up onto the roof. You have to help me, Mrs Davenport. I'm an old man. I have a heart condition. Please. I know you're a good woman underneath; I don't care what you are.'

Alice dragged herself to the kitchen using her hands, sliding on her backside, and grabbed a tea towel hanging on a nail near the sink. It had a few coffee stains on it but was almost clean. She tied it tightly around her knee until the fibres locked into the wound, stemming the flow of blood. The sweet, metallic taste lingered on her tongue and the inside of her mouth was tender to the touch – in steeling herself for the pain, Alice had taken a chunk out of the inside of her cheek.

'Keep your temper,' she said, but the banging continued.

'I don't want to break the door down, but I will,' came the cry from outside the front door. 'I have a hammer. I'll use it. I just want to talk. Just a conversation. Please.'

Alice steadied herself up against the counter. The voice sounded just like Mr Hutchinson. Exactly like Mr Hutchinson. She hobbled to the door, dragging her cut leg behind her, leaning against the walls for support. When she got to it, she looked through the spyhole.

'Mr Hutchinson?' she said. 'Is that you?' Outside there was silence for a second and then the voice again.

'Let me in, kid. I need to talk to your mother.'

'She's not here,' said Alice. 'It's just me.'

'Who's looking after you?'

'No one,' said Alice. 'I'm looking after myself.' The blood-damp tea towel loosened around her leg and dropped to the linoleum. A squirt of red leaked onto the wall. She bent down to pick it up and wrapped it around again, the bandage wet-slapping against her leg.

'Open the door, please,' said Mr Hutchinson. 'We need to talk. Now.'

Alice sat on the sofa and watched as Mr Hutchinson gulped greedy mouthfuls from a can of soup like a baby bird gobbling worms. When he had finished, he opened and closed his mouth. He rested back in the chair he had claimed as his own and rubbed his stomach. The chair used to belong to Alice's father.

'Do you have any more?' he asked, looking around. 'How much have you got?'

'Not much,' said Alice. 'What day is it?'

'Monday,' said the old man, as if that meant something, and helped himself to a packet of biscuits. A dribble of tomato soup ran down his chin and he scraped it up with his fingers then licked them clean.

'Power went out about a week ago,' he said. 'There's no one else left in the building. Where's your mother?'

Alice looked down at the floor.

'I don't know,' she said. 'She went out to work and she hasn't come home yet.'

A strange look came over Mr Hutchinson's face.

'How long have you been all alone?'

'Since the Storms started.'

After he had eaten, Mr Hutchinson seemed a lot calmer. He reached out a hand and touched Alice gently on the shoulder, then tousled her hair.

'It's Alice, isn't it?' he said. 'You must be very scared.'

'I'm OK,' said Alice. 'I'm nearly twelve, you know.'

'Then I suppose I'd better be here to take care of you.' Mr Hutchinson cast his eyes around the flat. 'Your mother might not come back...

soon.' He put his arm around her shoulder and pulled her close to him. He smelled like a combination of pipe smoke and the mouldiness of Prospect House.

'I'm OK,' she said, not sure whether to be angry or happy that Mr Hutchinson thought that, at her age, she needed to be taken care of. She'd done all right so far.

'I know, Alice. But you'll be under my care now,' said Mr Hutchinson and smiled. Alice pressed her fingers hard against the tea towel to stop it slipping down her leg. At first it had stung sweet and sharp but now it was starting to ache down to the bone.

'What happened here?' said Mr Hutchinson.

'Nothing. I fell.' Alice felt tears prick in her eyes, but she blinked and they disappeared into the depths of her insides. Mr Hutchinson peeled back the tea towel.

'Ouch,' he said. 'That looks nasty. We need to do something about that, it's very deep.'

'Something like what?' said Alice, a nervous judder in her chest.

'I was in the army,' said Mr Hutchinson. 'Saw action all over, mostly the Gulf. Other places too. I've fixed worse than this. Does your mother have any alcohol here?' Alice looked blankly at him.

'I think there's some upstairs,' she said in a whisper.

'Oh, I am sure there is,' said Mr Hutchinson. 'In the spare bedroom, the one on the far end – am I right?'

Alice nodded. She didn't know that Mr Hutchinson had ever been to their flat. The pain in her knee was beginning to throb; she felt sure it was making a dull, just about audible sound but she couldn't be sure. Her eyes were closing and she felt sleepy but she wanted to stay awake now that there was somebody to talk to – Mr Hutchinson was the first real person she had seen in days.

When he came back downstairs, Alice's eyelids were heavy and behind her eyeballs felt gritty and itchy. She could hear him rattling around in the kitchen drawers and when he appeared, the old man carried one of the bottles of clear liquid, the white sheet from the bed and a black pair of scissors that used to sit in their kitchen drawer. Alice rubbed her eyes.

'Couldn't find any antiseptic,' said Mr Hutchinson, brandishing the bottle of vodka, 'but this will do just fine.'

Alice jumped up and the tea towel slid down her leg.

'I think I'm OK,' she said faintly and sank to the floor.

'You've got a nasty cut there,' said Mr Hutchinson, starting to cut the sheet into strips. 'Lay down flat on the sofa and we'll sort you right out.' Alice used both arms to lift the injured leg up onto the cushions. It was heavy and dull, like her eyelids, but hurt a lot more.

'Here, take a sip of this.' Mr Hutchinson held the bottle to her lips and, before she could protest, tipped her head back and held it there while the harsh liquid slid down her throat. 'It'll help with the pain,' he added and Alice gagged as he held his hand over her mouth. It felt hot and warm inside her stomach, burning away the pain in her knee. She coughed a little and he took the bottle away for a second before replacing it again.

'Once more,' he said and she glugged down the vodka. Within moments she felt woozy and sick but relaxed, and the pain seemed to throb away gently in the background without the harsh sting.

'I feel sick,' she said as she pushed the bottle away.

'That's to be expected,' he said. 'Now hold onto something.' Alice screamed as Mr Hutchinson poured a sliver of vodka onto the wound and rubbed it with a cut strip of the sheet. She held onto the couch with both hands.

'Stop!' she screamed. 'It hurts.'

'Nearly there,' he said, rubbing harder. 'We need to make the wound clean.'

By the time Mr Hutchinson had finished cleaning and tying the tight white strips of sheet around it, the bleeding had subsided and Alice felt giddier and sicker than before. When he was done, he sat on the couch next to her stroking her hair, taking big gulps from the bottle and muttering words that Alice couldn't quite make out. Her leg was propped up on the pillows and her head ached as she drifted in and out of a sleepy place.

'Shh,' said Mr Hutchinson as he tipped the last dregs of the bottle into his mouth, 'we're going to be all alright.'

'I want my mother,' said Alice. 'I want to go home.'

'Oh, but you are home,' said Mr Hutchinson, putting his arms on her shoulder and her chest. He pressed down hard until Alice could barely breathe.

'You are home,' he soothed, 'and I'm all you've got in the world.'

Chapter Four

The FreeScreens

Carter

In the darkness of the shelter, Carter slowly got to his feet, the images of the Deadlands and the children of his own he had never met still scorched onto the inside of his head. His eyes were watering and his mouth was dry. The light of the FreeScreen in the shelter flickered on and off, casting a soft orange glow out into the darkness. Apart from the soft hum of electricity that ebbed out from the Barricades, it was silent.

Twins.

There had been no multiple births in the Community since the Storms. As much as it had been attempted in the labs, it was thought to be impossible. As much as his heart rallied against it, his mind raced with what had happened on that last night with Professor Mendoza's new student. The girl with the red hair. The Descendant.

A wet breeze whipped underneath his collar and over the smoothness of his face, droplets catching his eyes as he looked down the path. He smelled the air. Soon it would turn to heavy pellets and then hail again. Often the soft rain led to hail and if he didn't make it to the Community and inside some reinforced shelter, it could get dangerous.

Carter didn't want to remember as much as he did – it had all been over in a matter of seconds as the sun bled back behind the hills on his last night in the Community, fifteen years ago. He made the shape of the twins' names with his mouth – Ariel and Lucia – over and over again until his mind was filled with nothing else. He would get their address, visit them and, now that they were grown up, he would have no obligation of responsibility towards them. He felt something he couldn't quite quantify – there was an element of pride, of excitement. But his heart ached with anticipation of the impact it would have had in his absence. They were his – they were a part of him. He had never really imagined that he would have his own children; that was never a part of his plan. Of *their* plan.

But however hard he tried, it wasn't just the twins he thought about. He wondered how she was. Isabella.

'I've told you before, Carter. Stay away from the Lab Made.'

The sound of his grandfather's voice echoed in his head and he pulled himself together. He was tired and he needed to get back to the Community. But he would get the twins' address first.

Carter traced his fingers across the soft fibre of the screen, watching the cursor follow the swirl. The FreeScreen was a truly great invention – to date, the best Contribution ever produced by a Contender. He clicked on their names and waited.

Carter had been nine years old when the Industry had installed whole walls of FreeScreens in all public and private buildings through-out the Community. It had been talked about for a long time but their introduction had been the most recent Contribution of the new Controller General, Alderney, and Carter remembered it well – it had been less than a year before the disappearance of his parents.

Carter had followed the seventeen-year-old who had beaten Professor Mendoza with his FreeScreens Contribution around the Community until he had taken permanent residence in the underground offices and was rarely seen in public again. Alderney was what they called Neo-Industry, part of the strong-work-ethic group from the old times. Carter had watched him speak in front of the crowds, gaining their complete attention within seconds of opening his mouth.

'How did you come up with your Contribution?' Carter had asked him once as they'd walked through the Community.

Alderney had turned and smiled at him with perfect ice-white teeth. 'I looked for what was missing,' he'd said and sent Carter on his way.

The day the FreeScreens had been installed, Carter had woken up one night as his mother, Jacinta, had paced through the rooms downstairs.

'It's an intrusion,' she'd said to his father, Nikolas, in a whisper. 'Back to the old ways. I don't like it. A screen in every house?'

'It could be worse,' Nikolas had replied. 'At least this way we'll know what's going on. And I suppose they're not that different to televisions. Apparently *they* were a revelation in their day too.'

After that, the voices had lowered to a hush and Carter hadn't been able to make out any more of the detail. The next day his mother had been teary. He'd spent most of his time following the Industry engineers from home to home, trailing behind them as they'd worked in their crisp blue overalls. He'd watched as they'd pre-treated walls with a plasma adhesive and then painted over the plasma with a grey-white solution that enabled the screen to be seen in three dimensions. While the wall had dried, one of the engineers had gone to collect the screen. It had come in a small, round microfibre covering that shimmered like liquid silk in the palm of his hand. After he'd brought the box in carefully, he'd set it down on the floor before two engineers gently worked together to unfold the webby fabric into a massive cloth, which became harder, the longer it became exposed to the air.

'Twist,' the chief engineer had instructed, and they had turned over the graphene plate, working every fold and crease out of the fabric until the hardening screen was ready to fix to the wall. The junior engineer had balanced it on the palm of his hand, sometimes turning it and catching it on the tips of his fingers.

'Why do you do that?' Carter had asked curiously, watching the revolving plate. 'What if you drop it?'

'Twisting binds it in the light,' the junior engineer had answered. 'Without light the screen would be useless.' He'd flipped the screen over and caught it on the top of his index finger. 'And I never, ever drop anything.'

'What if it gets hard in the wrong shape?' Carter had asked, mesmerised by the spinning of the screen, which had been getting larger each time he'd looked at it, now taking the engineer's both hands to turn it in high circles above his head.

'It won't,' the spinner had told him, his eyes fixed on the centre of the plate.

They had been in and out of the house within half an hour, leaving no trace of ever having been there, except for the small cylindrical sliver of microfibre that the screen had been wrapped in. It had hardened into a thin ring of multicoloured light that had shimmered in the light. It had been the most beautiful thing he'd ever seen. Second most beautiful, he'd thought on reflection.

Now, under the cold white moon, Carter started to shake as nausea combined with the cold air took hold of him. Lines of text gleamed brightly on the screen. The twins' address was an old house in the South Quarter that showed five residents. Carter rubbed his hands together, listening to the regular ticking of the rain on the shelter. As soon as he could get there, he would. He wondered if they looked like him and what they knew already about how they had come into being. He imagined what their faces would look like when he arrived at their door; whether they were as good at censomics as he was. Whether one of them, too, might be Controller General one day. He breathed deeply. He still wasn't sure the realisation of their existence had sunk in properly. It hoped it would when he saw them.

The rain shower that had started picked up its rhythm. His eyes began to close; the tin-picking was as soothing and regular as a heartbeat. He thought again about the strange girl and her message. And then he thought about Isabella.

'Move, Carter,' he whispered to himself. 'Move.'

The rain came hard then, in thick, ugly pellets. Pellets that could, in twenty minutes, become ice crystals with the potential to pierce the skin. Since the Storms, there had been few deaths, but there had been enough that it was never worth taking the chance. He picked up speed, legs getting stronger with each step. Sloshy rivulets of water twisted underneath his neckline and down his back, making him gasp, but he didn't stop until the track wound its way around the pine forest that bled out the sweet, heady smells of wet conifer.

The first part of his Contender training to be Controller General would be physical – he'd need to prove himself fit and able to lead the Community – and now was a good time to start. He began to run faster, pushing his body to the limit. He felt the muscles in his legs tense and ache and the stiffness in his joints release. Although he'd not used his body in many years it still retained much of the strength it had before. He ducked and weaved across the path, taking longer strides, testing out the power of his legs.

Under the cover of the trees, the rain was bearable and Carter stopped to catch his breath in the lamp-lit forest. His lungs hurt and his legs were tired but physical exhaustion had never beaten him yet. He pushed onwards through the semi-darkness, black branches overhead holding the weight of the water and letting it out in deep plunges when the weight of it got too much. He got caught by the tail end of one leafy evacuation and the backs of his legs were almost pushed from under him. But he kept moving as quickly as he could. He knew, though, that he wasn't yet fast enough.

But, in just under an hour, for the first time in over fifteen years, he was back in the centre of the Community, the paved hub with its main podium and fountain garden known as Unity Square.

Carter found that after fifteen years, Unity Square had changed. The small podium had been enlarged and there were bigger, more imposing screens. At each corner of the square, hidden in the shadows, he could make out the shape of Industry officials. One nodded in his direction.

'Welcome back, Carter Warren,' said the man. 'Glad to have you with us.'

'Glad to be back,' said Carter, looking up at the cameras on each of the buildings around the square. 'Has there been a serious Storm threat recently? Looks like a lot of surveillance.'

The official almost smiled. 'Just keeping everyone safe,' he said. 'We all have a part to play in that.'

Carter nodded goodbye and walked around the edge of the square. Most of the inside house lights had been snuffed out and the glow from the street seemed dim and uninviting. With the exception of the officials and those moving out for the night shift, the streets were dark red and empty of conversation.

Two sides of the square were taken up with double-sided FreeScreens that reflected Community updates into the shallow puddles on the street. A thick crack of thunder echoed around the buildings of Unity Square and the sky shifted from a deep black to a feathery charcoal as a final outpouring of rain was unleashed across the angled roofs and into the drainage catchers. For a second there was silence and the FreeScreens went blank before the main colour of the screen shifted and the threat level of the rain moved back from red to amber.

Carter watched the news for a while, mesmerised by the huge screens as they showed releases, deaths and the bald crown of a baby streaked in blood. Then, there he was on the screen along with some of the faces he recognised from the Transporter – Harrison and Osian amongst others. A young girl smirked and put one thumb up towards the camera. The volume was a muffled growl under the last of the rain but he could hear the scratch of narration above the splashes. His name was one among many others that spilled out across the square.

'... Carter Warren, Osian Woolcroft, Jude Yavez and, lastly, Japheth Young were all released into Wood Community this evening, satisfying this quarter's request to balance the Model. And, to satisfy curiosity, it can now be confirmed that Jenson Jeremiah, Elizabet Conrad and Carter Warren have been selected to compete for the next election for the position of Controller General.'

Carter felt his whole body breathe a sigh of relief as the voice continued.

'All three Contenders, selected from different time periods, have been released this evening, and for different reasons. We are entering a new phase of our development here in the Community and we need a leader with the strength to guide us and help design this special transition. Each of our Contenders has unique qualities that could make each of them the best to lead us. In the coming days or weeks, we will find out which one of them can transform our Community to the next level.'

So it was confirmed. Three Contenders – all released this evening. Carter zoned in and out of the broadcast, exhausted. His heart beat faster as the news sank in. He'd had no real doubts, but the feeling of elation was magnificent. He wanted to shout and scream and throw his hands into the air. But more than anything, he wanted to tell his parents, to show them who he was now. Instead, he smiled to himself and let the feeling of excitement soak into his soul.

Carter was two streets away from the address on his card when he saw the figure of the woman. She stood, her back hunched a little, staring down at the earth. As he approached, he could see that her sandy-blonde hair was thin in places and caked in dirt. She moved slowly, scuffing her feet into the ground. His heart sank as she turned around.

'Carter Warren – what a surprise,' she said. The slight lisp that had once turned the corners of his mouth into a smile was now thick and raspy. In one hand she had a full bottle of fire fuel. As he stood there watching her, she opened it, sniffed it and replaced the lid.

'Isabella,' he said slowly. 'What happened to you?' He was unable to hide his shock. The excitement of the announcement drained from his body at the sight of the once beautiful, strong young woman.

'I noticed you were back.' She gestured towards the FreeScreens in Unity Square that were playing the announcements on loop. 'You haven't changed.'

'Nothing changes down there,' said Carter, awkwardly moving from one foot to another. Her eyes were darkened, circled and she carried a small light out in front of her, highlighting her painfully thin figure and the pockmarks that dotted her skin.

'Oh, but it does, I *promise* you it does, and more quickly than you could imagine,' she said.

'What's happened to you?' asked Carter, sadly. 'You look terrible. Things seem... well... different. There are guards everywhere and—' He broke off mid-sentence as Isabella put one finger to her lips and her eyes flicked up towards the FreeScreens in the square.

'Have you seen anyone else?' she mouthed, finger still against her lips.

'A girl,' said Carter, his voice hushed, 'and she talked about you. Who is she? What's going on?'

Isabella looked at him closely, up and down, her eyes piercing his heart. She turned around and moved in close to Carter. It was hard not to smell her now, a draughty stench of mud and sweat.

'We can't talk about that here,' she said, looking around her. 'But you can come to me and we can talk more. A lot of time has passed.'

'Why can't we talk here?'

'I came to find you, you know,' she said, ignoring his question, her eyes filling with tears. 'I thought we could have caught up. But you were... busy.' She bent down to scratch her feet. They were bare except for a strap between the first two toes, attached to a thin grass sole that was worn through. Home-made, not Industry issued.

'I did what I had to do,' said Carter, uncomfortable. Something felt terribly wrong in the Community. On top of everything, his head ached and his eyes were tight. Isabella looked dreadful, older, and so, so sad.

'You're a bright boy,' said Isabella. 'You can work out what happened. I live on the Fringes now, out by the South Barricade. I'm only allowed in here at night. Or, rather, they don't throw me out at night. I take my chances to see what's available, you know. Even someone like me needs things. You should come and see me sometime. Sometime *soon.*' The last word came out with virtually no sound, but the way her mouth formed the word, it seemed almost like a threat.

'I'm not sure I'll be able to do that,' said Carter hurriedly. 'You know the rules about spending time out at the Barricade, and as a Contender for—'

'Yes,' snapped Isabella. 'Well, you can't be associating with a Lab Made like me when you're about to become Controller General. I'm sure you met the current incumbent, Anaya Chess, at your underground dispersal. She was obviously a terrible choice.' She laughed out a sound that was more like a grunt.

'What do you mean, Isabella?'

She laughed again. 'The Industry are blaming Chess for the state of things. She made some desperate attempts to increase security in the last year but it's way too late for her. They're going to send her back underground. Carter, that should have been your job. It should have been your turn to come out of the Catacombs last time, not now. Now it's too late.'

Carter winced. 'I know and—'

'It's not safe here,' Isabella interrupted with a calm resignation and rubbed her palm across Carter's. 'Come and see me.' Then, without any further goodbyes, she left with the bottle of fire fuel in one hand, dragging a piece of wood behind her and whispering something inaudible in her wake.

'Wait,' he started but she was already out of earshot.

He watched her go, checking bins and behind homes until she melted into the blackness. There was something terrifying about the state of her – living outside on the Fringes could do that to a person, with little to eat and no shelter. He knew what had happened before he went away had hurt her. But Isabella? There had been a few older people he'd known of who had stayed out there for a few weeks, a month at the most, but they'd always come back. Been brought back. And besides Isabella, the odd girl had also said something about the Fringes. He didn't know much about that area – just that it was out along the edges of the Barricades and that it had been prohibited to spend time there, even in Gilbert Pinkerton's time as Controller General. But he knew he had no choice but to go.

When he was a teenager, the place to hang out had been the Blue Hills overlooking the Deadlands. They had spent so many evenings there, against the wishes of his grandfather, but that was not anywhere close to the stinking river. Back then when he was young, there had been none of those warning signs telling people to keep away from the Barricades; people just knew of the dangers and to steer well clear. They didn't need reminding.

He looked upwards at the shifting sky. Something didn't feel right. Children out near the drop-off station, the beautiful Isabella walking around half-dead in the blackness of night, talk of living out near the Barricades – none of this should be tolerated by the Industry. And none of it would be, when he became Controller.

As the moon shifted out from behind a cloud, the streets around Unity Square were quiet again. The soft dewy rainfall cooled Carter's headache as he walked towards the back of the Academy and around the path towards the address he'd been allocated. A light gleamed brightly through the window in the downstairs room then flickered as the FreeScreen inside switched channels. From the outside, the house looked small – the kind of dwelling you'd expect to find a Lab Made living in, rather than a Descendant like himself. He swiped his card over the door pad. As the door opened, he saw a shadow cross the room and a man stood up in the doorway to greet him.

'Carter Warren?' he asked, looking him up and down.

'Yes,' replied Carter. The man put his hand outside to feel the cool night air then moved aside so as to let Carter in. No hand swipe. He was well built with a thick mass of curls that tumbled down over his eyes and around his shoulders. His voice was firm, strong and slightly cold.

'I'm Alexis Ackerman. Your room is upstairs on the left. Rulebook's on the table next to the rester and there's a chunk of microsnacks in the fridge. I work at the synthetics plant on floor two. They brought some clothes over for you but you're going to have to pick up anything else you need yourself.' Before he'd finished the last sentence, the man was halfway up the stairs.

'Thanks,' said Carter, his legs melting into the sofa. 'I'm just going to sit down here for a while.'

'No need to report your movements to me,' said Alexis, unbuttoning his shirt. 'I'm Lab Made so our paths aren't likely to cross much. My ancestors weren't lucky enough to have children born to them as yours were. You're free to do whatever you want. Just don't wake me up before the morning; I've stayed up late enough as it is waiting for you. You have a meeting with the current Controller General tomorrow morning at nine so you'd better get some sleep. Goodnight.' And with that, he disappeared up the stairs and into the room on the right-hand side.

The door slammed and Carter sank into the soft arms of the rester.

As he drifted in and out of sleep, he heard the FreeScreen broadcasts remind everyone in the Community about the dangers of the Deadlands. The broadcasts infected his thoughts with dreams of claw-toothed creatures that clawed at the Barricades and demanded to be let past to feed and roam inside the Community. The warnings were fierce and regular. Carter dreamed of the sunken towns outside the Barricades that festered with nuclear waste and bred empty-eyed owls with poisoned talons and pale reptiles that spat venom with dart-point accuracy. He dreamed of his parents, drowning in a swirl of water and of the nose-less brother Silas whom he had never met, who ate his mother from the inside out and snarled at him and stuck out a forked tongue.

And then there was something else. In the background, or inside his head, there was a woman's voice talking. Calling to him.

'Carter Warren,' she yelled. 'We live near the Barricades. Come and see me some time.'

'Who are you? What do you want?' Carter heard himself say to the woman.

'You'll find us,' she said. 'You'll know why.'

'I don't know what you mean,' said Carter. 'Who are you?'

'We're the Lab born. You'll find us,' she taunted and disappeared into the moonlit night.

Drenched in sweat, Carter let out a yell and woke up. The FreeScreen buzzed with a loud, electrical hum, all programming finished for the evening. Seconds later, Alexis pounded down the stairs and cut the power to the FreeScreen.

'I told you not to wake me up,' he growled. 'We'll be leaving here at eight. Now get some sleep.' He punched his feet back up to the room on the right, leaving Carter sprawled on the sofa, shivering, a bead of sweat on his lip.

The woman's cackle reverberated in his head.

'Come and see me,' she said. 'And come soon.'

Chapter Five

The Rescue

Alice

The next morning the rain had started again. The pounding that felt like crushing rocks was no longer just inside her head but outside on the windows as well. Mr Hutchinson was standing over her, drinking soup out of a can.

'Last one,' he said, stirring it with his finger. 'There's some fruit there that's starting to go off – you should have that for breakfast. We've both got a long day ahead of us.'

Alice blinked the crust out of her eyes and looked down at her leg. A sharp pain shot from her knee to her thigh and radiated through her body.

'It still hurts,' she said.

'It will for a while,' said Mr Hutchinson, 'but we need to keep moving. We need a plan, soldier. Firstly, I'll go up onto the roof and collect some water. That's where you got it from yesterday, wasn't it?'

'Yes,' said Alice, 'but—'

'And we need supplies,' said Mr Hutchinson. 'We're partners now, aren't we?' One hairy hand slid out from behind his back and patted Alice on the head.

'I don't know,' she said. 'What if my mother comes home?'

Mr Hutchinson shook his head.

'She isn't going to be coming home, Alice. No one is. This building is empty apart from us; they've all gone. Most of them weren't at home when the Storms started and others just got flooded right out. Those first two days were so heavy it was like the sky was spitting rocks. You know Lydia Duncan from the second floor?'

Alice nodded. 'The lady with the pink hair?' she said.

'That's the one. Well, a giant hailstone hit her clean between the eyes and carved a hole in her head so big that you could see all the way through. She was on her balcony at the time – tipped right over the edge into the water. That was very early on. There were others…' His voice tapered off and Alice pulled the blanket around her.

'We should try to get out,' she said. 'Try to find other people.' As the words spilled out of her mouth, she suddenly realised that being in the flat with Mr Hutchinson until the rains stopped might not be the most comfortable of options.

'We won't get out yet,' said Mr Hutchinson. 'The lift shaft is full of water. So are the stairs. And it's rising. We'll never last out there. We have to stay here until the flood subsides. But we need a plan. And we need food. In the army we had plans in case of times like these. We should definitely have a plan.' His voice became more animated the more he spoke. 'And I've been thinking—'

'Do you have any water?' Alice cut in. Her head still pounded with the effects the vodka, and her throat felt like it was bunged up with sherbety chemical-tasting sand.

Hutchinson handed her a glass. 'Last one,' he said. 'I'll get some more in a moment. But we have work to do today. And we need to act quickly – the rain will only get heavier. I've been keeping a diary.' He pulled out a crumpled notebook and flashed it in front of Alice. 'I've always kept a journal, ever since my days in the Middle East. Stops you from going, well, stir-crazy.'

Alice licked the inside of her cheek and felt along the ridges of the gash she had bitten into.

'My leg hurts,' she said. 'It *really* hurts.'

'I know,' he replied. 'But it's nothing a strong girl like you can't handle. We have to be brave.' He stopped for a second and handed her a pear. 'What's your name again, Davenport?'

'Alice,' she replied, licking out the sweet fruit juice. 'My name is Alice.'

'Alice,' he said absently, flicking through his book. 'Do you want to play a game?'

Alice shrugged, sucking on the pear. 'I guess so.'

Hutchinson smiled. 'Well, that's great to know. So this is how it's going to go: I'll call you Davenport and you can call me Hutchinson – or Sir. And we're going on a mission.'

Alice looked at him and nodded. 'What sort of mission?' she said.

Hutchinson licked his pencil. 'Today is a Tuesday and on Tuesdays the rain tends to be light enough until approximately five-thirty, except for the odd heavy shower, of course. After that, it would be unwise for us to attempt any activity on either the balcony or the roof. Timing is everything in this game.'

Alice rubbed her eyes. She swung her legs over the side of the sofa and pulled on a jumper. When she pressed her injured leg on the floor, it took her weight but not without significant pain. She screwed up her face.

'What are we going to do?' she said. There was something almost exciting about a mission.

Hutchinson smiled. 'Do you know where the Middle East is, Davenport?'

Alice shook her head as he beckoned her towards the hallway.

'Come with me,' he said and grabbed her by the arm.

Alice half-hopped, half-limped to the stairs as Hutchinson strode up towards the bedrooms. He stopped halfway, opposite the map.

'*This* is the Middle East,' he said, pointing at the map on the wall. 'Here is Iraq, here is Syria, and the country to the left there is Jordan. Now, I want you to concentrate on Iraq. This is where I was stationed – the first time. I wasn't a young man even back then, I'll let you know, but I was strong, Davenport, I was strong.'

Alice watched as Hutchinson's eyes clouded over and he pulled out his pipe from his pocket. He struck a match and the faint smell of eggs wafted down the stairs towards her.

'Can I get another drink?' she said. 'I'm really thirsty.'

'Pay attention, Davenport, I need you to focus. Your first mission will begin shortly but now I need you to concentrate. Now, just look at Iraq. In the south we have Basra – wonderful place, fine people – all gone. We are here, in the north, in Mosul. Some survivors, you see. And in the middle there is Fallujah. We don't know much about Fallujah. Are you getting my drift here, Davenport?'

Alice shrugged her shoulders.

'I'm not sure I do,' she said.

'Sir,' said Hutchinson. 'Address me as either Sir or Hutchinson when you speak to me.'

'I'm not sure I do, Sir,' said Alice. She ran her tongue over her teeth. They felt sticky and there was a terrible taste in her mouth.

'Let's get straight to the point, Davenport. We are here in the north, you and me, in Mosul. Basra, to the south – floors one to five – is underwater. And then there's Fallujah. We don't know for sure whether there are any survivors in Fallujah. Team Hutchinson is on a discovery mission.'

'I thought you said that there was no one else here,' said Alice, confused. 'Sir, I'm not sure I understand.' Her head felt light and airy and she leaned on the wall for support.

'You will, Private,' said Hutchinson. 'Now, let's get some refreshments and then we'll make our plan of attack.'

On a clean sheet of paper in his notebook, Hutchinson drew out a sketchy map of the building.

'The water has made it as far as here.' He drew a line in the floor plan and scored out the floors below the line. 'We won't be going anywhere further down than this.' Then he drew another line just below the top two floors. 'There's nothing on either of these two levels, I've checked them all. But we need to search the properties below this line. Problem is—' he scratched the inside of his ear with the pencil '—the problem is that the stairs are blocked. When the Storms started, the cretins on the eighth floor barricaded themselves in to prohibit anyone coming down from these two floors and stealing their food – wardrobes and the like stopping up the stairs like a great big constipated colon. So we're going to need to go another way.'

Alice watched as he supped on the second bottle of vodka. He looked over at her and tipped the bottle in her direction. Her stomach retched at the thought.

'No thanks,' she said.

'Sir?'

'*Sir*,' she said and let her gaze melt into the lined notebook on the table in front of her. Hutchinson was deep in concentration and not smiling at all.

'We're looking for tobacco, alcohol and any foodstuffs you can lay your hands on. Only look for things that are tinned and preferably don't need mixing with water. Anything fresh will have gone bad by now – and absolutely no meat unless it's in a can. You'll have just under an hour to get in and out. Make sure you bring me back something strong. There'll be a reward in it for you if you do.' He put his hand on Alice's leg. 'We need to trust each other now, Davenport,' he said and then touched the side of her face.

Hutchinson made them wait for exactly fifteen minutes after smashing the bedroom window two floors down before making the next move. He swung the large basket he'd attached to the rope back and forth until the hole in the window had seemed big enough to push Alice through. Her head swirled as Hutchinson lowered her over the balcony. The rope dug into her hands and as she crouched her legs into the basket, she could feel them shaking beneath her. The pain in her leg was nothing compared to her fear of falling into the deep grey swirling mass below.

'Lean inwards,' called Hutchinson. 'Get a grip on the ledges and I'll go slowly.' Alice could almost hear him smiling. 'Chin up, Private,' he called cheerfully. 'We'll have you back on dry land in no time!'

As she neared the window, the wind whipped up and swayed the basket back and forth. Alice closed her eyes and waited as Hutchinson took the strain and steadied the basket until she was level with the window. Taking the hammer, she tapped around the edges of the broken glass, levering them and then pushing inwards like Hutchinson had shown her.

'You ready?' he called. Alice could just about hear his voice as it was eaten by the wind. The swing of the rope threw her almost entirely into the room and she used her hands, filled with splinters of glass, to pull herself over the window ledge and straight onto the bed. It was the smell that she noticed first. Next, it was the clusters of flies that buzzed along the ceiling of the room and then out into the cloudy sky like musical notes along a stave. On the bed was the stinking corpse of a dog, already long dead. Letting out a screech, she threw herself onto the floor, shaking.

'All right, Private?' called Hutchinson.

'Fine,' shouted Alice, her heart beating like a drum. She tugged on the rope to signal her arrival. Hands shaking, she untied the basket from the rope. Pulling open the bedroom door that had been jammed shut, she made her way downstairs, head spinning and stomach churning.

In the kitchen, the cupboards were empty except for two tins of dog food. Disappointed, she kicked the base unit door, which bounced open. Under the sink there were the dregs of a half bottle of whisky. Alice opened the bottle and sniffed. The rancid liquid burned her eyes and she shoved it into the basket. The front room had been completely trashed and the windows broken, an icy wind whispering through the curtains. Like Hutchinson had instructed, she walked out through the rim of the door and climbed over the wooden fencing separating the back balconies. But the next flat was exactly the same. And so was the next. By the time Alice reached the fourth flat, she had been gone for over half an hour and all that she had was a drip of whisky, the dog food and a can of processed peas that were out of date.

In the last flat in the row, the windows weren't smashed. As she climbed over the balcony, she called out, first in a whisper and then more loudly but no one answered. Taking the hammer in one hand and covering her eyes with the other, she banged on the glass until it shattered into pieces on the floor. When the last pieces fell, and there was no other sound, Alice crept through into the front room. She stepped over the glass, which crinkled underneath her feet.

It smelled even worse than the bed she had landed on when she had first arrived on the eighth floor. The walls were papered with cream-and-white roses, faded yellow with decades of smoke damage and wear. On the floor, in front of the electric fire, was a pile of half-burned books, charred around the edges and damp. The front door had been barricaded with a sturdy wooden table and a large bookcase. A chill ran through Alice's bones.

Someone had to still be in the house.

'Hello,' she called, but there was no answer. In the kitchen, the cupboards were not over-healthy but there were some cartons of cereal, biscuits and chocolate. Alice filled the basket and then opened one of the small bars of chocolate and inhaled the sweet, deep smell of cocoa. It melted in a delicious frenzy in her mouth and she savoured every piece. She chewed it, sucked it and swallowed, the sugar tingling through her fingers to the roots of her hair. For a moment she was delirious – until she remembered the barricade at the front door.

The stairs were as old as those in number 59, but creaked twice as noisily. Each step let out a distressed moan as she pushed her foot downwards, as lightly as she could without hurting herself or creating too much noise. Balancing her weight on the balustrade, she picked her way gently upstairs. The smell of decay was overpowering. It was a sweet, ugly smell; more potent even than the rubbish chute at the end of her balcony. Pulling her T-shirt over her face, she picked onwards, the smell hugging her brain and her lungs. It was only when she shoved open the bedroom door that the horror hit her.

The couple in the bed were embracing; skinny brown arms the colour of creamed coffee poking up above the covers. An empty bottle of pills stood on the cabinet next to them, and one of them, a man she presumed, was still clasping a bottle of spirits, one arm over the bedspread, the other around the person next to him. There was the whistle of the wind and the call of a bird somewhere in the distance. Standing as far back as she could, Alice pulled on the bottle, wrenching it out of the withered hand. As she turned to leave the room, she hobbled back to the bed and carefully pulled the duvet over the couple.

'I'm sorry,' she whispered, eyes filling with tears. Alice swallowed deeply and ran without stopping to look in the other bedroom. She didn't stop moving until she was back in the first flat with the jagged window.

Putting what she had found in the basket and tying it to the rope once more, Alice watched out of the window as Hutchinson pulled it up carefully, steadying it against the raw breeze that brought with it the overwhelming stench of a city in decay. While he unpacked the basket she thought, for a moment, that he wasn't going to send it back down for her and that she was going to have to stay there on level eight with the couple in one flat and the dog in the other. For the briefest of moments, in the quiet of the afternoon, Alice was terrified of being alone.

'Hutchinson,' she shouted. 'Sir, where are you?' But there was no answer and the only sound was a cold wind whipping around the tower. When the basket returned, relief overwhelmed her and she anchored it with one hand, climbing in with the other, levering her legs with the sway of the wind.

'Thank you,' she said quietly. 'Thank you.'

'Well done, Private,' said Hutchinson as he hauled her through the window. 'Mission one complete. But this lot won't last us long. Tomorrow, we'll go down to level seven.'

Their dinner was a relative banquet – tinned peaches and peas with a small glug of canned cream.

'Fit for a king,' said Hutchinson, eyeing the bottle of rum she'd stolen from the bony fingers of a dead man. 'Fit for a king.'

Less than an hour later, the rain turned to hail. Big, thumping chunks of ice that battered the wooden boards across the windows that Hutchinson had strengthened after they had eaten. The flat was starting to look like a prison.

'Those hailstones were vicious,' he said, stepping in from the balcony. 'And it looked like it was going to be a nice day today.' He took a large swig of the rum. His eyes were bloodshot and wild-looking.

Alice shook her head and sat down on the sofa. 'I'm tired,' she said and curled up with the blanket around her.

'We'll need to change your bandage before you go to sleep,' he said and stripped the blanket from her legs. He picked up the scissors and started shredding the rest of the sheet on the floor.

'I don't want to,' she said. 'Sir.'

'Don't disobey me,' he said in an angry voice. 'You will sleep when I tell you to.'

Alice scowled. 'It's my house,' she said under her breath.

Hutchinson's eyes bubbled and a thick drool of spit gathered at the corner of his mouth. His fabric-ripping became more frantic and exuberant.

'Your house?' he shouted. 'This is a situation of war. And in situations of war there are often things that we don't want to do, but we do them anyway.' He grabbed a length of sheeting and turned it into a makeshift gag. Alice kicked and screamed as he wound it around her head, tying it in a tight knot. Then he grabbed her knee and massaged the cut with his thumb. She tried to scream again but it got lost in the cloth.

'But we have to be brave,' he said. 'Now hold still.' As Hutchinson moved over her, undoing his belt, Alice pushed and squirmed but he had her pinned down, stinking of rum and peaches, traces of cream on his face, whiskers like a vicious tiger.

'You're my little girl now,' he said and reached for the rum, holding Alice with his bony hand.

'Get off me,' she screamed from under the gag and he laughed; a deep, throaty laugh that chilled her bones to the core.

'You're your mother's daughter, aren't you?' he said and he leaned slightly off balance to swig the drink. It was enough. In the splintering of a second, Alice reached down towards the carpet for something, anything, to beat off Hutchinson. Her fingers found the blunt, black metal scissors that her mother had used for making clothes for her when she was a little girl; scissors that had belonged to her grandmother, and had been carefully carried from house to house, holding a legacy of history in their dull metal blades.

With everything she had left in her, Alice reached around and plunged them into Hutchinson's side, just below the armpit, driving them through the thin muscle until they hit bone. He didn't scream or shout but instead he wheezed out a long, monotone growl. It was terrifyingly easy, frighteningly simple.

Then she pulled the scissors out and pushed them back in again until his blood dripped over her and he slumped, breathing shallowly on top of her.

'Help,' he mouthed. 'Help me.'

Using the scissors as leverage she pushed him off onto the floor. It wasn't as physically hard as she thought it might have been – had she considered it in advance – but the disgust of his filthy, ugly body was enough. She stuck the scissors into his heart one more time and left them there, pointing outwards like a sundial as the evening crept into twilight.

'Goodbye,' said Alice, her hands shaking and numb. Hutchinson's chest rose and fell and then rose again. And then he, and everything around him, fell silent.

Alice stood by a crack in the wooden covering of the balcony and breathed in deeply. Everything was cold and dark with just the lap of water outside. She watched as the pieces of wood, toys, trash and the shadows of dead cats bobbed up and down around the fifth floor of the tower block. And, once again, she was alone.

It was three days after the fight with Hutchinson that they rescued her. Rats had eaten their way through the bottom of the door and had started nibbling at anything they could find on the floor. She had hauled the remaining provisions upstairs and curled up on the worn mattress in her room, with a chest pushed up against the door. Hutchinson's blood had pooled on the living room carpet and, while she knew he was long dead, there was something reassuring about an additional piece of furniture between his body and her bed, while she slept.

On the second day after she had stabbed him, her leg felt a lot better and she went up to the roof to get some water. Running low on food, she tried going down the stairs towards the ninth floor. Just like he had said, the ninth floor was empty and there was a jumbled barricade of furniture separating the two floors. But it hadn't been put up to stop people going down. It had been built to stop people coming up. He'd barricaded himself in, thought Alice. He had barricaded himself in.

Crazy, insane old man. As horrible as it all was, she knew she had done the right thing. But she would draw the line at eating him, however hungry she got.

When she heard them shouting on a loudhailer from the boat, she thought it sounded like a call to prayer; musical, rhythmic and beautiful. It was late afternoon and the rain had fizzled into a soft, sheeted blur that you could stand outside in without getting bruised.

'I'm here,' she shouted from the hole in her mother's bedroom window, and she held up the bloody bedspread out into the water to make sure they knew she was real. A real, live person.

'Is there anybody with you?' a man shouted.

'No,' called back Alice. 'I'm all alone.'

'We're going to throw a rope up to you,' shouted the man. 'Is there anything you can secure it to?'

'I have one here,' yelled Alice through the window.

'Good work,' called back the man. 'We have to hurry, the rain is coming soon.'

Alice grabbed the rope that had the basket attached and fixed it to the leg of the bed. Then she smashed through the window, just like Hutchinson had shown her, and lowered the rope as low as she could. She made it almost as far as the seventh floor. The man in the boat had an inflatable mattress pulled behind them and, when she reached the end of the rope lowered from the window, Alice jumped, landing squarely in the middle of the mattress with a dull bounce. A woman in a waterproof suit hauled her in and sat her on the boat.

'Was there anyone else in there?' she said.

Alice looked up at her and then back towards the block of flats.

'No,' she said, and then added truthfully, 'no one who could be saved.'

She shared the boat with three other survivors – two young boys and a middle-aged woman who fussed over her.

'I'm OK,' she said and held her mouth in a completely straight line.

'You don't need to worry any more,' smiled the woman. 'You're safe now.'

Alice nodded and realised that the woman was saying it more to reassure herself than anyone else.

The last thing that Alice remembered before the boat pulled up to the compound was the cat. It floated past the boat, tail high in the air. It was white with black spots – or black with white spots; later, Alice couldn't exactly remember. It swirled around and got tangled up with the leaves and twigs that had been scraped from the pavements, bumping up and down in the swell. She watched until it disappeared past the boat and out of sight. And then, she really, truly and properly began to cry. Her tears seeped down her cheeks and into the well of the boat, between the dirty shoes of the two boys, and underneath the warped wooden seat that the woman sat on. She closed her eyes and let the tears run down her face until there was nothing more left to come.

When she awoke it was dark, and thick rain had made the deep water a dark grey-brown. The tops of buildings rose up out of the water like swan necks.

'Where are we going?' said Alice, nervously.

A woman steering the boat pointed into the distance towards a small funnel that loomed just above the line of the water.

'What's that?' said Alice.

'It's the chute to the Paradigm Industries Facility,' nodded the woman. 'You'll be safe there.'

Alice wasn't sure what safe was any more but the woman gave her two bread rolls containing lukewarm hot dogs that Alice thought were the sweetest and best thing in the world. But they weren't like anything she'd ever tasted before.

'These don't taste like hot dogs,' she said.

'That's because they're not,' replied the woman quickly and steered the course of the boat closer to the chimney stack of the building that stuck out of the water.

When they reached the docking station, they were pushed into the chute and landed on a platform from which they entered the facility through a special door in the wall. Above everything else, Alice remembered being pushed into the chute; it was round and made of grey metal the colour of a whale. As she put her legs into the slide, she looked back quickly at the black night, the thick, lapping water, and the moon half-covered with dense cloud.

Later, Alice could remember that blackness so clearly. It loomed and blossomed inside her head, sometimes pinpricked with stars and other times lit by the pale October moon. Alice remembered it every single day – because it was the last time she saw the sky for five whole years.

Chapter Six

The Contenders

Carter

When Carter woke the next morning, he could still feel a dull throb inside his head and an ugly aching in his lower legs. As he opened his eyes, he could see the substantial bulk of Alexis casting a grey shadow across his bed, darkening the room to the quality of twilight – although Carter could just make out the dawn light behind the window covers.

'I have just under an hour to start work. You have your orientation with the Controller General. That means we leave in ten minutes to get a Transporter from Proclamation Plaza. Welcome back.' Alexis smirked and threw a set of clean clothes onto the bed then left the room.

As he sat up, Carter realised that the aching in his legs was nothing compared to the loneliness he felt in that moment.

Outside the window, there was the regular rhythm of feet stomping their way to work or wherever it was they went at that time in the morning; Carter wasn't sure he cared. Peeling back the window covers he could see a thin, wispy mist that hung in the air as the cold yellow sun hoisted itself above the horizon. He tested his legs on the floor, stretching them before putting his full weight on them. From downstairs he could hear the shuffle of rushed activity and he picked up the fresh clothes from the bed. They were medium-duty work wear, functional and second-hand, in the same dark colour Alexis has been wearing last night. They looked several sizes too big for him.

'Are you ready?' came Alexis's voice up the stairs. Carter stood naked in the middle of the room and glanced once more at the overalls.

'Almost,' he said and pulled on the trousers that hung off him like food sacks. He wrapped around the waistband and folded up the bottoms.

'We leave now,' said Alexis and opened the front door. Carter took the stairs two at a time and, more by luck than design, landed at the bottom upright and ready to go. Outside as they joined the ranks, the air was crisp and cool and there was a low hum of conversation as the tide of workers swept out onto Unity Square and down the main street towards the central Transportation station. It reminded him of the morning he went away.

But this time, instead of their own clothes, every single one of them wore identical work suits – the same one that he was wearing himself.

'New uniform?' he asked Alexis who was already steps ahead of him. 'We used to all wear our own clothes.'

'This is what the adults wear now,' Alexis responded. Then he looked squarely at Carter and added, 'You *are* an adult, aren't you?' His eyes narrowed before he dropped his glance and weaved back between the crowds as far ahead of Carter as he could get.

To access the main platform at Proclamation Plaza, the crowd had to pass through a wide, low arch that carried the magnets above them. In the main tunnel, smaller passages curled off in other directions, headed for Transporter platforms to different sections of the Community. Determined not to lose either his trousers or Alexis, Carter followed, his eyes tracking the distance between them, as well as the distance between Alexis and the tunnel. One soft surge of the crowd behind him closed the gap and Carter found himself channelled into a tunnel with his trousers around his knees.

'Get yourself a belt and a sense of direction,' said Alexis as they surfed up the tunnel with the others towards the platform. 'Tomorrow, Carter Warren, you're on your own.'

'I'll be glad of that,' said Carter, sick of Ackerman's rudeness. 'But for now, you can lead the way.'

'I'll take you to the orientation room and then I have to work,' said Alexis. 'And when you're done for the day just head for the Transporter terminal; it will take you back to Proclamation Plaza. The Controller will introduce you to Lilith McDermott. She's your mentor.'

Then he popped a block of microsnack in his mouth and turned his back to Carter. After that, no further conversation passed between them for the remainder of the journey.

Without any windows, Carter couldn't be absolutely sure whether the Transporter was above or below ground for the majority of the time. Although for the last ten minutes when the air was filled with the same stale stillness that he had felt on his ascent from the Catacombs, he was fairly sure that they were going deeper underground. There were two stops before his – the first was Power; the second, Manufacturing. At each stop, about a third of the passengers left, and when the doors slid open to reveal the entrance to the Food Plant, Carter was the last to leave the Transporter for the second time in less than twelve hours. Alexis led the way through a series of corridors until they reached a room marked Orientation.

'I'll be fine from here,' said Carter. Alexis nodded grumpily and disappeared down the tangled maze of tunnels. As he lifted his arm to knock, the door slid gracefully open.

'Carter Warren, so nice of you to join us.'

It was the same voice that he had heard the night before – the voice of Anaya Chess.

'Yes, Controller,' he said, and watched as his name was scored off automatically on a large electronic board at the front of the room. There were six places, two others crossed off and three that remained blank.

'Take your seats,' said Chess. 'We're about to start your Contender orientation.'

Carter made his way to one of the benches that were laid out in rows, running from the door to the other side of the room. In front of each bench was a thin table with a screen embedded in it. The two others on the bench moved along to accommodate him. At the far end, he recognised one boy who had been on the first Transporter with him. That must be Jenson Jeremiah. Next to him sat the girl, Elizabet. All the other benches were empty. The Controller stepped out from behind a screen at the front of the room, her thin hair braided into tight cords around her head. It pulled back her skin, making her seem her twenty-seven or so years, rather than the much older-looking woman who had spoken underground.

'Good morning and welcome,' she said. 'As you know, my name is Anaya Chess. For all three of you, this will be your first full day back in the Community and the first for several years to actively contribute to our society. There are three additional Contenders who are not with us today – depending on how you fare over the next week will depend on whether they become part of this process too.'

She glanced around at the walls, but Carter could see nothing there.

'As you know, you have been chosen because of your skills, knowledge and the leadership you have shown as young adults during your time in the Community. The time has come for us to select a new Controller General and you are the best candidates both above and below ground for what we need at this time in our evolution. Each of you has demonstrated an aptitude for learning significant levels above your peers, and a keen interest in the areas important for sustaining life within our Community. You are strong, determined, brave and smart – but only one of you will make Controller General. For your information, you are the youngest ever group of Contenders – new blood, so to speak.'

As Chess broke off to look at each one of them, Carter took the opportunity to do the same. There was the boy from the Transporter – he was short and stubby-looking with deep brown eyes and flawless dark skin, and Elizabet, a spindly yellow-haired girl who appeared even younger than he did. Between the three of them, they couldn't have looked more different. Carter guessed that personality-wise and politically, they were probably complete triangular opposites too; that was how it always worked.

'Over the next week you will each have time to work on your Contributions – the one that presents themselves as the most impressive and impactful will likely win the day. Those of you who are not selected into the role I shall be vacating will be expected to contribute to the education of our next generation.'

'Professors,' said Elizabet under her breath and rolled her eyes.

The boy from the Transporter looked across at Carter and eyed both he and Elizabet up and down. The girl twirled a twig-like finger around the hair that fell like fronds in front of her face. She almost looked through Carter.

'So what's today all about?' she asked, looking across the row. 'I guess this is where the training for the others starts? I've started mine already.'

Chess stepped closer to the row and looked her closely in the eye. 'Well, then, I expect you will be at your peak during this process,' she said. 'But your mentor will also guide you.'

'I don't need a mentor,' said Elizabet. 'I can do this on my own.'

'You will all need your mentors,' said Chess dismissively. 'Any other questions?' Carter had plenty but thought better of asking. He shrugged and, before he could say anything, the boy on the end raised his hand. When he spoke, his voice was low and quiet – hardly good for rousing a crowd. Carter had almost written him off.

'How come there are six Contenders?' he said in a slow, deliberate boom. 'Even three is unusual. There have only ever been two. What needs to happen to bring the others into play?'

Chess smiled, although there was a dark cloudiness in her eyes. 'This is a very unique selection,' she said, 'unlike any other. Although you may not know it, our Community is on the verge of a very important change and, to do that, we need a different kind of leader, someone very special. I can tell you that you will need to be able to take our Community to the next level of its evolution. We will be expanding outside of our borders and tackling a few issues we have identified on the inside of the Barricades. Some disquiet amongst our people, you could say.' She looked a little embarrassed. 'You will have to undergo significant personal challenges and—' she lowered her voice a little '—I can tell you that the role of Controller General is the hardest job that has ever existed. Are you brave enough to take that on?'

The room fell silent and Carter found himself nodding, along with the other two Contenders.

Chess looked at the girl.

'Anything else to say, Elizabet?'

The girl looked up.

'I'm brave enough,' Elizabet said. 'The question is—' she looked across the row at Carter and the boy from the Transporter '—are they?'

Carter smiled, irritated already. 'Bravery isn't everything,' he said. 'So let's get to it.'

'Well, now, Elizabet,' said Chess. 'That sounds like a challenge to me.'

Just then the doors clicked open and two Industry officials walked in. Without saying a word, one of the officials handed across a silver tablet and left the room. Chess flicked her finger across the tablet and smiled.

'Your initiation begins here,' she said calmly. 'I have some information for each of you here – a simulation, if you like, and I will need you to plan your responses. Elizabet, you will go first, then Carter and finally, Jenson. This will require you to dig deep into who you are as individuals and what is important to you.'

Elizabet stared straight ahead, her eyes clear and bright. Jenson was looking down at his hands, rubbing his palms together slowly. A divider in the room opened, revealing three work areas, each with the name of the Contender above. Carter's booth was coloured yellow and faced Elizabet's directly, which was pattered with white birds.

'Make your way to your work areas and I will visit you individually. In the time you have, I suggest you think about everything you have been in your lives until this point and the new person you will have to be to take on this, *specific*, challenge.'

Carter stood up and pushed back his chair. The others followed and they made their way to the booths – he could see that Jenson was already shaking. He sat down at the console and watched as the screen flashed into action. As the images cleared on the screen, the figures formed into faces he knew – pictures of his parents, his grandfather, his Academy friends. He strained his eyes to see the emotion in the footage that moved quickly in front of his face. He hadn't ever seen them on a screen before and had almost forgotten the brightness of his mother's eyes. She stood, holding hands with his father, staring out at the Barricades, and Carter watched as they kissed and walked backwards towards the Community. Then the screen changed and there was a five-year-old Carter being lifted up into the air by his grandfather, staring at the clouds. He almost felt like he remembered that exact moment: the lightness, the blueness – a perfect blend of a day. The film faded and there were his parents again, this time with someone else, someone he knew but couldn't quite place, somewhere close to the Industry headquarters. His mother was crying, holding her swollen stomach, and his father's eyes were red. The footage played over and over again and Carter felt his throat thicken and his own eyes prickle with tears. He looked around at the other Contenders – Elizabet was talking to Chess quietly, her shoulders shaking but her gaze fixed firmly ahead. Carter could hear a mumble of words but couldn't make out the detail, until her final outburst. She pulled at her hair and banged her palm against the screen.

'I can't!' she screamed. 'I just can't. It's wrong; it's just WRONG.'

Jenson kept his head down and Chess smiled over at Carter.

'Concentrate on your own screen please, Carter Warren,' she said. 'Your time will come.'

When his time came, Elizabet was sat in the corner of the room with a wry smile on her face and Jenson had his face in his hands. Carter couldn't see what was on either of their screens but whatever it was, it had been big. That was good. Chess sidled over to his booth.

'Carter,' she said. 'I need you to focus on the screen and tell me what you would do in this scenario. And while you are doing this, place your index finger against the scanning chip of your personal card. This will help us to understand your motives.'

'What do you mean?' said Carter. 'You can read my mind?'

Chess laughed. 'No, no, nothing quite like that. But your card makes us feel closer to you, and it will guide your on-screen character to make decisions.' She laughed again and took Carter's hand and placed it on his card. The screen rolled into action again and Elizabet began to shake her head again in the corner of the room.

'Is she OK?' asked Carter.

'That's not your concern,' said Chess. 'Now it's your turn.'

On the screen there was a close-up of Carter's mother. Then, as she turned away from the camera, rain started to fall from the sky. Heavy, thick balls of ice pelted against her back and one caught her on the left side of her head. As she fell to the ground, the camera angle widened and there were a group of children, Carter's Academy friends amongst them. In the distance, he could make out a shelter and, then, Carter himself ran onto the screen. He wasn't sure how old he was, maybe twelve or thirteen. He stood there staring at his mother on the floor.

'This didn't happen,' he said. 'My mother was already dead.'

'Think about what you are seeing,' said Chess softly. 'What do you do next?'

Carter watched as a trickle of blood seeped from one of his mother's eyes. He could almost smell the scent of her skin and the softness of her energy. The version of Carter on the screen knelt down next to her and put one arm under her shoulder. There was a scream from the group of children and one, Isabella, fell, clutching her arm as the ice rained downwards.

'You want me to save one of them,' he said to himself and pressed his finger down into the card. The boy on the screen stood up and looked over at the children. They were younger looking than he remembered and Carter was older, stronger. As the ice rained around him, he shouted across at the group.

'Run to the shelter,' he said. 'Go quickly.'

'Carter,' begged his mother. 'Don't leave me, please. Save me.'

He knelt back down and ran his fingers through her hair. The line of blood ran as far as her neckline and pooled on the ground. There was another scream from the children.

Chess rubbed his shoulder. 'With complete power comes great responsibility,' she said and took a step backwards from the booth.

Carter swallowed.

'I have to do what's right,' he mouthed and held his mother's hand tightly. He pulled her towards him and tried to lift her. She was much lighter than he had imagined. It would be easy enough to take her to the shelter.

'I love you, Carter,' she said. 'We can be together again, like a family.' Her eyes filled with tears and something jolted in Carter.

'I don't think I believe in love,' he said. 'I believe in what's right.'

Sheet hail started to fall all around him and the rain was getting stronger. Isabella screamed again, this time as a spear of lightening hit the ground near to where the children had gathered. Carter hesitated for a second and then dropped his mother, who shrivelled into a ghostly pile of rags. He ran towards the children, herding them into the shelter. As he did so, the screen went blank and a bead of sweat trickled from his forehead onto the desk in front of him.

'Good start,' said Chess. 'A little slow, but you got there in the end.'

'You wanted me to save the future over my past,' said Carter, breathless.

Chess looked at him steadily. 'You'll do what you have to do,' she said. 'And that will make you a leader or a failure. The choice is yours.' Carter looked at the clock on his screen – less than three minutes had passed since he started watching the footage.

'Is that it?' he said.

Chess smiled. 'That was just the warm-up,' she said. 'Now we get into the interesting stuff.'

There were the usual set of tests that Carter had expected – electronic circuitry to be rewired that, surprisingly, Jenson mastered more quickly than the other two, and some synthetic mixing to create new strains of plant material.

From the time he'd spent during his visits to the Industry Headquarters as a young boy, Carter knew he had aced that one completely. He couldn't hide his smile. Synthetics was a great deal more valuable than electronics – the points Jenson had won would be worth very little. But, from the look on her face, Elizabet had done exceptionally well too. The Industry technicians cleared away the materials and, just briefly, the three of them were left in the room alone.

As the door closed, Elizabet glanced over at Carter, her eyes changed to tight and angry.

'Wait until we start on Censomics,' she said. 'We'll see who's best placed for Controller General then. I know the Model better than anyone.' She threw off her shoes and did an elegant, athletic handstand against the wall, her thin arms much stronger than they looked. She lowered her body downwards, allowing her arms to take her full body weight before she pumped them back up again.

'Cryonics will come first,' said Carter, with slight disdain, 'and that carries some fairly big points too. And, by the way, I—'

'Yes, you fixed the Model when you were, what, seven or eight?' said Jenson in a deep, bored voice. 'We've all heard about that. Your reputation precedes you.'

'That may be true,' said Elizabet, kicking her legs down again and standing upright. 'But I'm also related to one of the original Scouts and he was there when the Model was first developed. He oversaw its design in fact. He was more important than anyone.'

Carter recalled her surname – Conrad. Filip Conrad. Again, he tried to dismiss her. 'That was over eighty years ago,' he said. 'It doesn't mean you have any more insight than anyone else.'

'It's not always *what* you know,' said Elizabet as if she were telling someone a secret and smiled a sweet, sickly grin back at Carter.

When Chess came back into the room, the three of them were sat in an awkward silence. She popped her head around the door briefly.

'There will be one final challenge today, but this will come later this afternoon,' she said. 'I'll just get you some refreshments before I take you to meet your mentors.'

Carter looked at Elizabet who had kicked up another handstand, poised with one leg against the wall and the other in the air, eyes closed.

'When do you come from?' Carter asked her, curious.

'I'm from a long time before you,' said the girl. 'That's all you need to know.'

'You don't *need* to tell me anything. I was making conversation.'

Elizabet opened her eyes briefly, flashing a smirk at Carter. 'You're a Warren, aren't you?'

Carter looked at her sharply. 'You knew my father? My mother?'

Jenson stared at them both.

Elizabet laughed and let her body sink to the floor elegantly before bouncing upright. 'I know of your family, yes. But long before your father. The Warren I knew was…' she laughed to herself. 'He wasn't that great.'

Carter let the tension in his body release before he spoke, ignoring her comments.

'So do you have an idea for your Contribution?'

'Of course; I've had it for years – but I shan't be telling you the details.'

'I don't want to know what it is,' he said. 'But if you've been around for that long, you might want to make sure it's still relevant to the world – things do change, you know.'

Elizabet nodded.

'They do,' she said. 'And they will. Things are going to be very different when I'm Controller General. Starting with the Model that you think you know so much about.'

As Carter started to speak, the door opened and Chess came back into the room carrying a plate full of synthetic foods and handed them to the Contenders. Jenson was still looking outwards blankly and refused to have anything to eat. Chess ignored him and started talking.

'Thank you for your work this morning,' she said. 'The results are being processed as we speak and will feed through to the final evaluations. As you know, this is about who you are as individuals and what decisions we can expect you to make if you are elected as Controller General. Everything here is designed to find out exactly who you are. Are *you* sure of who you are?'

Carter looked at Elizabet, who was dipping boeuf sticks into a sauce and popping them into her mouth one by one.

'That was interesting,' she said, her mouth full of food. 'Do we get to do that again?'

Chess shook her head. 'I'm afraid not, Elizabet. Most of the other work will be done directly with your mentors who have been chosen to bring out the best in you – and I am sure you are eager to meet them. For those of you who may have had previous mentors, you should sever all ties with them. Your new mentors are experienced returners who have served this Community well. They will answer any questions or concerns you may have. And—' she paused as they were about to leave '—you each have a challenging road ahead of you. I suggest you concentrate on your own journeys and don't focus on each other. Now you will meet your mentors and I shall see you later today.'

And with that, she was gone. Carter and the others were shunted by a security officer out of the door and directed down a flight of stairs towards the Synthetic Food Plant. Jenson was taken first, still quiet and miserable. Then Elizabet was siphoned into a side room.

'Goodbye, Carter Warren,' she said. 'I'm sure you'll make a great professor.'

Carter smiled at her. 'And so will you,' he said. 'I'll make sure you get a good position when I am Controller General.'

She flashed a sarcastic grin at him and then was gone.

He wondered whether she, like him, had always wanted to go through the process and what it had been like in her time as a child growing up with his distant relatives. He wound his way down the next flight of stairs until they reached the bottom floor.

'In here,' said the guard. 'Your mentor is still on her shift.'

The Synthetic Food Plant clicked and buzzed with the patting and shaping of material by the machines and the manipulation of various levers by those operating them. One button added flavour, another included different materials to differentiate textures, and a pair of grab claws defined the shape. Carter scanned the floor and on the far right he could just make out the lumbering shape of Alexis. The guard directed him to the middle of the room, next to a girl with white-blonde hair and an old man in his forties with wizened fingers who stood on one leg and then the other, operating his machine with rapid dexterity. As he moved closer, the woman started to speak.

'Carter Warren?' she said, not taking her eyes away from the machine for a second. 'I'm your mentor, Lilith McDermott – but, please, call me Lily. We've been waiting for you and it's so good to finally meet you.' There was genuine excitement in her voice and something else that sounded a little like relief.

It was partly the shock of seeing an almost ghost-like image of the old Isabella and partly tiredness that suddenly sparked irritation and anger in Carter.

'My mentor? You can't be more than, what, sixteen?'

Lily stopped the machine, smiled brightly at him and took off her gloves, touching his hand softly with her own. The clicking sound of metal whirred to a stop.

'I'm eighteen, actually.'

There was a bright sparkling in her eyes that was so much like the young Isabella might have had, it made Carter's heart beat fast. But the young Isabella was gone and other than the brightness of her eyes, the two were very different. Lily's hair was long and light, tied back neatly, and her lips were perfectly rounded. She seemed efficient, direct and calm. Good qualities for a mentor. Then he remembered the professor.

'What about the professor... Professor Mendoza?

Lily smiled and shook her head. 'I'm afraid she's no longer with us. She has been called to the Catacombs. And, in her absence, we've been electronically matched to each other because the Industry believes I can contribute to you, get the best from you and complement your skills more than anyone else in the Community today.' She flashed him a self-assured smile. 'And I've been around a bit too. This is my fourth tenure, just so you know.'

'Fourth tenure? How can that even be possible?' Carter asked, puzzled. He'd heard of a couple of people being frozen for a second time, voluntary punishment for breaking minor rules in the Industry Code of Conduct. But never *three* freezings – and never by choice.

Lily grinned back at him.

'Let's just say I've got a great deal of experience and I'm here to help you. My job is to make sure that you, above the others, become Controller General. But there'll be plenty of time to talk later. We'll need to get to work straight away – you have a Contribution to prepare for. How did your orientation go?'

Carter felt himself soften slightly. Lily clearly wanted to help him, it seemed.

'It was tough,' he said. 'But nothing I couldn't handle.'

'And the other Contenders?'

'I think the boy isn't going to be a problem but the girl…' Carter stopped for a second. 'There's something about her – something special. She's smart, really smart, but it's like she knows something more. Like she can anticipate what's going to happen next.' Carter thought back to her almost predictive replaying of the electronics exercise. 'She's, well, she's different to other people.'

'You all are. That's why you've been chosen.'

'But she seemed… like she was from somewhere else. I just couldn't quite read her.'

'And don't try to. This is about *you*, remember. And what *you* can bring to the Community. The next step will be for us to run through what your ideas might be for your Contribution and then we need to get you making some decisions.'

'I can make decisions already,' said Carter. 'I'm here, aren't I?'

Lily smiled and pushed the hair from her eyes. 'You are indeed, Carter Warren. You are indeed.'

'So right now I'm going to do something useful. Show me how to work that machine and then we can get out of here and start work.'

'Well, food shaping should accelerate your physical reactions, speed up your adaption. Then I am assuming that you'll be reassigned to somewhere more—' she paused for a second, '—fitting to your circumstances and aspirations.'

He nodded his head slightly.

'But for today, we are glad to have you on the team. This—' she gestured to the old man two machines away '—is Morton Dickenson.

Carter nodded to the old man who raised one wrinkled paw in his direction.

'Welcome to the Plant, kid. I'm a Lab Made, but don't hold it against me.'

Carter smiled. He might not be around for long but it was nice to find someone who seemed generally pleased to meet him.

'Hi Morton,' he said and held out his hand. 'I'm Carter.'

They rubbed palms and Carter was left was the overwhelming smell of chemical rosemary powder and kelp sauce. Within minutes it had permeated his own work shirt, his mouth mask and the space between him and Lily. The old man Morton looked at his clothing in mock disdain.

'Take this, kid,' said Morton, handing Carter his belt. 'You need it more than me.'

'And even a great leader needs to know how to make food,' said Lily with a laugh and went back to her position.

Morton grinned at him, showing gums that were as red as his hair.

Carter glanced over at Lily, hands firm on the machine, and a warm glow enveloped his body.

'A bit like Isabella, ain't she?' said Morton, grinning and flashing the room a glimpse of his gums. 'Her mother was a Delaney too. Shame about poor Isabella. But that's love for you.'

Carter stopped dead, mid-pour.

'What did you say?'

The room went quiet. The question had sounded a great deal more confrontational than he had meant it to.

Morton looked around, tufts of hair on his head puffing about in the breeze coming from the ventilation fans.

Carter turned to face Morton.

'I don't think I believe in love,' he said, repeating his grandfather's words. 'Love doesn't get things done. And there's no love possible between a Descendant and a Lab Made.' The second point came out more quietly. As he looked around for Lily, Morton laughed at him.

'There's always love,' said Morton and turned back to his machine, nodding to himself and smiling. 'A girl, or a boy or something. Anything that keeps your heart beating while you're underground. They said we'd die without it; it's the one thing that we still have. The one thing they can't stop. And it blindsides you when you are least expecting it.'

'I'll be sure to watch out for that love thing,' Carter replied cautiously and the old man whirled around, switching legs as he did so.

'You need any advice, feel free to come to me, son,' said Morton with a wry smile. 'I can let you know what you need to know.' He winked at Carter and carried on with the chicker, feeding it through slowly, all the while keeping his gaze directly forwards.

'I think I'm all OK,' said Carter and turned back to his machine.

'You think?' said the old man. Then he whispered something that Carter could barely hear and shuffled around in his pocket.

'What?' asked Carter. 'I didn't hear you.'

Morton coughed hard, pulling his identity card out of his trousers clumsily and dropping it onto the floor, just as two of the Industry security guards headed directly towards his machine.

As both he and Carter bent down to pick up the card, Morton spoke in a hurried whisper, his words cutting Carter like the icy shards of rain that fell from the skies. There was no mistaking what he said, even after the guards took the old man Morton out of the Food Plant and into the lifts. The words echoed in Carter's ears:

'I know who you are. You're Jacinta Warren's son and you're here for the Uprising.'

Chapter Seven

The Facility

Alice

The first place they took Alice to was cold and damp with metal walls that were covered with pictures of red and yellow hot air balloons that soared upwards into an invisible sky. It was called the Playroom, although there was nothing in there to play with. There were rows of small bunk beds with hardly any space between them, each covered in thin plastic covers that made Alice much too warm at night.

At one end of the room was a large bathroom that had plastic shutters for doors. Most of the other children were younger than her but almost all of them cried like babies in the beginning, sometimes all night. Different children came and went. They cried for their parents and they wanted to see the sun. Alice knew that there wasn't much point in crying; it didn't bring you what you wanted and it usually caused more trouble.

For the whole of the first two weeks there was no school, which should have been a good thing but it also meant that they weren't allowed to leave the room very often. The only adult they saw, apart from the porters who brought them food, came twice a day. She was called Miss Kunstein, a spiky-looking woman in a long coat with tails who took them out of the room and down some corridors past the laboratories, through a tunnel, and the wrong way along grinding, black travel belts. They walked for two hours every morning and for two hours every evening. Kunstein always walked upfront alone, swishing her long coat through the miles of cavernous passageways. The underground facility was huge. The network of tunnels extended deep under the city and into the heart of the earth.

'Daytrip time,' said Miss Kunstein as they left one morning. 'Alice, you lead.'

Alice walked on ahead through the maze of corridors, turning left and right, following the course they had taken every morning in the two weeks since they had arrived. At each junction, although both ways looked the same, she always took the correct one. Somehow, she could feel the corridors like she'd been able to feel the hum of the streets of the city, never getting lost. When they got back to the Playroom, Kunstein let all of the others back into the room then turned to Alice.

'How did you know the way?' she asked.

'I just did. We walk that way every day.'

'We pass through eighty-seven junctions, Alice, and each one looks almost identical.'

Alice shrugged. 'I know my way around places. It's what I do.'

Kunstein smiled in a strange, knowing kind of way. 'You've had to find your way around quite a bit, haven't you, Alice?'

Alice bit her lip and said nothing as the door opened. It was only when she woke up in the middle of the night, hot and sweating under the plastic cover, that she remembered where she had met Kunstein before.

It had been the day they'd gone to the museum and Alice's mother had soaked herself in perfume that smelled like violet creams. The museum had been one of only two buildings that stood more than a couple of storeys tall in that part of town. They'd climbed the steps surrounded by grand white pillars and, as they'd stood in the doorway facing the rain, Alice's mother had pointed outwards.

'Look, just there, you can see Prospect House.' The dreary tower block shape of the flats had loomed black and imposing against the other surrounding buildings. Alice had nodded. Even across town it had carved an ugly, dirty shadow across the skyline.

They'd crept into the museum and waited as the security man spoke into a scratchy radio and ushered them through the turnstile. He'd thrown an icy stare at Alice's dirty, drippy footprints as she'd sloshed past.

'She yours?' he'd asked her mother, nodding his head.

'Yes, but she won't be no trouble. We can still… you know?' Her voice had trailed off and got lost in the domed entrance hall, eaten up by the portraits of fat, bearded men that had watched them with empty glances.

'Keep her out of the way,' the security guard had instructed. He had a sharp uniform and a shiny head that was clean of hair although he had a wisp of furry fluff above his top lip. Alice had put her hand over her own hair and gathered up the soaking mass into a ponytail.

'See you a bit later, then,' Alice's mother had said to the guard with a weak smile.

'My break's in ten minutes,' the guard had grunted, going back into his security booth. 'And don't shake yourself in there, you hear me?' he'd called to Alice from behind the glass, narrowing his eyes as she and her mother had disappeared through the door and down a curved flight of stairs that extended deep underground. When they'd reached the bottom, a warm rush of air had whooshed to meet them and Alice had thought that she'd felt a moth flutter across her cheek.

They'd gone through a low corridor and down some more stairs until they'd reached an alcove where there were two archways covered with thick red curtains. Over one there had been a felt-tip pen note that said *Private* and the other had a sign that read *Natural History*.

Alice's mother had pushed open the curtain to *Natural History* and they'd walked on until they spilled out into a room full of pastel-pink marble pillars etched with leaves and reeds that had curled over the edges of the ceiling and gripped onto the walls with firm, emerald tendrils. She'd wondered if the pillars were holding up the whole world above her.

Along each side of the room, crystal cases had been packed with stuffed animals; hundreds of pairs of glassy eyes had locked on Alice as she'd stepped carefully through the centre. In the first case on her left had been a blue and gold kingfisher, its beak shining with the silver-finned fish that had dangled out of it. Alice had gulped.

'Is it real?' she'd asked her mother.

'It was, but it isn't any more.'

They'd stood there at that first case, warming their fingers on the glass cabinet, which was being heated by the bright light focused on the kingfisher. Alice had watched as her fingers had pulsed back into life, red and stinging, and she'd pressed them hard against the glass to stop the tingling.

Next to the kingfisher there had been a case full of butterfly cocoons that had looked like they were made of cotton wool, soft grey-white and empty. Beside them, pinned helplessly against a board, had been hundreds of butterflies and moths. Alice had focused her eyes on them in the gloom until she'd thought she seen one of the wings lift sadly off the board.

She'd pulled her mother's sleeve. 'They're beautiful,' she'd said, horrified. 'Why would anyone do that to them?' Her mother had dragged herself from her own reverie and smiled, ignoring what Alice had just said.

'I have to go and do some business now,' she'd whispered and crunched her fingers slowly. 'You just have a look at the other animals and I'll be back soon. No wandering off now, just wait in the café upstairs when you're finished, OK?

Alice had nodded and wandered through the museum, following the corridor past all the other cases until she'd reached the lift at the end that led to the café. When it had stopped at the top, she'd stepped out of the creaking carriage and found herself a table, watching as the fan in the ceiling whirred around rhythmically.

A sign on the wall in shiny red plastic had said *Only customers that have made a purchase at the café are invited to sit here*, so she'd wrapped her hands around a three-quarters empty mug still on the table. She'd squeezed the last of the heat out of the cup and kicked her feet against one of the other chairs, licking tiny sprinkles of sugar and powdered chocolate off the edges of the mug. It had tasted good.

'I'm waiting for my mother,' she'd said to the waiter who'd come to wipe the table. He'd scraped a crusty cloth across the film of dried coffee and carrot cake crumbs and straightened the chairs without saying anything, before going back to the cappuccino station.

'She gon' leave you?' The waiter had run his rag over the nozzle of the cappuccino machine. 'She gon' chat with Mr Security in his *love* box?' The waiter had made the word love loop around his mouth a few times before he'd spat it out and then made a whooping sound when he was done. Alice had scrunched up her shoulders and shrugged.

'Maybe she ain't never comin' back,' the waiter had said and flashed a perfect white smile, giggling to himself as he'd stacked the plates into piles according to size.

'She always comes back,' Alice had replied fiercely, biting her lip hard. The waiter had smiled and raised his eyebrows.

'One day she won't,' he'd said and tucked the cloth into his waistband. 'I got tha' evil eye, I know everythin'.' Cackling, he'd set about putting the cups and mugs into a similar order. Alice had turned back to the coffee cup she'd been holding and swirled around the dregs.

That was when she'd seen her. She hadn't noticed the lady at first, sat in the corner with her hands also fixed around a mug. She'd been dressed in a long black coat that was wrapped around her tightly and done up all the way to her neck. Her eyes had gleamed dark and hard as she'd watched Alice.

'What's your name?' the woman had asked her.

'Alice,' Alice had replied slowly.

'You're a brave girl, out here all on your own.'

'I'm not afraid of being on my own,' Alice had said, defiantly, even though part of her was. 'I've been to lots of places on my own. I take the Tube from Prospect House all over London.'

'You do? And what are you doing here?'

'I'm taking care of my mother. I take care of things.'

'That's good to know.' The woman had got up from her chair just as Alice's mother had arrived to collect her. 'That's very good to know, Alice. Maybe we'll meet again soon.'

Now, Alice shivered; she was sure it had been Kunstein.

The first week underground was the hardest. It was tough, not just because she missed her mother, but because she missed all the little things about their life. She missed biscuits and the map on the wall in the flat and the green blades of grass in the park and her blue dress with the embroidered red rose. Sometimes she even wondered about the man with the evil eye in the museum and whether he or any of the coffee cups had made it out intact. But most of all she missed the view from her balcony and being able to look out across the city, watching the way the river snaked around the outside of her world in the far distance, hugging it tight like a noose.

Like the Underground and the subways of south London and the dark maze of city streets, Alice knew how to navigate the network of tunnels and corridors with rooms that you needed a special pass to access. Her card gave her access to almost nowhere and came with instructions from a broad-shouldered man with a grey suit. He gave them a welcome talk in the great hall.

'My name is William Wilson,' said the man, surveying the crowd. 'And welcome to the Industry Headquarters. This will be your new home—'

'Until when?' shouted a man near the front.

'… until we are able to establish a safe and secure environment above ground. You will already be aware that the meteorological activity over the past few weeks has rendered all areas north and west of London, and all low-lying areas – including the city and surrounding areas – uninhabitable. We have also detected that, as a result of structural damage caused by the significant weather fluctuation to Drakewater Nuclear Facility, there has been some leakage of toxic waste material.'

A rumble broke out among the crowd and Wilson rolled down a shiny white screen from behind him. Some of the younger children were crying.

'Are we safe here?' called the boy from the crowd.

Wilson straightened his tie and coughed.

'This facility is completely protected against all kinds of threats. We have been developing the underground environment here for over fifty years.'

'Is it a bunker?' The boy at the front had pushed his way forwards so that he stood directly in front of the stage.

Wilson smiled wryly.

'Ladies and gentlemen, this is not a bunker. Nor is this a government-provided facility. As you may know, Paradigm Industries are a private group of companies that undertake a range of market-focused activities including media and communications, biochemical and biomedical advancement, banking and finance, and construction and change consultancy. We have pioneered the exploitation of subterranean business development and own a significant proportion of the under-city landscapes across the south-east. This has enabled us to—'

Wilson broke off as a man began to shout from the front of the crowd. 'We don't care about your market share this, or your consultancy that. We just want to know what's going on. Where are the politicians? Has anyone called the army?'

Wilson moved right to the front of the stage so that he stood directly opposite the man.

'Mr... Allerton. Graham Allerton, correct?'

The man, Graham Allerton, nodded, his mouth wide open.

Wilson moved so close to him that Alice thought he might fall off the stage at any moment.

'How do you know my...?'

Wilson ignored the man and gestured to him to move backwards.

'Mr Allerton of Grantham Drive, Camberwell. I can only offer my sympathies regarding the loss of your wife – so close to the loss of your daughter less than a year ago.' His face softened. 'Car crash, wasn't it?'

Allerton nodded and dropped his jaw further.

'I…' he began to say, but little, if anything, came out of his mouth.

'But Mr Allerton, you are not the only one and there are many confused and frightened people in this hall. It is my job to let you know that whilst you are our guests here, you are all safe. Those of you with us today are the lucky ones. Anyone who has remained above ground will not be so fortunate.' Tears streamed down Allerton's face and he stepped back into the crowd as Wilson started again.

'You will all need to prepare yourselves for some bad news. Due to the damage done at Drakewater and other facilities both here and overseas, significant contamination has taken place. Forecasts suggest that the Storms will continue for several months – if not years – and life as we knew it has changed forever. Only facilities such as these will provide any level of protection and, unless they are fully equipped, these are unlikely to provide any long-term solution. Our priority now is you.'

Alice didn't really understand much of what William Wilson was saying but she didn't think it sounded like they were going to be leaving the underground den anytime soon.

As the lights went down, William Wilson announced that they would be watching a short film about the facility that they had made a few years ago for marketing purposes and that it would help them to see how safe they were. A lightning-flash logo zoomed across the screen and then the music started – a low, soft drone of notes that underscored the documentary. A sharp voice cut through the hum as a swooping camera glided through long, grey corridors, up and down staircases and past room after room.

The facility, built using new techniques and new polybrand materials developed by Paradigm Industries, is unique. No facility combines research, manufacture, recycling, power and habitation in such a way. Not only is it the largest facility of its kind in the world, it's the only one fully equipped with its own power-production atmosphere processing plants, designed to withstand significant external pressure.

Alice bit her nails individually until nothing was left above the finger lines except a row of red half-moons. The hands of the watch she had stolen from a stall at the Frederick Street market dragged around the face. Sometimes, her watch was the only thing that marked out the difference between day and night. It was so difficult to tell the time without sunshine.

As the film rolled towards the end, Alice yawned. Graham Allerton hadn't made a sound during the programme and the woman next to her who had been crying was asleep. William Wilson puffed out his chest and moved back to his podium at the front of the stage. A klaxon sounded that woke up the Great Hall in one, immediate blare.

'Thank you for your attention everybody. Over the next few days you will be allocated a personal living space. But until then, please continue to treat the communal bunks as your home. Any possessions should be surrendered to enable us to maximise our resources here and we will make our best efforts to house families together or within close proximity.

'Each level within the facility has hundreds of miles of tunnels, some of which can be used for recreational exercise and others that are entry prohibited. It will be very easy to get lost – and if you can imagine being lost in a large city with no recourse to refreshments or facilities, it could become dangerous. If you have any questions, please refer them to your case officer when we issue you with your personal identification cards today. Thank you for your time and attention.'

As she lay in bed thinking about Kunstein, Alice felt the plastic of her card in her pocket. It hadn't been difficult to swap her key card with the one the food porter had clipped to his belt when he arrived with the evening meal. In fact, it was easier than shoplifting at the market – no one here was expecting her to do it.

She climbed out of bed, swiped her card on the door, slid it open silently and crept to the end of the corridor. When she got to the first set of stairs, she started to climb upwards, tiptoeing as quickly as she could without clanking her feet on the cold metal staircase. In the dim quiet of the service stairwell, for the first time since she'd been flipped like a giant fish from the window of her flat, she was alone.

Alice stood motionless in the silence for a few seconds and devoured it in great gulping chucks. Then she started to move again, this time more quickly, to the upper levels that were forbidden to anyone not employed by Paradigm Industries. She knew that the alarm would be raised, but under the circumstances it would be worth it to spend some time alone.

By the time the alarm came, she had found out enough. And it came quickly. Short, sharp blasts on the klaxon and then a long, loud blare. But as the cool air of solitude crept around her she felt calm and, although she knew there would be trouble, she was fairly sure that the punishments wouldn't come much worse than her previous fate of being marooned in a house alone with a deceased and decomposing Mr Hutchinson. And that thought alone instantly calmed Alice.

Chapter Eight

The Children

Carter

'Where are they taking him?' Carter asked Lily. 'And what was he talking about?'

Lily pulled down a lever on her machine, carefully shaping the chicker into cubes.

'He's just a crazy old man,' she said dismissively. 'His workmanship is still excellent but his mind has all but evaporated. He's made it to a good age really, but too long underground and not enough drugs. He was one of the earliest ones, you know?'

Carter pressed the stop button on the man's machine that was still running.

'How old is he?'

'Forty something or thereabouts – he's had a few blackouts in the last week or so; that's why he was allocated a position next to me. I covered for him as much as I could but the last time he was raving about monsters and all kinds of things. The Industry said they'd give him one more chance before…' Lily's eyes filled with tears and Carter put a hand on her shoulder.

'Before what?'

'Before he would be taken for his final freeze.'

Above the whirring of the machines, there came a long, whining drone of a sound and then a voice spoke clearly across the whole room.

'Carter Warren, please report to the initiation room immediately.'

Lily nodded towards the door. 'You'd better be quick,' she said. 'This will be your last test of the day. They may call you back for more, depending on how you get along with the next stage but this may be your last chance to impress them directly. It's back up the stairs to the room at the top. And focus.'

'I always do,' said Carter and shut down his machine.

When he got to the room, the other two Contenders had not arrived. All the tables and benches had been removed and three of the walls had been transformed into giant screens made up of thousands of dashboard metrics. Carter recognised it immediately. It was the Model.

He watched as the charts and graphs flickered up and down fractionally, measuring the amount of food available, populations split by age, gender, suitability to simple tasks, health and every other thing imaginable – as well as air quality, time and weather. He stood mesmerised by the pixels that danced across the screen, changing every second. He was so engrossed that he didn't even notice when Elizabet, Jenson and, lastly, the Controller General entered the room.

'Right then,' said Chess. 'You all know what we're looking at here. This is a delayed feed from the Model. As you are aware, we employ hundreds of analysts to monitor this data on a constant basis but, ultimately, when there are decisions to be made, it always falls upon the Controller General to make the final call on any critical actions. Therefore you must all be experts.

'I'm already an expert,' said Elizabet with confidence. 'I'm a direct Descendant of—'

'Yes, yes, we know,' said Chess, interjecting. 'Now, for the last task of today, each of you is going to monitor the entire Model, making the necessary changes to ensure that you maintain an absolute equilibrium across the Community. The decisions you make today, of course, will not have any direct impact as you're all using the same direct copy of an offline version. It will be speeded up so that you can see the results of your changes immediately. However, you should treat this simulation as if it were real life. *We* will be.'

Jenson's eyes flicked back and forth across the screen. 'How do we control it?' he said.

Chess handed them each a tablet. 'You'll use this,' she said. 'There are five key mechanisms – Synthetics, which controls food and materials production; Electronics for power; Land Grab, which monitors expansion and contraction; Behaviour Location of our citizens based on their card data; and, of course, Cryonics, which controls freezing and release. Combined, these make up the overall Censomics data, which you will all know as Population Control. Behaviour Location is a new one – recently developed.'

Jenson looked troubled. 'You want us to monitor the whole thing?' he said. 'That's impossible.'

'Nothing is impossible,' said Carter. 'We just need to work together. Right?' He looked at Elizabet who was focused on the data.

'As long as you let me tell you what to do,' she said, not looking at him.

Carter laughed at her arrogance. 'If you know all the right answers, you won't need to tell me – I'll be doing them already,' he said.

'Enough bickering,' said Chess. 'The challenge has already started.'

The levels on the screen moved slowly as Carter started to find his way around the control. There was a deficit of food so he increased production, moving more of the population into work mode.

'We need more people,' said Elizabet. 'I'm going to unfreeze four hundred.'

'There's not a thawing due until next week according to the rota,' said Jenson, flicking through his tablet. 'You'll have to wait.'

'I can order one – I'm Controller General,' said Elizabet.

'Wait a moment,' said Carter. 'That's madness. We don't have enough food as it is – according to the production data, we can't feed the people we have.'

'Too late,' said Elizabet decisively. 'Thawed. They'll be here tomorrow.'

'What age and demographic?'

Elizabet looked down at her small screen. 'Doesn't say,' she said.

'You have to specify,' said Carter, irritated. 'I thought you were an expert at this.' He looked at the data, shaking his head. 'They're all over thirty – they'll consume and not produce effectively.'

Jenson pointed to the top left-hand corner of the screen. 'We've got bigger problems than that,' he said. 'There's trouble out near the Barricades.'

All three of them focused their gaze on the Behavioural sector, which was glowing red.

'What's happening there?' said Elizabet.

'Lack of food, I'd guess,' said Carter. 'It's making people agitated and they're looking for a way to rebel.'

'Send in Terrorist Security,' said Jenson. 'It's the only way.'

'No,' said Carter, his mind on Morton. 'We need to find out what's happening first. We need to know the reasons why they're rebelling.'

'Ever the peacekeeper,' said Elizabet snidely. 'Just shoot them. The rebels need taking down.'

'I know that,' said Carter. 'But unless we understand their motives, then how will we stop it happening again?'

'Times are different now, Carter,' snapped Elizabet, flicking a switch on the control panel. And, by the way, Jenson, Terrorist Security is not the only way. There are other methods for ensuring we get the information we need. Some of these rebels need to be kept alive and out in the Community, for the time being, so that we can obtain the information we need. We just need to ensure they are—' she hesitated '—controlled. There are ways of doing that.'

Within moments, the indicator on the screen turned from red to amber and then, eventually, to green.

'What did you do?' said Jenson.

'See there,' said Elizabet, smiling and pointing to a detailed graph. 'We needed more Lab Mades released – ones with low level IQs and skill sets to stabilise production in the plants.

'But they're not using any resources,' said Jenson.

'I know,' said Elizabet, smiling. 'I got rid of them as soon as they'd outlived their purpose. If I tell you any more, it'll spoil my Contribution.' She giggled. 'But it's safe to say it involves the Lab Mades.'

Carter felt a pain grow in the pit of his stomach and he shuddered. He didn't even want to know what her Contribution was, but he did know was that there was no way he could let Elizabet beat him.

As the afternoon wore on, the days ticked through the Model. The unfrozen returned to the Community to consume resources and the disquiet in the Community increased. The top right-hand corner glowed a continual blood red.

'We need to make people happy, content,' said Carter finally. 'Or expand into the Deadlands; give ourselves some more production space. Remember what Chess said?'

'No,' said Jenson and Elizabet in unison. 'There's nothing good out there.'

'And people don't need to be happy,' Elizabet added. 'They should just be grateful for what they have.'

Carter frowned at her. 'Happiness is important,' he said. 'And we need to freeze some more people – including the older generations – until we can stabilise resources.'

Between them they quickly selected a few hundred. 'You know this will give us more problems,' said Jenson. 'There aren't enough births happening. When the young people grow up and we have to return the older ones, they'll consume without producing and we'll have the same issue again.'

'Then we don't return them,' said Elizabet. 'We remove them.'

Carter shivered at the thought of his grandfather, his parents even. In Elizabet's mind, they were completely expendable. And the rebels too. There was something about her cool, calm confidence that sent a chill down his spine.

'There has to be a better way – a different way,' he said. 'There's no humanity here.'

'Well, if there's a better way, Carter Warren,' said Elizabet, 'you find it.'

'I will,' said Carter quietly. 'I definitely will.'

Within three hours, the Model of the Community was at breaking point. Chess walked into the room, smiling, eating a stick of carrotina.

'Good work,' she said glibly. 'It didn't take the three of you very long to destroy everything we have.'

'He stopped me making the right decisions,' said Elizabet, gesturing towards Carter.

'Yeah,' added Jenson, his eyes still fixed on the screen.

Chess flicked a switch and the walls faded into blackness.

'And that's why we only have one Controller General,' she said. 'A decision made by more than one person is a compromise for all.'

Elizabet opened her mouth to add something but closed it again, content her point had been made.

Chess looked at the blackened screen and shook her head.

'What's next?' said Jenson.

'Nothing more for today,' said Chess crunching her carrotina. 'You can leave now, but do start to think about your Contributions. And enjoy the last of the evening sunshine – it's been a while since any of you have seen it.'

By the time Carter had boarded the Transporter back to Proclamation Plaza, the sun was already starting to dip its burning orange hump back below the edge of the horizon. He hoped deep in his heart that he never had to see either Elizabet or Jenson again – and definitely not as Controller General.

Lines of people were making their way home under the cover of a calm autumn evening, most of them channelling their way towards Unity Square. He breathed in the sweet air that carried traces of lavender. Lavender usually meant only one thing: a baby had been born. A First Gen – someone directly descended from the first group of people, beside the Scouts, to see the outside world after the Storms. A direct relation of someone who had been on the Ship. He fell in line with the stream of people headed north to the square, dazzled by the melting yellow rays of the sun and the thick sweetness of the air. He glanced at his reflection in one of the pools by the fountains and was startled to see the exhaustion etched on his face.

At Unity Square, hundreds were gathered around the screens where a girl lay panting in the final stages of birth. He didn't remember how many births he'd watched, but each one filled the whole Community with a dizzying rapture. There was a collective intake of breath and, at the first glimpse of the tiny head projected onto the FreeScreen, the crowd screamed. As the girl made her final push, the bloodied baby was paraded simultaneously into every home, bawling red and scrunched for all to see. When there was a birth, there was no turning off the coverage, even if you tried to cut the power. It was all beamed in remotely. The screen showed a small crowd lined in rows to congratulate the parents and their families. There were almost as many Industry doctors as there were onlookers. Above ground births were so rare that when one was happening, there was no switching off.

'Lucky to catch the re-run,' said one woman, tears in her eyes, pointing at the screen. 'I was at work for the live birth – it happened at ten this morning. Poor girl, there were only a few people from the night shift to watch her. If she'd been a Descendant they would probably have given us some time off to see the live screen.'

'All healthy?' said Carter, watching the reactions of the crowds.

The woman nodded. 'Yes.'

'Then why are there so many medics around her? Has there been a contamination?' He remembered a health scare back when he was younger when an animal had breached the Barricades and all pregnancies were rescanned to check for infections and deformities. He wondered how the birth of his own children had been, and what it would have felt like to have been there. He felt something akin to relief that he had not had to stand beside the girl with the red hair, holding her hand and maintaining the terrible charade. But there was some regret too, that he'd not been there to see the two tiny lives begin their journey in the Community.

The new parents on the screen looked terrified, yet proud.

'Was the birth… not successful?' he added.

The woman looked over one shoulder. 'You've not been back long, have you?' she said.

Carter shrugged. 'Just since last night.'

She looked at him closely and her smile faded. 'You're *him*, aren't you?' she said. 'Well, Carter Warren, those aren't medics, they're Terrorist Security. They attend every birth these days, since the snatchings. It's written into the code.'

With that, the woman gathered her dark grey shawl around her shoulders and hurried across to the other side of the square, where a group had gathered around the edge of the FreeScreen. Carter thought about what the old man Morton had said about an uprising and the strange cryptic conversation with the girl and then with Isabella. His blood ran cold. The Community was falling apart and, more than ever, it needed him to bind it together as Controller General. Without any doubt, he was the person to mend this.

Seconds later, he felt the uncomfortable stare of the whole group and he slipped down into a side street, away from them. As he left, he glanced back at the screen as the baby was taken away for registration and, within minutes, its clean, gurgling face was back once again, this time with a name scrolling across the screen: Zillah McDermott.

The path to the south of the Community became more rugged the further away from Unity Square it got. Most of the land had once been a housing estate so there was a lot of old crumbled tarmac through the forests, although most traces of the old world had disappeared. Many of the tallest buildings had fallen during or directly after the Storms, but there were one or two that still stood as a reminder. In the south, there was the tall, glassy pyramid shape that speared out of the Black River and could be seen from almost every part of the Community. It was closest in the south and, although the top had broken off many years earlier, it was still there, lurching out of the water and reflecting shards of light across the Community. All of the professors, except for Mendoza, had advised their classes to avoid looking at it.

As he walked, Carter could feel he was getting closer to the Black River. It was still a long way off but he could smell the darkness rising above the treeline. Birds scattered overhead and darker clouds peppered the early evening sky. He hoped it wouldn't be too far before he found the twins' address.

When he reached it, he discovered that the house was one of the older reclamations from the early days with a sturdy metal roof and solid brick walls. These houses were bigger than all the others – usually reserved for Descendants, to encourage them to procreate.

Carter's father had given up theirs so they could be closer to Unity Square and it had remained empty and decaying, for years. Sometimes they'd visit the house late at night, often with Isabella and her uncle Rufus, his father's friend, in the far north of the Community.

'Sit here and do your homework,' Carter's father had said, tucking him onto a stool in the kitchen. But Carter had crept downstairs, as he so often did, to see what his father was doing.

He'd watched from a crack in the door while Rufus Delaney had forced open a small door in the kitchen floor, covered by a large, smooth stone that had led down a flight of stairs to a tiny room. From where he'd hid, Carter had been able to see something so terrifying, so alien, that he'd ran back to the bedroom he'd been placed in and done the same piece of homework over and over until his father had come to collect him. It had been chemical mathematics. And he'd counted and counted and counted. He hadn't even had to listen to the conversation between his father and Isabella's uncle to know that it had been something frightening.

'This is dangerous,' he'd heard his father say. 'You can't tell anyone about this.'

Carter had imagined that Rufus Delaney hadn't had much chance to say a word to anyone as he'd been called for freezing that same week. He'd held Isabella while she'd cried, until another uncle of hers had come to collect her and, after that, Carter had seen less of her outside of their classes at the Academy. The house had been deemed unsafe and demolished. Luckily, anything dangerous that had remained in the house had been probably destroyed too.

Carter looked up at the house, the house where he knew he'd find his twins. From the window, a flickering of light gave way to a shadow that quickly disappeared. There was someone watching him within.

Above him, the soft patter of rain had started and already a film of water had gathered over his clothes. He moved towards the door. Before he got as far as the step, it opened and he was bundled inside the house and up a set of creaking stairs. A boy with the same white-blonde hair as his pushed him into a room and down on one of the resters without saying a word, then checked the window covers and stood by the doorway, listening.

A shrill voice trailed up the stairs and through the open door into the room.

'Lucia? Is that Lucia? Is she back?'

The boy creased his forehead and held a finger to his lips. Carter could see that his hands were shaking too but were quite discoloured; the mottled green brown of dirty water.

'No, Grandma Jescha, it was just the rain on the door.' The boy's voice cracked a little as he spoke.

Carter looked around; although the house wasn't typical Community accommodation, it was certainly fitting of a Descendant, but this room – more than any other he had ever seen – was incredible. One of the walls was covered in coloured drawings; landscapes, animals, impressions of the Catacombs. The landscapes and the Catacombs, he could confirm with certainty, were fairly realistic but the rest was fantastical. And absolutely illegal. Drawing in this way had been outlawed since the very beginning. Everyone knew that. He looked at the boy, horrified.

A bowl of water, full of ragged cloths, sat on the floor. Carter could just about tell that the other walls had been rubbed clean of script and designs.

The boy plugged the gap where the door didn't quite reach the floor with the remaining clean rags that lay scattered around. He worked quickly and silently but when he eventually spoke, his voice was tuned with an urgent concern.

'Did she find you? Where is she?' The questions forced themselves out in a mouthy torrent as the rain outside increased to a gentle tap on the windows and the roof.

'Ariel?' Carter spoke slowly and softly, mindful of the effort that the boy had made to ensure that whoever was downstairs did not hear them.

'Yes, of course I'm Ariel,' he said with irritation. 'Did you see Lucia?'

Carter took a deep breath. 'You're my son.' He exhaled loudly, the words sounding soft and strange – almost like a question. They sat there, fairly equally proportioned with less than twelve months between them.

'Where's my sister?' Ariel's whisper gained in gravity and he grabbed Carter's arm. 'I need to know where she is. She's in danger. Did you find her?' Outside, the tap of rain increased to a thick, regular thud and there was the tinny sound of rain against metal above them.

'I don't know,' said Carter. 'I've been away. Underground. I didn't even know about you until last night.'

Ariel dismissed him with his hand.

'We all know where you've been. Lucia went out last night to find you. She didn't come home. Something's happened to her. I can feel it.' Ariel's voice was swallowed by the tap-tap of rainwater that was beginning to turn to ice.

The girl at the shelter. Carter's heartbeat quickened.

Downstairs, there were raised voices followed swiftly by the rise and fall of a woman crying. Carter wondered whether the girl with red hair was in the house. One of the pictures on the wall was of her; long fire-flames of auburn flashing out of the wall towards him, although one arm was part way through being erased. Alongside the girl, careful script had been etched into the wall: *Veritas liberabit vos.* The words swam and bulged out towards him. The pounding of the hail on the metal room clattered towards its crescendo and the house seemed almost to shake as it reached its heaviest point.

'Her?' Carter heard his voice, small and distant, disappear into the ice storm. 'She was there at the Transporter drop-off.'

'Lucia? What happened? How was she?'

'She was...' Carter paused. 'I had no idea who she was. Tell me everything you know.'

'I will,' said the boy, 'but we need to do this quickly. The Industry will be here soon and anything we might have been able to do to help my sister – your daughter – will have been lost.'

The rain relaxed into a soft, steady slap against the windows as they talked and Carter helped Ariel rub the last traces of bright paint from the walls.

'She made these colours, these diagrams herself?' said Carter, astounded and horrified.

'Yes,' said Ariel, a trace of anger in his voice. 'I don't know how she learned to do it but she used flowers and plants that she found out near the Barricades. There's a lot I don't know about what she's been up to. Or the people she seems to be spending her time with.' His hands were still shaking and his face was smeared with paint residue and angry tears.

'She was still alive when I saw her,' said Carter. 'And whatever happened with the Transporter – and I can't be sure – but she wasn't there when I woke up. I should go and look for her.'

'Well, you could, but if we don't clear this mess up there won't be any reason for her to come back. They'd lock her away for disruption – if they saw any of this.' Ariel gestured towards the last pictogram – an orangey-yellow creature like the last vestiges of an autumn sun. Its mouth was open, showing clean, white teeth in a bright-red maw. Carter ran his fingers over the colours and shapes.

'This is incredible,' he said, his eyes wide. 'And illegal. Did you not report it?'

'She was beginning to go crazy in here,' Ariel said, changing the subject. 'Her ideas got wilder and wilder. We tried to stop her. She talked about revolution. About an uprising. It was contagious. Some of the other stuff she drew—' he paused '—it was like she was deliberately trying to get herself punished. You know they could expel her? Force-freeze her? Anything. There are people here who are trying to cause trouble, who deserve it. But not her.'

Carter shrugged and thought of Isabella. 'Things are different. Wrong.'

Ariel grunted. 'You finally worked that out? Of course people are different. The cracks started to appear after Chess came into power. Her Contribution was a failure – people have been starting to doubt the Industry. That's why you're here. The rumour is that you're going to unite the people.

'That's the plan.'

'You have to. Otherwise we could find ourselves going back to the way things were before, with all this…' Ariel waved his arms towards the murals on the walls. 'People turning on each other – it's like before. We know a better way and this, what we have now, is it.' The boy was calm and eloquent despite being visibly upset.

'But what does this have to do with Lucia?' he said. 'Where does she fit into all of this?'

'She had ideas that there were others like her,' said Ariel. 'And it's not just her; there are lots of them living here in the Community. Her ideas would have got us *all* killed. So about six months ago, Jescha took her to a Clinician and people started to ridicule her, saying she was just like her mother. She got some attention, bad attention. So we told people she had been cured. We're Descendants so we're more likely to be believed.' He turned away from the paintings.

'What do you mean, like her mother?'

'Samita, my mother, is special – she's different. I guess you were too eager not to see that.'

Carter felt his cheeks flush red.

'So what happened next?'

'Lucia was under home curfew,' said Ariel. 'And I knew that she was going to do *something*. I didn't know what exactly, but something. When she knew you were going to be released, she said that she thought that you would be the one to help her. And then, yesterday evening, she disappeared.'

Carter crushed up his forehead in confusion.

'What do you mean she disappeared?' he asked. 'From where?'

'She was locked in this room,' said Ariel. 'So somehow, she had help.'

Downstairs, the wailing had given way to silence and Ariel pulled the rags from under the door, putting his ear to the ground.

'When it's been twenty-four hours, we have to formally report her as missing, presumed absconded,' he whispered. 'Jescha is waiting until the last second of the twenty-four hours has expired before they call. We haven't slept since the door log said she'd left before nine last night. She has half an hour left to come home.'

He looked at Carter. 'If the Industry finds her, and she's been doing something illegal, she'll be charged with treason. And frozen for good – Descendant or otherwise.'

Ariel's eyes pricked with tears. Carter gently laid his palm upwards and they touched in a familial bond. He thought about the girl with the red hair. Whatever had happened to the Community, to Lucia and to Isabella, he knew it was his time to make things right.

'Who is Jescha?'

'Jescha Davenport is our biological grandmother. She's our formal guardian. She's brought us up since, well, since we were born when it became clear that Samita couldn't take care of us. She wanted us to stay here in her home rather than board at the Academy like the Industry wanted.'

'But what about Samita?'

Ariel bit the finger of one hand nervously and rubbed at the last corners of the painting with a rag in the other.

'Samita? If she hadn't given birth to us I imagine she'd be in the Clinical Quarter or underground. Jescha was allowed to keep her here because of us. In her condition, she didn't react well to being a mother. We were the first set of twins to be born since the Storms and the attention was too much for her.' Ariel looked at the floor. 'They didn't pick up her differences when she was younger. At least, Jescha never reported it. If they had, she probably wouldn't have been allowed to reproduce and we'd never have been born. No one even quite knows how she got herself to your going-away ceremony, although one of the tutors at the time took her along to the Medics for a test and, well, the rest is history.'

Carter flinched. 'She was there with my professor, Mendoza,' he said. 'We…' he hesitated. 'It's a long story but we…'

His son looked at him quizzically. 'Couldn't you tell she was different?' he asked. 'When you talked to her?'

'I didn't really…' Carter stopped. Few words had passed between him and Samita that evening. 'I didn't notice anything,' he said, finally.

Ariel shook his head.

There was no mistaking that the boy was his son. Sitting there on the rester, their faces reflected in the dirty water, they could have been mistaken for twins themselves.

'I'll make this right,' he said, 'when I am Controller General.'

'You're confident it's going to be you?'

'I am. I've seen what the other Contenders have to offer and it's not enough. Nothing is more important to me that getting the Community back on track. We can't have things like they were before.'

'People have put all of their hopes into your return,' said Ariel. 'Much more than the other Contenders. It's because of us, you know.

Nobody believed at first that twins would be possible – they believed that there would be something wrong when we were born, but there wasn't. We were normal – at least, until Lucia started hanging around with a group of people at the Fringes. Elections aren't even properly due for another two years; Chess has only been in position for ten. They're going to vote her out once the successful Contender's Contribution has been proved and they're ready to take office. Chess can't handle the situation with the rebels. People say you're the one to end this once and for all. You can't mess this up. '

Carter thought about the people he'd met so far – not all of them had been as happy to see him as Lily and his son.

'And I'd steer clear of any trouble makers, any people from the Fringes if I were you,' said Ariel. 'As you can imagine, they're not exactly excited to see you back. Stay away from anyone who could drag you down.'

'I need to help Lucia.'

'Did Chess make you take those tests?' said Ariel. 'You know what's important, don't you? More than anything, you need to think about the Community – that's the best way to help her. But you can start by helping me clean this wall. We don't have much time to finish this before Jescha calls the Industry to report her missing and they'll be in here checking for evidence of my sister as a rebel. You'll want to be gone before then. And with any luck, they'll find Lucia before daybreak and send her to the Clinicians. It's better that they think she's missing, than a dangerous revolutionary. The Medics are the best people to help her now.'

When it was time to leave, Carter pulled the door closed silently. Without the light of the moon, the blackness of the shadows cast slippery shapes across the path that crunched through the broken tarmac in the forest, towards the city.

Carter took the path back towards the north, treading quietly through the pine. After less than a minute, there was the thump of heavy feet hitting the ground, and a slip of torchlight in the darkness shone out from the trees. Momentarily, Carter was blinded by the brightness.

'Lucia?' he said cautiously. 'Is that you?' The light came closer, boring directly into him. He shielded his eyes. 'It's OK, you know. I can make this all OK.' There was the cracking of twigs as the figure stepped towards him.

'No, it's not Lucia. It's me.'

Carter recognised the voice immediately. It was his mentor.

'Lily, what are you doing here?' She crunched her way towards him through the leaves and pulled him along the pathway.

'I'm saving you from yourself,' she said angrily. 'You shouldn't be here. We need to leave. Now.'

Chapter Nine

The Families

Alice

When they found her missing, the alarm sounded loudly. With the alarm screeching in the background, Alice, looking significantly younger than her eleven years, pulled the trick that she had used so many times before. It had always worked when she'd been caught shoplifting – especially at the markets. She screwed her fingernails tightly into the palm of her hand and thought about Charlie, the Jack Russell puppy that her father had bought her years before. Within seconds, the tears started to fall in heavy torrents and her shoulders heaved and shook.

'Take her to the infirmary,' said one of the men with a disappointed tone. Alice let her legs slip to the floor and she squeezed out more tears and short, breathy screeches. Two of the men did their best to comfort her and they put her onto a trolley and into a card-operated lift that shot downwards into the bowels of the Industry structures. She carried on sobbing and lurching until almost an hour after a doctor had shone lights in her eyes and certified her as needing some solitary rest.

'She can stay for twelve hours,' said one of the men who had brought her to the infirmary. 'And then she goes back in the Playroom.' The door clicked neatly as they left the room, and in the cool, quiet darkness she let her breathing subside to a satisfyingly regular beat. Her mouth formed a tight smile. Even though she had only been gone from the Playroom for twenty-three minutes, it had most definitely been worth it.

She thought one more time about the puppy. Her father had bought it for her before he died. That was when they had lived miles and miles away from the flat in the clouds with the map of the world and the park with bare trees. Her father had brought Charlie home from work, just a scrap of brown-white fur and a floppy pink tongue. Her mother had slanted her eyes but her father had wrapped his arms around all three of them and all the doubts about having a dog melted away into nothing. Every morning before school, Alice would take Charlie out into the garden and chase him around the cherry tree, throwing globs of blossom at his stubby brown face while he'd jumped and barked in his screechy puppy voice. Charlie had slept under Alice's bed, making a snuffling snoring noise that had sang her to sleep most nights.

But then her father had gotten sick with the cancer. Alice's mother had tried to care for him but he'd kept getting worse, coughing up chunks of livery-coloured spit, his tongue lolling out of one side of his mouth like Charlie's, but not in a playful way. He'd died fifteen weeks and four long days after bringing home the puppy, and Alice's mother had had to sell the house to pay off their debts and buy a polished onyx headstone with his name carved on it.

What was the point, thought Alice, of that headstone now? She imagined it anchored under acres of water-sky, sitting alongside supermarket trolleys and broken glass with her father flying high in his coffin, floating amongst the clouds made of buildings.

Her mother had cried constantly the day that they'd moved into the tiny flat in the clouds. She'd laid on the sofa watching as Alice had packed up the things that they'd needed into thin cardboard boxes while men who were not her father had carried them into the blue-and-white van to the estate. Charlie had sat on her lap in the van, licking at her fingers and wagging his metronome tail in a happy love-beat.

Inside, the miserable grey walls had reeked of despair and the lift had broken. As she'd watched the men climb up the stairs, dumping their boxes on the communal balcony, Alice had placed her hand on Charlie's belly and felt his strong dog heart. A thin drizzle had begun to blow across the sky from slate grey clouds that hung like fog. The rain had melted through the cardboard of the packing boxes, peeling them apart and leaving her toys, the kitchenware, their bedding and her mother's pimpled dressing gown open to the elements. Charlie had licked one salty tear from her face and she'd smelled the hot fur on his head.

Nine floors below, she could see her mother and the men who'd carried things talking behind the van. One of them had put his arm on her shoulder; little stick arms and dark featureless faces that were just silhouettes against the late afternoon grey blanket. She'd hardly recognised her pale, thin mother who had plastered on a thick red lipstick and was wrapped deep in the arms of a blob of a man. As she'd watched them, something had whistled past her ear and flown like a condor in the sky. It had been their washing-up bowl.

'What we got 'ere?' a voice from behind her had asked, and she'd whirled around to see a group of boys kicking open the remnants of the slippery boxes, strewing their contents across the balcony. Charlie had let out a tiny yapping bark, shiny teeth smiling. Alice had backed herself against the wooden rail of the balcony and locked her eyes to the floor. The boy who had spoken had flashed his broken gums.

'Nothing,' she'd said quietly and looked across at her front door, but one of the other boys had already taken up his post there. He'd stood just inside the door, arms folded, blowing gum bubbles. Alice had rubbed her fingers over Charlie's ears.

'Oh, there's no dogs allowed here,' the boy had said. 'Didn't no one tell you that, girl?' The stump-toothed boy had had a long, deep scar above his eye that had gone all the way across into his hairline where it had disappeared into a thick tuft of blackness. Alice had shaken her head.

'Like I said, this is my estate and I say no dogs.' And, without warning, the boy had snatched Charlie from Alice's arms. The dog had whined and called for Alice and she'd reached across to pet him.

'Now you see it,' the boy had said with a smile. 'And now you don't.' With two hands he'd lobbed Charlie off the balcony. There had been a howl as he'd flown through the air, clipping a tree as he'd fallen. He'd landed with a sick thump and a screech on the concrete by the adventure playground. For a second there had been silence, except the falling of leaves and soft whip of the wind. Alice's mother had looked up and screamed at Alice who was all alone on the balcony. The boy with the wiry scar and his ugly friends had gone, disappearing into the cold grey air like apparitions as quickly and silently as they had arrived.

In the darkness of the Infirmary, a single tear edged down her cheek. For the first time since she had arrived, Alice began to think about how, since the Storms, everything had changed and would never be the same again. They were all trapped here, locked inside the capsule, waiting for the world to return.

But before being taken to the Infirmary, during her twenty-three-minute expedition in the corridors and walkways of the Paradigm Industries head office, Alice had discovered many things.

The first was that there were areas of her new underground home that were not just forbidden but were secret and private, even to some of the people who worked there. When she had reached the eighth level above the residential plazas, exhausted, she had looked for somewhere to rest. A tiny grille on one of the ventilation tunnels had been left ajar and, when she had slid it back, she'd found that there had been enough room inside to squeeze a little way into the steel tube without blocking it entirely. She'd laid there in the cool air shaft feeling the freshness blow against her legs and through her hair.

When she'd closed her eyes she'd thought she could hear the sea, shushing louder and quieter, until she'd realised someone else was in the reception plaza. Her heartbeat had grown to a thunderous roar as she'd pulled the wire meshing as tightly as she could and wriggled as far into the shaft as her body would safely let her.

Through the cross-hatch of the grille she had watched as two men and a woman clicked open a series of retractable doors to reveal a lift: a lift in the centre of the level that didn't appear on any of the other floors other than as a steel tube through the middle of the whole installation.

'Going up?' one of the men had asked as the woman ushered them into the lift.

'Yes,' she'd said. 'Broadcast starts in five minutes and we're late already.'

'It's carnage out there,' the man had said.

'Like it wasn't crazy before?' the other had asked, and they all laughed in a way that had made Alice shiver.

'The government should have listened – I told Wilson that years ago, when the whole global warming thing first started, but he knew they wouldn't.

'He's in his element now, right?'

'Sure – I mean, they didn't cause the Storms, but him and Kunstein have this whole thing figured out. I mean, they were the only ones who had a plan.'

'Is that plan still viable?'

'Depends on who they choose, I suppose – and hell, it won't be one of us; we're way too old.'

'Just do what they tell you,' the woman had instructed, 'and there's a chance we'll get out of here alive.'

The silver doors to the lift had closed and the three sets of outer doors had folded back into the wall, creating a seamless red-and-black montage of brick-and-wood decoration. Pushing aside the grille, Alice had climbed out of the shaft and run her hands along where she had seen the doors join together and fold back in on themselves, but there had been nothing. It had been then that the alarm had sounded.

After her hysteria had stopped and the doctor had agreed she was suitably sedated, Alice had been allowed a visitor. Miss Kunstein had arrived at the Infirmary with a tiny piece of chocolate. She'd sat down on the bed, her long black coat discarded on a chair by Alice's bed.

'I hope you are feeling better,' she'd said quietly, placing the unwrapped chocolate on Alice's pillow. 'And I hope you'll agree that your *adventure* was a waste of time. There's nothing of any interest to children here; it's an organisational facility – lots of machines, dangerous chemicals and very, *very* busy people.'

Alice had been able to smell the square of chocolate so strongly that her tongue had felt slippery and hungry. She'd wanted to ask about the museum but instead, she'd bitten down on her lip.

'I'm sleepy,' she'd said.

'And you can sleep soon,' Miss Kunstein had told her. 'I just want to check your understanding. There's nothing to be worried about, nothing to go looking for and no reason to be out of your room at night. Is that agreed?'

Alice had swallowed the saliva that had been building between her teeth and nodded.

'Yes,' she'd said in a soft voice, digging her fingernails into her palms, already patterned with lines of dried blood. Miss Kunstein had leaned over and kissed her on the forehead.

'I shall come and collect you in the morning. It's a big day tomorrow – we are moving everyone into more permanent accommodation and introducing everyone to their new families. You'd like a new family, wouldn't you?'

'I don't know,' Alice had replied truthfully.

'Well, we'll see what happens next,' Kunstein had told her. She'd smiled without moving her eyes and glided out of the room with her tails swishing quietly. Then there had been silence, and the sound of a thudding heartbeat. And then nothing.

Alice Davenport's new family came in the form of Lucinda and Ian Watson. Lucinda had been rescued first, hauled off the roof of the firm of architects where she had been clinging to a satellite dish for two days when the floor had collapsed inwards on itself, and Ian had followed three days later.

He'd thrown himself into the water after a rescue boat when it had failed to hear his cries for help for him and his son. After exhaustion had got the better of him, he'd tried to swim back but he'd ended up spending a night in the freezing water, causing him to lose the hearing in one ear and the fingers from one hand. He'd still shaken uncontrollably almost a month later. It had taken a number of weeks for them to be reunited in the Ship – Lucinda had already been allocated a new husband by the time Ian had been released from the infirmary, but due to the unsuitability of the new partnering, they'd been able to stay together. However, their son Dylan had never been found.

The Watsons had been allocated three new daughters in total, Alice being the eldest. The other two, Jennifer and Serena, had known each other before the Storms and quietly kept themselves to themselves which, Alice thought, was for the best.

Each level had its own great hall – a low-slung round wheel of a room with a large steel pillar at its core that had electronic screens all the way around it. Circles of seats like ripples on water edged out from the middle, and eight aisles cut directly into the rows in perfect symmetry. The seats folded in on themselves and retracted into the floor when the room needed to become an exercise hall.

Sometimes, during the day, the screens around the pillar showed films, usually all about the different Paradigm Industries, but every day at 4.00 p.m. there was a live broadcast from five different static cameras of the devastation and carnage in the outside world. The picture was a desolate one: grey and fuzzy pictures that were watermarked by the constant downpour above. The broadcast was shown for half an hour and most of those who could bear to watch it at all left in tears. Alice, on the other hand, had watched every single broadcast in the four weeks she had been inside the facility without sadness or regret. Even the one time she thought she had seen her block of flats slip downwards off the screen and into oblivion, she still felt the queer rub of satisfaction that she always got as she watched the weather eat through everything outside their giant underground capsule.

But after four weeks, the cameras malfunctioned. One by one, they stopped sending the signals back to the facility. The network of over fifteen thousand cameras that had covered the whole city stopped working and plunged Alice back into a sad darkness. Instead, the briefings would now all come from the Controller General, William Wilson.

'Today,' said Wilson, 'we will be enhancing the living conditions within this facility beyond what any of us thought possible. Today is the first step in developing ourselves as the first fully functioning subterranean community in the world.' There was the regular low murmur of uncertainty mingled with excitement.

'Do we have to stay in this dungeon?' someone called. Wilson ignored her.

'For those of you who have been keeping in tune with current affairs, you will know that the detailed forecasts undertaken by our meteorological departments suggest that there will be no immediate end to current prevailing weather trends. In addition, the issues we have identified with Drakewater suggest that, even though the facility is a number of kilometres away, there is likely to be significant impact on the environment.' Alice wished that sometimes William Wilson would just speak the plain truth. *Yes. We're going nowhere.*

A boy near to Alice bit on his knuckles and she could see tears in his eyes. A girl sat behind him, and put a hand on his shoulder. As Alice looked around, she could see other people linking hands, touching palms, holding each other in a quiet calm as the voice of William Wilson continued.

'We have been unable to make contact with any other outside agency,' he said. 'We have made attempts both inside and outside this organisation and this country. There are no other facilities like this in the world that can offer the level of resource and protection you will find here. I can't guarantee the quality of the cooking—' he broke off and, open-mouthed, the crowd faced front. Nobody laughed. 'But I can guarantee that there will be enough to last us a number of years if we are careful with the resources that we have. But this facility does not run itself. We are going to need you to work in our food production areas, our mineral extraction plant, as teachers, childcare assistants, doctors, counsellors, water purifiers, laundry staff and the like. Many of you will be able to use your existing skills and others will train for new ones. In return you will receive safety, food and a home for your family.'

A red-eyed boy seated midway back stood up.

'That's all well and great, sir, but I don't have a family. My family are dead and I ain't got a thing in the world to live for.' He was a thin boy with broken glasses taped together with plaster, and the standard oyster-grey trousers and T-shirt that were issued every few days. Alice loved the way the suits smelled chemically clean and fitted her perfectly.

'And that is why we will give you something,' said William Wilson, his voice beaming. The boy sat down and pressed his fingertips to his forehead. 'Based on the information you provided us when you arrived, you have been allocated a functional family, one with which you will be able to create a lasting bond. Today, you will be leaving the communal bunk rooms and will be placed into your new individual accommodations in the west and north quarters of this facility.'

'What if I don't want to?' said the boy, a sullen frown on his face.

'We are living in a different world now,' said Wilson. 'We must want to work together, to live together, to survive together. Or we all die together. We are not your government, your educators, your lawmakers or your providers. You are here by our invitation and we welcome you warmly – but you are not obliged to stay.

'You have a unique opportunity to start again and, for those of you who do not feel that this life is for you, we can arrange for your exit from the facility. I will, however, remind you that our highest level with access to the world outside is twenty feet deep in water that has a current toxicity level strong enough to dissolve skin.'

Wilson cleared his throat.

'The choice is yours.'

Chapter Ten

The Investigation

Carter

Lily sat with her back against one of the broad oaks a good way off the path. It was so dense with trees that Carter could barely see her face.

'Right now, you have to forget you have a daughter,' she said. 'Showing that you care for her, looking for her or trying to do anything for her will ruin your chances of becoming Controller General. The Industry already knows about her. Associating with her is going to prove to them that you value your family more than the Community. You have to choose.'

Carter squinted through the darkness. 'But bearing children is one of the most contributory acts a citizen can do. Surely the twins are an asset. Should I just abandon her?'

'Yes,' said Lily. 'Well, not exactly. She's unpredictable, rebellious and she doesn't reflect well upon you. The boy, well, I'm not sure about him yet. But you have to prove yourself, show that you know what's important to the Community.'

Carter felt Lily's hand on his shoulder. 'I know this is all pretty confusing,' she continued, 'but believe me, you're the best person for this.

Above all else, you have to trust your instincts and do what you know you need to do. There are people who have sacrificed a lot to put you in the position you are in today, and they expect a great deal from you.'

'My parents weren't there for *me*,' said Carter. 'It changes a person.'

'Sometimes for the better,' said Lily. 'Look at the kind of person you have become without them. You learned how to separate unhelpful emotions. You have the whole Community depending on you to quash this rebellion.'

'Why?' asked Carter. 'What happened to make people change so much?'

'It started about ten years ago – maybe more,' said Lily, letting go of his hand. 'A group of people got together and started to spend more and more time out near the Barricades – sometimes even after curfew. Their behaviour at work became secretive and they started to come into work tired, unable to be fully productive. When a few officials went out there, they discovered they had been creating things – useless things. Art, drawings, and they'd even started to make some noisy instruments.'

'What do you mean?' Carter looked incredulous at how much effort had gone into this rebellion – effort that could have been carefully channelled into sorting out the real dissatisfactions in the Community.

'I don't get to hear everything,' said Lily. 'I'm too *Industry* to gain the full confidence of anyone who might be doing something deliberately rebellious – they know I'd have to report them. But even I get to hear some things from my sister, although we don't talk too much and she never names the people she knows. She's been part of a few of the groups but not too recently, not since she became pregnant.'

Carter remembered the name of the baby on the FreeScreen and the security – Zillah McDermott. 'Your sister was the one giving birth?' he said.

'Yes, she had the baby this morning – it was an attempt to calm her down, bring her back into order. She's been under curfew for the last few months to keep the baby safe. But before that, there was something, a whisper of them making instruments – for musical purposes. And these weren't just children – these were adults, grown men and women making music, singing for pleasure and having night parties.'

Carter turned to her slowly. 'Parties?'

Lily nodded. 'They were becoming animals again,' she said. 'Work levels began to fall and they started to focus on themselves, not on each other and not on our Community. They all thought they were different, individual, *special*.'

'Was it mostly…?' Carter half-hated himself for asking. He had never wanted to see the differences between himself and the others lower down in the Community, even though his grandfather reminded him so often how important it was.

'Lab Mades? Yes, but not all. Some First Gens started to join them later. We're only talking small numbers, but it was enough. And many of the Lab Mades understand that without the Industry, they wouldn't even exist, so they rallied against the rebels. They were faithful.' She sighed. Against the night sounds and the sharp smell of trampled nettles, Carter realised he was holding his breath in anticipation. He released it in one long wheeze.

'What happened to them?'

'It grew slowly. For the first couple of years, only the close families noticed any difference, but gradually, to the mentors, it became more obvious. I referred a few to the Clinicians and there was some medication that could help, but many others were referred for freezing to minimise the spread of the threat. Some of them became mad with the sickness and killed themselves.'

'Why didn't the Industry do something more quickly?'

Lily looked around. 'In the end, many more were frozen for their own safety.' She smoothed her hair. 'We shouldn't really talk about this,' she said. 'But I'm going to tell you because you need to know what you're up against. When this whole thing started, one of them climbed out onto the Barricade and was torn to pieces by a pack of wolves on the other side. She had some wild ideas about opening up the Community and breaking down the defences.'

'That's why the signs are there,' said Carter. 'The signs at the edges of the Community.'

Lily paused. 'We couldn't even recover the body for disposal. It was at that point that the Industry really had to put in safety mechanisms. They increased the electrical current circulating through the Barricade and put in procedures to stop the gatherings. It's not talked about publicly, but there are always rumours. The most recent one was that your daughter knew something important and that she would try to get a message to you.'

'She did get a message to me' said Carter, 'but nothing that sounded particularly rebellious.' And he explained about what had happened at the drop-off point. Lily listened, her eyes angry.

'Did you report seeing her? And did she talk about a way out? A plan? Anything?'

'No,' said Carter. 'She mentioned the Barricades, and told me to go and see Isabella, but nothing much else. I didn't think there was anything to report.'

A bird trilled in the trees above them, accompanied by the buzzing of a tiny engine. Carter looked up. It wasn't a bird at all.

'It's the night drones. They use the energy from personal information cards to find where Community members are. We should go,' said Lily. 'They're out looking for dissident conversations. Let's stop this now, and work on some tasks.'

Their pace back through the trees was regular and calm, punctuated with directions from Lily about how Carter's training would progress.

'We're going to start with some oration,' she said as they stopped in a clearing. 'That's key to gaining people's trust.'

Carter shrugged. 'I'm a great public speaker,' he said confidently. 'Let's work on something I actually need help with.'

'You've just passed the first test,' said Lily, smiling. 'Not wanting to impress me with your strengths, but showing a desire to improve your weaknesses is good. However, next session we'll need to do some practice on your speaking – you have to be absolutely word-perfect when you address your crowd for the first time. But what do you think you need now?'

Carter nodded. 'Well, my biggest weakness at the moment is physical strength, but also mentally I don't feel as sharp as I was before. So much has happened while I've been away. If I'm going to fix the Community, I need to understand the rebels.' He paused. 'I still have some catching up to do.'

Lily nodded. 'Well, the physical I can help with. When it comes to working out what's happened while you've been away – you need to understand that the Industry has had to make some changes and how important they are. The rebels, and their influence within the Community, are very different from when you were last here. They've destroyed Chess – she was just too weak to be able to quash their rebellions fast enough.'

'But I'm a Descendant,' said Carter, indignant. 'And I'm a Warren. My families were there at the very beginning.' He stood proud.

Lily smiled. 'All Contenders are Descendants. But there are complications with your family – both now and in the past. You know that. You need to prove that you are over all of that.'

'You mean my parents?'

'I mean your parents, your children and your past. And maybe where you'll struggle over Elizabet. You have a lot of residual memories and relationships that you need to make peace with and, from what I hear, she's working through that stage very quickly.'

'What do you mean?'

'Elizabet has less work to do. Now don't be fooled, she also has some demons but she has a strong mentor and some clear direction. She'll just need to know how to follow it. You have a missing daughter, dead parents and a reputation that's going to get you into the wrong hands if you're not careful.'

'There's nothing wrong with my reputation!' Carter felt anger rise inside him.

Lily laughed. 'Remember I know everything about you, Carter. It's my job to know. Samita may be the mother of your children, but I know your heart was always with someone else. And not a Descendant. I know you considered breaking the rules for Isabella.'

Carter was thankful that the darkness hid the crimson flaring in his face. 'Isabella was my friend,' he said shortly. 'Nothing more.'

'Maybe,' said Lily. 'But I suggest you stay away from her. Your name and your associations can play a big part in selection, Carter, and yours isn't your biggest strength right now. Nothing is more important than your Contendership. You have better insight and skills than Jenson and Elizabet put together.' She snapped a tree branch in her path. 'Make sure you don't screw this up.'

Carter pushed all thoughts of the sweet, kind girl from his childhood out of his mind and away from the clearing towards the deep thickness of the forest.

'What now?' he said, finally.

'Next test,' said Lily, spearing the tree branch into the ground. 'We run a circuit of the wood to strengthen your muscles.'

Carter pushed on his heels and began to run, the tendons in his ankles pulling hard as the adrenaline coursed through his bloodstream. Lily was fast and the pain in Carter's chest was overwhelming as he moved forwards after her. They darted through the dimly lit treeline, him following the crunching of twigs ahead and the swiftness of the air trail she left behind her. For what seemed like hours they ran, until he could no longer hear her and, as he slowed, he careered into her back, knocking them both to the floor. They rolled between the trees until they came to a stop on a patch of damp grass.

'What the…?' started Carter.

'Next lesson.' Lily smiled in the darkness as they lay amongst the leaves. 'Be vigilant. Always.'

There was a rush and a whirl of twigs as Carter disappeared into the darkness.

'Something you'd do well to remember,' he shouted behind him as he darted around the wood, retracing the path they'd followed, slowing his pace a little until Lily came up behind him again. He forced himself to move faster until he felt his legs burning as the weakened muscle worked harder to push him onwards.

'You're getting there,' she said. 'But there's more to this than being able to run fast, you know.'

They slowed down to a halt near a small group of thin trees that led out onto a bare patch of balding grass.

'So what's next?' Carter asked. 'I want to keep going.'

Lily pulled her card out of her pocket. It glowed with a bright orange pulse.

'Well, there's a Level Two Storm due in around ten minutes. We can either circle back to the Community or you can take this opportunity to build a shelter that will withstand the rain – created from what you have here. When you next meet with Chess, you could be asked to make anything, do anything. But a shelter is always a practical favourite of the assessors. I'll give you eight minutes.'

Carter looked around. They had stopped in a clearing with little loose foliage or branches and already he could feel the soft patter of rain. In the distance was the growl of thunder.

'The Storms can come at any time,' said Lily. 'You can't always guarantee safe distance or that the predictions are correct.'

Carter looked up at the sky. 'There's dark cloud coverage,' he said, remembering his meteorological lessons at the Academy. 'The rain will be longer, but lighter than a Level Three or Four Storm. Underground shelter is out – it will fill with water in no time. There's a chance of lightning so tree shelter won't work. The right choice is stone with twig-work.'

He looked around. To the left of the clearing, where an old village used to be, were the crumbled foundations of an old farmhouse. Sizing up the oddments of stone, he began to lift and pull them into position, grinding the edges quickly so that they fitted together neatly, packing the edges with mud that he rolled and shaped with the rain. By the time he was ten years old, he'd been the fastest and most effective shelter builder in the Academy, but years of inactivity made his fingers fumble a little as he turned over the last remnants of stone. The shelter was now waist-high but still it had no roof. The rain continued to get harder.

'You can still run away,' said Lily.

Carter rubbed the sweat and rain from his eyes. 'I never run,' he said.

One of the first things he had learned in the Academy had been how to recognise things that were out of place – anything from the old world that didn't belong any more. In the early days, when the first of the Scouts came back above ground, they'd disposed of everything that would remind people of the mess that had been made of the world. But clearing a whole civilisation took time and, even when Carter was young, there had been things still buried, things left behind.

'Report everything,' Professor Mendoza had told the class. 'Report it to me and I will make sure that it is disposed of properly. For everything you find and turn in, you earn special credits. Keep anything and you will be punished.'

He had learned to visually identify every uneven bump and lump in the ground where something seemed unusual or out of place, and as his fingers moulded mud carefully into the gaps in the stone, he scanned the edges of the clearing. To the far side, the natural cadence of the land undulated softly. Balls of ice started to fall all around him.

'You have about five minutes,' said Lily hiding herself behind a curved rock. 'Remember, this could be a decision between life and death if the Storm were stronger.'

Carter let his eyes glide across the landscape. To the other side of the clearing, a rock jutted out from one side of a tree, covered in thick green moss.

'There,' he said and ran out through what had become sheets of tiny balls of hail. Scraping his hands underneath the tree roots, he pulled at the thin rock. It came away in his hands easily – not a rock at all but a large piece of metal from long ago. As he raced back to his part-built shelter, the ice pounded his temples, slapping against his eyes. He fixed the makeshift roof on top with some stones and flung himself inside the shelter, listening to the pounding of the ice above him. Within seconds Lily was behind him and inside the tiny stone structure, smiling.

'Not bad,' she said. 'But next time you'll need to be much quicker.'

Carter looked down at his hands, bleeding and caked with mud. He tapped on the wall with his fist.

'Bit out of practice,' he said, proud with his efforts. 'But it'll hold until the rain stops.'

They sat there watching the ice turn back to a thin rain and then eventually slow to a halt. Although it had always been the same since the Storms, Carter never ceased to be amazed at how quickly things could change, sometimes with little notice. As the darkness of the night clouds cleared, they sat there watching the moon. Lily tapped the stone wall of the shelter.

'You know that you must do whatever it takes to win this. All three of you Contenders have an equally tough road to follow but your journey is yours and yours alone. Bravery and focus is paramount.'

'It is,' said Carter, looking directly at Lily in the darkness. 'And I am ready. Let's go.'

For over an hour they walked through the small wood crammed with trees. Through the fractured conversation and the cracking of twigs, Carter let his mind wander back to the night before he went away and each time he started to recall the details, he pushed it back. He focused on his footsteps, counting each one as did – a habit he'd started just after his parents died. He counted to block out the thoughts. The road path would have been much easier but, for the most part, he was thankful for the cool silence and the temperate stillness inside the ring of trees. By the time they reached the lights of the southern edge that led to Unity Square, Carter had counted to ten thousand and, with each step, he thought about Isabella.

'Your methods of distraction are good,' said Lily as she turned off the square towards her house. 'But you need to improve them.'

'I…' began Carter, but Lily was already gone.

When Carter awoke, the sun was streaming through his window and he could tell by the freshness of the air that Alexis had already left. He lay there for a second watching clouds scuttling across the cobalt sky, feeling his body warm and still on the rester. He felt good, relaxed, seconds before he realised the warmth was actually dampness in his bed and was coming from last night's clothes. Before he could pull on a clean suit, a bleeping pulsed in his pocket. He pulled out his personal information card:

You are required to attend a meeting at Industry Headquarters. You must leave now.

Carter hauled himself down the stairs and out of the door into the sharp rays of the white morning. The sun had already cut through the morning mist, chasing it into nowhere. As he turned into and then past Unity Square, he broke into a run towards Proclamation Plaza, his lungs heaving hard and his ankles turning over at every other stride. The streets were almost empty; most of those on the morning shift had left already and those on the evening shift hadn't yet returned.

As he ran through the tunnel, he could just see the silver outline of the Transporter waiting to leave, glistening in the sun. With one last spurt, he pelted towards the stop and through into the carriage. As he slumped breathless into his seat, the door closed and the carriage pulled out towards the Industry Headquarters. When he arrived, two

Industry officials flanking the door entrance barred his entry to the Plant with their strong, stubby arms.

'Carter Warren. Come with us, please,' one of them said, and they moved aside, locking in unison behind him.

The interrogation room was deep underground with round observation depressions at regular intervals in the walls. A long real-wood table ran through the length of the middle; three chairs, two occupied, were placed on one side of the table and one sat opposite.

The officials led Carter to the only unoccupied seat on the far side of the table and they each took one of the other – considerably more comfortable – seats in front of him. Next to him was Ariel and beside him was a young woman with a shock of red hair, twists of scarlet weaving around her pale cheeks. Her eyes didn't leave the grainy texture of the wood as she drew circle after circle with a bony index finger.

Carter's heart skipped a beat and then sank. It was Samita. She was older than he remembered, obviously, but in his mind she had been more beautiful, softer and more delicate. His heart was still and he felt nothing more than sadness for what he had done. The woman seated before him looked troubled and strange.

'My name is Malcolm Wilson,' said one of the officials. 'Which makes me First Gen. And this is Murphy. I am a relative of the original William Wilson, of course – names are so important, don't you think, Carter?'

Carter looked at the pair. 'Can you tell me why they're here?' he asked, pointing at Ariel and Samita. 'If this is about my Contendership, then where are Jenson and Elizabet?' He tried to be cool, keeping his eyes away from the spiralling motion that Samita was making on the table. It was unnerving.

The officials looked at each other and one spoke in a gruff tone.

'This is not about the position of Controller General. We are here today to discuss the disappearance of Lucia Warren-Davenport. We have not yet located her and as a matter of security, both hers and that of the Community, we need to understand how we can find her.'

Murphy picked up a slate and began to read from the screen.

'At the request of her guardian, Jescha Davenport, we have been focusing this investigation on supportive recovery but we now have to consider this to be an active attempt at escape and therefore treason.'

Samita continued to run her finger around in a spiral shape on the table, following the grain carefully. One of the officials started questioning her first.

'Samita Davenport...' he started.

The woman with the red hair lifted her head from the table and looked at the space between Murphy and Wilson. Her green eyes looked dull and lifeless.

'Related to an original Scout. What good fortune.'

'Am I in trouble?' she slurred. Trouble came out as *trubber.*

Carter looked her up and down – there *was* something different about her – not usual. Her eyes darted from one side of the room to the other then fixed back on the table. She was just like some of the people he'd seen once in the Infirmary. People who were classified as special and kept safely away from the Community by the Industry. The analysts he'd been working with had told him that they had their own special Community inside the walls of the headquarters.

'No,' said Wilson. 'You're not in trouble. But we do need your co-operation to assure us that we do not have a problem here.'

'What sort of problem are you talking about?' said Carter. 'Can't you just use the Model to track her card's location?'

Samita snapped her head around to look at Carter. He caught her eyes for a second before she cast her head downwards again, back to her spiral-drawing on the table.

Wilson etched indistinguishable words on his slate, squared his jaw and cleared his throat.

'Please be reminded that you are all here under the Community Charter, sub-clause, *Protection of the Community Environment*. As the immediate family of Lucia Warren-Davenport, who is under suspicion of being a dangerous and dissident citizen, you are also currently being considered for segregation. And potential, immediate freezing. I'm sure I don't need to explain to you what that means.'

Carter opened his mouth to protest but managed to stop himself before he spoke. He swallowed deeply and kept calm. 'Whatever I can do to help, obviously,' he said.

The room was silent except for the scratching on the table.

'Well, Carter Warren, second day back in the Community and you're already under investigation. Congratulations. I'm sure you expected to be here under different circumstances.' Wilson paused for a second before Murphy picked up.

'Dissenters,' said Wilson, scribbling on his slate, 'such a rare and selfish kind. Not only putting the Community in jeopardy, but they leave without their loved ones. Their only thought is for themselves.' He looked at Murphy. 'Selfishness is a dreadful thing, don't you think, Murphy?'

Murphy nodded gravely and clicked his teeth. 'Sad people,' he said.

Carter swallowed deeply and shook his head before the realisation dawned.

'I see,' he said. 'This is all part of my training, isn't it? This interrogation? To see how I respond?'

Murphy's mouth broke out into an uneven grin.

'Our Controller General in waiting,' he said. The transitory smile that had looked uncomfortable on Murphy's lips was swallowed up by an ugly, empty frown that spread across his face.

'Training?' said Murphy. 'I suggest you take this very seriously, Carter Warren.'

'Do whatever you need to,' he replied earnestly, working hard to suppress his annoyance at Murphy and Wilson. 'No special privileges. I understand that this is your job and that what you are doing is very important. If I can help you find her, I will. I have nothing to hide but I also have no time to waste.'

Wilson looked impressed. 'Has she been in contact with you?'

Carter shook his head. 'Not directly. I saw her at the Transporter stop but she disappeared before I could talk to her. She didn't say anything I could understand.' He looked directly at Murphy. 'I'm sure there's security footage of that area that can be scanned – you probably know all of this already. I would be disappointed if that's not the case.'

The two interrogators looked at each other uncomfortably.

'How did you know she was your daughter? You never actually met her, did you?'

Carter shrugged at Wilson with an open smile. 'I didn't. And while I had hoped to contribute to the Community by providing children on my return, I wasn't aware until I saw the FreeScreen that I'd been successful already. Lucky, I guess. Do you have children, Wilson?'

Wilson smiled back at him with some conviviality. 'Not yet, I'm afraid, Warren, although I've been matched with another eligible First Gen so we're hopeful for some good news soon. But you? First multiple births to occur in the Community since the Storms – there was one hell of a ceremony. Shame you weren't here to enjoy it. It was a blast, wasn't it, Samita?'

Samita kept her eyes firmly fixed on the table and started drawing shapes with her finger again.

Murphy picked up the thread next.

'But it's not the first time that one of the twins has gone missing, is it?' he said, addressing her directly. 'There was also that unfortunate incident with an old friend of Carter's. Isabella, wasn't it?'

Samita flinched slightly at the mention of her name but said nothing.

'You remember, don't you?' said Wilson. 'The time Lucia ran off with Isabella? When Isabella kept her out all night.'

'She did *what*?' Carter pushed back his chair in genuine shock. 'What happened?'

'From what we understand, about seven years ago—'

'She was abducted,' interrupted Ariel, sullenly. 'That *woman* abducted her.'

Carter turned to his son. 'Isabella took away my daughter?' he exclaimed. 'Why?'

Ariel narrowed his eyes at Carter. 'Because.'

'Because what?'

'Perhaps because she's unstable,' Wilson interjected. 'She's a rebel. She was trying to recruit her.'

Carter shook his head. 'That doesn't make any sense,' he said. 'Lucia would have been very young – eight maybe? What use would she have been?'

'She did it because she wanted to ruin our family,' burst out Ariel, and Samita looked up. 'Because of you, Carter Warren. She was jealous. You and her had something together. You and that crazed Lab Made Fringe dweller.'

Everyone in the room looked at Carter. He sat perfectly still, his heart pounding in his chest. Her sparkling eyes, short blonde hair, the way she laughed at him and always believed in his ideas and theories. The nights they spent in the hills, the way she stroked his shoulder and nuzzled her head into his neck.

His mouth opened into a wide smile, hoping his heart didn't betray him. 'Isabella? The girl I was at the Academy with? Nothing happened between us at all. She may have been a little obsessed with me and we were occasionally homework partners, but nothing more. As Ariel says, she's a Lab Made. I'm a Descendant.' A dark, sad pain leaked through his heart and into his bones. 'I could never be romantically interested in someone like that.'

The questions continued. Murphy and Wilson appeared to be enjoying themselves, Carter thought; his only wish was to get out of the room and into the fresh, pale sunshine outside to start work on his Contribution, to continue his training. Being in the underground confines of the Industry reminded him too much of the fifteen years he'd spent in the Catacombs. And he wasn't in any mood to repeat that.

'I will ask you one last time,' said Murphy, staring intently at each of them. 'Do you know where your daughter is?'

'No,' replied Samita and Carter in a firm and unintended harmony, then looked at each other.

'Touching,' said Murphy. 'Well, I think we've all heard enough for today.'

'Does that mean we can go?' said Carter, scraping his chair backwards.

'It does indeed,' said Murphy, 'for now. As soon as we locate Lucia, we will be in touch. Depending on how and where we locate her will dictate whether we need to consider charges against any of you.' He nodded at the family and tapped Carter on the shoulder.

'Chess will be in touch with you soon to discuss next steps. In the meantime, I suggest you continue working very closely with your mentor – she may look young but she has *a lot* to offer you – if you understand me. We await a transformational Contribution to our Community. Make your choices wisely.'

Carter nodded. 'I think I do,' he said with confidence. 'And I certainly will. Now show me how I get out of here.'

Two Industry guards came into the room and accompanied the party through spine-like corridors to a Transporter stop. The station was still and empty except for one man with dark circles around his eyes and a pair of stained cream pants. There was an awkward silence before anyone spoke. Ariel looked at Carter.

'There's nothing more to say,' he said. 'Except, good luck I suppose.'

'It's not luck I need,' whispered Carter. 'I need to understand what's going on here.'

Samita looked up from the table. Her nails were worn bare and her fingers were bright red.

'You're in trubber,' she said. 'Big trubber.'

'What does she mean?' said Carter.

'She's terrified by the Industry,' said Ariel. 'Completely unfounded, but she blames them for everything that's happening.'

'Where is your mama?' drawled Samita. 'She gone away? Like my baby?'

'My parents are dead,' said Carter.

'No, they not,' said Samita. 'They in better place.'

Carter rolled his eyes at Ariel who put his hand softly on the woman's shoulder. 'Mama, stop now,' he said. 'You don't even know who this is.'

Samita pulled her hair back from her face and looked at Ariel directly.

'Yes, I do,' she said clearly and with absolute accusation. 'I remember him. Mendoza told me he help me. But he went away. He is Carter Warren.'

Carter held his jaw firm as he looked at the twins' mother.

A single carriage pulled in almost immediately and they all got on. Carter stood separately from the others, leaving the man from the platform free to sit cross-legged on the floor in front of him.

'One carriage,' the man said to Carter.

'Yeah,' said Carter, nodding and looking over at Samita who sat, eyes transfixed out of the window into the blackness, repeating something to herself over and over.

'You know what one carriage means?' said the man quietly, without waiting for a response. 'Means that this is not a very busy station, you know, in terms of departures. Not a lot of traffic going in the outwards direction, if you get my understanding. I think we need to consider ourselves to be the lucky ones today, don't you think? We weren't the only ones in there, you know. I heard them. Before they took them away.'

The thundering of the magnetic tracks shrouded any reply that Carter would have made so he remained silent, looking at the reflection of Samita in the window as the Transporter thundered through the darkness. There was something he was thankful for and something he was sorry about but in the thick blackness of the tunnels underground, he struggled to determine which exactly was which.

Their goodbyes were polite but awkward. They left in the opposite direction to Proclamation Plaza. As he turned to watch them leave, he heard Samita shouting something and he watched as Ariel put his arm around her.

'They are bad people,' she called. 'I remember what happened that night, I remember. 'Do *you*, Carter Warren?'

Chapter Eleven

The Ship

Alice

Alice's harmonious family life with the Watsons, as it turned out, was relatively short-lived. They weren't bad people; they just weren't *her* people. After a while, Alice couldn't remember what the feeling of having a family felt like. But she knew it wasn't this. She stayed a respectful emotional distance from them all, struggling to be both polite and engaging on any level.

Lucinda Watson was a nervous, mousy woman concerned with her appearance. She was concerned enough to spend time worrying about it, but didn't care sufficiently to do anything constructive to change it. She irritated Alice even more than her own mother had.

'These suits are so unflattering,' she would say each morning in the place of *hello* or *how are you*. There were no mirrors in their new apartment, but she would peacock herself up and down the corridors glancing in any shiny surface that reflected a full-length image.

'I think they're OK,' said Alice the first time Lucinda mentioned the clothes. She liked the snugness and the regularity and how everyone looked the same. When the tight film-wrapped packages arrived on her fold-down bed in her room each week, she spent some quiet time breathing in their cleanness and soft simplicity. After the first time Lucinda complained, Alice would just nod and smile, adoring the synthetic cotton softness of her brand-new clothes.

The thing that she loved the most was the fact that, for the first time she could remember, whatever she had was exactly the same as every other child who lived on the Ship. She had no more and no less than anyone else, which made her the same. And that was perfect.

Alice couldn't be sure, but she thought that it was probably Jonah Daniels that had been the first to call the underwater, underground facility *the Ship*. She sometimes wondered whether it might not have been better for the name *the Ship* to have been *the Submarine*, buried deep in the cornerstones of the earth, but *the Ship*, for some reason, was what stuck. Jonah knew a lot about all things maritime. He'd *said* that he'd spent a whole summer on the Princess Aurelia with his sister Scarlett who'd worked cruises as a dancer and he knew all that there was to know about boats and liners and life on the open seas.

'There were crystals and diamonds melted into the staircases, and musicians who played smoky jazz all night in the bars,' Jonah had said. 'Sometimes, after the shows, Scarlett would let me stay up with her and listen to them. They were cool.' The cabin room had been silent as the other children had listened, mesmerised by Jonah's account. Billie-Jo Hatherall, Jonah's new sister, had broken the quiet.

'Oh, *sure*,' she'd said, rolling her eyes. 'Sure she did.' Jonah had ignored her and looked at Alice.

'Cruise ships are made in this long oblong shape. All along the edges are the cabins and on the inside are the restaurants and shops and stuff. See?' Jonah had licked his finger and ran the outline on the floor in front of Alice. 'And there are staircases here, here and in the middle, that run all the way from the top decks to the engine rooms. See?' Jonah had pointed to sections of his map that were fading back into a grey floor, the colour of angry clouds.

A few seconds later and Alice had no longer been able to see any of the drawing at all.

'This place is just like one big ship,' Jonah had said. 'It's one big massive cruise ship floating across the ocean. The cabins on the outside are where we live and all the classrooms and the restaurants are in the middle.'

'But it's not a ship,' Billie-Jo had protested. 'We'd feel it moving if it was.'

'My sister said that you don't feel a cruiser moving after a while,' Jonah had replied. 'Anyway, I wasn't saying it *was* a ship; I was saying it's *like* a ship, stupid.' He'd shot a glance at Billie-Jo who'd screwed up her eyes.

'Mama says you have to stop calling me names,' she'd whined. 'And you have to stop talking about your other sister because she's dead and gone.'

Jonah's eyes had splintered with anger and tiny beads of sweat had pooled on his forehead.

Alice had thought he looked funny when he was mad, like a tiny little madman and not like a boy at all.

'She is not dead' Jonah had pulled each word from his throat like knives. 'She's on her cruise ship and she's sailing around looking for me. A boat is the best place to be in a storm and she's gonna be there waiting for me when we go up top. We're going to watch the open sea for dolphins and listen to jazz and see things you'll never see down here, Silly-Joe. You're nothing like my sister and you never will be.' His eyes had glittered with a dangerous anger that made Alice's blood shiver. Billie-Jo's lower lip had quivered.

Alice had opened her mouth to speak but before she could say anything, Jonah had pushed past them, leaving Billie-Jo with tears gleaming in her eyes.

'I'm gonna tell Mama on you,' she'd screeched, pulling out strands of her own hair in frustration.

'She's not my mama and she isn't yours either. Whether you call yourself Hatherall or not,' he'd said in a quiet voice, but a voice that was loud enough to make Billie-Jo spill over into tears.

As Jonah had kicked his way down the corridor, Alice had put her arm on the little girl's shoulder and watched as the boy who didn't want to be her brother had disappeared into their cabin.

Whether it had come from the conversation with Jonah and Billie-Jo or from someone else, the name *the Ship* had stuck around and soon it was being used in briefings as well as in casual discussion.

In her dreams, Alice saw the Ship cutting passages through the dark earthy depths, bound for the crisp, green lands of South America or Australia.

She imagined the Ship rising up through the waves of layered clay and rock aiming for a cloudless blue sky, coming to rest, nestled in the hefty arms of a verdant valley. She imagined the thick oak trees and the smell of summer butterflies winding their way through the peachy blossoms of giant cherry trees towards the salty taste of the sea. It was calming, relaxing and, above everything else, the Ship was home.

The Infirmary was the busiest place on the Ship. Most evenings as Lucinda sat with Alice in their small front room, she would entertain her new family with her insightful personal diagnoses that varied wildly from mild depression to extreme psychopathy.

'And then there's Helen Hatherall on Deck Seven,' she'd said as Alice had sat learning the base chemistry she'd been set for homework.

'She has *completely* lost it,' she'd said. Ian had looked up from his synthetics manual.

'Isn't this information supposed to be confidential?' he'd asked. 'I'm sure that Helen Hatherall wouldn't want her state of mind being discussed around our dinner table.'

Helen Hatherall was Jonah and Billie-Jo's new mother and Alice wasn't keen on hearing anything about her. She'd let her eyes run across the length of her slate without properly reading any of the words.

It hadn't really mattered because Alice was finding it easy to absorb the information in her new classes. Everything seemed to make more sense to her than before. Work and school were more interesting and distracted her from people like Lucinda and Ian who drained her energy and were just like her mother in their own ways. Studying gave her a focus and she was able to dissolve the strings between her and most other people until she no longer really cared about anyone. Except Jonah.

Because Jonah wasn't like most of the other children on the Ship. Most of the other children moved around the corridors in great masses like packs of domesticated animals waiting to be handed their feed, huddling together for comfort or solidarity. Especially in the early weeks – the weeks that they later all referred to as the on-boarding – children of all ages gathered like companies of badgers or peeps of chicks following around the Industry staff like some strange imprinting experiment. Some gathered on the floors like a bed of clams while others basked on the chairs in crocodilian congregations, snapping at the younger fry darting around the corridors.

Alice kept herself completely away from the groups that merged and changed with every day that passed. But Jonah was different. Most of the time he drifted from group to group, smiling and nodding but not staying for any longer than an hour or so, when he would move on to the next group.

He was short for his age, shorter than Alice. Skinny with fluffy, unruly hair, he was good at school but always failed to complete his homework on time. And whenever they sat in the bright square classroom on Deck Sixteen, he'd spend the whole time staring out of an imaginary window in the wall. But despite his strangeness, Alice liked him. She liked his soft, sometimes squeaky, voice, and the way he would glance over to her, away from his imaginary window when he thought that she wasn't looking. There was something special about him.

Two days after the incident with Billie-Jo, Alice took her tray and joined him on the floor underneath one of the tables at the back of the canteen where she found him staring outwards at the legs of the other children as they passed. She had noticed that underneath the tables had become his new favourite habitat.

'Are you waiting to pounce?' she said and set down her tray.

Jonah looked at her with a confused, empty grin.

'Why would I do that?' he asked.

'You don't like anyone here, do you?' Alice bit into the corner of a synthetic biscuit. It tasted mildly of tangerine and she spat the mouthful out onto her hand, wiping it on the back of her trousers. It didn't matter; she'd get an identical pair of clean ones tomorrow.

'Do *you*?' he asked, eyeing the spray of crumbs on the floor and the half-eaten biscuit on Alice's plate.

'Some of them are OK,' said Alice and then realised that, actually, she would struggle to think of the name of an exact individual she liked. Everyone was just sort of, kind of, OK.

'Name one,' said Jonah. 'Can I have that?' He gestured towards the biscuit.

Alice wrinkled up her nose.

'Be my guest,' she said. 'Everything tastes of oranges down here, don't you think?'

'I hadn't noticed,' said Jonah and stuffed the rest of the biscuit into his mouth. 'I liked oranges. My parents ran a fruit shop.'

'My parents...' Alice stopped, unsure what to say next. 'My parents were dead, so I'm no worse off down here. I like it here. It's better than before.'

She picked at her fingernails, scraping out imaginary grits of dirt with her teeth. When she looked up at Jonah, his shoulders heaved up and down in regular sobbing throbs. The crying was raw and looked like it had come from somewhere deep inside him. Between the uprights of the table, Alice could see most of the other children making their way back to the classrooms, stick legs clicking towards the door and out into the corridor.

'I hated my parents,' he said as snot webbed out from his nose and his eyes melted with tears. 'I hated them because they weren't cool. But that Helen woman I live with, she's *crazy*. I just want them to come back.' A loud sob escaped his mouth and scrunched his eyes into thin cracks; looking nothing like the little madman she had seen shouting at Billie-Jo.

Alice hovered her hand in the air, unsure where to place it, and finally rested it on Jonah's left ankle. As his breathing and moaning became louder, a crowd of legs came closer. Alice watched as the group of legs marched and gathered around the outside of the table they were sat underneath. She shook Jonah's ankle and put a finger to her lips but it was too late. A gaggle of heads appeared where the legs had been, Billie-Jo amongst them.

'Aye-aye shipmates,' said a booming voice that came with an ugly smile. 'Little baby Jonny want his mummy and daddy to come and get him?'

Alice felt Jonah's leg stiffen and saw his fists turn white.

'It's his sister he wants to come and kiss and cuddle him,' sang Billie-Jo. 'He cries for her every night *and* he wets the bed.'

A couple of the faces around the outside of the table clenched in uncomfortable recognition for a second, then, as the others started sneering, they joined in. Jonah's face, already blotched with tears, turned raw like sunburn. One of the boys pulled him out by the arms and they all stood up around him. From under the table, Alice could see them, poking and kicking at him, laughing as he lay there, wide-eyed, imploring her to do something, anything.

'Are you a soldier?' said one of the boys, pulling back his leg, 'or are you the cry-baby Billie-Jo says you are?' He landed Jonah a heavy slug in the stomach with his foot.

Alice felt a cold blue anger drip though her veins and into her fingers that were clenched into tight fists, the fingernails ripping tiny half-moons into her palms. She uncoiled her body from underneath the table and pulled herself upright until she felt twice her usual size. The group whirled to face her and Billie-Jo smiled sweetly.

'Hi, Alice,' she said. The twinkle in her eyes faded when she saw the empty hollow of anger in Alice's face.

The boy turned towards Alice.

'Leave. Him. Alone.' Alice's words shot from her mouth like hard, cold bullets. Above her she could feel the weight of the whole city pushing down and rising back up to meet the stars. Her eyes were seared metal, boring holes into the figure that stood in front of her. For a moment there was a silence and a scar-faced boy, foot half-raised ready to kick again, lowered it slowly and turned on her.

'Who are you, his little girlfriend?' He laughed loudly and his voice echoed around the room. Billie-Jo wasn't laughing any more. A foamy fleck of spit from Alice's mouth landed on the boy's face as she turned to face him.

'I'm Alice Davenport,' she said, her hands shaking and her lips cutting hard, white lines into her icy face. 'And I'm telling you to leave him alone.'

The boy laughed and pushed Alice backwards, leaping on top of her and pinning her down with one arm. She could see the gleam of teenage muscle pushing out from underneath his suit. He pushed her hard against the floor until she could almost feel the imaginary movement of the Ship.

'Alice, Alice full of malice, came like a slum-dog into the palace. What makes you think I'm gonna listen to a girl like you?' he said. A broad grin revealed stumpy teeth and he rolled dead eyes back into his head.

Alice straightened her back and ran a damp tongue around her dry mouth. In the absence of a pair of scissors, the words came tumbling out. With everything she had left inside her, she snarled at the boy.

'The reason you're going to listen to me is because I know you. I might not know your name or where you come from or what your story is, but I know you. I know you and I know every boy like you. You were the boy on the bus who used to spit in the old lady's hair. You were the boy who used to wait in the tunnel and steal the busker's money. You were the boy in class who never listened, then made out the teachers were no good. And then you were the boy who never learned to read and write properly. You were the boy who hurt my Charlie.

'You were also the boy whose parents never gave a toss where he was at night, never took him to the dentist, and left him on his own when they should have been taking care of him. You're going to listen to me because we're not that different, me and you. Do you get it?

You're going to listen to me because I know that if you weren't being that stupid little boy, you could be something else. And *here*, you can be. You don't have to be the poor boy who has to steal or sell drugs or rob old ladies or hurt people because *in here*, we're all the same.

'In here, there are no cool trainers or rich parents or fancy schools. Or cricket or gaming machines or cheap lipstick. No gangs, no football and no drugs. For kids like you and me, in here is *better*. In here it's *equal*. We have got a chance.'

Alice exhaled like the last empty breaths of a balloon and heaved the startled boy off her, standing upright and strong and letting her hands flop by her sides. One solitary tear pooled in her right eye.

The room was silent except for the occasional sniff coming from the boy who stood opposite her, crumpling at the knees. Billie-Jo's jaw was slung open. They all stood there without speaking for what felt like an eternity. And then the boy began to cry.

'I'm sorry,' he said. 'I'm sorry.'

'Everyone, back to class. Now!'

The shrill voice of Miss Kunstein rang through the canteen, shredding the silence. The boy, his nose streaming, held out his hand to Jonah and pulled him up from the floor. Jonah looked at Alice with glowing eyes. They left in silence. Billie-Joe fled down the corridor towards her classroom and the rest followed her. The room was empty.

Miss Kunstein bent down and pulled out the tray with the remainder of the food from under the table. She handed it to Alice.

'Alice Davenport, you can stay here for a moment. You don't seem to have finished your lunch,' she said.

'I'm not hungry any longer,' said Alice. 'Can I go back to class?' She could feel the tiny red fingernail arcs spotting blood into her palms and she wiped them onto her trousers.

'That was very, very brave,' said Miss Kunstein, handing her some tissue.

Alice wasn't sure whether to dry her eyes, blow her nose or dab her palms so she did all three, in that order.

'It's just the truth,' she said. 'Things are better here for me than they were before. I eat better, I sleep better and I learn more. It's better for a lot of people. They just don't understand that yet.'

Miss Kunstein put an arm around her shoulder.

'I've been watching you,' she said. 'If you continue with your studies the way you have been, I think you'll be destined for some great things here, Alice. Do you think you'd like to take on some responsibility on behalf of Paradigm Industries?'

Alice shrugged and nodded all at the same time and, as she did so, she felt the anticipation of what might be to come weigh heavy on her shoulders. But at the same time, it gave her some purpose. A place she might be at home.

'That's settled then,' said Miss Kunstein, and pulled her skirts around her as she glided out of the room. 'I'll call for you when I need you. Be ready.'

Chapter Twelve

The Truth

Carter

The air was cold and a sharp breeze blew the foulness of the river through the Community and out into the Deadlands on the other side. In the late afternoon, Carter stood there, replaying Lucia's words in his head.

'Go to the Barricades,' he said to himself. There was something else she'd said before the strange words. Something had struck a chord in him so old and so deep. He sliced through the memories he'd remembered when he first came out from the Catacombs, the things that had slid their way through the freeze to the front of his cortex.

And then there was what Samita had said. '*I remember what happened that night, I remember. Do* you, *Carter Warren?*'

His last thought underground had been about the night before; the formal goodbyes at the Freezing Preparation Evening and crowds of people that always attended a mass submission to the Catacombs. Hundreds of people had been there, many of them going away at the same time as him, with their friends and families. Descendants stood together on the high podiums, Carter at the centre, with the hundreds of First Gens in the general population. The Lab Mades stood at the sides.

Carter had been to two Freezing Preparation Evenings before his own – they were held rarely but they provided the people of the Community with the opportunity to say goodbye to those going underground and to ask questions of the Professors about the process. They were organised by the Industry, looked forward to by the whole population. The seldom-used recreation space was opened up and invitations distributed through the personal information cards on the same day that the call-ups were announced. Carter's entire Academy class had been invited and most of them had been there, along with their guests.

Along each side of the recreation centre there were trays of different types of synthetic foods – chicker, boeuf, duckler, carrotina and the best kinds of sweet fauclate that hardly ever came in the food baskets. Carter hadn't seen any for years – until that night. He just loved the sweet, soft way that fauclate melted in his mouth and got stuck in-between his teeth. It was delicious and a perfect reason to celebrate at those special evenings – because there was always a lot of it.

The Controller General always opened the event with a speech about the values of the Community. Carter had watched as Bobbie Alderney strutted onto the podium beside them to cheers and applause from the crowd.

'People of the Community,' he began. 'Another momentous evening is upon us.' There were further cheers and cries from the audience and he waited for them to settle down before he continued.

'Three hundred and seventy-five of you have been selected to spend your tenure in the Catacombs as willing volunteers to support the Industry in creating and maintaining the most successful civilisation in human history.' He paused. 'You should all be very, very proud.'

He hadn't seen Samita arrive or at any point during the speech but he had seen her at the fauclate tables with Professor Mendoza, picking her way through the different flavours and licking her fingers, the golden red threads of her hair reflecting in the lights. As he approached the table, the professor put her arm around Carter's shoulders, guiding him to the quiet still of the shadows.

'I'm proud of you,' she said. 'And your parents would be too.'

Carter remembered the way the professor had looked at him. It was with strange, almost maternal care as she'd held him tight into her shoulder.

'You want to be Controller General, don't you?' she'd said.

'Of course I do.'

'And you know I promised your parents and your grandfather I would do everything in my power to ensure that you fulfilled your potential.'

Carter had nodded.

'And that you can trust me and the Industry with your life.'

Carter had nodded again. 'Of course,' he'd said. His teacher was the closest to a mother he'd had since his parents had died.

Professor Mendoza had looked at him intently. 'Do you know why you are here today?' she'd said, ushering her other students back towards the tables.

'Of course,' he'd replied. 'I'm fifteen and there are no Controller General elections scheduled for at least another eight years, meaning I would be too old to be put forward when the time came around if I stayed here. So I have to go to the Catacombs until it's time.'

The Professor had smiled. 'Carter,' she'd said, shaking her head. 'You sometimes seem to forget how important your heritage is. Most people...' she'd stopped for a second. 'Most people would give up everything to have a chance to be a Contender. And I mean *everything*, Carter.'

'I don't know what you mean.'

The professor had looked behind her and pulled Carter to one side. 'They know about you and Isabella,' she'd hissed. 'That you're more than just friends.'

'But…' Carter had shaken his head. 'We *are* just friends, nothing more,' he'd insisted. 'We always have been.'

'I – and many others have seen the way you look at each other,' the professor had told him. 'Even since you were small neither of you paid enough attention to the importance placed on you as a potential Contender'

'I…' Carter had begun. 'We never…'

'You may have fought against it, Carter, but love is a very strong emotion and one day it would have been your downfall. You seem to be forgetting that nothing in our lives is to be hidden – not an emotion or a feeling or an idea. These are the rules. Which is why the Industry took the decision it did.'

Even in the most complex of classroom discussions, Carter had never seen the professor looking so serious – and afraid almost.

'They are planning to freeze you,' Mendoza had quietly told him.

'I know that,' Carter had replied with confidence, as the re-runs of the Controller General's speech had begun to play. 'So that I can be the right age when the next election start.'

'No,' Mendoza had responded, slowly. 'That's not the current plan. If they ever release you, it will be when Isabella is dead – or when you can no longer be attracted to her.'

Carter had felt his heart sink deep. 'But why? We've done nothing wrong. They can't, I need to be back here for the next election in, seven, maybe eight years' time, I…'

'They know, Carter. They know about what you promised her.'

The promise. The words had only left his lips the night before but the intention had been carved into his heart from the moment he had met Isabella. So often they had met in the shadows of the hills overlooking the Barricades. They'd barely had to say anything, as each had always known the other's most intimate thoughts and feelings that had transferred between them.

But that night they had talked about it as they had traced the outline of the sunset until the stars emerged, hard and white.

'People are people,' Isabella had said. 'Why does it matter if nearly a hundred years ago you were born to someone who came out from underground a few days or weeks before me?'

'It just does,' Carter had replied. 'It's the way things are.'

'But it shouldn't be. I'm just as smart as you, as fast as you and way more curious. I've been two years ahead at the Academy since I started and still I don't get to compete.'

Carter had shrugged. 'But at least when I'm Controller General I can try to change that.'

'*If* you become Controller General…' Isabella had interlinked her fingers with Carter's. 'What if you don't come back?'

'I've been trained my whole life to be Controller General,' Carter had explained. 'Alderney's tenure will be complete in between five and eight years. When I get back, you'll be twenty one, maximum, and I'll be Controller General.'

'But we'll never be able to have children of our own. Even if you changed the rules, Carter, I've been tested and…' She'd blinked away tears. 'I just can't.'

Carter had put his arm around her shoulder and pulled her into him. 'That's OK,' he'd said softly. 'A Controller General can't have both worlds.' He'd felt Isabella sob softly as he'd repeated the words his grandfather had mentioned many times. 'The job is too demanding and I can't afford distractions. I don't want anything to jeopardise my chance to change things. But maybe when I've completed my tenure as Controller General and things are different. When we're older we can look at other methods, you know?'

Isabella had shaken her head. 'They'll never allow it anyway,' she'd said. 'They'll still probably make you reproduce with another Descendant. It's what they do. They want to keep the bloodline as pure as possible.

'I will change things. And I don't want children if it has to be without you.'

They'd sat there in the cool, late evening, watching night birds circling over the Black River and the sounds of the Community quietening into darkness. Carter had pushed his hand into his pocket and pulled out the hard, sparkling ring of trophene and held it to the moon. As it had caught the light, it had glittered a hundred shades of blue, green and yellow, swirling inside the hardened material like the surface of a FreeScreen. He'd held it out to Isabella.

'Trophene,' he'd said finally. 'It's indestructible. And multi-dimensional. And forever.'

Isabella had taken the ring from him and slipped it onto her finger. 'It's beautiful,' she'd said, a tight knot forming in her throat. 'Thank you.'

They'd sat in silence for a while, Carter inhaling the scent of Isabella's hair.

'When you come back, things will be different, won't they?'

'Yes,' he'd said. 'In a good way. And when they are different for everyone, they will be different for us.'

'Will you kiss me? Just once?'

Carter had looked deep into Isabella's eyes. 'You know I can't, it's against the rules. They'll freeze both of us forever if...'

Before he'd finished his sentence, her lips were on his, soft, delicate and warm. For the briefest of seconds he'd felt her tongue touch his and the sky had exploded into a thousand fragments of light.

'Come back for me, Carter,' he'd heard her say somewhere in the distance. 'In eight years' time, come and find me.'

'I promise,' he'd whispered. 'I promise.'

Carter had shaken off his memories and looked at Mendoza with shock on his face. As the words of the Controller General had faded into the night, the FreeScreens had sparkled into life again, displaying the clinical clean cells of the Catacombs and a friendly band of assistants welcoming each individual into their sleep chambers. Along each side of the square base of the recreation centre, around a hundred Industry Experts had stood taking questions and providing reassurance to those about to leave their friends and families.

Mendoza had smiled in a strange, sad way. 'They've known about you both for a while,' she'd said quietly. 'Yes, you've been very careful to not have physical contact with Isabella until last night, but they have known. Your grandfather tried to warn you many, many times.'

Carter had looked around him. Everything had seemed so normal still and yet his whole world was crashing down around him. His heart had beat fast as the desperate panic set in.

'Laugh,' Mendoza had said. 'Look normal. Don't show any sign of what we're talking about.'

Carter had grimaced and tried to smile widely. Everything had felt so strained and terrifying. His face had turned a pale white and felt ice cold.

'You're going to lose everything because of that girl,' Mendoza had told him. 'Everything you have trained for, everything your parents went through to raise you the way they did. And you are going to lose your life – not to mention Isabella's.' She'd looked beyond angry, exasperated to the point of despair. Her face had looked strange, strained even. 'We are going to lose everything unless you do exactly what I say.'

'Anything.' Carter had swallowed deeply, his palms damp with sweat. 'Anything.'

'Firstly, you need to forget any allegiance you have to Isabella. She may be smart and you may think she is your equal in so many ways but she's Lab Made. You know what that means. She and her ancestors were made and developed chemically in the labs. She *has* no real ancestry. We make thousands of her kind a year. And more than that, she can't reproduce. Even if you were allowed to be with her, your generation would not continue. And it must, Carter, it must. You are born with some of the most important DNA that ever existed. She must be dead to you from now on, or your actions could kill you both.'

Carter's lips had felt dry, and they burned... the memory of Isabella's kiss like grey ash on a fire.

'What can I do?' he'd said, 'how do I make this right?'

'There is one thing. *Only* one thing, Carter. Nothing you can say today will convince the Industry that you are willing to forget Isabella. Unless you follow my instructions, it is likely you will be kept down in the Catacombs in the Terminal Freezing section, only to be woken up in the event of an extreme shortage.'

'What can I *do*?' Carter had hissed. 'Tell me and I'll do it.'

Mendoza had gestured towards the girl with the red hair. 'Samita,' she'd said, 'is in a similar predicament to yourself – albeit the circumstances and details are very different.'

Carter had looked at the girl. Her spirals of red hair had waved in the breeze. She'd shivered in the moonlight, her fingers moving more quickly high in the sky, tracing the outline of the stars.

'What do you mean?' Carter had asked. 'Who is she?'

Mendoza had looked across at the girl and then back at him with deep intent. 'She's a Descendant too – a Davenport – one of the absolute strongest genetic lines.'

Carter had thought back to the history lessons where they'd all had to map their family trees. The Lab Mades had sat that exercise out and been forced to ooh and aah as the Davenports and Conrads in the room had presented their direct lineage to the other students.

'So why does she need me?'

'She and her mother came to me some days ago, looking for help, urgently. She's a very special case and it's unlikely she will survive spending time in prolonged sleep. Emotionally, she would not survive well without her mother. She's scheduled for the next Freezing and, as you know, there are no other circumstances that will prevent her from being taken down into the Catacombs. Pregnancy, for her, is the only option. And, if her pregnancy were to be discovered *after* you have been frozen, you would be allowed to stay underground until the next election, having proved that the brief liaison between yourself and Isabella meant nothing, and still be in line to compete for the next Controller General position.'

'What if she doesn't... you know...' Carter had felt his voice shaking a little as he'd spoken '... have a baby.'

'Well, we have no guarantee of success. But this is our only option.'

Carter had breathed deeply and exhaled. His heart had felt like it was smashing into a thousand pieces.

'And Isabella, what will happen to her?'

'Remember the very first classes we did at the Academy? Emotion Containment lessons? If she is smart, she will use those tools to forget you, just as you need to forget her. Just like the work we did when your parents died, Carter, you need to focus on closing your mind to her and to everything she may have ever meant to you. You need to forget her.'

'But…' The lull of talking and deep discussion around the recreation centre had begun drawing to a close. Some people had even left already.

Mendoza had looked Carter deep in the eyes. 'We are running out of time,' she'd said sharply. 'You need to move fast.'

Carter had looked at the girl who'd nodded back towards him and waved.

'You want me to… do it? Here? Now?'

'You do *know* what you need to do, don't you, Carter Warren?' she'd said. 'I'm sure the mechanics of this operation have not escaped you during biological science classes?'

Carter had sighed and nodded. He did know, but the kiss from Isabella had been the only emotional contact he'd had with a girl in all his fifteen years. The professor had beckoned over the girl who'd stood next to Carter smiling nervously. Mendoza had pointed them in the direction of a small door that had led out into a small wooded area right at the back of the recreation centre.

'This entrance is never used,' he'd heard Mendoza saying through the darkness. 'Now, Samita, you are ready for this like we discussed, aren't you?'

'Ready,' had come the response and then there had been a nod from the professor, a sliver of a moon and a calm, cool breeze and then Professor Mendoza was gone.

Suddenly it was just the two of them and the sound of twigs crackling as they'd fallen beneath a pine tree and his lips had met hers in a vibrant embrace. It had happened quickly and was over in seconds. The act itself had been devoid of pleasure but it had been painless and quick. Painless right up until he was standing again and the girl was rearranging her clothes and then, it had hit him.

From behind a tree he'd seen her. Beautiful, sunny-blonde Isabella, her face empty and blank for a moment before the dreadful realisation really and truly drained into her bones. What she'd seen made a sound come from her mouth that had made Carter's blood curdle in his veins. She'd howled and wailed in the kind of pain that was only ever talked about when people discussed being frozen without drugs. And had stood watching the newly formed convenience couple, her mouth wide open, still screaming.

Carter's mouth had opened and closed on the words but nothing had come out. Samita had got to her feet and disappeared into the darkness. Behind Isabella, he'd seen the shape of Mendoza comforting her.

'Forget him now,' he'd heard as the professor had guided Isabella to the path. 'Forget him – he was never yours to remember.'

He'd watched the tears streaming down Isabella's face, darkened with anger and distress. The screaming had stopped but she'd mouthed three soundless words through the darkness at him as she'd turned around.

'I loved you.'

When Carter had awoken the next morning, he'd pushed every thought of her from his head. Every thought of *it*. Of what happened. And, when the scent or the sound of her had infiltrated the cortex of his brain, he'd repeated to himself, over and over.

I did it to save you.

I did it to save us.

He'd repeated it softly to himself until he was surrounded by Industry guards. The same guards that had then taken him on the journey through the Community and then to his cell in the Catacombs. The distraction with the crying man, Pablo, in the tunnels had been a perfect way to show his allegiance to the Industry, to demonstrate his beliefs to Alderney.

I did it to save you.

He'd thought he'd been saving Isabella's uncle, Rufus Delaney too, out at the old house in the woods. At least that's what his grandfather had said when he'd told him what he'd seen down in the dirty basement when they'd met up there that night.

'You're saving him from himself,' his grandfather had said. That was the night before they'd sent Rufus Delaney to the Catacombs.

And, there, in the cold afternoon light of Proclamation Plaza, fifteen years later, as he watched Samita trail into the distance, her words still rang in his ears.

Bad people.

And Carter knew that he had to talk to Isabella about what had happened – before it was too late.

Chapter Thirteen

The Industry

Alice

Jonah's new mother, Helen Hatherall, was the first suicide on Level Seven. Jonah had turned up to class dry-eyed although Billie-Joe, hysterical, had been excused for the day.

'I didn't see anything,' Jonah had said, eyes fixed to the floor. 'They took her away before, you know, it happened. They don't have proper funerals here – they just push them off the edge of the Ship.'

'How did she…?' Alice had asked but then wasn't sure exactly that she wanted to know. Jonah had shrugged his shoulders.

'I didn't see anything,' he'd repeated. 'The people who came for her said that she poisoned herself, but they didn't say how or with what.' His eyes had clouded over with a dull, lifeless sediment and his bottom lip had started to shake. 'I didn't even like her,' he'd continued, 'but she was all I had.'

'Will they…?' Alice hesitated for a second. 'Will they send you another new mother?'

'I don't know. Maybe. I suppose someone will need to take care of Billie-Joe – and George can't do it. He couldn't even take care of his own wife.'

Alice had sat down on the floor next to Jonah.

'It's harder for some people,' she'd said. 'They just can't deal with it. It's easier for us – we had less to lose, I suppose.'

Jonah had looked up at her, his eyes burning with anger.

'It might have been easier for you but none of this is easy for me. All I want to do is run around in the park or kick a football or ride my bike. I hate this stupid place; it drives me mad. I think I'm the only one who cares what things used to be like. Everyone's getting on with things like it's normal to eat that rubbish and live with people you don't even know. I feel like the only crazy person.'

'We're all mad here,' Alice had told him. 'Every one of us.'

In the months that followed, there were at least twenty more suicides that Alice heard about: all adults over thirty, although apparently this was less than had been expected by Paradigm Industries. And even she knew that there were probably more. The leadership team at Paradigm Industries, or the Industry, as they became known on board the Ship, did everything they could to make the situation better but, as Alice realised, there were some shipmates that just weren't suited to life on the open seas.

Life became a regular rhythm of ups and downs. Education was intense and structured and, in contrast to Alice's previous experiences, absolutely compulsory. She learned the practical skills of survival: food and nutrition, how to extract the minerals from the earth to create energy, how to create synthetic compounds and transform them into materials, and – most importantly – the politics of management.

'You will make a great leader in the new world,' Miss Kunstein had told her. 'You are a fast learner and you have the adaptive skills to make our good people great. You will achieve things beyond your wildest imaginings.'

Alice had nodded. And as much as she wasn't sure about Jonah's adaptability, by the time they had been underground for eighteen months, the pair had become virtually inseparable.

After two years they had almost forgotten what the smell of a fresh spring breeze on their skin felt like and, although she craved the sweet, hay smell of cut grass and the grazing sound of a skateboard on gravel, Alice loved the regularity and simplicity of life on board the Ship.

'Sometimes I'm not sure I want this to end,' she said to Jonah one evening after classes had ended as they sat outside the classroom. His hair, tousled over to one side, only half-covered the disbelief that mapped across his face.

'What do you mean?' he said. 'I'd go crazy without the hope of getting out of here. I only live for the hope of what might be left outside.'

Alice slipped an arm around his shoulder. 'Hope is a dangerous thing,' she said. 'It's hope that got us into this mess in the first place. Instead of doing something about the planet, about wars, about the madness, people just hoped things would improve. Hope doesn't make things better; hope just stops people from acting. It's like the lottery – you remember the lottery?'

Jonah nodded. 'But the lotteries gave people a chance, right? They gave people the chance to win their way out of poverty – that has to be a good thing.'

Alice clicked her tongue against the roof of her mouth.

'Wrong,' she said decisively. 'It stopped people from trying harder to achieve. All that hope was a waste of energy and a waste of time. My mother was a hoper – look where that got her.'

They sat there, backs against the cool metal of lockers in the Academy room. At times, Alice thought she could feel a breeze of cool air wafting through the corridors, that reminded her of afternoons at school and her life before the Storms. There were things she missed: Charlie the puppy and his moist nose, the smell of candy floss, wet pavements that reflected rainbows, and occasionally the sound of her father's voice. She could hardly remember what that sounded like any more. And she hated herself for it. Every time she tried so hard to hear his deep, treacle-sounding voice inside her head, it turned into the crisp, cruel tones of Hutchinson, barking orders that felt like a hard thumb pressing into her bruises.

But most of what she missed had started long before going underground. Cool summer nights in the garden, the way grass felt underneath her skin and riding a bike – they had all gone years before. And the weirdest part was that the longer she was on board the Ship, the less she missed them.

She interlaced her fingers with Jonah's and, as he turned to face her, his lips bruised hers. Gently and without definition, but in a way that made her stomach feel full of glitter and her eyes go dizzy.

'I think I might love you,' he said. 'Despite your crazy ideas, I don't think I could get through this without you.' Then he kissed her again, this time deeply and with all the weight of the world above them pressed onto her lips.

Alice held his hand tightly as the delicate beauty of the silence enveloped them.

Sometime in the third year, Miss Kunstein became Kunstein. Along with many other things, the titles that had once demarked the outlines of gender melted into the distant past like smoke in the sunset.

Alice and Jonah became known as a couple, although they never spoke about it to anyone. Alice wasn't even sure how she would explain the fact that there was a safeness in the nostalgia of her old life that she felt with Jonah that she didn't feel anywhere else on board the Ship. How she would explain that one night, before the curfew, they had found an old storeroom and danced to a tune they hummed themselves. They'd danced awkwardly with hands on shoulders and around waists, like in films they'd seen when they were children. When they'd finished dancing, they'd melted into each other for a moment and cried together. They never spoke about it afterwards, and it never happened again.

On what she thought might have been her fifteenth birthday, Kunstein took Alice into the Control Room that squatted twenty floors below the residential areas of the Ship, buried deep in the bowels of the core structure. As the lessons started back after lunch, Kunstein clipped open the hidden lift doors that Alice had seen in her first week on board the Ship and they stepped into the glass box that smelled of diesel and dried flowers, and nothing like the smoke-filled and urine-stained elevator that rarely worked in Prospect House.

They slipped downwards so quickly that the jolt snatched the breath from Alice's lungs and, as the vanilla and lavender circulated through her senses, she believed that it might have been the most beautiful scent in the world. Without realising, she clung to the skirts of Kunstein's ample black cloak and held herself against the wall of the lift tightly, scared of what might come next. But as the doors opened, and she saw the corridors bustling with the Industry scientists, she felt calm… different even.

Kunstein directed her through the corridors and into a side room that led around the edge of the Ship and then back towards the middle. She tapped a code into the next door and led Alice through.

'Security,' she said, and as Alice stepped into the shell of the room that took up almost the whole level and was vaster than any other on the Ship, she realised that Kunstein had brought her to the Control Room. It gleamed and whirred with metallic brilliance.

'Would you like some tea?' said Kunstein, offering her a tall cup of something that smelled strangely similar to coffee.

'No, thank you,' replied Alice, and she looked around at the walls while Kunstein sipped the odd liquid that frothed over the edges of the flask.

'What exactly am I looking for?' asked Alice as they pored over monitors, dials and switches that covered the whole of one wall of the cavernous room. For the first time in years, Alice realised she was looking at something that was happening outside of the Ship. Kunstein kept her eyes fixed to the screens as they sat there together in silence, the only noise was the quiet clicking and shushing of the machinery that kept the sunken craft in operation. Alice thought that she could almost feel the floor moving. Kunstein pointed to the screens and traced her finger around the shapes and colours.

'Here,' she said. 'Look here.' A whirl of colour glided past the main screen on a background of dark blue and black.

'Why me?' asked Alice. 'Why would you show all this to me and not someone with more experience? There must be engineers, mechanics, scientists, bankers – all kinds of people here on the Ship, but you're showing me. I don't understand.'

Kunstein smiled at her.

'That is exactly why,' she said. 'We can use those people's skills, believe me. But what would they want to do when they got out there?'

Alice thought for a second.

'They would use their skills to build everything back up from scratch,' she said. 'Start again, recreate, develop. Make everything real again.'

Kunstein pointed to one of the screens; it was barely recognisable as the inside of a supermarket. Alice remembered Mr Shah's neat rows of tin cans and overpriced, wiped clean vegetables. She wondered if he made it back up North. And what up North might be like now and whether people were as mad as bats, like he'd said.

'Exactly,' said Kunstein. 'And how would that help people? Not at all. They have become used to things as they are in here. They would never be able to adapt to that level of complexity again – assuming we could even recreate it in that way. And, by the way, we couldn't. There just aren't enough of us.'

Alice laughed to herself. She didn't want anything back the way it had been.

'Back to your question of *why you* – well, it's not just you, Alice, that we're looking at to do this. There are others. We need people who are young, fit, flexible, smart and, above all, want things to change. *Demand* that things change. A situation like this changes people – those who lived the lives of the privileged, well, some of them are resentful and angry. Not at the Industry, but at anyone who would deny them the elite position that they became accustomed to. You know, Alice—' Kunstein flicked a few switches on the dashboard in front of her '— some people will go to their banks when we get above ground and look for their money.' She laughed a deep, hefty laugh. 'Can you imagine?'

Alice thought about the grand, marble buildings in the City, stocked with currencies of paper and metal that no longer meant anything, and smiled with a nervous uncertainty.

'But surely, maybe, someone would swap it with them for something?'
Kunstein nodded.

'Maybe some would. But do you understand; it doesn't mean anything any more. And in truth, it never did. It was something we made up to trade with. But if no one has anything to trade any more, what's the point?'

Alice felt the ideas trickling around inside her brain, settling, unsettling and then concreting themselves as the conversation progressed.

'So...' Alice watched the colours on the screens swarm around in the depths of the water in the supermarket, backlit from the camera '... why did we bother with money in the first place?'

Kunstein pointed to a gargantuan flippered fish that darted in between the checkouts.

'Why, exactly,' she said.

All afternoon, Alice watched the monitors and learned how to alternate the views of the cameras across the different screens to watch the flooded city at different angles.

'The levels are falling,' said Kunstein. 'In the last twelve months, the water has subsided significantly. It's still not safe, but it will be.'

'When?' said Alice, watching the still, dark depths. In the silence of the room, punctuated by light, airy clicks, it was eerie and serene. It reminded Alice of an aquarium. And it didn't look safe at all.

'When this light—' Kunstein pointed to a solid oval button on the wall that blinked amber '—turns to green. It measures water level, land mass, air quality and, most importantly, radioactivity. We can't account for other things, of course, like structural safety of the buildings or what animal life may have survived, but it's a good start. We installed part of this after the Storms, you know: an ingenious piece of intelligence equipment.'

Alice nodded in agreement, although she couldn't quite be sure how accurate it was.

'After the Storms? Did you manage to test it?' she asked, watching the supermarket. There was the skeletal outline of a body on the floor, a huge rucksack on its back; or, she thought, it looked like it might have been a body at some point in the last few years.

'We have completed what tests we could,' said Kunstein. 'And I like the way you think. I truly believe you're going to be a very useful asset to the team.'

Alice wasn't sure. She wondered if she, untested, would be any more useful than the thick-glassed, oval bulb on the wall.

'We could be talking months,' said Kunstein. 'Two years at the most, but based on the forecasts so far it could be as little as nine more months here for some people. For those who will be leaving first – and that could include you – they could be outside, breathing fresh, unfiltered air. Clearly, a great deal of work will need to be done to make the environment inhabitable again. But before that, we will need to agree what we want to create. Physically it won't be a blank canvas but, in terms of how we shape society, we might have a great opportunity in front of us. Do you understand what this could mean Alice, for you and others like you?'

Alice nodded although she wasn't altogether sure.

'I think so,' she said, her head swimming with fish.

'Other people,' said Kunstein, almost without stopping, 'people like Helen Hatherall, they were not born for this new order.'

'None of us were,' Alice interrupted.

'True,' said Kunstein, 'but what we are about to create can be learned, if people want to learn. You wanted to learn, didn't you, Alice?'

The fish that had glided back onto the screen opened its jaws wide, revealing a sharp row of white teeth. Alice drew back from the monitor a little as it snapped its jaws tight shut around a smaller fish in the fresh produce aisle. She remembered that she hadn't even thought about Jonah all afternoon.

'Yes,' she said and leaned back in her chair.

'You didn't just *want* to learn; you knew that you *had* to learn,' continued Kunstein. 'In fact, you were open to it. You created that space for yourself. Do you understand what I mean?'

Alice didn't, but she was too mesmerised by the screens to argue. She watched as the indicator levels on the dashboards rose and fell, changing colour, shape and dimension. There were entire sections dedicated to water purity, sanitation, air quality and emissions levels for both inside the Ship and outside in whatever was beyond the flooded wasteland in which she used to live. It was just like she had learned at school, but it was all real and there right in front of her.

'Your curiosity and your skills make you very special, Alice,' said Kunstein.

Alice snapped back to the screen and watched as something large-bodied swept across the screen in front of her.

'What do you want me to do?' she said quietly, without looking up. Kunstein smiled, a sharp curl of lip lifting over bright white teeth.

'Your training has already started. But when the time is right, and it's safe, I'll want you to go out there,' she said. 'I want you to go out there and bring something back for me.'

Alice turned around in her chair and looked up into the deep black pools of Kunstein's eyes.

'What is out there that could possibly be of any use to us after it's been drowned under so much water?' Alice's scorn rippled through the room and for a second she thought she saw a flicker of regret in Kunstein's eyes.

'I want you to bring back our humanity,' Kunstein said and then turned a switch, forcing the screen Alice was staring at to fade through charcoal grey and then, eventually, to black.

Chapter Fourteen

The Message

Carter

As the late afternoon crept into evening, the paleness of the earlier clouds swept into a bright orange blaze across the horizon. In the distance, Carter could just make out some of the buildings of the old city across the river, disintegrating into the Deadlands. Those buildings had always been there, the ones that had survived the Storms. The shattered clock building, the bridge and most of the broken wheel had eventually slipped back into the Black River. Now there were only a few of the ones that he remembered from his childhood still carving dark shadows in the distance. Even since he'd been away, the landscape had changed. Even buildings had moved.

Carter doubled back through Unity Square and down into a side street not far from Drummond Row. He took his personal information card and slotted it into a gap in the wall near a bench, leaving a pile of leaves to mark the spot. No one needed to know where he was going.

The extra security, the drones, the threats of freezing, the ideas of rebellion – like Lily had said he needed to find out what had been happening in the Community since he'd been away. There was only one person he could trust to tell him the truth. If she would even speak to him. And even though he knew it was dangerous, he needed to let her know the truth too.

He wasn't sure exactly where he might find Isabella – if he could find her at all – but the ruins of the old house in the forest, as Lucia had mentioned, would be the place to start. As he travelled further south, the houses thinned out into small storage barns and then into nothing. Tall grasses took over, bordering the pathways, and Carter kept close to the edges, away from the glare of guide lights, drone cameras and the Transporter tracks. In the trees there was the rustle of birds in the branches overhead and the smell of lavender and garlic as he crushed through the plants, releasing the calming purple and pungent fragrances out into the clouds.

Whenever he had travelled there with his father it had always been late evening and Carter had dawdled behind, walking backwards and watching the line of the Community disappear into the trees. He tried that again, but the landmarks weren't the same and he wandered around in the twilight, pulling on the memories, the scents and the sounds until he felt he was halfway close. He almost tripped over the foundations of the old house; the path had crumbled into dust and the inch-high walls were overgrown with thick ivy and roots.

'I wondered when you'd come.' The voice cut through the air and made Carter jump back in shock. It came from somewhere deep in the earth, and then filtered through the scrubby bushes to where Carter stood.

'Isabella? Are you there?' Carter kept his voice to a whisper. There was the scratching of insects and the sound of a light wind through the branches of the trees above him. Then there was nothing again and it was silent.

'Isabella?' he called out. He heard the sound of twigs snapping and more silence. He resisted the urge to run away and tried to ignore the deep thumping in his chest.

Eventually, she crawled out from a hole in the ground that had been covered by rough bracken and branches, forming a hidden bunker. Had he moved five or so paces to the left, he'd have fallen straight in. There were streaks of mud down her face and her arms were caked in grime. The rags she wore were torn and filthy but more than anything Carter wanted to place a hand on her cheek and kiss her gently.

He still remembered the softness of those deep scarlet lips and the silvery white-blonde hair which made them look as though he and Isabella belonged together. She hauled herself up until they stood eye to shoulder. She straightened herself and something in her bones clicked. She looked over his shoulder, her eyes glassy. Inside him, Carter felt a thick, heavy sadness.

'Do you know exactly why you are here?' she said. 'I am assuming that you are not here by accident?'

Whatever she looked like, her voice, *that voice*, was the same. The voice that had made him promise.

'I had a message,' he said, slowly. 'From my daughter.'

'Why didn't you tell me that when I saw you earlier?' Isabella's voice was quiet and her eyes were sad. 'Why didn't you come to me as soon as you got here? You *promised*.'

Carter paused for a second. 'Things have changed around here. So many things…' He swallowed deeply, pain rooting deep inside of him. 'Lucia told me to come and find you. I just didn't know at the time that it was her or what she meant. But I'm here now. And I need your help.'

The sadness in her eyes bore through him and he stepped backwards. There was a break of clean air between them.

'What happened to you?' he said in a slow, steady voice. 'Why are you like this?'

'The unravelling of a life can sometimes happen almost immediately, and sometimes over many years,' said Isabella. 'It just depends on circumstances. On your story. On our story.' Her voice was scornful and icy sharp.

'So tell me yours,' said Carter, brushing the dirt from his clothes.

'Mendoza told me what you did. What you did with that girl. She *showed* me, Carter. Do you know what that did to me?' She stopped for a second. 'I've had fifteen years to be angry with you and yet still it feels like yesterday.' Isabella picked dirt from her nails and rubbed the fragments of earth into her clothes. 'And now look at us.' She shook her head. 'I'm damaged, I'm almost thirty, my life is nearly over and you're still the Industry golden boy you always were, a father of twins—' her voice broke off '—and you come to *me* for help?'

Carter shook his head. 'Did Mendoza explain to you why I did it? Did she tell you?'

'The reasons don't matter, Carter. The pain is still real.'

He could hardly bear to look at her. Her eyes were dull, the bright sparkle extinguished and the inquisitive beauty that had always been so prevalent had been snuffed out completely.

'Why didn't you box up the pain, like Mendoza taught us?' he asked. 'Emotion Containment? Start your thoughts from another place…' The methods had seemed so real to him as a ten year old, but looking at Isabella he felt foolish even talking about it.

'Do you think that actually works, Carter?' She spat on the floor. 'Nothing about the Industry works. Not in the way you think it does.'

A thin, cool wind whipped through the trees.

In his world, just a couple of days had passed since he and Isabella had been sitting on the hills, watching the stars prick through the black sky.

'When your parents died, and your grandfather stopped you from seeing me because I was Lab Made, what did we agree?'

Carter swallowed. 'We said we would still see each other at the Academy.'

'What else?' Isabella's voice grew louder.

'That it didn't matter about me being a Descendant and you being...' he stuttered over the words... 'about you being Lab Made. That we believed all people should be considered equal.'

'What else?' Isabella was almost shouting.

'That I would become Controller General to change things. For everyone.'

Isabella smiled but behind her eyes was the same glassy expression.

'You're too late to change things for me,' she said bitterly. 'You were expected to be released seven years ago, to compete against Chess when Bobbie Alderney stepped down. I was still waiting for you then. We came to find you.'

Seven years.

'We?' Carter remembered what Ariel had said when they had been called in by the Industry guards. 'You abducted Lucia?'

Isabella rolled her eyes. 'I did *not* abduct her,' she said severely. 'The girl came to *me* a few months before that, asking questions about you. Wanting to know more about her heritage. She told me it was for a project she was doing at the Academy but I could tell it wasn't that at all. She wanted to know more than the usual ancestral stuff they talk about in class. She wanted to know about you.'

'What did you tell her?'

'I told her everything, Carter.' Isabella shook her head. 'If I help you, you need to listen. You need to do what I say.'

He looked at her, the once soft lips holding a defiant, angry line across her face and a pulse of guilt punched him. 'You broke your promise to me once,' she continued. 'But I had to wait until *you* came to *me*. You came so you must want answers.'

'I do,' said Carter. 'I need to understand what's happened – what's happening.'

'Yes,' said Isabella. 'So will you do what I tell you? Will you act on it? Do you trust in me like I blindly trusted in you?'

Carter swallowed deeply. As broken and sad as Isabella looked, she wasn't desperate. Her eyes were still honest and her face still determined. She didn't seem crazy or maniacal. She was, in a mournful but beautiful way, still his Isabella. He nodded. 'I will do what you tell me,' he said. 'I trust you.'

The woman, now so much older than him, smiled a little and pushed her lank hair back from her face. 'We might not have much time,' she started. 'But if you're still going to be Controller General, there are some things you need to know.'

'Is this anything to do with the rebels? With the uprising?'

Isabella nodded.

'If we'd known then what we know now…' Her lips formed a half-smile. 'Remember when we watched that film with the original Scouts? When we were partners in the classroom?'

Carter nodded. 'Of course I do. I remember it like it was yesterday.'

'Except it was fifteen years ago.' Isabella brushed a frond of splitting hair from her eyes. 'Well, you need to know that most of it wasn't true. Not even then. The Deadlands aren't like that any more. The Industry is not what you think it is, and the Model? It's corrupt.'

After the last couple of days, Carter wasn't entirely sure he disagreed. 'But that's the system, Isabella,' he said. 'How else would we survive; how would we know we had the right people?' He wanted to reach out to her, but she kept herself curled away from him, distant, and laughed a hollow sound.

'Do we need to know *everything*, Carter? This *system*… may have worked once, back in the early days, but right now, it's a mess.'

'We wouldn't be here without the Model, without the Industry,' he said quietly but without conviction. 'Our ancestors would have all drowned in the Storms or starved on high ground. Without the Ship there would have been nothing.'

'That may be true, but aren't there enough of us now? Isn't it time for something different?'

She ran her fingers through her hair and pulled out a few strands, letting the wind carry them away. They caught the edges of a branch and hung there before disappearing into the soft breeze.

'Why do they provide us with food, Carter?'

'Because it's not safe to eat anything that grows.' The answers were simple, words that they had rehearsed.

'Yes, Carter.'

Isabella's voice sounded distant, like an echo of a heartbeat carried on the wind. If he closed his eyes, she could almost be the same person as before. But he didn't close them. He couldn't.

Isabella rooted around on the ground then stopped to pick a half-formed fruit from the ground and popped it into her mouth with a crunch. She laughed at his expression, her teeth full of seeds.

'How do you know it's not safe? Have you ever tried doing anything the Industry tells you not to? As benevolent as they are, they don't deliver food packs out to the Fringes. I've been eating tree-grown fruit for years now,' said Isabella. 'And roots and grasses. Sometimes, out by the Black River, we catch the occasional bird that flies over.'

Carter felt sick to his stomach. 'That's disgusting,' he said. 'And it's forbidden.'

His voice escalated above the trees, breaking through the canopy and floating back down the path. Isabella pulled him closer to her.

'That's the point,' she said. There was a fluttering of wings in the trees overhead and they both looked up. Carter's mouth felt dry, like it was full of feathers.

'*We?* Do you mean Lucia?' As the words fell from his mouth, he knew already.

'When you weren't released for the last Controller General Contendership, I came out here and I swore I would never leave this house. Lucia followed me out here – she talked about you incessantly, talked to anyone who had known you to try to find out more about who you were. We waited for hours at the Transporter drop off station together, both of us so desperate to see you. She is a good girl, brilliant – a genius.' Isabella gritted her teeth. 'It pains me to say it a little, but she is so much like you, Carter.

'She was only eight when Chess became Controller General, but she forced her way to the front of every live speech, questioning whatever she could with anyone who would listen. When they told her to stop challenging – to stop asking – she came here. She couldn't understand how someone like her mother could have been used in such a way by Mendoza, how her mother had to be hidden away, to pretend to be something she was not, how Jescha was afraid to get her help in case she'd be taken to the Catacombs as soon as she and Ariel were old enough. She didn't understand what made her more worthy of Contendership than one of her friends whose great-great grandmother had been conceived in a test tube and implanted into one of those germinators, but could map every subsequent generation since.

'When no one would listen to her, she came out here at night to find out about the Deadlands. She would get as close to the Barricades as she could, just to get a glimpse of the outside. To get a glimpse of where the Davenports and the Warrens originally came from.'

'How much does she know?' Carter asked. 'What did she find out?'

'Before he died, your grandfather tried to talk to her. Filled her head with terrible stories about monsters and what a traitor *his* father Richard had been and lies about you. He tried to make her believe that when you were Controller General, you would stop the rebels and you'd send all the Lab Mades to the Catacombs. That it was the best thing for us.

'Grandfather Milton knew I'd never do that.' Carter looked shocked.

'Lucia didn't believe him. She only visited him that one time and, after that, she wanted nothing more to do with him. Like I said, she's a very smart girl.'

'Do you know where she is now?'

Isabella sighed. 'Not for sure. She could have made it out already. But your daughter, like many others, idolised the idea of you and she never even knew you. She thought that you would be the one to save us all. Ironic that people on both sides believe that, isn't it?' Isabella paused and smiled, her lips tight and hard. 'There are people in here, Carter who want something better for their lives. Just like you did once. Just like your parents did.'

The mention of them made the pit of his stomach ache. 'My parents were careless,' he said. 'They got themselves killed.' His face grew hot and red in the growing darkness.

Isabella sighed again.

'Your parents were heroes,' she said. 'But they were very, very unlucky. You're out of the Catacombs now, Carter; you need to wake up.'

There was something desperate in her voice that Carter recognised. Something urgent.

'What are you talking about?'

'I'll tell you,' she said. 'But you won't believe me. And I am only doing this for your daughter and the rest of them in the hope that you will see sense. But you'll have to climb down here into the bunker with me. The drones will come soon.'

They sat together half-buried in the hole, covered by a shield of twigs and bracken that was enough to disguise them from a distance. At one point in its long history it had been some sort of well, hidden in the thick plants that had grown up around it. Isabella pulled branches over to form a thin lid. It reminded him of the late nights, back in the old days, watching pink clouds drift across the sparkle of the Barricades. The nights when they sat together on the hill made of old rubble and the ash of things burned, nights that were secret and out of bounds. Of times when they had talked about how he would become Controller General and change the world.

'This won't hide us for long,' she said. 'But it's better than being out in the open. Do you know about the extra guards? And the drones?'

Carter nodded. 'I saw one the other night. They're new.'

'Yes,' said Isabella. 'They're looking for signs of rebellion. Signs of dissent.' She grabbed a stick and started scratching it into the plants that grew around the inside walls of the well.

Carter narrowed his eyes at her.

'There is so much that's hidden in here,' she said, 'dark things, on both sides. Like what happened to Professor Mendoza and what's really across the Barricades. And why things that used to be so important here are banned, prohibited.'

'Things from before.'

'Yes,' said Isabella. 'Things like art, music, creativity, travel, games, books. All the things that our ancestors loved and cherished. Why do you think we can't have those here?'

Carter knew the standard answer but after everything he had heard, he wasn't entirely sure.

'All those things were dangerous,' he said. 'Books were full of lies – and games, music and art just wasted time. They didn't make food or shelter. What use were they?' Although the words came easily, Carter had the same feeling, again – that he was trying to convince himself.

'That's what the Industry would have you believe,' said Isabella. 'Your daughter loved to paint. And she was good at it. Very good. Even against old-world standards she was of an exceptional standard. But she's not the only one. There are people here making sounds, Carter. Can you imagine it? Sounds that are not just the dull ache of talking but beautiful sounds, like the birds.'

What she was describing could have them both sent to the Catacombs just for discussing. There had been talk, a year or so before Carter's parents had been killed, of creating a visual display in honour of the Industry, to celebrate the creation of the Community. The organisers were put on trial for conspiracy to create dissent. Groups that were not in pursuit of work or education were not allowed. And music, the potent emotional mood-enhancer, was considered to be one of the most destructive drugs of all. His grandfather had told him how it created emotions that were not there before and caused people to act in ways that they would not have done without it.

'Your daughter,' said Isabella, 'now *she* can sing.'

Above the hole in the ground, Carter could hear the sounds of the evening gathering. Sounds that were familiar and safe. His heart was beating louder through his shirt than any of them.

'How did she know how to do these things?' he said. 'All these things are forbidden. Who taught her?'

Isabella smiled with a sweetness of reminiscence.

'We learned them,' she said. 'We learned from what people left behind. Do you remember what you saw here when you were a child? You came with your father to see my uncle, Rufus Delaney. They were planning the revolution even then, you know, Rufus and Nikolas. Do you remember what they had?'

Carter stared into the soft earth, his eyes wide and black. 'I was doing my homework,' he said slowly. 'When I went to find my father and your uncle they were in the cellar, with boxes and boxes of books.'

Isabella picked a handful of thin, stringy plants that grew from the walls. 'When you were young, your father hoped you'd grow up to lead the revolution with him.' She laughed coarsely and spat into the ground. 'But my uncle was right – you were too *Industry* for that. And I... well, I was too *tainted* after what happened to him.'

'They thought that I would lead the revolution?' said Carter. 'Why me and not you?'

Isabella shrugged. 'I guess I was too obvious, being a Delaney, a Lab Made. Your father thought he could get you in under the radar, being so perfect, so *Industry*.'

'Your uncle was frozen,' said Carter, squinting in the dark. 'And they tore the house down – the whole thing – because of the books.'

For the first time he saw that there were tears in Isabella's eyes and the corners of her mouth trembled.

'My uncle was killed,' said Isabella. 'They destroyed the house because *you* told your grandfather about the books. And then he told the Industry.' The evening air was quiet and warm as the stars began to gather in white clusters through the trees and branches above them.

'We managed to save a handful of them and bury them in waterproof casing in the forest before they came,' said Isabella. 'Your father had hoped that when Professor Mendoza became Controller General, they could introduce books back into the Community and start exploring beyond the Barricades, but when she failed and Alderney got in, things turned ugly.'

Carter could barely understand what he was hearing. '*How* ugly?'

'Things were strict enough when we were teenagers. It got worse after you left. The Industry put Chess in charge to try and soften the way things looked but it just made some people more determined. Lucia could see that something was wrong from a very early age – all questions and curiosity. I told her to be more careful. Some of the so-called rebels actually work for the Industry, spying on the rest of us to work out how best to expose us. I said to Lucia that it was important to work out who you could trust. She was brave, just like your father, Carter – he'd have been so proud of her.'

As much as he didn't want to hear the answer, Carter needed to ask the question. 'What happened to my parents?' he said. 'What *really* happened to them?'

Isabella dragged a stick through the dirt. 'No one really knows,' she said. 'The few allies who knew what their intentions were don't speak about them. Most likely, they were killed by the Industry. When your mother was found to be carrying your brother and scans showed that he was, well, imperfect, she was scheduled to go to the Catacombs. But she wasn't going to go quietly. My guess is that the Industry orchestrated the attack in the Deadlands. I just don't know.

'Your grandfather was different to them and different to you. He was Industry, like the boy, Ariel, wants to be. He wanted to see you become Controller General, but as time went by, his mind and his commitment had begun to deteriorate. They couldn't risk him ruining your chances. But it was his time to go, he'd had a long life.'

'What happened to my grandfather?'

Shock and disbelief came over Carter in waves. He wanted to know everything, but at the same time he wished he hadn't heard any of it. Everything he had ever believed in felt like it was coming crashing down around him.

'What happened to your grandfather is the least of your problems. You need to deal with what's within your power to change. And to do that, there are some things you need to know right now, and some things that can wait.' She took a deep breath and exhaled loudly.

'You said you wanted me to listen to you,' Carter said, trying to be patient. 'And I am doing that. To do what you told me to. What is that exactly?'

'You have a choice,' said Isabella. 'The Industry wants you to unite the people. There are a few rebels gathering – their main aim is to find out what's beyond the Barricades and whether they can make any kind of life there. If you're going to be a leader of either side, you'll need to know what's out there before you choose which one. And in choosing, you'll need to be committed. It might be too late for me but you can still change things, Carter.'

She stared at him boldly and then smiled in the beautiful, crooked way that he had loved from the moment they had first met. His heart melted. Everything he trained for, everything he had worked so hard to achieve seemed to be falling through his fingers. The main reason had always been her and without her to fight for, he couldn't imagine being Controller General. But at the same time, he couldn't imagine anything else.

'This whole thing is bigger than just *us*,' she said, reading the creases in his face. She ran one finger delicately along his shoulder. 'There are hundreds of people like me, Lab Mades, who are made to do the most menial of jobs here, who can't use the intelligence so many of us have and—' she bit her lip '—and can't love who we want to because almost a hundred years ago our ancestors were created in a way that we didn't choose to be. That has now become frowned upon by the Descendants. You know that's wrong, Carter, and that everything has to change.' She paused. 'You promised.'

Carter exhaled heavily. The determination in Isabella's face, her deep commitment despite the brokenness of her own situation, pulled at his heart. Everything she had always been was still there inside of her while everything inside of him felt fractured and different.

'I've always trusted you,' he said. 'Always believed in you. But what you're talking about here could get me frozen again. Or killed.'

'Would you want to be just another failed Controller General? Or a hero, like your father wanted you to be?'

Carter looked into Isabella's eyes. 'I wanted to do this for you,' he said bitterly. 'For us.'

The woman shook her head sadly. 'It's not just about us any more,' she said. 'You want my opinion? Save us all. And do it in full possession of the facts. Go out there into the Deadlands and find out the truth for yourself. If you're still intent on being Controller General, you'll have much more to unite people with or to challenge the Industry. You'll have been there and seen what's on the other side of those Barricades.

Your knowledge of what is out there will be more of a Contribution to this Community than anything anyone else has ever seen or done.'

'There's a chance I might not survive out there,' Carter said slowly, his mind almost made up. 'There's a good chance I might not come back.' He wondered what there might even be to come back for, without Isabella.

'Well, you definitely won't survive in here, not knowing.'

'I've survived so far.'

Isabella laughed. 'There's surviving and then there's *living*. None of us just want to *survive* – what would be the point of that? We want something more, something joyful. Something to survive *for*. We had that in the past; our lives had *meaning* when we could create something for ourselves. If you give people what they are seeking, Carter, then they won't need to go looking for it.'

In the darkness of the hole in the ground, Carter felt excitement and terror building in equal measure.

'How easy is it to get out there? Is it even possible?'

'Anything is possible, Carter. Didn't Mendoza teach you anything?'

'Mendoza? What did she know? She didn't even make Controller General.'

'True,' said Isabella. 'I mean, she dedicated her career pretending to tutor you to become a Contender while really schooling you to lead the rebels and then, when the Industry sends you to the Catacombs as a punishment for loving me, jeopardising your chance to become the most influential Controller General in history, she risks everything by finding a way to prove to the Industry that what you felt for me meant nothing and you were prepared to impregnate another girl without giving it any thought.'

Carter swallowed hard.

'Mendoza was leading the rebels?' he said, incredulous. 'That can't possibly be true, she was a Contender for Controller General herself.'

Isabella shrugged. 'Like you, she wanted to become Controller General to change the world,' said Isabella. 'Her motivations may have been different but she wasn't alone. There are lots of people who want change, Carter. She was a great woman.'

He thought back to his days in the classroom and how Mendoza had seemed so *Industry* to him. How she had looked at him during the Freezing Preparation Evening. His mind whirled with confusion as he tried to make sense of what Isabella was telling him. And what Mendoza had said that night: *we are going to lose everything unless you do exactly what I say.*

'I thought you hated Mendoza,' he said, finally.

'On a personal level, I hated what Mendoza did, but I do know why she did it. It took me a long time to come to terms with it – or at least to understand the reasons. But then, when Alderney stepped down and the Contendership started without you seven years ago, my heart broke.' A tear pooled in the corner of one eye. 'I was only twenty-one. There might have still been a chance for us if you'd come back then. That's why the Industry waited until now to unfreeze you, Carter. They wanted to wait until I was too old for you. As much as I hated Mendoza's actions, she didn't do it soon enough. Either way, I lost you.'

As terrifying as the prospect of what might lay outside the Barricades was, the thought of not knowing and letting his parents and Isabella down again was equally, if not more, distressing to him. And there was something about the recent changes in the Community that were unprecedented, something that was building to a transformational crescendo that he couldn't avoid. He would need the upper hand against both the Industry and the rebels if he, Carter, was to change anything. In the murky half-light there was still something of the girl he used to know. The girl who had, and always would be, his main reason for Contendership for position of Controller General. He pushed his back into the earth wall behind him; it felt firm and solid against his body and gave him strength.

'You're right,' he said, finally, feeling his heart beat fast. 'I *have* to go into the Deadlands. Now tell me how.'

In the darkness of the hole, Carter could just make out Isabella's smile. 'Part of me always knew you'd do what was right,' she said. 'Even without me.'

Carter breathed deeply. 'This is a way out without a Transporter and without the Industry, right?'

'Yes, there's a secret tunnel nearer to the Barricades. I started it years ago and then I got a little help from the few people I could trust. We dug it through until we could join up with one of the old subway passages that ran under the river in the west of the old city.

'There's another side alcove that we tapped into at the end of the tunnel that leads into a maintenance shaft. We took it all the way, apart from the last bit. We cracked the final passageway just before news of your release came out. Lucia wanted to wait for you. She thought that you should be the one to lead the people out of the Community. You're going to have to be careful – make sure there are no drones around. They've been looking for the entrance for weeks now. It must stay hidden.'

Isabella coughed hard and Carter looked at her in half-disbelief.

'How far away?'

'The entrance is very close to here, hidden between the two black moss-covered rocks and covered with branches thick enough to hold your weight. No one would notice it, not out here. You should resurface far enough away from the Barricades for you to escape without being spotted.' Pride sparkled in Isabella's eyes.

'If that's true, how come nobody has been out there yet?'

'I don't know for sure that nobody has,' she said.

'Who knows about this?'

'Now? The others have been taken for freezing. So it's just the three of us.'

'Me, you and...' Carter allowed some of the pieces inside his head to fall into place.

'Lucia, yes,' said Isabella.

Carter scratched around in the dirt and then touched her hand gently. 'Will you come with me?'

Isabella shook her head. 'I can't,' she said. 'It really is too late for me.' She lifted up her clothing to show the creamy brown of her skin with the silvery metallic line running through it, framed with a yellow bruise and a lick of pus.

Carter shivered. 'What is *that*?'

'It's a tracker. And a death trap. If I go close enough to the Barricades, it will electrocute me from the inside out. I can't even try to get out of here unless I can have this removed.' She pulled at the metal that was meshed into her skin.

'Don't,' said Carter, grabbing her hands. 'Leave it alone.'

'You have to go without me. And make this happen, Carter, for all our sakes.'

Carter looked at the wound. 'Did the Industry really do that?' he said. 'It's barbaric. Inhumane.'

'As inhumane as splitting up families? And banning creativity? As controlling as who you can love? The Industry will stop at nothing to protect itself, Carter. They keep me alive as a punishment to show others.' She swallowed deeply. 'I offered myself up for freezing when you didn't come back the first time. I didn't want to live without you. It was Lucia who gave me the strength to carry on. But they told me that if I did anything more, broke any more rules, they would kill her. I couldn't risk that, Carter. She's special.'

Feeling the softness of her skin against his, Carter felt his heart weaken. He reached out and touched her hand gently. Around one of her fingers he felt something solid, cylindrical. He pulled her closer to him and ran the tips of his finger over her hand.

'You remember that?'

Isabella gently removed the hardened ring of slivery microfibre that had been baked in the sun and handed it to him. It was the tiny piece that the FreeScreen fitters had given him as a child.

He held it up to the failing light and, through the greyness, Carter could just see their initials carved into the surface.

'We can't go back in time,' said Isabella, taking it back and placing it on her finger, 'but there's a part of me that still wants you to change the world – my world.'

For a moment, there was a deep silence and then he kissed her gently on the lips, soft and warm.

'I will change the world,' he said. 'I promise.'

Carter pulled back the branches that covered the well hole and looked into the pinpricked sky, as black as the river he could hear in the distance. Something skittered in the trees and the air smelled different, cleaner almost.

'I'll go now,' he said, his mind and heart racing. 'I'll find the way out. And I'll find Lucia. And then when I come back, things will be different. Happiness is what's important – not just ours but everyone's. I will change what the Community understands happiness to be.'

Isabella nodded.

'Your father would be proud,' she said. 'A new proposition for happiness.'

As he pulled himself upwards, he held out his hand to help Isabella from the corner in which she was crouched. Then he remembered something.

'Lucia said strange words to me before she disappeared. I couldn't understand them. It was in some other language.'

Isabella thought for a second and then smiled to herself.

'*Veritas liberabit vos?*'

'It sounded like that. I'm not sure.'

Carter watched as a smile crept over her face. It started in the corners of her eyes and then brightened in her soft, green eyes. She looked just like he had remembered her, the first time he had been compelled to wheel his body around in the classroom on the first day of his Censomics class. The day that his heart had throbbed hard against its chamber and made his cheeks pulse crimson.

She touched his hand gently with hers and cleared her throat. When she spoke, there was something about her words that both excited and terrified him in equal measure.

'It means *the truth shall set you free*,' she said, her eyes sparkling in the starlight as she played with the ring on her finger.

Carter closed his hands over hers and looked up into the night sky. 'Yes,' he said quietly. 'It will.'

Chapter Fifteen

The Preparation

Alice

It was several planning sessions and almost fourteen months to the day after her first excursion to the Control Room that Alice was woken up in the middle of the night by Lucinda Watson, who looked sick and terrified. Her thin curls, greying and worn, dragged down towards her neck. Ian stood staunchly behind her, a hand on one shoulder.

'There's someone here for you,' she said in a frightened whisper. 'Did you do something wrong?'

Alice turned over on her rester and rubbed the creases from her eyelids.

'Is it Kunstein?' she asked, although she knew exactly what was happening. She could feel it. Her fingers tingled with an apprehension and an excitement she hadn't felt since the first time she had escaped along the corridors of the Ship and watched the secret conversations of the Industry elite. This was her time.

The thick muscles on her arms pulsed with excitement as Alice stepped into the room. Although they'd been through training individually, she knew them all. They had been selected on her recommendation to Kunstein.

'Is it the gym tonight?' Lucinda would call absently as Alice left each evening.

'Netball,' she would call cheerfully back before making the sixty-floor lift ride to the shooting range where Wilson would line up targets and shout encouragement as she fired shot after shot into the round circles of paper.

A great deal of what she had learned in microbiology and synthetics classes would help outside with food preparation, but it was the hard, physical workouts that she knew would be the most useful. There was even a swimming pool – the biggest she had ever seen – way down in the depths of the Ship. There, twice a week, she donned scuba gear and sank into the sparkling depths of the underlit lake that glowed white in the darkness. She was now expected to be an expert in things she had never dreamed of doing – climbing, diving, shooting. And she excelled at them all.

The ten Scouts were called to the main hall on the fifteenth floor of the main building and asked to assemble into their teams. There were two groups of five, each comprising a mixture of Industry professionals and hand-picked residents of the Ship, including Jonah who, puffed out in his thin translucent suit, paced back and forth checking his breathing equipment and radio over and over again. The two Industry officials Alice had never seen before.

Jonah looked the most nervous; his eyes flitted from one person to another and every few minutes he wiped his palms down the softness of his suit. When she had been asked to pull together a group of people whom she trusted, people who were genuinely committed to something new, Alice had picked Jonah – more because she was scared of what would happen to him if she left him behind. But, like her, he needed a chance. And for him, this was it.

'What if it doesn't work?' he said. 'What if we get radiated from whatever came out of the nuclear places? What if there's still water everywhere? What about all the dead people?'

Alice grabbed his hand and pulled him over to sit next to her.

'You've done the training and seen the footage – you know that it's going to be carnage out there, right? But the radiation levels are safe and the water levels have almost equalised. The landscape will have changed and we probably will see—' she lowered her voice '—dead people. But there won't be zombies and monsters or anything from the movies. This is our chance to see the sky. Imagine that – the actual *sky*.' They held each other for a second and through his suit she could feel his heart beating.

'It'll be OK,' she said softly. So softly that not even Jonah could hear it.

The creases that had held Jonah's mouth in a cold nervous line broke out into a half-smile and he lifted off the microfibre hood with its firm-fitting skullcap.

'The sky,' he said. 'I can't imagine it. That's the problem – I really can't.'

There was a quiet in the room as each held their own thoughts in quiet contemplation, punctuated only by Jonah's short wonderings. He looked upwards at the ceiling. 'But what if…' he started.

'It's OK, Jonah,' said Alice. 'The worst monsters are those we create ourselves. You should stop letting your imagination go crazy – we will deal with what we have to deal with.' She almost believed it herself. 'And you can take off the over-suit for now,' she added with a quick grin. 'We won't be leaving for hours yet.'

When the doors slid open with a soft grating slipping sound, four people walked out into the centre of the room with broad smiles on their faces. Alice recognised two of them, William Wilson and Kunstein – whose first name she had never known – but the others weren't people she ever thought she had seen before. One of them winked at her and nodded his head in recognition but she ignored them both and looked straight ahead.

'Good morning,' said William Wilson. His voice sounded less tinny and marginally friendlier in person, Alice thought. But not enough to make her particularly interested in getting to know him in any depth. There were some mumblings of good morning and an exchange of formalities. He switched on a screen that linked directly to the Control Room. Alice had since spent most afternoons with Kunstein in there, reviewing the protocol and developing plans. The screen focused directly on the red button, which now radiated a perfect shade of bottle green.

'This,' began William Wilson, 'is a momentous day. As you can see, at approximately three thirty-seven a.m. this morning, the water levels that we have been so closely monitoring dropped to what we consider to be an acceptable level. For the past six months, weather patterns have stabilised to what we would expect for this time of year and in this new climate patterning. Air quality is actually of a higher standard than when we last breathed it without purification assistance and there have been no dangerous predators spotted on the cameras in the last two weeks.'

'What about radiation?' Jonah's voice sounded hollow and small in the big room, scratchy and childlike in the oversized trousers of his protection suit. All eyes turned towards him, and Alice thought he looked delicate, vulnerable. In that moment, more than any other, she loved him.

'Just coming onto that, Jonah,' said Wilson with a curt snap in his voice. 'The radiation levels that we have been able to manage using the remote equipment and sentinels indicate that everything above ground within a radius of at least five miles of exit point four, where you'll be leaving the Ship, is safe. But I suggest you wear the suits for your own protection. Just in case there's something we haven't managed to monitor.'

Alice looked over at Jonah. His dark grey eyes, the colour of lead, watched every movement on the screen intently, thick with a cloud of worry and concern.

'You don't have to do this,' she whispered to him. 'There are others who would love to be out there; let them have the chance if you don't want to.'

Jonah stood up straight and pulled his shoulders backwards.

'I'm not going to let you go anywhere without me,' he said defiantly. 'You might be in charge of this whole thing, but you're not going alone.'

After the first briefing, they were taken to a classroom adjoining the main hall and given a demonstration of various pieces of safety equipment, some of which, Alice imagined, they could never possibly need. She fiddled with the paper-light suit, barely believing that it could protect her from anything – apart, perhaps from when she knocked her knuckles against the smoothly curved skullcap attached to the outer edge of the hood. It was a daring fusion of what felt like household cling film and plated steel.

'Is this trophene?' asked Jonah.

William Wilson nodded.

'Hardest and most flexible substance to have been created to date. We piloted its use on the mechanical scouts and sentinels. This is its first use as a fashion accessory. Maybe we should patent it?'

Wilson laughed somewhat more heartily than was appropriate and Kunstein shot him a sideways glance.

'These support suits have been through a rigorous design and development process,' said Kunstein. 'You have nothing to worry about at all. They have everything you need to make this first expedition a success. There is an automatic Geiger sensor in the suits you have been provided with, to warn of any unexpected rises in radiation levels,' said Kunstein, 'and in your hoods there are cameras and a small amount of processed oxygen, which will allow you to breathe underwater.'

'We're not going swimming,' said the boy who Alice recognised from her floor. Filip Conrad. He'd come from another floor less than a year earlier. He was taller than her with jet-black hair and slightly crooked teeth. His accent was clipped and European. He looked at her sideways and added, 'Are we?'

Alice shrugged back at him. 'If we do, I don't think it will be intentional,' she said, grinning at him.

Kunstein looked at them with mock annoyance.

Jonah's irascibility was significantly more genuine and he narrowed his eyes in grumpy irritation.

'If you do not need any guidance in how to approach a half-drowned world, Filip, then please do let us know,' said Kunstein.

He turned a pale shade of pink.

Jonah said nothing but continued to frown, his eyes black with jealousy.

'Let's get down to business,' said William Wilson. 'We have a lot to cover in the next two hours. Alice, Filip, as our two team leaders, I am expecting exemplary behaviour from you both. And—' he gestured to the others in the room '—I expect the rest of you to support them one hundred per cent. With absolutely no exceptions or you'll be dead – or, worse, back to the Ship.'

Around a few trays of food, they talked strategies and objectives. William Wilson projected a map onto the wall that was more patches of open blue than it was land. The thin snake of the Thames that had previously wound its way through the city was shown as a thick arc, encircling the two districts and completely flooding others. The whole thing looked a completely different shape to anything Alice remembered.

'This is what we have to work with,' said Wilson. 'We are here, towards the north side of the city, south of the main curve in the river. This area surrounded by the red dotted line is where we know to be immediately safe from radiation or anything critically dangerous.' He stopped for a second and curled a thin tongue over his lips.

'I cannot tell you how exciting this is,' he said. 'I'm sure you understand that this is probably the single most important task you will ever undertake in your lives. What we're doing today is testing the water… so to speak.' He chuckled again but this time glances from Kunstein, Alice and Filip cut him short. He turned back to the screen and Kunstein continued.

'Team A, headed up by Alice, will take this route—' she traced her finger across the screen '—but you will all leave using exit shaft number four. The shaft runs upwards from the highest floor underground and will lead you directly into one of our divisional sub buildings, on the fifth floor. From what we can see, that building has been pretty well preserved, with the top floors remaining above the water level for most of the last five years. Depending on the state of the building, once you have exited the shaft, you should be able to use the stairs to get out onto the street. This will place you here.' Kunstein tapped the screen with her finger. Every pair of eyes in the room remained fixed on the map.

'Old Arnott Road,' said William Wilson. 'At least, that was what you used to call it.'

'The area in a one-mile radius of this is now known as Area X,' said Kunstein. 'Your first job will be to investigate whether what we have observed on the monitors in the last few months is accurate and representative. Your second job will be to identify and secure a base camp. Over the coming weeks, we will need to build other teams that will help with the reconstruction work and it will not be energy-effective to keep returning them to—' she paused '—to the Ship as you like to call it. But we will need teams of people we can trust. As you can imagine, this is a very delicate situation. So we'll need to work together and that might mean making some very *difficult* decisions. Team B, headed up by Filip, will follow this route.'

Alice bit the skin around her fingers. Everything felt like it was shifting too quickly for her to understand. Suddenly, she and Filip were in charge, with the backing of Kunstein under the strategy of Wilson. Jonah was melting into her background. The idea of her mother and her life before seemed like a different world.

'At this point in time, we will not be notifying the general population about our plans. We will, however, be letting them know about our intention to place you in isolation training, in preparation for an ascent, although we cannot and will not be specific about timescales, thereby ensuring that your nearest and dearest do not worry about your wellbeing. We also have a team of people who will be joining you – some of our finest engineers – who will help you to set up your base while you are there. They're behind-the-scenes kind of people so they won't be missed here.'

'Is the plan the same?' said Alice.

'To the letter,' said William Wilson. 'Firstly, I need you to get out there and test the air with your samplers to get an independent measure – but your suit scanners should do the rest. We'll use the readings to get germ and bacteria ratings within Area X and then take a look around. Remember what we agreed was usable – metals, core materials and combustibles for energy. We'll run a collection service from the shaft back here to our storerooms in the core underbelly of the Ship. But more important than anything else is our need to cleanse this town. To remove all traces of what it was before. Try to remember that the biggest danger to us comes not from anything outside, but from ourselves.'

Alice looked across at Filip, who was nodding seriously. He was older than her, seventeen or eighteen maybe, and was taller than anyone else in the room – William Wilson included. His eyes were as dark as the inside of a wishing well, pooled, secret and almost pure black. He twisted his wrists around until they clicked.

'You want the city razed to the ground, right?' For the content of his question, the tone of Filip's voice was irreverently casual. Alice let her usually carefully guarded respect for him creep up a notch. There was something so certain, so direct about him that was absent in Jonah.

'*Razed*,' said Wilson, 'is quite an emotive word. I myself prefer *cleansed.*'

'But you want us to get rid of everything, not just the bodies?'

'Everything that will not be productive in building our new community.' Wilson prowled slowly around the edge of the room, almost as if he was drinking in the questions that they had not yet asked. Alice watched as Kunstein's eyes moved from her, to Jonah, to Filip and then across at the others who sat in the room, each face showing a slightly different set of emotions.

'Remember why we are doing this,' she said. 'Can you imagine the chaos of returning the people we have here to the world up there?'

She looked upwards and Alice expected the ceiling to dissolve into a window of clear glass, revealing a city of trees, drunk with grief, felled to their roots and bodies littering the streets.

'We need to start again,' said Alice. 'Whatever we had is gone and it's our job to clear the way for the others.'

Wilson nodded firmly, looking pleased, and the others on the team visibly relaxed.

'I know it's going to be tough,' said Kunstein. 'But we have special work to be done. And a great deal of it. You will need to identify a space within which we can dispense of *unwanted material*. Initial surveillance points to this area here.' She waved her hand towards the west of the map. 'It was known as Butterfly Valley. There was previously a landfill site here. I would imagine it will be far enough away from the initial borders of our new community. As we expand and develop, we may need to reconsider, but for now—' she looked at Alice '—I would suggest you use this.'

Filip clicked his wrists again. 'When you say *unwanted material*, you're talking about bodies, right?' Alice watched as he looked directly at her, eyes unwavering until he winked at her, not caring who was watching.

Wilson nodded.

'There won't be many bodies left, but there's no getting around the fact that we lost a lot of lives here. And we absolutely cannot build our foundations on a city of broken bones. You'll start the pyres like we discussed, for anything that will not produce toxins. The *aftermath* and anything we can't use for building or recycling will need to be concealed. Start with the Butterfly Valley site, as long as it proves usable, and we'll look at what comes next.'

Alice felt a fizz of excitement in her chest. It felt like the moment when you hurled yourself off a rope swing into an ice-cold river and everything felt fresh and clean and new. She hadn't imagined ever feeling that again. Her feet twitched nervously against the slick polished surface of the classroom floor, and for one glorious second she imagined the uneven contours of dewy grass beneath her feet and the call of birds overhead.

'Are we looking for others?' said Jonah. 'What about other survivors?'

'All observations indicate there aren't any,' said Wilson. 'There have been no attempts at communication and...'

'But what if there are?'

Alice looked at William Wilson, who was flicking through the screens of his slate. He didn't look at Jonah when he answered but his response was clear enough.

'Outsiders pose the second greatest threat to our new community,' he said with the air of a military battle commander.

'You want us to kill them? Are you serious?' Jonah sat back in his chair and pushed away the slate on the desk. He looked at Alice. 'I'm not killing anyone.'

Filip cleared his throat and cracked his knuckles against the desk.

'Killing is not our business, Jonah,' he said. 'But defence is. So, like Wilson says, we defend to create. Anyone we find won't have been through the programme that our people have here; they won't understand about the new world. We'll have to do what we can to educate them. It's all about communication and it's all about change. You see?'

Alice nodded. 'He's right.'

Jonah's face changed from one shade of green to another while Alice raised her eyebrows and looked at Kunstein, who seemed equally impressed. Filip smiled at Alice.

'Agreed, Filip. I think we all understand each other,' said William Wilson, and performed one of his rarer smiles that started with his teeth and ended close to, but not including, his eyes.

'We'll give you another hour to formalise your plans before we go to the tunnels,' said Kunstein. 'Please be in your suits and ready to go when we return. Your sustenance packs are being prepared, which will give you everything you need including a communications pack. Be ready to move. You are the future now.'

When Kunstein and Wilson left the room with a clip of heels and a swish of black cloak, Jonah sidled over towards Alice and touched her arm. In the starkness of the mission ahead, and the thought of being outside the Ship, the sweetness of his touch felt childlike – in a way that she no longer did.

'Why isn't there anyone on this team over eighteen?' he said, pulling up the arm coverlets of his suit. 'You know, like any *adults*?'

Alice looked at him. He looked so small and vulnerable that she wanted to pick him up and hold him in her arms. She resisted, however tempting it seemed.

'Jonah,' she said, 'didn't you ever wonder why there was a dispro-portionate ratio of age groups here on the Ship?'

Jonah shrugged. 'I just thought... I guess I don't know what I thought.'

'There are hundreds of us,' she said. 'Between five and eighteen. Maybe more, I don't know for sure. But what I do know is that when this happened, the Industry had a plan. They had a better plan than any government or army or religious organisation. They saved everyone they could but they saved more of the people they thought could make a difference, could build a better place for us to get back to. Children are cruel and imperfect but they can also create change in a way that is much more transformative than anything the previous generations could have dreamed about. In the last five years here, this is what we have been preparing for, dreaming of, constructing. Some of the people who live on the Ship were born here; some of them have never known anything but this. Imagine what we can do, Jonah. Just imagine it.'

Jonah pulled his arm away. 'You sound like her,' he said and cast his eyes towards the door. Alice raised an eyebrow, pursed her lips and smiled.

'That's the nicest thing you've ever said to me,' she said and stood up to walk to the front of the room. She cleared her throat to get the room's attention and then smiled the broadest grin, arms outstretched in front of her.

'Okay, everybody,' she said with ardent jubilation as the room swelled with excitement. 'Let's get these plans moving. Team Davenport is on a discovery mission.'

There was a ripple of excitement as William Wilson and Kunstein came back into the room.

'Stay in touch,' they said almost together and shook each of the Scouts hands in turn. Kunstein cupped the curves of Alice's face when she came to her and looked into her eyes.

'Be strong,' she said and Alice was almost certain that there was an ice-like tear forming in her left eye.

Each had their suit checked and tested by one of the silent engineers who had accompanied them and then they were led, in single file, to the very edges of the Ship. An engineer flipped back a panel in the wall, revealing a tight vertical shaft – the same shaft that Alice had squeezed herself into almost five years before.

She could sense Filip behind her, the feel of his breath on her neck through the thin coverlet suit, and she turned around.

'Everything in order?' she asked. 'Is your team ready?'

He smiled at her and nodded.

'Nervous?'

'Excited.' He smiled.

'Me too. You have any concerns about your team?'

'None. You?'

'No.'

'Then let's get on with it.' Filip flashed another smile, the corners of his mouth turning up to reveal shark-like white incisors against blood-red lips. There was something about him, thought Alice, that reminded her of something, but she couldn't quite place it.

'If you need anything, use the leader communication line,' she said. 'The range isn't great on the first day so I don't think we should stray too far apart.'

'I concur,' said Filip and she saw the smile again. As she climbed into the shaft and started her ascent on the ladder, she took one arm off the rail and flapped it into the darkness.

'Goodbye, Ship,' she said softly and pressed her hand flat on the edge of the shaft. 'Sail safe.'

Behind her, the nine other Scouts took their places on the ladder and, one by one, crept upwards from the warmth and safety of the Ship into the unknown skeleton of a world from which they had fled five years earlier.

Chapter Sixteen

The Escape

Carter

Lily was waiting outside on the street when he got home, slinking back in the shadows. She emerged from the darkness and pulled him with her before he'd even had time to speak. The air was laced with juniper and the coolness was nothing like the stuffy, putrid aroma of the hole he'd been in earlier.

'Move,' she said. 'They'll be here any minute.'

They moved quickly and silently through the streets and out towards the wood.

'Who will be here?'

'The Industry; they're coming to get you. Your card has been still for hours and word is that Elizabet is about to finalise her Contribution – it's complicated and may be quite controversial but it will certainly change the Community in a way not seen since the very early days.'

'What is it?' Carter remembered what she'd said about Lab Mades and he felt an aching twinge in the pit of his stomach.

'It's a genetic modification programme,' said Lily, looking around. 'Her mentor came to me as he had some concerns about her approach

but if she can develop the changes to the Model she's looking for…'
Lily could barely disguise her concern.

'What changes?'

Lily took a deep breath. 'In at least one of her previous lives, Elizabet
was very close to one of the genetic professors, a doctor. This doctor
pioneered the technology to create and grow foetuses outside the body.
She took genetic material from anyone and everyone she could and
created the Lab Mades. It took a great deal of work and a lot of failed
attempts but in order to grow the population quickly, she cultivated
the babies in special cases in the Catacombs.

Carter nodded, impatient. 'We learned most of that in the
Academy,' he said. 'What has this got to do with Elizabet?'

Lily took a deep breath. 'As a junior member of the Community, Elizabet was mentored by the doctor. She helped grow the original Lab Mades.'

'So what's her Contribution?'

Lily paused and they rested beneath a small oak tree. 'She hasn't
disclosed it in full. But…' She shook her head.

'What's her plan?'

'She's going to round up some of the existing Lab Mades who've
exhibited rebellious tendencies for genetic testing – to see if she can
isolate the gene that makes them… different.'

Carter stared at Lily, open-mouthed. 'And then what?'

She shrugged. 'Her mentor thinks she'll breed a new set of
genetically modified Lab Mades – with reduced intelligence and no
propensity for anything other than doing exactly what the Industry,
or Elizabet, wants them too.'

Dread eked into every fibre of Carter's body as he thought of Lily.

'She has to be stopped.' Carter felt his mouth get dry as he spoke.
'She can't win,' he added, wishing desperately he could warn Isabella.

'I agree,' said Lily, beckoning him on through the wood. 'Which is why we need to forget about her and focus on you. But before we start, there are some things you need to know. At this point, the race for Controller General is just between the two of you. Jenson has failed his personal challenges and has displayed some health issues so he's been sent back to the Catacombs. And, Carter, the Industry have some concerns about you.'

'What concerns?'

'They think you're going to be approached by the rebels – so they want me to bring you in. Tomorrow at the latest.'

'Bring me in where?'

'Industry Headquarters.'

Carter breathed in deeply and quickened his pace.

'But I have things to do.'

'What things?' Lily rounded on him and looked him squarely in the eye.

'Well, I need to start my Contribution for one thing. If Elizabet has her idea formulated I must…'

'You can do that at the Industry Headquarters,' interrupted Lily. 'They have all the resources there and…'

Carter held his hand up to stop her. 'It's not that kind of Contribution. And, anyway, if the rebels have plans for me, then surely I need to address those and not run away from them.'

Lily looked behind her. 'Carter, this isn't a request; it's an order.'

'Why are you telling me this?'

'I'm telling you so that you can be prepared and answer any questions they might have.'

'Is that your job, to tell me?' Carter looked at her quizzically. 'Why are you here?'

Lily hesitated. 'It's my job to make you as successful as you can be. But, no, I shouldn't be telling you this. I just feel that if you have all the information, you can probably make the right choices. You are going to need to know everything if you're going to be Controller General.'

Carter winced slightly. 'There's no "if". So what would the Industry say if I mentioned that you'd told me all this?'

'What are you getting at, Carter?'

'Can I trust you?'

'You have to. I'm your mentor. And what would the Industry say if they knew I'd given you inside information? They'd send me back to the Catacombs. You should know that.'

Carter hesitated and looked around. 'Then I'm going to tell you something. And I'll explain on the way there,' he whispered. 'But you have to trust that I know what I'm talking about.'

She nodded. 'On the way where?' she said. 'They'll be looking for you soon.'

They stopped at a FreeScreen terminal just outside the forest. The light flickered green – no rain due.

'We've just got to check something. I promise you we'll be back before the electronic surveillances are done. But first I need you to contact the Industry and tell them you've checked on me, that I'm fine and understand the situation. And that I am committed to becoming Controller General and will be at the Headquarters first thing in the morning. But we have to leave our cards here.'

Lily shook her head. 'Not carrying your card is a criminal offence,' she said. 'We could get into serious trouble. I should report you; officially you're under my charge.'

'You won't report me. In a few months' time, I will be Controller General,' said Carter. 'And then I'll decide what counts as trouble.

This is more important than anything you or I have ever had to do before. If you want to be in my counsel then I can arrange it. No more Catacombs, no more working at the Food Plant; if you're with me on this then I will arrange something a lot more appropriate to your skills. Just trust me on this one. It's important.'

Lily looked at his usually pale-blue eyes, now serious and almost violet in colour.

'I believe in you,' she said quietly.

They took the back roads to the south, flitting in and out through the trees, staying away from the tracks and keeping as close to the outside perimeter as possible without tripping the torches that floodlit the Barricades from the inside. It wasn't until they were clear of the last of the homes, long past the darkened windows of Jescha's house, that Carter could tell Lily about Isabella. They shared a clutch of carrotina and some pieces of boeuf from the cloth bag Lily had brought. He told her almost everything. Leaving out the kiss they had shared.

'You know that *creature* is medically insane, don't you?' Lily twisted a curl of hair around her finger and let it go in a pinch. 'Nuts,' she said, 'completely and entirely. She's exactly the type of person Elizabet will want to eliminate.'

Carter weighed up the conversation in his head. Everything had made such perfect sense to him when he'd been with her but he was keen not to alienate Isabella.

'She may be; she may not be. Either way, I have to know. I have to know the truth. How else can I end this uprising unless I've been out there?'

Lily pursed her lips. 'I'm sorry. She may have been a friend of yours when you were children but it's well known around the Community that she's trouble. She has been for years, ever since you went away.'

Carter turned to her. 'Trouble,' he said. 'Like how?'

Lily held his gaze tightly and paused. 'Well, firstly, she was accused of trying to abduct a child a few years ago – your child, Lucia, to be exact – although they couldn't prove that malicious intent was involved. The girl claimed she went out there of her own accord. And Isabella herself has been under investigation several times. Her family are well-known serial offenders – most of them terminally frozen. Her uncle, in your time, was frozen for dissent, and once she even tried to climb the Barricades. The Industry doctors did everything they could for her but they believed it left her, well, mentally unstable – a combination of the electricity and her existing mental delusion.'

Carter nodded his head slowly. The Industry would have made their version of events well known. 'Maybe. But if there *is* a way out of here, as Controller General, I have a right to know. And I have a right to find out what happened to Lucia, to my parents, and to everyone who's so disenchanted with this place. Something has gone terribly wrong here.'

Lily shook her head in frustration. 'That was always the problem of the human condition – wanting better, wanting faster, wanting more. Isabella is obsessed with bringing the Industry down. I suppose she showed you her magnetic belt, the inhibitor?'

Carter cringed as he thought of the sharp, metal strip interwoven into Isabella's skin.

'Is that what you call it?' he said, beginning to get angry. 'It's disgusting. It's inhumane.'

'It's not pretty,' said Lily. 'But it's the only way she could be stopped from attempting to climb the fences. Even though they're electrified, she kept trying to climb them. The fences were only intended to provide a warning jolt to stop any animals from the Deadlands coming in, but the current had to be increased to stop her from trying to destroy them – and herself. Do you know how dangerous it would be if there were an open passage between here and the Deadlands? It would be catastrophic for the Community.'

Carter flexed his arms outwards. 'Well, I'll soon find out,' he said.

They walked and whispered as the navy blueness of the evening gave way to a pure black blanket sprinkled with a smattering of stars and the odd lace-white cloud.

'I'm not sure about this,' said Lily. 'The repercussions are wider than you think.'

'I understand exactly what the repercussions are,' said Carter. 'And whatever happens next is bigger than me; it's bigger than the Community. This could be a whole shift in the paradigm of what we know.'

Lily started out into the darkness as they walked.

'I'm coming with you,' she said, breaking the silence.

'I don't need you to,' said Carter. 'This is something I need to do for *me* – for the Community.'

'I'm your mentor,' said Lily. 'You're my responsibility right now. And, besides, I want to. I want to be there to see it. And if you decide to position me well in your counsel, then even better.'

In the darkness of the forest, the cool night air was refreshingly soft. From the branches came the deep, throaty sound of owls. In the loneliness of the forest that was broken with the remnants of old, shattered buildings and smashed tarmac, Carter looked up at the millions of stars that peppered the sky and the fullness of the moon. The night had never looked so beautiful to him.

'First of all, I want at least to check whether the tunnel Isabella mentioned is really there. And, maybe, if I can understand that world and I can bring a small part of that world back – the part that made people happy – then I can make that my Contribution: a new proposition for happiness. But I need to know what we've sheltered them from for the last twenty years. And why.'

'And you think you can do that in one evening?'

Carter hesitated. 'If I have to. But if I can't, then you'll need to come back and cover for me. But at least one of us needs to be back before sunrise to keep the Industry happy – and both before nightfall tomorrow.'

'What about the tunnel?' said Lily. 'As soon as we open it up, then we put the Community in danger.'

Carter cleared his throat and his voice was strong and certain. 'If it *is* there, then we're already in danger. I need to get it closed off, contained. I need to ensure that no one leaves here again without permission. And I'll show people that what they have is better than what they think they want. An idea is always more attractive than the reality.'

'True. So you're willing to go this far to become Controller General?' Lily looked at Carter seriously.

'I promise you,' said Carter, looking up at the sky. 'The next person to lead this Community will bring to it something so compelling that nobody will want to leave again. Or we all leave. Together.'

In the darkness above them there was the twitter of a nightjar flitting across the branches.

'They only come when the rains are due,' said Lily. 'There could be a storm on the way.'

'The indicators said no, but we need to go anyway,' he said. 'When I get what I need, we'll come back and I will present my findings to the Industry. Having people voluntarily unite is infinitely better than the horror that Elizabet has planned. Whatever we find will either make or break this.'

He sounded excited, delirious almost.

'You know that if something happens out there, we might not be able to come back,' said Lily. 'We can't take any risks with the rest of the Community. Are you prepared for that? We'll never survive out there.'

Carter smiled.

'Well, I won't survive in here, not knowing. And you keep forgetting who you're with,' he said. 'I am Carter Warren, remember?'

'I'm not sure you know what you're doing,' she said.

'Well, I do. And I always have.'

They finished the last of the carrotina with some water. Lily pulled out some fauclate from her pocket and broke it in half, handing one slab to Carter who began to nibble at the corner, deep in thought.

'We need to move quickly,' he said, 'if we're going to be back before anyone notices we've left.'

They took a route directly through the forest that descended into pitch-blackness. The few night birds that flew in above the Barricades and had made temporary resting places high in the trees chirped their night noises as the pair passed below them like silent ghosts. Carter stopped her from moving any further.

'From here we need to follow the tracks,' he said. 'We can't risk falling into any holes like the one I was in earlier. A twisted or a broken ankle and we're finished. We need to be especially careful from here on in.'

They crept through a thicket of sweet ferns and out onto the track, which wasn't much more than old brown fronds trampled down into the earth. Lily tapped the floor with her feet.

'Seems pretty solid,' she said. 'No secret tunnels or hidden passages here.' Carter paced around slowly in the darkness, testing each footfall gingerly.

'Isabella,' he hissed. 'Are you here?'

'She'll be long gone,' said Lily. 'It's a surprise she hasn't died from some infection already. The Industry did it for her own safety, but it looks like it might be what kills her in the end.'

Carter thought for a moment and then squared up to Lily. 'How do *you* know so much about her?' he said.

Lily ran her fingers through the ferns.

'What do you mean? Everyone knows about her. She's pretty well-known across the Community.' She stroked the fronds of the fern thoughtfully.

Carter looked away, back towards the place where he had seen Isabella earlier.

'She's not who you think she is.'

Lily laughed.

'Don't you get it? She's a liar, a dissident, a fraud. You can't believe anything she says. And who knows what sort of trouble she's got your daughter into. The Industry have been taking the best care of her that they could without committing her to underground storage, but it has to happen sometime.'

Carter pushed thoughts of Isabella from his head. But still his words came out as fractured sentences.

'Let's try and find the tunnel. Prove how much or how little truth there was in that. She talked about unrest – about people wanting to leave.' He thought about what Morton had whispered to him in the food production plant. *He* hadn't seemed that insane. 'Either way, I need to know.'

They inched around the clearing on their hands and knees, tapping the floor as they went. It was Carter who found the entrance first, between two flat rocks, just as Isabella had said. The moss that covered them was thick and warm, tiny tendrils of growth inching up to meet his hands as he pushed down gently. On one side of the entrance there was a gap, loosely covered by ferns that had been dragged over the top from below, concealing the opening.

'Someone has been down there,' whispered Lily.

Sitting on one of the rocks, Carter used his feet to kick apart the branches that covered the rest of the entrance, then got down on his knees and separated the twig-work. Lily pulled back the last of the base logs and less than an hour after they had started the search, they were sitting alongside a square-shaped opening in the ground, wide enough for both of them to squeeze through.

As Carter lowered his body down by the wooden handholds that had been forced into the wall, a damp earthy smell filled his nostrils. There was something acrid and decaying and the warm air was stuffy. Lily came behind him, pulling a cover of sticks over the entrance to hide the hole as best she could. When Carter reached the ground he stumbled over something both soft and hard at the same time. He kicked the lump towards the entrance to the tunnel and let out an involuntary yell.

Above him, Lily called down.

'Are you all right?' Her voice echoed and boomed in the tight space of the hole and shook him even further. Carter realised he was shaking and felt stupid.

'Yes, I think so. Lily, there's something here. I think it's…'

'Wait until I get there.' She scrambled down after him and they stood in the almost pitch blackness. The shape didn't move.

'Do you think it's her?' Lily's whisper capitulated Carter's worst fears.

'I don't know.' They stood there, the sound of a solitary owl cooing above them, out into the blackness. Slowly, half-crouched, Lily inched herself forwards, feeling the way with her hands. Carter held his breath and could feel his heart smashing inside his chest. There was a gulp and then the weak halo of moonlight that had been filtering through the hole disappeared. He lost sight of Lily completely.

'Lily!' His whisper echoed around the cramped space and out into the tunnel. Nothing came back. 'Hey!' he shouted. 'Come back.'

Still, there was nothing.

'Lily!' Carter rushed forward into the space of the tunnel, crashing into Lily who was on her hands and knees just a few feet ahead of him. He tumbled over her crouched body and landed face down in the pile of rags on the floor.

'It's OK,' said Lily, her voice sounding alien and overly loud in the darkness. 'It's just supplies – look. This is where Isabella must have stored some of her things.'

The sack had been made from old clothing, well-worn but firm. Feeling his way inside, Carter pulled out an almost full bottle of fire fuel, flint lights and thick, chunky stumps of wood.

'At least someone was prepared,' said Lily. 'I'm guessing you didn't bring anything like this?'

Carter shook his head and wrapped a rag around one of the sticks then dripped fuel around it. Striking the flints together with a haphazard zing, the torch flew into life, blinding them momentarily.

It bled a bright orange glow, the colour of an autumn sunrise, into the blackness. A family of tiny beetles scurried across the wall and under one of the makeshift struts.

For a silent moment they sat there transfixed in the silence: the beetles watching Carter; Carter watching the beetles. Now they had light.

The tunnel that led westwards towards the Barricades wasn't quite large enough for either of them to stand upright in, but it wasn't so small that they had to crawl. The outer edges had been stepped up with a wooden structure, a ribcage of sturdy branches to stop the earth crumbling down around them and snuffing out the vein of a tunnel that curled forwards towards the outer edges of the Community. Carter held the torch out in front of him, letting it absorb the darkness and create an orb of light that was nothing but whiteness. As their eyes became accustomed to the gloom, Carter looked at the outline of Lily in the darkness and shivered at the thought of how much Isabella had changed.

'Come on,' she said. 'We need to go.'

Apart from the occasional fork in the passageway where one twist or the other led to a thick boulder blocking the way, the tunnel continued to lead west until they neared the edge of the river bend, the tunnel curving against a red brick wall that had been smashed through into little more than a crawl space.

Carter went first, on his back and in reverse, watching the flickering of the torchlight reflect against the ceiling. He shivered as he watched Lily go through and, when they were on the other side, the tunnel widened out into a dank, semi-circular construction with a solid floor and dripping ceiling. This tunnel hadn't been hollowed out of the earth by hand. This was from the old days.

'Subway,' he said. 'People used to walk under here because it was too dangerous above ground. But if this is water from the Black River seeping into the brickwork, it could be poisonous.'

Sticky dark shoeprints stood out in front of them on the smooth surface of the floor. Carter smiled.

'But not that poisonous; someone's been through here before. We're going this way.'

Lily looked at him uncomfortably. 'Who do you think that could be?' she said.

'I know who I *hope* it is.'

Covering their heads, they pelted through the tunnel, their speed helped by the relative evenness of the tiling and their desperation not to catch any of the droplets of water on their skin. A sheer wall of dark grey trophene rose up to meet them as they raced, breathless, towards the other end. Carter banged his fists against the wall.

There was no way through.

'This can't be it,' he said. 'Check the side walls. Isabella said something about another side tunnel.' He shone the light against the damp walls as they padded back and forth, tapping the edges until they finally hit the alcove set back into the brickwork. Lily went first, ducking through the low side tunnel leading west as they crawled back into the dark, hand-dug shaft.

'We're past the river now,' said Lily. 'We're in the Deadlands.'

Carter shrugged.

'Technically, the Deadlands is only really the land above ground. The Industry Headquarters extends out underground beyond the perimeters of the Community Barricades; it has to. The Catacombs and the Plants are pretty far into the Deadlands, it's just that they're underground.'

As the tunnel snaked out into the underbelly of the Deadlands, Carter felt the air becoming clearer and softer on the throat. He breathed in deeply and then exhaled.

'The air here is better,' he said. 'It's like there's a current running through the tunnel. It must meet the surface somewhere, or at least have some sort of channel that's feeding it.'

'I think we should rest,' said Lily. 'Gather our strength before we get out there. I've been on shift all day and I'm hungry.'

Carter looked at her. She seemed exhausted and let out a long sigh.

'We should go on; who knows what's on the other side – and we don't have much time.'

Her face cracked. 'Please, Carter.'

Carter squared on her. 'If we can't get out or it's completely unsafe, then we'll go back,' he said. 'Depending on how far they've dug through here, there can't be more than an hour each way. We'll be back at Unity Square by sunrise.'

'Then let's take ten minutes. I need to sit down for a while.'

'Fine,' said Carter. 'But only for a short while.'

They sat there in silence on the soft earth and Lily reached into her bag, handing Carter a flask of water.

'Even a Controller General needs to drink,' she said. 'Go on.' She looked around nervously.

Carter reached for the water, his mouth dry and parched.

'Don't worry. I think that whatever is out there will answer a lot of questions – for everybody.' In the cool darkness, his eyes felt soft and heavy.

Lily sat next to him and rested her head on the wall of the tunnel. 'I'm tired,' she said. 'Aren't you?'

Carter yawned and settled himself against the opposite wall. There was a deadness in his legs and he let his body relax.

'You're going to make a great Controller General,' whispered Lily.

Nodding, Carter felt the corners of his mouth twitching and, within seconds, he was asleep.

Although somewhere in the crevices of his reverie he heard the violent crash of wood and earth, it was the sharpness of Lily's screaming that woke him. The sound was like icy, bony fingers dragging him through stony ground and it pulled him kicking from the deep sleep he had settled into on the floor. Rubbing cold sweat from his face, he leapt up, his head searing with pain.

'What's going on?' he shouted and thrashed his arms around the edges of the tunnel until he found the torch and the bag containing the flints. As it flared into life, he could see Lily, arms and legs streaked with brown earth, scrabbling at the wall of the tunnel.

'It's gone!' she screamed. 'The tunnel has collapsed!'

As Carter brought the torch around in a circle, he could see that Lily wasn't clawing at the wall but at a mound of earth that had fallen thick against the floor of the tunnel. The walls and roof had collapsed inwards, barring the way back from where they had come.

'Go! Run *NOW.*'

'We're going to be buried alive,' screeched Lily, stumbling to her feet. 'We're going to die.'

'We're not going to die,' he said pulling her along as they made their way through as quickly as they could. 'There's air here, and a breeze. It's faint, but there's a breeze.' He waved the torch over the wall of rubble and earth. The struts had collapsed and were lying broken on the ground. Dust and splintered wood filled the tunnel all the way to the roof and Carter hurriedly rubbed the dust from his eyes. He pushed Lily forwards into the tunnel, stumbling behind her.

They moved quickly and in silence, punctuated by the spitting of the torch and the occasional trickle of earth from the roof of the tunnel onto the floor. Having to crouch down low and half-crawl through the space, Carter could feel the gradient of the tunnel sloping upwards at a gradual incline towards the surface. His heavy legs ached and his muscles were sore.

'Handmade tunnels like that are never safe, not at this depth,' he said, moving forwards. 'We must have fallen asleep.'

'You had a blackout,' said Lily. 'It happens sometimes when you first come out of the Catacombs. You were out for about half an hour. I closed my eyes for a moment and the next thing I knew, the tunnel came crashing down.'

Carter rubbed his eyes and looked sideways through the darkness at Lily. He didn't remember falling asleep – in fact he remembered nothing more after taking a drink of the water from Lily. It was possible that he'd had a blackout but he'd not experienced any of the other symptoms that occasionally accompanied an awakening. The tunnels were a dangerous place to be with someone he could trust, let alone anyone who might have drugged him – but Lily had taken a risk to be there with him too. There was nowhere to go but forwards, making sure he monitored her movements. He nodded back at her.

'Well, I can't afford to have another blackout. We need to keep moving – no more stopping until we get to the other side.'

As they trudged through the tunnel, saying very little to each other, Carter mulled over Lily's actions. She was there to protect him – she wouldn't have taken the risk to go beyond the Barricades otherwise. But there was something else. Within about twenty minutes, Carter was almost certain he could see what he'd feared most of all. In front of them was a dirty red-brick foundation wall blocking the way ahead, with a small hole just large enough to squeeze through smashed into the blocks. A large log, its end covered in brick chips leaned casually against the wall. Beyond that, he could just about make out a tiny shard of grey-blue light creeping through dark, heavy floorboards, dripping out into the tunnel. There was a spent torch near the thick pole of wood, burned down to its last embers.

Carter moved forward, following the path of the torch as it slipped down through the crack and past the angle of the shattered wall. And then, seeing the terrible, horrific shape, he screamed and then howled, his heart pounding and his legs shaking.

Directly in front of him, against the wall, was her body. As a single flicker of light floated down, it landed on the dull stare of the lifeless face of Lucia Warren-Davenport, sat propped upright against the wall next to a pile of shiny coins and a faded book. Her dark red hair was strewn with blood, her wrists slashed and broken, the veins emptied on dusty floor, covering the black-and-orange rusted pair of scissors that lay on the ground next to her.

Chapter Seventeen

The Emergence

Alice

'It's gone,' said Jonah. 'It's almost all gone.'

They stood at the foot of what had once been the Museum of Natural History as a circle of crows cawed loudly from the parapets at the top. Most of the stonework on the outside of the building had crumbled around the edges; big gashes had zebra-striped the stone where torrents of water had poured down roofs in gushes on a daily basis, month after month. Pink streamers of light threaded themselves between the clouds, casting a psychedelic glow over the remains of the shattered city.

There was something so beautiful in the way the devastated cityscape basked in the sunrise and, as the ten of them sat there in their pristine white suits, looking at the shadowed depth of a skyline they could barely remember, they cried. Alice was silent but let the tears trickle down the inside of her helmet into the shoulders of her suit, and she stood with her back to the buildings and her face to the sky, letting the sun dry her cheeks. Jonah held his head in his hands, while Filip stood on part of a crumbled wall looking out at the road, shaking his head.

His voice echoed into her ear through the in-suit communication.

'You all right, Davenport?' She looked over in his direction and nodded her head. Jonah lifted his head to watch the exchange between the two of them, unable to hear the words, then lowered it again onto his arms, hugging himself together tightly, teeth clenched.

'I'll live,' said Alice quietly.

'I know,' said Filip and held one hand out towards her.

The journey from the top deck of the Ship through the shaft and out into the bright light of the morning had been less ceremonial and far more straightforward than Alice had imagined.

It had taken less than a couple of hours to ascend slowly – hand over hand – and, when she'd reached the round metal grate with its slightly worn rubber seal, she'd almost been disappointed that it was over. When Alice had clicked open the manual combination, like a safe, the small circular door had opened. As she'd popped out onto the floor of the room less than half a metre below and sat back watching the others tumbling down the tiny step, hysteria had taken over and she'd laughed continuously until her stomach had ached and her cheeks had burned.

Very little that had been discussed underground as part of their training could have prepared them for that first morning. As they'd poured out of the Industry building to sit on the museum steps and watch the sunrise, Alice had begun to feel a bond with Filip, and at the same time had realised that a distance was growing between her and Jonah. Everything felt different above ground and Kunstein had been right: things would change now, and there would be some very difficult decisions.

Delicate ribbons of pink glittered across the skyline, filtering in and out of what buildings remained in the distance.

'I'm fine,' she whispered to Filip into the communicator and then walked over to where Jonah was sitting on a step, looking out into the silent road. Filip didn't respond but walked to a pile of rubble on the opposite edge of the museum where the others had gathered in a group.

Alice could hear him humming gently through the communicator, a song that she hadn't heard for years that made her heart lift and fall.

The streets were strewn with washed-out cars, plastics and mounds of unidentifiable items. They looked like a bizarre form of art.

'It's where the street lights were,' said Alice, tipping her head. Jonah looked at her.

'What?'

'When the wind gusted the water, and it was deep enough, everything gathered around the street lights and swirled around like a sink hole. Then it got sucked downwards by the current and made these… things. Look at the lines of them at the edges of the street.'

They walked closer to the clump sculpture nearest to them. It was part smashed-up car, part rags and bones and the remainder contained what looked like the insides of a children's clothes store.

'They sold curtains made of that stuff in Greenham's,' said Jonah, pointing to a speck of material preserved under crushed glass on what used to be the dashboard of the car. 'I recognise the design.' He reached out his arm and pulled the tiny sliver of cloth and pressed it to the skin of his helmet cover.

'What's going on between you and Filip?' he said quietly.

Alice felt her body stiffen.

'Nothing,' she said. 'Nothing at all.'

'But it's a different nothing to what's going on between us,' said Jonah and let the piece of material flutter off into the soft wind, spinning like a sycamore helicopter back into the debris. A second later it had disappeared out of sight. Alice looked until she could see the rise of a tower block or two in the distance. The sight of one in particular gave her ugly butterflies in her stomach.

They set up a camp in the Industry building they had emerged from, down the street and directly opposite the museum. As Alice's team hauled the last of their supplies up the shaft and into the containment room, Filip's team secured the entry and exit points with steel plates and barricades. Around the walls of the containment room, a few floors from ground level, there were plastic-wrapped pull-down beds that were still in relatively good condition. In fact, in comparison to some of the other buildings, the one owned by the Industry was in excellent shape.

'Is this the way we came in?' said Alice to Filip.

He nodded slowly. 'I think we came in through the windows on the far side.'

'Which must mean that the lift is on the top floor. We just need to reactivate it like Kunstein said so that they can send supplies from the main Control Room and we can send down anything that we need to.'

'How do you do that directional thing? Your mind must be just a criss-cross of maps.'

'I can find my way around,' said Alice, smiling.

'You sure can,' said Filip and threw her one of his tight, crooked smiles.

When they were done, Alice and Filip gathered everyone into the containment room. She looked across the eight faces in front of them, all now familiar from the briefing sessions that had been held on the Ship. There were the two Industry workers, Grenville Jones and Walford Jeremiah, the oldest of the Scouts. She and Filip had been allocated one per team. Alice had been offered Grenville Jones, the least geeky-looking of the two. He had half-apologetically semi-bowed to Alice when formally introduced. She had smiled at his unnecessary deference and welcomed him to the team warmly.

The others on her team she had chosen herself: Jayden Woolcroft, one of the strongest and fittest on the Ship whose thick bulky muscles gleamed in the light; Quinn Fordham, a quiet mathematical genius who was always top of the resettlement and community modules. Alice had suspected that she'd been helping develop and program the systems in the Control Room – Kunstein had all but told her as much. And then there was Jonah. Kunstein had expressed her reservations about Jonah – at times vehemently – but Alice had insisted, no, *demanded*, that Jonah be allowed to join her team.

'I can only allow ten people in total and that includes you, Filip and two of our existing people,' Kunstein had reminded her. 'You don't want to include any... deadwood.' Alice had looked at her with clear, dispassionate eyes.

'Neither do I,' she had said. 'Jonah comes with me.' And the decision was made.

It was still only mid-morning when they had completely secured the containment room as their base camp. Stuffed into the lockers disguised as wall panelling, just as Kunstein had described, were the weapons and ammunition. Most of them Alice left secured in their containers, coded with the detailed alpha-numeric combinations that she and Filip had been schooled to remember. But she did take two handguns. The dull metal was cold and hard, the colour of an unforgiving night sky. She handed one to Filip and watched as he ran his finger down the barrel.

'Hey, hot shot – threat to life emergencies only,' she said. 'I know you were top of the class but remember what Kunstein said.' Filip nodded, slipping the gun into the holster around his waist.

'We shouldn't have gone outside without them when we first arrived,' he said. 'I remember Kunstein saying that too. We've got to stick to the script, Davenport. We might think we know the world up here but since we left, it's become a very different place.'

'And I've become a very different person,' said Alice, slotting the gun into her holster.

After their first meal above ground, Filip locked down all the provisions and secured the sliding door that led to the shaft as Alice briefed the teams with what Kunstein had told her.

'This first night will be the hardest,' she said. 'Temperatures should be warm enough that we don't need the additional blankets stored here but it will *feel* different out here. We'll debrief before bed but I want everything prepared for either sleep or defence. When we return to base this evening, whatever we have come across today, those two things must be foremost on our minds. I am going to need one volunteer from each group to work on the base – uploading images, setting up communications, etc. Quinn – you're it from our team.' Quinn blinked, smiled and continued fusing the wiring together that she had been working on since they had arrived.

Filip pointed towards a bulky, sullen-looking girl with a determined line of concentration painted across her face. Even the hair scraped back into a tight ponytail was under control. 'And, Kelly,' he started, 'you can be ours. Don't you be hassling Quinn, OK? You'll both have work to do.'

The girl flushed and shared an intimate glance with Quinn. There was something about some of the romances that had begun underground that made them deep and untouchable, unconditional, even.

Alice continued with half a smile on her own face until the topic drifted into a bleak reiteration of the rules.

'Today will be mostly about orientation and exploration before we start locking down the boundaries of the new community. There's going to be a pretty significant clean-up operation and we need to understand how to manage that. Quinn, we'll need some calculations over the next few days that can help us with the waste disposal metrics and whether we need to expand the perimeters.'

There was nodding in agreement and a short round of applause before Filip stood up to join Alice.

'You have all been chosen for a reason,' he said, looking at each one of them. 'For your skills and your vision and commitment – for who you are *and* what you will bring to this expedition.'

Alice glanced across at Jonah. He was leaning back in his chair with his body postured to the front in assumed engagement but with a gaze that was lost in the swirl of leaves that had gathered outside the window. It was the same look he'd had in the classroom when he'd sat gazing, as if through a window, at leaves that were completely imaginary. But now they were real and there was something hypnotically simple about the way they turned over chaotically in the breeze, dancing uncontrollably in a fluttering, loosely co-ordinated conga, line after line weaving in beautiful circles. She realised that Filip was still talking.

'We will see things today that we never expected to see,' he said with a calm, simple resignation. 'Things that will startle us and may disturb us. We have all been through the same training, have been given the same support and will have the same goal. As Alice has already said, today is about orientation but it is not about risks. Do everything in pairs and do not take any chances. The air is clear and everything within three miles is radiation-light but the suits will protect against any chemicals that might have spilled out from the buildings so, for now, keep them on. Treat the scenes with respect but try not to lose your heart in this city – nothing exists in the way it did before. And finally, and most importantly, if you encounter anyone else, remain calm. Sweeps have not shown any survivors but we need to remain vigilant. Remember; refer anyone to me or Alice and we'll engage in negotiation. Right, Alice?'

Alice was grateful she'd tuned back in with enough time to answer Filip with confidence. 'Absolutely,' she said.

While Filip took his team east, Alice, Jonah, Jayden and Grenville headed west across the city and towards the river. Alice paired herself with Jonah up front while the other two followed them closely behind, matching them step for step. The thick, black sludge that caked the streets squeaked in the warm of the sun under their feet as they squashed out any residual air from within the cracks in the mud. Pieces of buildings that had been shattered by the heavy rainwater lay spread-eagled across the pavement while others sat staunchly squat in the cool sunlight, windows smashed but otherwise erect.

'Most of these will need to be destroyed,' said Alice. 'They're rotten to the core.'

A selection of cars with cracked paint stood motionless in the roads, some on their sides and others on their roofs, one still with a laminated 'For Sale' sign in the windscreen. Above them, a hawk circled in a lonely spiral, screeching petulantly as if desperate for them to look up. It spun around and around and then disappeared somewhere beyond the stone grey sky across the flood plain and into the dense safety of the woody copse that separated the housing estate from the river.

Every few blocks there was a shuffling sound that usually revealed itself to be little more than something insignificant discarded in the wind. At the corner of most intersections, there was a pile of human and animal matter; broken femurs, skulls, prosthetics, false teeth, jawbones, hipbones, jewellery, knuckles, tailbones, snouts and sockets. Crushed and wave-battered with no discernible features and none preserved in position. Muddled together they formed a delicately balanced installation of modern life until the current of a breeze rearranged them into a new format, a different adjustment. Alice watched as they sighed and settled like pre-historic sculptures. But it didn't make her feel sad. It didn't make her feel anything. Jonah linked her arm tightly and she smiled and returned his grip, the corners of her mouth just visible. Inside the mask, she watched as he breathed quickly, in-out-in-out-in-out.

'All OK with team two?' she whispered through the communicator to Filip.

'Yes,' he replied and then responded, 'Everything as expected with team one?'

'Uh-huh,' she said. 'So far, so good. We'll have made the river in an hour.'

As they reached the edge of the city, the smell of the river rose to greet them. The overwhelming stench of dead fish that had been prevalent in the bowels of the city became stronger and increasingly more disgusting. Interspersed with the trash and bones and melee of the old city, there were fragments of fish skins and skeletons like sawdust sprinkled over a carpenter's workbench. Alice avoided stepping near them, around them or alongside them. They both smelled and looked disgusting.

'Try not to touch anything that looks like it used to be alive, until we work out toxicity levels,' said Alice. 'Remember your training. These suits are pretty durable but—' she hesitated, '—a test in test conditions is no real test at all.'

It was early afternoon, when the sun was bleeding past its zenith, casting a trail of silver and orange, that they came across the first of the cruisers. It was wedged cleanly between the roof of a supermarket and the city library, which both stood about five storeys high on the other side of the river. In the years before, the cruisers had been used as casino ships, drifting out into the middle of the wide loop of the river further downstream, taking tourists back and forth from one side of the city to another, enabling them to do a little mid-afternoon gambling during their journey. Alice remembered that her mother had once taken her on one of those boats; she'd spent the whole time alone, throwing up over the side of the cruiser, while her mother had been busy with two of the deckhands. Jonah walked down towards the very edge of the river, eyes fixed on the boat teetering above them.

As it towered across the other side of the filthy, swollen river, the bow that protruded from the edge of the buildings cast a long shadow across the pavement and out into the road. The hull was battered, with chipped and peeling paint where the bottom had been scraped over the submerged rooftops of iceberg-esque buildings. There was a huge gaping hole in one side, which spewed out some precarious mechanics like nautical intestines, dripping downwards towards the water.

On one side, the clean black script that was once etched like a signature into the side of the boat was now a dull, faded series of unconnected, indistinguishable letters. They all stood there in silence, agape, looking at the giant body above them as the sun filtered rays around its edges. Alice moved closer to look at the giant hull above them.

'Must have got wedged when the waters subsided,' said Grenville. 'We've seen some others like this on the screens – nothing this spectacular though.'

'It looks like the pictures of Atlas,' said Jayden. 'Like the whole heavens are on the shoulders of the supermarket.' Alice laughed and looked upwards at the freakish, circus scenario.

'It's one of the things we're going to have to deal with,' she said. 'One of the gigantic, crazy problems that we will need to find a solution for.' Grenville nodded, his mouth still open.

Alice thought about the incomprehensibility of it; how five years ago, the removal of a boat from the roof of a supermarket would have been someone else's problem – anybody else's problem but hers. But now, in the bright sunlight, she felt an overwhelming responsibility to fix everything. The hawk that had followed them earlier circled in the sky above them, drifting on its wings and making the occasional call. Alice wondered what the whole sorry scene must look like from up there, in the quiet of the clouds with just the whistle of the wind and the occasional gurgle of the river.

It was because her eyes had been drawn upwards, caught by the sun and the boat and the madness, that she missed what was obviously out of place. It wasn't until she heard the splash of water that she or anyone else realised that Jonah wasn't with them any longer.

He was in the water lying face down on a splintery pallet, paddling with his hands through the murky depths. The hood of his suit was off and he was trickling water through his thin, floppy hair as he moved arm over arm towards the supermarket on the other side of the river.

'Jonah!' screamed Alice. 'What are you doing?' Her voice was agonised, drained against the splashing as she watched him inching further away from the shore.

'It's Scarlett,' waved back Jonah through mouthfuls of black sludge. 'My sister Scarlett. She's on that ship, I can see her. Look, it's the Princess Aurelia.'

Filip's voice came through on Alice's earpiece.

'Davenport,' he said, 'what's happening?'

'It's Jonah,' she breathed heavily, 'he's gone rogue. You need to come. Quickly.'

'I'm on my way.'

Alice looked around desperately for something to use. 'Jayden,' she shouted, with a note of panic. 'Get some wood and make me a raft. I'm going after him.'

'You can't go alone,' he replied Jayden. 'It's too dangerous.'

Grenville nodded. 'Who knows what's out there,' he said gravely. 'You need to let him go.'

'You know I can't do that,' said Alice, determined. 'I would never do that.' She dragged across some loose wood planks that looked like they might once have been scaffolding.

'Jayden, fix those together,' she said, urgently. 'That's not a request, that's an order. I need to move fast.' The boy ran into one of the buildings and came out with a handful of rope. He deftly fixed the wood struts together and pushed it onto the water.

'I'm coming with you,' called Grenville. 'We're all coming with you.'

'No, you're not,' said Alice, definitely. 'Wait here until Filip arrives.'

The water was thick, viscous and black. It no longer looked like a river but more an oily snake slithering around the outside of the city. Alice pushed out the shell of a boat onto the surface as he handed two thinner pieces of wood to use as oars.

'Whatever you do, don't touch the water,' said Grenville, shaking a tiny test tube with some grey-brown drops in it. 'It's toxic; possibly hallucinogenic, with the waste that's in there. There's some evidence of some life and whatever lives in there is likely to be pretty dangerous. 'Stay safe,' he added.

Even though the river had probably doubled in width since the Storms, Jonah had made it almost halfway to the other side; Alice could hear him laughing and singing to himself as he splashed towards the shore. His arms were now fully out of the suit; Alice could see his shoulders above the pull and ebb of the slow, thick waves.

'Jonah!' she screamed again. 'Come back!' He stopped for a second and Alice thought she heard him call her name. But it wasn't her name. It started with a wailing, then a chant and eventually, it became a song. Just one word, over and over: Scarlett. Scarlett. Scarlett.

'How do you think those buildings look, structurally?' Alice said to Grenville with urgency. He shrugged.

'They would have been waterlogged through all five floors,' he said. 'The joists would have been weakened, the architecture damaged – but that one's holding the boat. I don't know.' Almost before he had finished speaking, Alice had gone, pushing out into the water after Jonah, striking the wooden oars hard.

In the first few minutes, she gained good ground on Jonah, straining her muscles hard as she'd been taught below deck on the Ship. But as she reached the halfway mark, Jonah had climbed out the other side and he was wringing out his suit on the bank, wearing just the thin grey uniform that he'd been issued with.

'Wait!' cried Alice. 'Let me come with you. I can help you.'

Jonah strained his eyes across the river at her.

'She's here,' he called, waving and smiling, 'waiting for me, just like she said she would be.'

Alice turned around and watched as the small frame of Jonah slipped inside the supermarket, stomping through crushed glass and disturbing a crowd of ravenous pigeons. They flew out of the smashed shopfront in an explosion of movement, circling over the edge of the water before heading further west towards the forests on the outskirts of where the city used to be.

She paddled her little boat faster, the faces of Jayden and Grenville getting smaller and paler as she got further from the shore of the east bank. With the exertion of exercise, Alice felt her skin baking inside her suit. She longed to feel a cool breeze on her bare arms. In her ear came Filip's voice.

'It's the water,' he said. 'Don't touch it, don't let it get inside your suit, and whatever you do, don't get into it. The effluent from Drakewater somehow infected it – it's dangerous. It's mood-enhancing, hallucinogenic. You should have waited for me.'

She looked back at the shore. Now there were more people, maybe ten or fifteen. Her mother was there, and Hutchinson. He had his notebook out in front of him, making plans. Charlie sat on a patch of yellow grass and barked, one side of his head bloodied and sore. But there was a noise inside her head, a buzzing, like a song that wouldn't go away.

'Davenport, Alice, it's me, it's Filip. Keep your mind focused. You're almost at the other shore. Stay with me, you can do this. Concentrate. I need you. We all need you. I'm on my way.'

Alice squeezed her eyes tightly shut and then opened them again. This time there was just Jayden and Grenville. She rowed faster, harder; she could feel the blisters forming on her hands as she dragged the pieces of wood through the water. Within a few minutes, she had beached on the other side and, breathless, she hauled herself and her boat onto the muddy pavement above what used to be the wharf dock that was submerged in the depths of the new Black River.

The inside of the supermarket was strewn with rubbish, bones and a covering of dirty, squelching moss over which muddy footprints led to a useless, flapping fire escape door toward the back of the shop. On the spiral that wound upwards, prints dripped out the shape of Jonah's boots going upwards towards the roof, the click of her own steps unnerving in the echoes of the shadows of the stairway.

When she reached the fourth floor, the puddles were thinner, less wet and led outwards to the roof. She heard Jonah before she saw him, singing loudly from deep within the body of the cruiser.

'Jonah,' she called, 'where are you?' His head emerged from a hole on the second deck, followed by a shower of poker coins that landed at Alice's feet.

'Look,' he said with a demonic laugh, his eyes wild and glazed, 'the chips are down.' A dark rash had spread across his cheeks and his skin was starting to break out into thick, pus-filled boils. Already, his thin hair was weeping in great tears from his head. Alice stopped as he threw the last of the red and green plastic coins at the floor.

'What are you doing?' she said slowly, looking at the curve of the boat between the two buildings.

'My sister Scarlett is here,' he said cheerfully. 'I always wanted you to meet her. I told her you were going to be my wife until you met Filip. When we got down to the river, I could hear her calling to me. She told me to take my suit off so that I could hear her better. She's here, you know, in the boat.'

Alice looked past Jonah and into the broken hull of the boat through the jagged gaps gouged out by the buildings that had been underwater as it had lolled about above. It was empty and silent.

'Why don't you come back with me?' said Alice quietly. 'We can help you.'

'Oh, no,' said Jonah, his tone laced with a decisive vehemence that Alice had rarely seen in the five years they had been together. 'I won't be coming back across the river. I have to stay here with my sister in the boat. We're going to wait for the water to come back and then we're going to sail away – to the Caribbean or somewhere warm.'

'You're not going to be able to do that, Jonah,' said Alice.

'Yeah, and who's going to stop me?' said Jonah, jumping down from the boat. He grabbed Alice by the hand and pulled her towards the edge of the supermarket roof. The soft swishing sound of her protective suit slithered through the air. Below them the river looked like a thick black ribbon, winding its way through a dirty tea towel of land, pockmarked with devastation.

'Keep calm, Alice,' said Filip through the communicator. He sounded close, comforting even. A blood-specked trickle trailed from the corner of Jonah's left ear.

'We could go together,' he said. 'You and me and Scarlett. You'd love her, Alice; she's just like you. Pretty and kind and good. She's a good person, Alice. I used to be a good person too. I used to be someone else before this.' He looked out across the horizon. 'Where am I?'

Tears welled in Alice's eyes as the city below her danced in the giddiness of height and depth and she could smell the dampness of the sweat from Jonah's body mixing with the toxic, foul-smelling water from the river. In her heart she knew it was only a matter of time.

'It's OK, Jonah,' she said, biting back the saltiness of her tears. 'It's going to be all right. We can go now and everything will be OK.' She leaned back from the edge of the building, one white-gloved hand holding his, gently leading him back towards the fire escape.

'Scarlett,' he said, looking at Alice, 'are you there?'

'Yes,' said Alice, 'I'm here. Come on, Jonah, let's go.' They managed two steps before he suddenly let go of her hand and pushed her backwards onto the floor.

'You're not Scarlett,' he said with a vicious snarl, 'you're Alice, Alice full of malice, came like a slum-dog into the palace. What did you do with my sister, you evil little bitch?' The poison streamed from his mouth and landed not just in the fountains of spittle that hit her suit but in deep, sharp spikes in her heart. He looked five years old and not sixteen; gap-toothed, angry, inconsolable. The small face of the eleven-year-old underneath the table in the first year on the Ship flashed in front of her. She reached out her hand.

'It's OK, Jonah,' she said over and over. 'It's OK.'

'Where's my sister?' he screamed in a torrent of questions. 'Did you kill her like you killed everyone else in your life? Were you jealous of her? Like you were jealous of your father, taking all of your mother's attention? And your puppy too? Am I next, now that you have Filip to help you? Do you just hurt everyone who tries to help you? Now, where's my sister? What have you done to her? I want my sister.'

Alice felt her heart sinking to somewhere deep within her body, out of reach of Jonah's cold fingers of anger that clawed over her each time he spoke.

'It's OK,' she said again, her voice breaking, and silent tears wetting the inside of her hood. 'We can get you back and help you.' She leaned forward and held out her hand again, for the last time.

The lunge took her by surprise and, as Alice crouched on the balls of her feet, Jonah came flying towards her, knocking her closer towards the edge. Stone chips and gravel scudded under her feet, and fragments flew into the river below. He pinned her to the edge of the roof.

'You are not taking me anywhere. I'm staying here with Scarlett in her ship and we're going to dance and listen to jazz and watch the sun come up.' His voice was whining, childlike. Then there was the sound of the hawk overhead and, with Jonah on top of her rolling them closer to the edge, Alice froze. He had a jagged piece of glass in his hand and waved it over the front of her helmet, his soft, flopping hair falling out in chunks. The beauty and madness of his eyes gleamed in the sunlight as they straddled the edge like lovers on the brink of climax.

'Do it, Filip,' she whispered.

The desperate call of the hawk made them both look upwards.

From the street below came the crack of a gunshot and, what seemed like minutes rather than a second later, the side of Jonah's torso took the impact of the bullet. A fine spray of blood spattered onto the fabric of Alice's suit. She looked at Jonah and gulped hard.

'Alice,' he said in a whisper, 'I love you.'

'I know,' she said. 'I know.'

Then he lifted the weight of his body, off and away from her. He pushed himself upwards and sideways with one arm, as carefully as if he were disposing of a bomb, not one hair of his body touching Alice's. He put a hand to his abdomen where the blood was fast beginning to leak from his suit. Finally, with a sad, silent push, he levered himself gently off the edge of the building.

Alice looked over and watched his body sail through the sunlight and land with a dull thud. There was the sound of the shattering of glass on the littered pavement below. Jonah's arms and legs were dislocated in an awkward spider shape, back curved and head to one side, surrounded by smashed and broken bricks. The blood spread quickly across the road, trickling outwards like an uneven crimson map until it reached the river and became black.

Filip sat crouched on the road on her side of the river, shoulders heaving but with the gun still pointed upwards and a thin trail of smoke blending into the afternoon sun. The sound of the gun still rang with a zing in Alice's ears but the two words, *I'm sorry*, were clearly audible above the soft sobbing of the usually cocky voice of Filip that echoed through the communicator suit.

Chapter Eighteen

The Deadlands

Carter

As the tired flames licked slowly around the edges of the log torch, Carter sat with his palms against Lucia's and his damp eyes closed. Her body wasn't yet completely cold, but the wounds in her wrists were deep and final. In the dirt on the floor, three words were carved.

I AM SORRY.

'She killed herself,' said Lily decisively, putting a hand over the white-blue eyes of Lucia and closing them shut. 'She thought no one was coming to save her and she gave up. It's sad. Carter, I am sorry.'

Carter fingered the words in the dirt and formed the pile of coins into columns in a distracted malaise.

'From what I know of her, she wouldn't do that,' he said. 'She wouldn't.'

Lily put her arm around his shoulders. 'People can't survive out here,' she said. 'Without the security and the structure of the Community, they lose all sense of what to do.'

Carter shrugged her arm away and kneeled down beside Lucia. 'I've never seen a dead body before,' he said. 'I don't even know anyone who has – not directly, anyway.' The girl looked asleep. 'Do you think there's anything the Industry can do for her?' he added.

Lily shook her head. 'No,' she said quietly. 'No, there isn't.'

He flicked through the book by her side. It was full of old temples, ruins and stories of the old world. There in the pages were the words she had said to him:

Veritas liberabit vos – the truth shall set you free.

'She said that to me,' he said finally. 'At the Transporter stop. She came to find me. She wanted me to join the rebels.' He stood up and rubbed the traces of blood from her palms onto his trousers.

Lily moved close to him. 'What did you say? Why didn't you tell me this? Are you planning to lead the revolution?'

'If I am to lead anything,' said Carter, 'I need to know the truth. We have to go into the Deadlands. The truth is more important than anything now.'

Lily looked at the body.

'And what do we do with her?'

Carter's answer was firm and definite. 'She wanted to be outside. She comes with us.'

They squeezed through the space in the wall: Lily first, next the body of Lucia, and then Carter. They placed the girl on a chair as they sorted through what they found next. Inside the brick wall was an old cellar, full of empty glass bottles, barrels and crates. As the torch burned down to nothing, Lily lit another and held it high enough that they could see the whole of the inside of the room. It was a low, rectangular space with walls that were regular old red brick but painted a faded white around the inside. The ceiling was made of long straight planks of wood with a small square door in one corner that led upwards.

The room was packed full of oddments: shapes and items that Carter had never even seen before – a whole plethora of beautiful junk. Boxes, dried-out papers and the skeleton of some kind of animal with a long tail that lay curled in a corner. Everything inside the underground room had been whipped up, and knocked from the surfaces and strewn across the room. Between them they picked through it carefully, marvelling at the weirdness of the abandoned entrails of the old life.

'What happened to you, Lucia?' said Carter, looking around at the destruction.

'I think—' Lily gritted her teeth '—I think she got as far as this room and then she ran out of energy, she ran out of light and she had no idea where she was.'

Carter shook his head and climbed onto a table. He tried to push open the small door cut into the ceiling. Even with his full weight it only moved slightly. 'If that's true then she had absolutely no chance trying to move that alone,' he said, climbing down. 'She couldn't get out; she was injured and scared. She was waiting for me to come.'

He imagined Lucia, with no burn left in her torch, running from the Industry officials she thought were chasing her. Climbing through the hole in the wall and stumbling around in the pitch blackness, smashing and crashing into things, broken and wasted until all she could do was wait. His heart sank as he picked up the scissors and rubbed them clean of blood.

Lily rubbed her hand across his shoulder. 'None of this was your fault,' she said.

Carter scanned around at the mess of the cellar and then back to the outline of Lucia's face, running a finger down her jawline and across the thin, bony edges of her throat. There were features of his there; she looked even more like him than Ariel did.

'All of this was my fault,' he said. Bring me that piece of wood from the other side of the wall,' he said. 'We're going to need it to get out of here.'

Lily walked around the propped-up body of Lucia and through the crawl space, leaning away from the hand that pointed outwards. She came back with the stump of wood, flattened at one end, and handed it to Carter who was balanced on a chair that he had fixed on top of the table. He banged on the hatch and, with a few attempts, blasted through it easily. A cloud of dust caught his throat and his eyes and he staggered down from the chair, coughing. Through the dust, the shards of light from above shot through the darkness, illuminating the particles of dirt that hung in the air like stars.

When the air cleared, there was a hole. A square hole of light that spilled down through the grey emptiness that led upwards into the house in the Deadlands. Carter brushed the splinters of wood from his shoulder and looked up.

'What's there?' said Lily, climbing onto the table.

'I don't know; I can't see very much.' Carter brushed away the sticky dust from the edges of the hole and peered into the greyness. He hauled his body upwards, inching his shoulders through the small square door and then up into the room of a farm cottage on the western side of the Black River.

Through the smashed-out windows of the old house streamed the first white beams of a new sun. Any coverings that had once blocked out the day were long gone but, inside the house, some traces of the old life remained. He'd emerged into what looked like a kitchen; there were two signs still fixed to the wall that read:

A BALANCED DIET IS A COOKIE IN EACH HAND
and
I KISS BETTER THAN I COOK

Through an archway to an adjoining room, Carter found a pair of long, curved resters, rotten through to the springs, and on one wall a glass-covered printed picture. He ran his fingers over the surface – it wasn't part of a FreeScreen but was static. The faded outline was a picture of two young children dressed in strange clothes and smiling blankly out at him. He wondered why they were smiling.

There was a FreeScreen too, but it wasn't fixed to the wall. It was lying pregnant on its side, its innards – wires and cables – spewing out onto the floor. And, with the exception of the kitchen, there was a thick mud-infused material covering the floors that created dust explosions each time Carter stamped his feet in it.

'Carpet,' he said to himself quietly. He'd seen some once on an old FreeScreen broadcast. It felt soft and dusty underfoot. He moved across it slowly until he came to the stairway and pushed down onto them, ready to climb.

The wooden steps were creaky; some crackling under his weight. Inside the first room he went into, there were books lining the walls, hundreds of them, and shelves full of things that he had never seen before. Even now, out in the Deadlands, he felt a shiver of dangerous excitement at the sight of ornaments of the old world. Slowly, he reached out and picked up a book, pages flattened tight against the weight of the others in the stack.

His fingers trembled as he ran them down the black lettering on the spine. He mouthed the words to himself a few times before he opened the pages, the door to the old world. Colour flooded from the pages. Things Carter had never seen in his life before. The tips of his fingers started to sweat as he leafed very slowly through the pages. He knew that what he had stumbled upon would transform the Community forever. He tore open book after book, drowning in the words. He sat there absorbing the content in awe and wonder, lost in the world of the past. For a moment, he forgot about the Community, about Lucia, and, until the shrill, desperate shout came from downstairs, about Lily too.

'Carter, where are you? Don't leave me here. It's dark!' He edged himself down the stairs carefully and back into the kitchen to the hole in the cellar. He leaned inside and held out his hand.

'It's incredible up here,' he said.

Lily frowned at him. 'Help me up. Now,'

'Pass Lucia to me first,' he said. 'And then I have something amazing to show you.'

Without even realising exactly what he was looking for, Carter knew that he had found it. He and Lily sat upstairs and devoured the contents of the books, magazines, comics and journals they found throughout the house. He spent hours skimming through some and read other sections over and over until he had learned passages by heart. He memorised the rules of different sports, the fundamentals of religion, the history of musical instruments and theories of science and the natural world. He had example after example of ways to unite people, to bring them happiness, to create equality and unity right here in his hands: a new proposition for happiness.

When they went outside, the new day had already begun. The sun crept over the horizon and shot spurs of red light into the farmhouse in the dark corner of the Deadlands. The house itself was strangled by brambles that extended thorny fingers across the cracked guttering and wound its tentacles inside the rooms through broken windows. But even so, it seemed to breathe with life – with at least the idea of a new beginning.

Lily and Carter stood in the doorway as they watched the first sunrise outside the Barricades of the Community. In the far distance, they could see the twisted metal spurs glinting in the light, reflecting pearls of different colour across the surface of the Black River towards them. The harsh, imposing structure of the high walls, blotting out everything inside the Community was in stark contrast to the stunning hillocks across the far north-west that broke the horizon and a brightness that Carter had never seen before.

'This is more illuminating than any training,' he said. 'Imagine what it would be like to share this with everyone. It's… beautiful.'

Through the peppering of trees and grassland that had grown up between them and the river, there was a circling of birds that filled one corner of the clean stretch of sky. In the warmth of the late morning sun, they buried Lucia underneath a tree that bloomed with a heavy purple fruit that squashed easily underfoot, scattering tiny black seeds into the earth. Lily recited the names of the first Scouts and then they watched the rays of the sun settle high in the sky as a mark of respect. Something about the solemnity of the occasion shook him to the core. When the burial was complete, Carter took Lily back inside the house.

'What's missing from our world?' he said as they climbed the stairs.

'What do you mean?'

'What is here that is not there?'

Lily frowned at Carter. 'Nothing; we have food and shelter. It's more than the old world could claim. Remember the famine, the homelessness, the…'

Carter held up his hand to stop her. 'But people had something more than that. What did the old world have that holds so much appeal to the rebels?'

Lily lay on her back on the floor. There were tiny cracks in the ceiling that let the light through. 'I don't know,' she said, sleepily. 'I'm not a rebel.'

'You don't need to be a rebel to understand.'

'You won't make Controller General if you think like this.'

Carter sat next to her. 'Look around you, Lily. Look at this place and look at all this stuff. My grandfather told me that all of this was designed to make people's lives more complicated. Musical instruments, books, games, hobbies, interests. The Industry tells us that it tore people's lives apart and that's why it's all forbidden. But look at all these pictures. It wasn't that at all. The Industry got it wrong. Isabella was right.'

He picked up a book and opened it midway through. 'See these people here, they're playing a game. Football, I think it is. Look how they're doing it together.' He flicked through the pages. 'And here, this is an orchestra, making music. This is what the rebels have been trying to create – not something that tears us apart, but something that brings us together: something that makes us whole again.'

Carter felt excitement rise inside of him. This would change the Community; he could transform their whole way of life, with the support of the Industry behind him. These books would not be a threat – they would be what joined people together, made them equal. He imagined the Lab Made and the Descendants creating the most beautiful music, games, sports, collaborative projects that would depend on the strengths of all different types of people in their Community.

In some way, he would keep his promise to Isabella.

'Bringing people together is dangerous,' said Lily. 'It's like romance; it has no direct function. All the evidence the Industry has from the past has shown us how these things wasted time. These *activities* are dangerous – they detract people from what they should be doing. People will make the wrong choices, choose the wrong people to be with.'

Carter shook his head. 'Romance doesn't have to be dangerous. Love is what keeps us alive. What do you think people *should* be doing? This is *living*, Lily – and what's more important than living? Nothing. Don't you get it – what we know about the past isn't true.' He paused. 'Well, not entirely, anyway.'

Lily looked confused. 'But we *are* living, Carter. We're living in the way that the Industry has designed.'

'We're not living,' said Carter. 'We're *existing*.'

Lily looked around at the room – the ripped pictures on the walls and the shelves and cupboards full of things that she'd never seen in the Community. 'So how does this help you become Controller General? The Industry would reject it straight away. You'd be sent to the Catacombs for sure.'

'Then I'll have to convince them when I present it as my Contribution,' said Carter, his eyes lighting up. 'I'm going to use what we've found to bind the Community – the Industry included. Give the rebels what they want.'

Lily opened a cupboard door and pulled out a stack of magazines. She leafed through the pictures of people that looked so different.

'You mean you're going to take all *this* back to the Community and you think that'll change things? All these made-up stories and books about sounds and pictures that didn't even ever exist and bring them back with you to the Community?'

Carter nodded his head vigorously. 'It's a start,' he said. 'But it's more than that. These things… they're not evil or wrong in themselves. The rebels were right. The Industry might have made the right choice to change things back then, but that was over eighty years ago. Things are different now. Maybe we've evolved enough to make up our own minds again.'

Lily still looked doubtful. 'When would they do this – during work time? Instead of working? When they should be sleeping? I don't think the Industry would go for this idea. It seems like—' she struggled for the words '—I don't know, a waste.'

Carter shook his head. 'Maybe if the Industry isn't interested, the rebels would be?'

'What are you saying?'

'I'm saying that we need to be the ones to use this material before they do. If they brought this into the Community, people would believe in the rebels even more.' He pulled out some books from a bag he'd taken from one of the bedrooms and flicked through the pages. 'See, it's just the same as reading on a slate – you just move from one page to the next, looking at the pictures.' His voice drifted off, lost in a chord of chirping from the roof of the house.

'I think I like this one,' said Lily, lightly fingering the picture of a girl in a blue and white dress looking at her own reflection. 'What do you think Wonderland is?'

Carter smiled broadly at her. 'I'll let you keep hold of that one if you like.' He watched as she folded it and placed it carefully inside her bag.

'Thank you.'

'I've chosen five books, an instrument of some kind, and these pictures, too.' He unrolled a bright orange picture of sunflowers and another of an elephant and Lily held them carefully. She traced the outline of each flower while Carter picked out a tune on the tin whistle he'd found on the shelf.

'This is amazing,' he said. 'I'm bringing the past back to the future. A *new* future.'

As grey clouds began to pepper the early afternoon sky, they made their preparations to leave, gathering some water from a deep pond sunk into the grass.

'What do you think we should do?' said Carter. 'I mean, how do you think we're going to get back into the Community? Do you think we can dig our way back through the tunnel?'

'Not without the risk of the whole thing collapsing on us. It would take us days to dig our way back through there.' Lily looked upwards at the sky as a group of white doves skimmed in front of a ribbon of cloud.

'There's only one way through the Barricades, to the north-east of here, just outside the north-west corner of the Community. It's the tunnel where the Transporters used to come under the river to let the Scouts out. But the Industry still uses it for the auto-Transporters to take waste out into the Deadlands. It's sealed – but there's a holding area we can go to that opens at sunset each night. We can walk through the tunnel to the communication area and call for the guards. We can explain, tell them who you are and that we were trying to capture a fugitive – your daughter – and they'll have to let us through.'

Carter screwed up his eyes.

'How do you know about all this?' he said, his eyes firmly fixed on Lily.

She breathed deeply and put one hand over his.

'I've been out here before,' she said.

For a while there was silence while Carter let the reality sink in. She was on her fourth tenure; technically, it was possible. But it would have been so long ago.

'When?' he managed.

'Years ago, before I went to the Catacombs. Way before the Food Plant, I used to work as a Scout. I did a mission out to the north-east, near Drakewater, but we had to abandon due to radiation levels. I've done all the training so I'm probably just about the best person you could wish to be stuck out here with. It's much better not to be alone in a place like this. The dogs – they're less likely to attack if we move in pairs. Two bodies confuse them. It's what we learned.'

Carter cut his way down the path of the garden towards the end of the small wall that encircled the garden, barely visible under the pleated weave of creepers that held it tightly in place.

'Why didn't you tell me?'

'I didn't think you needed to know.'

Carter paused for a second. 'There hasn't been an expedition in years,' he said. 'Twenty years, to be exact. My parents were on the last one.'

Lily cast her eyes to the floor.

'That's why I didn't tell you,' she said.

'You were there – you were there when they were killed? How could you have been?' The realisation came to him in waves. The only sound came from the circling of birds above them.

'You need to tell me what happened,' he said.

Lily turned away from him and said quietly, 'You don't want to know. It was horrible.'

Carter felt a knot tighten in his stomach and his heart start to beat fast. 'I do. Tell me,' he said. 'Tell me everything.'

'I will, but later – when we're back on the other side. Not now. We need to focus on what you need to do out here and get back before we're missed. You need to keep focused, Carter. You still want to get out of here and be Controller General, right? You haven't worked your whole life so far to fail now.'

He felt his resolve strengthen. Failure was not an option – not for his parents, not for Isabella and not for the Community.

'So you'll know where we're going and you can get us back in?'

'I don't know this area at all, but if we stay close to the river we can follow it around to the north and we should make the entrance by nightfall. It'll take some convincing to get us in but as long as you're with me, I'm sure I can charm the guards.' She pulled some fauclate from her pocket and handed it to Carter as he nodded.

He took it from her and, as she looked upwards to watch the circling birds, he sniffed at the corner. It smelled normal, but he thrust it into his pocket without tasting it, keeping his eyes on Lily.

'We need to move quickly and take what water we can with us,' she continued. 'I doubt we'll find another fresh source anywhere near here. Anything we find from the old times is unlikely to be any good either.'

In the dust on the ground she drew out the shape of the river with a gnarled stick in a big S-curve that looped around a small sprig of lavender with its small purple flowers bending to the light.

'We must be near here.' She drew a cross in the south-west of the dirt map, outside the ring of the river. 'And we need to be here.' She pointed to a spot in the north marked by the bud of a nettle breaking through the soil. 'We don't have enough time to take the slopes to the far west so we'll need to cut through the valley, here, alongside the river.'

'Seems like the most direct route,' said Carter. 'What's the problem?'

'Dogs,' said Lily. 'A pack of mutations that came over from Drake-water when they ran out of food. They settled here not long after the land cleared. They bred with the few domestics that had made it through the Storms on this side and set up home. They're not the most dangerous creatures when they're alone, but they're aggressive in packs, and they're pretty fond of people. Not in the way they apparently used to be. You know they used to live in houses – with people? Are you going to bring that strange old custom back from the past too, Carter Warren?'

Even with the change Carter wanted to bring to the Community, he couldn't imagine that. Not for one minute.

'So we go around, skip the valley?'

'We won't make the tunnel before it closes. It's only open for two or three seconds on work days to let the Transporters from the Catacombs back above ground to drop off waste. Tomorrow and the day after are rest days, and two days of waiting out in the Deadlands without food and under attack, we'll be dead – plus there's no shelter if there was a storm.'

'And we need to be back in the Community tonight.'

Lily pursed her lips. 'Yes we do.'

'So teach me how to fight the dogs. Consider it part of my training.'

Lily smiled and pulled the scissors from the pocket of her trousers. They glinted dangerously where the edges still held any sharpness. 'We have this to start with. We'll use sticks and whatever else we can find in the house. Nothing will stop us reaching that tunnel before sunset.'

Past the ivy-rich outer wall of the garden, a path crept around to the east towards the curve of the river. The mashed-up woodlands were much different to what Carter had experienced in the Community; they were wilder and there was an abundance of variety. Bright red berries pinpricked the bushes and strange, maggot-heavy fruits bowed down the branches of trees. The birds were bolder, less skittish, and there were other creatures that lurked wide-eyed and big-eared in the undergrowth.

'Whatever you're thinking, don't try to eat them,' said Lily as Carter smelled the rotting flesh of a bunch of purple globes that hung from a tree in front of him. He scrunched up his nose. They were similar to those Isabella had eaten earlier.

'Why not?'

'Because they would kill you.'

He thought of Isabella's words to him. 'Have you ever done something the Industry told you not to?'

Lily laughed. 'I wouldn't eat anything that hasn't been synthesised. Who knows what it's made of? It doesn't smell like anything I'd want to eat.'

Carter smiled. 'And yet people did. They depended on the weather to produce crops to eat. It was a precarious business. Though I'm not sure we'd even be able to process this stuff any more.' He picked one of the fruit and squashed it between his fingers, staining them with a dark mauve juice that he rubbed across his lips, leaving dark lined stains. It tasted sweet.

Lily shrugged. 'Well, I hope you stay alive long enough to make Controller General.'

'I will,' said Carter. 'To help the Community, I have to.'

Crumbling buildings clustered around littered streets paved the journey north-east. Stunted houses with trees pushing eager branches through the roofs, and pavements split open by small, strong shoots left the way uneven and difficult. The paths, crawling with insects and the odd, darting rat-like creature, gave way to wide stretches of land peppered with piles of brick and stone. Birds took to their wings and fluttered out of sight while other creatures watched bug-eyed as they passed, hopping and diving into the undergrowth as they got closer. After some time, they reached a wide space filled with rotting cars. A faded sign with crippled blue paint read:

PARK AND RIDE

They paused in the opening, staring around at the rusting remains. It was then that the mournful howling started.

'Did you hear that?' said Lily, standing still and turning her ear to the wind. She grabbed Carter's arm tightly as a deep, throaty, growling sound came from the vehicles. 'It's the dogs. The wolves.' Her eyes narrowed towards the desolate metal structures.

He watched as, out of several of the cars, straggle-furred animals with hair the colour of raked leaves crawled, teeth sharp and angry, towards them.

'Move,' said Carter. 'Quietly – I'll hold them back.'

They toe-picked their way around the edge of the field, knee-deep in the damp, dew-sodden grass that swayed heavily in the breeze. The dogs eased themselves into a group, snapping irritably as matted tails flapped into wet noses.

'You need to distract them,' said Lily. 'Cause a scene – throw something at them. One bite and they'll infect us.' One wolf at the back howled and bit at the leg of one of the dogs alongside it as the rest of the pack watched Carter and Lily. Through the terror, Lily seemed calm, composed, almost.

Carter looked around, picking up some loose stone from the ground. He lobbed the chippings towards the closest two animals and watched as they flinched in annoyance. Then the snarling started, dripping white froth from their eager mouths into the swaying grass. As the dogs took a reluctant step back, waiting in anticipation, Carter scanned the horizon. On the other side of the car park he could make out a building with the outline of a ladder leaning against it. He grabbed his bag with the books tightly and pointed to the building with his other hand.

'Run,' he said under his breath. 'Make for the roof and I'll distract them.' Before he could pick up another handful of stones, Lily was gone, pelting long strides through the grass towards the ladder. There was some confusion amongst the pack as Carter aimed his next set of shots. The first few scattering of pebbles hit the foremost of the wolves and the animal let out a screech that chilled his bones raw. He picked another handful, stepped backwards and threw hard, catching some at the back.

For a moment they looked puzzled, unsure how to retaliate, and he left them with that as he raced after Lily, kicking through the undergrowth while they chased, teeth bared, across the gravelled car park. His heart was pounding and his shoes felt heavy, the bag bouncing against his legs. Ahead of him Lily was already on the flat roof, watching.

As his hands hit the ladder he could hear the animals snarling beneath him and he threw up the bag, hauling his torso to safety, arms arching and body breathless. A group of about twenty dogs, furious at being woken, circled the building, howling and screeching. Carter lay on his back on the roof watching the sky melt in and out, his eyes fuzzy with a sickening mix of terror and exhaustion. Above him, grey clouds wrapped themselves into ugly balls, threatening a downpour.

'You're safe,' said Lily quietly, her voice still shaking and breathless. 'We just need to wait for them to go away and the rain to start.'

Less than an hour later, the heavy pellets bombed down onto the roof and into the fur of the wolves. They waited until the slapping of the rain became too much and then retreated miserably back across the car park to the relative safety of the vehicles. Carter watched as Lily lapped up the rain as it pooled on the roof, dipping her tongue into the water and licking up the ice crystals, swallowing them whole. He copied her, grateful in some ways for the pain of the hail that left him pink-skinned, as it battered his arms and head.

'This is horrible,' he yelled through the timpani of hail. Lily held out her hand and looked up at the clouds.

'It's probably just a Level Two Storm,' she said, cupping her hand into his ear. 'It'll be a little painful on the skin but not deadly. If we can make it to the trees then we'll be sheltered enough and we can climb high into the branches if they come again.'

Lily took the slippery ladder first. Carter followed and they crept towards the muddy path and into the thin spread of woods that lined a track towards the north. Water trickled through the leaves at a steady rate until finally the rain stopped. There was only the sound of a rubbery squelching and the intermittent whistle of birds as they tramped down the path.

'It's not much further now,' said Lily, looking ahead. 'We probably have another hour before we hit the border.'

As they neared the Transporter stop at the north-east corner of the loop of river that wound its way around the Community, Carter stopped. The shelter was the same simple construction as that on the other side of the river where he'd been dropped off just days earlier. Surrounded by a protective film of trophene, there was a FreeScreen, scrolling news across the front.

'This place was just for the Scouts. It won't work properly without a card,' said Lily. 'It probably won't work at all after all these years. Leave it. Come on; we need to get closer to the tunnel, it's almost time.'

The opening of the tunnel was a large hole set back into the bluff of the embankment that rose high above the river. Layers of rich sediment deposited by the Storms had coated the hillock in a covering of white flowers and, save for the smooth trophene retractable lid, the whole surface was a sprinkling of intricate blossom, still wet from the downpour. From underneath the ground there was a vibration and then a soft rumbling.

Carter looked at the FreeScreen. 'Lily,' he called, his heart pounding and a sick feeling overcoming him. 'You have to come and look at this.'

'It's happening,' said Lily. 'It's coming soon.'

'No, you have to look at this, it's important.'

'Carter, we don't have time. When the Transporter passes through, you have to wait and I will explain to the Industry guard inside the tunnel so that they'll let us through. We only have seconds to slip past and inside before it shuts automatically. The guards are under orders to shoot unknowns so I'll go first and let you know when it's clear, OK? Here, why don't you let me hold the book bag?'

There was something in her voice that Carter knew was wrong. He thought again about the water she'd handed him in the tunnel.

As she moved in to reach for the bag, Carter moved it out of her way.

'It's not heavy, and besides, you have the pictures,' he said.

Everything that happened next was fast and confusing. The grate opened quickly, smoothly and with minimum effort. There was a rush of air – partly from the Transporter as it whooshed past and partly from the arrow-straight throw as the rusted pair of scissors arced from Lily's hand directly into his shoulder. Distracted by the pain, Carter held on tight to the bag as she tried to grab it, stepped backwards and almost missed the final glimpse of Lily as she pushed herself inside the tunnel. Before he could follow her, the lid snapped shut tight, leaving just a few strands of her hair floating on the breeze near his face.

In the distance, the Transporter was already a thread of black winding its way east towards Drakewater. He still had the bag of books, but Lily had gone.

Carter glanced at the entrance to the tunnel and then back at the FreeScreen. It was the headline that had first caught his attention that, at that moment, terrified him the most.

THREE DEAD IN REBEL ESCAPE PLOT
IDENTIFIED AS:
LUCIA WARREN-DAVENPORT
ISABELLA DELANEY AND
CONTENDER, CARTER WARREN

There was no more to the story, just the headline looping continuously. He stumbled backwards. The blunt wound in his shoulder throbbed even though there was hardly any blood. It had all been part of the test. She'd used him. She had tested him. He'd failed. And Isabella was dead.

'Lily!' he screamed into the smooth lid of the tunnel. He heard his own voice as distant, somewhere in the background of his own mind. There was a silence before the horrific confirmation and a parting sentence from Lily that made the blood in his veins run cold. Her voice echoed through from the other side of the tunnel.

'Go now, Carter. Run. Before I send the Industry to kill you.'

Chapter Nineteen

The Fires

Alice

As they crossed the river, Rachel Mendoza, part of Filip's team, and Jayden took turns rowing; big propellers-worth of water churned over in effortless crunches of waves, making the crossing in half the time. Filip had covered Jonah's body, slumped in the corner of the boat, with a sheet of green corrugated plastic that he had found on the street. The part-burned, mottled plastic magnified parts of Jonah's face, made the boils seem bigger and more gruesome than they were. As much as Alice wanted to look at him, wanted to remember who he was, she couldn't and turned her head away to watch the boat, balanced on the roof of the supermarket. She felt a numb pain in her hands that radiated throughout her body and made her eyes glow cold and white.

The strokes of the rowers became more pronounced as the boat that Filip's team had put together lurched closer to the shore. Nobody had said a word since Alice had staggered out of the supermarket, splinters of bone and small lines of hair stuck to her. Filip and Alice sat still, opposite each other with their knees touching.

'Put your hands out,' said Filip in a low voice so that only she could hear him through the suit. Her lip, which she had bitten hard throughout the silence of their return trip, held the metallic taste of blood.

'What?'

'Put your hands out. Flat, in front you. Palms upwards – just do it.' Alice put out her hands, the pink of her hands visible through the thin, clear grey skin of the suit glove. Filip placed his hands, palms downward, above Alice's without touching even a fibre of the suit. He left them there until Alice could feel the energy, the warmth that his hands generated between them – something unseen and alive that they had created. Then, slowly, he lowered them onto hers and rubbed them gently along the length of her hands until their fingertips touched. She looked up at him but his eyes were closed tight in concentration.

'Share with me what you feel,' he said through the suit. 'Let me feel it. Let me share it.' His voice was clipped and metallic but charged with everything meaningful.

Alice took a deep breath and poured out her emotions. She told him about Jonah, how she'd felt about him, what they had meant to each other. They had saved each other in the Ship, but out here, where it really mattered, she hadn't been able to save him. She cried until there were no tears left. When she finally stopped, she felt equalised, divided and controlled. But all the same, she knew that something inside her had died with Jonah.

Within twenty minutes they were all back on the east bank of the river, the rowers exhausted and Jonah's body already starting to cause an unnerving chill between them. Grenville and Walford carried him back through the city, holding his broken body on their shoulders as the sun beat down on them. Alice was silent for the entire journey, stopping at times to pick something up out of the piles of bones on the street and then lay it back down again. There was a cool sadness between them that the nine remaining Scouts could not contain.

As they neared Unity Square, there was a shuffling in one of the shops. It wasn't until they caught sight of a row of snouts snuffling from behind a wall and the first whining howl ripped through the alley, that they realised they were in trouble.

'Wolves!' screamed Rachel, terror echoing through the empty streets. 'Run!'

Those at the front of the pack that bounded out towards them had bald patches, stripped of fur, and the same bleeding sores that Jonah had got from the river. They snarled at the group with sharp yellow teeth. Without hesitation Alice drew her gun and pulled the trigger twice and the bodies of the lead wolves dropped to the pavement. The two others that followed received the same treatment, falling with a sweet whine and a limp onto the road opposite them.

'We need to get inside and get safe,' said Alice, out of breath, the gun in her hand shaking a little. 'Day one in the new world is done.'

Locked in the containment room on the fifth floor of the Industry building near Unity Square, the teams ate the first batch of synthetic provisions and removed their suits. Jayden and one of the others had painted Jonah's body in liquid trophene while they decided what to do with it. It was starting to harden.

'Remember, whatever happened to him, he was one of us – he will *always* be one of us.' Filip said to the teams.

There was an eerie silence as Alice came back into the room, opened a box of fauclate and passed it around the group.

'You know what's weird?' she said in a strange voice. 'When I went into that supermarket and saw chocolate on the shelves – even though

it was spoiled and I couldn't eat it – I didn't even feel like it. This—'
she held up a piece of the sweet, fibrous synthetic product '—is all I
wanted.'

'That's conditioning for you,' said Kelly, her arms around Quinn
who was tapping numbers into the model of a spreadsheet.

'No,' said Alice wryly, 'that's not conditioning. That's real choice.'

The first sunset above ground seemed to be the longest one any of
them had ever experienced in their days before the Storms. Through
the window cavity they watched the ball of fire glide slowly from the
sky spitting a band of red, pink and mauve rays down onto the city.
When the darkness hauled a dark grey lid across the sky, Alice pulled
down the bunks and they each sat with a slate configuring the plans
and eating the rest of their evening food allocation.

Within a few minutes of finishing refreshments, the group began,
one by one, to drop into a deep sleep, slates open in front of nodding
heads and tightly closed eyes. In the blackness, Alice felt a hand slip
down between the mattress of the bunk above her, ruffling her hair
and caressing her shoulder.

'Goodnight, Alice,' said Filip. 'Sweet dreams.' She reached up and
touched his fingertips, rubbing her palm gently against his.

'Goodnight,' she whispered back to him but in the depths of her
tiredness, although the contours of her lips made the shapes of the
words, no actual sound came out of her mouth.

Alice awoke sweating in terror with a stiff arm, her fingers still
interlaced with Filip's through the crack in the bunks. Through her
nightmares, Hutchinson's face was burned into her memory. Rachel
and Jayden were crammed into one of the small bunks and Quinn and

Kelly lay curled like kittens in the corner of the room. Outside, the sun was already blazing hot, although Alice thought it couldn't have been more than eight o'clock in the morning. The sight of the sun was good, although the glow of the natural light that brightened her was quickly brought down by the sight of Jonah trussed in trophene wrap on the other side of the room. She handed out day packs to her team and Filip did the same before she stood in front of the group, now down to nine.

'Our first priority is security,' she said. 'Not for us but for the others who will come. We need to secure a perimeter around this city and drive out anything that might threaten us while we are building our new community. The wolves we saw yesterday, I think, are an anomaly.' She looked over at the statisticians.

'I agree,' said Quinn. 'From the monitoring Kelly and I did of yesterday's expedition, there were no other significant signs of life.' She stood up and pulled down a map of the city she had drawn on some scroll paper, with the near-horseshoe shape of the river in thick, bold blue. 'While you didn't venture far north, both teams explored east and west – almost as far as the river in both directions. Unless the woods and copses to the north hold significantly different terrains, I don't think we're going to find any mammals other than those that have strayed into the area by mistake.' She looked at Alice. 'And I think we can eradicate those.'

'I will shoot anything that threatens our safety here,' said Alice in a hard voice. She beckoned the teams to the windows and pointed indiscriminately.

'So, now we've been into the old world and we've seen the beauty and the horror of what's out there,' she said. 'Not everything – but we've observed enough to know what we need to do next. What happened yesterday was horrific, but we need to keep strong. It is because of – and not in spite of – what happened to Jonah that the plan continues and is now even more important.'

Filip joined her at the window and pointed out into the street.

'Over the next few days, we want each one of these cars taken to the edge of the river and used to create a barricade,' he said. 'Layer them two or three thick in depth and height. If any of them are in drivable condition then do that, but it's highly unlikely. Otherwise, just push them. The Industry muscle team will be arriving tomorrow to help with the clear-up, but they will need direction. There's some usable winching equipment in the garage we found, about half a kilometre east of here. Walford, can you see if there's anything we can trailer over here?'

Alice watched as a dove landed on the steps below and pecked at the grass growing through the cracks in the pavement. It looked up at her and, for just a second, she wondered whether it had ever been to Prospect House. When she spoke aloud, her voice sounded louder and truer than it did in her head.

'We need that barricade electrified,' she said. 'I never want anyone on the other side of that filthy, hallucinogenic trail of poison that used to be a river.' She pointed to the horseshoe shape on Quinn's map. 'And where the loop ends, we continue the barricade around us so that nothing can get in.'

'And no one can get out,' added Jayden. Alice turned around to face him.

'Exactly,' she said. 'What happened to Jonah was devastating, a tragedy and something we need to have mitigating plans for. I don't want anyone else in that river or coming up here to find things that remind them of their old life that drives them crazy. No one.'

As the others gathered their kits to prepare for the day, Filip pulled Alice towards him, nestling one arm around her waist and looking out at the city. His hands felt different to Jonah's. There was something electrically adult about him.

'You knew that would happen, didn't you, what happened with Jonah?'

He licked a finger and rubbed some dirt from her cheek. 'Not that exactly, but something. You knew he wasn't ready to come back out here. That was brave.' His words fell like secrets against the backdrop of the noise of the others and Alice let her own hands slip to her sides. She let out a sigh that whistled between her teeth.

'Not that exactly, but something, yes. I had to know what someone like Jonah would make of a world like this. I hoped…' she let her voice stumble to a whisper. 'I hoped he would be all right. But hoping forces you to place your trust in things that do not exist. We can't afford to do that when the others come. We have to prepare them and prepare *for* them. Kunstein was right – we have to bring them into a transformed world where things are different, completely different. We have to make it so that the new world is who we all are.

'Right now, people are just starting to understand the devastation we were in before the Storms. But there will be some of them who think that if they could just get back to their old house or find their photographs or their favourite blanket, everything will be OK. We need to destroy everything; a world wiped clean of memories of the place – the world – that put them in this situation. It could be anything that triggers them – a landscape, a chocolate bar, a ship on the roof of a building…'

The conviction in Alice's voice was her mainstay. She bit down and waited for Filip's response. The pigeons, having had enough of their conversation, flew off the windowsill and out into the cotton-fresh blueness of the morning. Filip watched them disappear before he spoke. His voice came clearly – the tone not accusatory, but clear and straight; one of the qualities that Alice most admired in him.

'Was that Jonah's purpose on this expedition? Did you bring him out here to see how people like *him* might react to the world?' He spoke carefully, leaving the explanations to Alice.

'People like *him* are people like *us* but with less training,' said Alice. 'We are all the same in many ways – we just have different things that trigger us or set us in motion. Jonah's purpose out here was just to be Jonah, just like your purpose is to bring yourself and your skills. And he was all I had – he was what I brought. Regardless of which one of us pulled the trigger, we are both culpable, Filip. But I more than you – I brought him out here hoping that he would survive, and somehow knowing that he wouldn't. I just didn't expect it to happen so soon.'

Filip folded his arms around Alice's waist and held her tightly. The delicate way with which he did it allowed her to melt some of her sadness into him, and for the moments that they stood there, her shoulders softened. As they framed the open window, drinking in the vastness of the city, Alice began to get a vague idea of the scale and the scope of the dangerous work in front of them and, whilst it scared her to the core, she knew she must carry on.

That afternoon, they built the first of the pyres.

Starting in one residential corner of the city, the clean-up was formally initiated when they selected where to begin. Alice felt determined, practical and almost detached.

'When the others come we'll need houses to put them in,' said Alice in front of Kelly's hand-drawn map. 'They'll need something that they can create as their own in this new world. This area here—' she pointed on the map to a cluster of streets to the north-west of Unity Square '—was the residential area in the hub of the city. As they were on higher ground the structural water damage wasn't as catastrophic – we may not even need to rebuild these in the first instance. They're all two-storey, two-bedroom properties and they'll need clearing of all material items and repainting. White and with no distinguishing features. When we run out of white paint, use cream, antique then fawn. After that we go to other hardware stores. I want everything that we can't reduce to a raw material for reuse or recycling burned. That includes everything personal, everything with a label or a logo, a pattern or a sign. Everything symbolic, religious, iconic, descriptive has to be destroyed.'

A slow wave of agreement rose up from the teams. This was something they all knew had to happen, but something that had never been discussed. Alice was relieved she wouldn't have to justify the decision any more than she'd already had to with herself.

'What about books?' said Kelly. 'I used to love reading fiction, anything that wasn't real.'

Quinn squeezed her hand and shook her head.

'I'm guessing that's a no?' said Jayden. 'We have to start again, right?'

'Right,' said Alice. 'What we have now is incredibly fragile. In one, maybe two years' time, the rest of our people will be coming to join us – some even before then if we can get this right. We need to provide them with the best possible chance of survival. There are some children down there on the Ship who have never seen the sun. But they've also never been force-fed television or plastic toys or the complexities of a society that almost took us to extinction. For their sake more than anyone else's, we need to get this right. However painful it is, you have to consider the contents of those houses as junk, unless it has a functional purpose. Otherwise, it's junk that will stink and rot and decay through into our bones the longer we leave it there.'

She looked around at the dusty faces of the team. The emotions ranged from stark indignation to sadness. 'It's not that all those things were wrong – they were fun and they were interesting, but our lives are different now. We have to do something transformative, something completely alien to us so that we *really* start again and do not try to pick up where we left off. It's what we believe,' she said firmly and waited while each of them nodded in decisive agreement.

Starting in that one small street in the north-west corner of the centre of the city and moving outwards in painful, slow circles, they started to burn up everything that had ever meant anything. They took it in turns to stoke the fires with books and papers, plastics and flags, furniture, mattresses and everything that was branded with time. They carried, dragged and pushed everything they could manage from homes, supermarkets and offices. In the first few days they had cleared one small street around Unity Square and hauled sixteen cars from the edges of the city onto the verge.

The front door of the first house that Jayden went crashing through on their second day above ground reminded Alice a little of the house she had shared with her mother, father and Charlie the puppy in the country, in the days before Prospect House and the Storms. The small front room opened out into the lounge with a tiny kitchen at the back before a proud square of garden. But it wasn't the shape or the style of the house that reminded her; it was the front door, wooden and painted red with a small plastic sticker across the top that was the same, and made her heart beat faster in her chest.

The peeling plastic sticker with black writing with twelve swirly words:

You Don't Have To Be Mad To Live Here:
But It Helps!

You could buy them at every corner shop and even most of the market stalls in town. Alice remembered how her father had brought a sticker exactly the same home from work one day, just as he had brought home her puppy Charlie, and sweets, and a book about zebras that Alice had loved. She ripped the piece of plastic from the door and smashed her fist against the window until the last of the glass shattered and her fingers bled.

The door was warped at the edges and hung uncomfortably on the paper-thin hinges like a sweater that had been stretched in the wash. It didn't take much more than one rhino run at the door and Jayden's bulk flew into the house. The wood splintered into pieces. Alice remembered the hours she had spent with the blue paint-flecked axe making storm windows out of a wardrobe. Things, she thought, were so much easier to break here.

Downstairs, ornamental plates patterned with sour-looking horses, and dull metal ladles covered the length of one wall. Chintzy china animals, fractured into small pieces littered the thick, green carpet. A giant ceramic fox head looked up from the corner of one room. Alice wasn't sure she could distinguish the balance between mildew and the original colour. The other walls half-bowed under the weight of stocky shelves crammed with DVDs, videos, CDs and box sets. It suddenly occurred to her that she hadn't seen a feature film in over five years.

Upstairs was worse. Bedrooms stacked with unread magazines, un-played-with toys, unworn clothes. There were shoes – tens of pairs of shoes that were time-worn but almost brand new, and two pairs still in crumpled cardboard boxes. Quinn and Kelly leafed through a wardrobe, pulling out the remnants of dull faded material and measuring them against their bodies. Hats, leggings, scarves and T-shirts, all in different colours, reminded Alice that there had once been something other than the clean, grey uniform of the Ship but, for some reason, the idea didn't hold much appeal. Papers, crumpled and dirty, were strewn across the floor. The headlines on a magazine near the bed that caught Alice's eye read like a foreign language, something so distant and alien that she physically retched as the words streamed from her mouth.

TEN DAYS TO A FLAT TUMMY
HOW TO TELL IF YOUR HUSBAND'S CHEATING
GET FIT FOR YOUR MAN
OUTRAGEOUS CELEB PHOTO GOSSIP

Kelly, who was thumbing through the pages, registered a look of disgust on her face. Alice moved to the window and took a deep breath of air.

'Take it all down to the pyre,' she said. 'Get rid of every single thing. Let's create some good space.'

The fires burned for most of the day.

As Jayden and Grenville carried Jonah's body on their shoulders and placed it without ceremony into the flames, the teams fell silent. Quinn brought the last trolley-load of the evening as the rest of them sat around the fire watching the embers burn to dust. Kelly and Rachel helped her sort through the junk; piles of magazines, books, a suitcase, a lamp, a cuddly toy and worn black case with peeling fabric.

Alice picked up the case and opened it; inside, the rich, glossy mahogany of a violin shone back at her, threateningly beautiful and dangerous. Before she could toss it into the flames, Quinn snatched the body and the bow out of the case, letting her hands caress the thin wooden neck. And under the silver crescent of a white moon, she positioned the instrument under her chin and began to play.

Underscored by the percussive spit of the flames, the beauty of the notes spiralled up into the night and echoed under the stars. Quinn played, eyes closed, until every perfect sound was imprinted in the hearts of each of them like the grooves of a record. She swayed into the rhythm of the music, eating up the space in between the cadences and her audience until they were all one, moving in time together until the final draw of the bow across the strings.

Nobody spoke and nobody clapped; they just sat in silence around the fire as the final vibrations seeped outwards into the night and the strains of musical brilliance hung in the air.

'Bruch's violin concerto in G Minor, third movement,' said Quinn, tears streaming down her face, and threw the violin into the heat of the flames.

Alice watched as the bridge of the violin burned into nothing and the strings pinged back in a painful sharp pizzicato for the final time.

'There's something I need to do,' she whispered to Filip, slipping her arm into his. 'Something for me. I need to bury my past, just like Quinn has. And if you won't come with me, I at least need you to cover for me.'

Chapter Twenty

The Betrayal

Carter

From outside the entrance to the tunnel, Carter felt his face burning in anger.

'Lily!' he called and banged on the trophene door. 'I get it. It's part of test, right?' There was a silence before she spoke: a silence that seemed to last for hours.

'I'm not supposed to talk to you now.' Her voice was different – hard, and delivered in a cold monotone. 'They'll be here to collect me in less than five minutes. If you want to survive – in whatever way you can – I suggest you run. You're lucky I haven't killed you already; although that might have been kinder than leaving you out there with the wolves.'

'You think I didn't know there was something going on?'

There was a crunching on the other side of the tunnel. Lily's feet kicked gravel against the door while she searched for something to say.

'Carter, I was your mentor, your running mate,' she said finally, 'brought in to test your loyalty. If you failed, I got to take your place. That's the benefit of having six Contenders. Three out in the open and the other three, well, masquerading as mentors. Our *job* was to get you to break. It's the new process. The way the Industry ensures we have someone stronger than Anaya Chess in charge.'

'She was the wrong choice – I'm not.'

'Chess is too weak. She should have introduced more stringent measures when she had the chance. She showed too much sympathy with the dissidents and so the Contender rules have been changed. I was there to help you, gain your trust and to find out how quickly the rebels would try to recruit you. Your love and trust in Isabella let you down, just before you were frozen. And it's let you down again. It – she – has always made you weak.' Her voice sounded hollow.

Carter pushed his palm on the trophene firmly, feeling the heat of the sun absorbed by the trophene warming his palm. It felt safe, secure, disarming. And it made him even angrier.

'You'll never make Controller General. If you were that good, they'd have given you a chance before this – you've been around; even you told me that.'

There was a sarcastic laugh from the tunnel.

'You're even more self-absorbed than I'd heard. As much as you think you're the great saviour, you're just bitter. Angry that your parents left you, jealous that Isabella understood more than you, and so self-assured that you couldn't stop yourself thinking you were bigger than the Industry. I told them you would be trouble; that's why they gave you to me. But there *is* something about you. I can see what Isabella saw in you. Maybe it's just the eyes…'

Carter balled his fist and punched the ground until his shoulder ached and the sides of his fingers began to blossom with a blue bruise and the green blood of the grass.

'Just let me in,' he said, 'and I'll forgive you.'

This time Lily's laughter was loud and emphatic.

'Forgive me? There's nothing to forgive *me* for. It's you who should be begging for forgiveness. Do you think you're ever going to be allowed back in after what you've done? You broke the rules, Carter. Your intention was always to break the rules; you knew that when you left your card behind. You knew that you were putting our Community at risk by coming out here. It was a test; you know that. You are a rebel – you want to do things your own way. Just like your old girlfriend, just like your daughter.' She paused. 'Just like your parents.'

Carter thought about what Isabella had said. 'What about my parents?' he shouted. 'What happened to them?'

The cruel laughing had stopped but Lily's voice was still hard.

'You're the absolute double of your father, Carter. He was a good man, trusting in so many ways. But your mother… well, she caused complications. They were what ended the missions to the Deadlands for everyone else and why the rules inside the Community had to be strengthened. They were *why* this idea of an uprising first got traction. They were the start of things, Carter. Something *you* could have put an end to.'

Carter's palms were sweating and he felt sick. 'They were good people,' he said.

'It was on the second day of the mission that they tried to escape. Your mother was due to be sent to the Catacombs but your father had other ideas. They had a plan to make for the west and start a new life together, to have more children and bring them into a world with no boundaries. But not with you, Carter Warren – they left you in the Community. *You* were not required.'

Carter felt the strings of blood in his veins go cold. 'It's not true. They were in an accident—'

'Your birth was hailed as a success,' Lily said, interrupting him midsentence. Her voice was like a knife. 'But the scans showed that her next child wasn't going to be as lucky. The medics said he had gills like a fish and webbed feet. A malformed Descendent would never be tolerated so she was due to be frozen and the child terminated. That was the plan – but somehow she found out.'

Her accusations came out like bullets.

'It was no accident; they planned it all. And it was no accident that I shot them. I was under orders, of course. It's what I do, Carter Warren. Your father was killed instantly, but your mother… well, it took a little longer. The other Scouts were, thankfully, already inside the Transporter so it wasn't difficult to propagate the story about wolves when we got back to the Community. But then there was your daughter.'

Rage shot through his head and his body, bringing a pain he'd never experienced before. He forced himself, against every instinct inside him, to push back the anger and keep asking the questions.

'What about my daughter?' Carter thought about his parents, smiling as they'd left him that morning, all those years ago. Kissing him on the head. Knowing that they had no intention of seeing him again. He felt the anger building again and clenched his fists tightly.

'Well, as I had a connection with the family, I was brought out of the Catacombs in preparation for your return. And you were given to me as my main assignment – they only told me that the situation with your daughter had got out of hand after they'd briefed me about you. I never imagined we'd find your daughter alive. That was a shame – so young.'

'What?' The inside of Carter's head felt cold and his arms were numb. The first of the evening mosquitoes lifted off the water and started to gnaw into his skin.

'I'll claim self-defence but I don't think anyone in the Industry will care. After your eagerness to swig the sedative in my water, it was really easy to set up the roof fall once I'd seen there was a way out. To be truthful, I thought the girl was already dead but she was just asleep.'

A rage built up inside Carter, like an explosion of stars. His breathing was staggered, harsh, but Lily didn't stop. Her voice was sneering, cruel.

'She probably didn't even hear me coming; for all her rebellious instincts, she didn't even stir until I slashed her wrists. Then, when I pulled down some of the struts in the tunnel, it was enough of an emergency to make you find the way out. My orders were to destroy the tunnel, destroy the revolution and retrieve the girl – preferably *with* you rather than against you, but, Carter Warren, there's a big part of you that wants this for yourself and not for the Community.'

Carter banged hard on the lid with his fists. 'I will get you back for this,' he said, his voice low and full of rage. 'You will regret this.'

'It's not about you, Carter,' said Lily with cold, calm definition. 'It's about me. After this Contribution of yours that I'm making, I wouldn't be too surprised if I even make Controller General, especially for quelling the rebellion – which I intend to do by discrediting you.'

Carter banged hard again. 'You're crazy,' he shouted. 'Crazy.'

'Crazy is all relative, isn't it?' said Lily. 'Some hours ago that's what you thought about Isabella. But maybe, just maybe, she wasn't that crazy after all.' Lily's voice became more muffled as she moved away from the sliding door that separated them. 'You should leave. There's nothing for you here. You're tainted now.' Her voice was final, echoing though the cavernous tunnel and muffled by the thickness of the door.

For the first time since his parents had left him, Carter felt desperately alone.

'You will pay for this. I will be back for you.'

'You won't. Not for very long anyway. You don't have the skills to find food, to defend yourself or to be alone. You'll probably die of loneliness before you die of starvation. But that is the choice you've made. You must have known that coming out here would mean an end to your life in the Community, not just your shot at becoming Controller General. You've broken the most important rule by leaving. And by loving someone you shouldn't have. You have no right to lead us.'

There was a silence on the other side of the door as Lily's words reverberated through the grass verge and out into the warmness of the setting sun. 'When the guards come to collect me, they'll kill you – if the wolves don't do it first,' she added quietly, 'because, officially, you've been declared dead already. But there's a part of me that pities you. Go now if you want to live and never, ever come anywhere near the Barricades. You have about two minutes of your life left. Goodbye, Carter Warren.'

Picking up the scissors from where they had fallen after striking his shoulder, Carter moved back towards the dark shape of the shelter cast against the horizon. Four or five paces in, he sped up until his walk became a jog and then a sprint. Breathlessness sent pains through his chest and his shoulders but he kept running until he reached the leafy cover of the trees. And then he threw himself onto the piles of earthy undergrowth and screamed until his whole body ached.

When Carter opened his eyes again it was dark, but a bright, icy moon had arched itself across the sky and cast a flood of white light across the trees. Under the pale mist that gathered in the upper branches, he could hear the scuttling whisper of small animals in the dense undergrowth.

The pain in his shoulder had gathered some traction and it felt sore, and the dry, gravelly tenseness in his throat irritated his trachea, making him cough. As he did, the skittering became more intense, and in the background he could hear other, less light-footed animals moving amongst the fallen leaves and broken branches.

There had been something about his dream that had woken him. He'd been climbing, hand over foot over a hill of broken bones glued together with moss, leaves, and a covering of bright sunshine-yellow gorse that glowed as he walked. In his dream he had felt the ground underneath him shifting and breaking as he'd moved against it, slippery as ice, towards the top of the hill. On the hill was a row of glass shards like the one that had stuck out from the river on the west side. Above him, there had been a figure, back to the sun, that had cut a clear outline against the white light.

'Isabella,' he'd called, 'Isabella, is that you?'

When she'd turned around he'd seen her as she was before, in the days when he had sat behind her at the Academy desperately wanting to stroke her hair. The shadow of Isabella had turned around, the eyes playful and shimmering in the brightness of the dream. As she'd turned around, the golden haze of the gorse and the white paper-like flowers on the sides of the hillside had bent and shaped themselves into bells and chimed his arrival.

'Carter Warren,' she'd said softly. 'You've missed your chance. I'm gone now.'

Then the face had melted into the blackness of the sun shadow and Isabella had become Lily, laughing and calling him. And the tiny white flowers had became bones: knuckles and teeth of long-dead Lab Made children, nipping at his ankles and scratching him with their sharp pincer-like spikes. He'd tried to kick them away, to step backwards.

'Leave me alone!' he'd shouted. 'Leave me alone!' And then he'd turned and ran. He'd ran fast, away from the jumping bones and the figure of Lily who had stood barking in a throaty howl. In the distance, three trees had loomed ahead of him, tall and dark. Carter had ran to them, grabbing the trunk of one tightly in his arms, feeling the rough bark against his skin. The branches of the tree had folded around him, pulling him tighter and closer until an old, familiar voice had warmed his heart.

'Carter Warren,' the voice had said, 'what a surprise to see you here. Do you remember me?' Carter had hugged the tree that had become an old man.

'Grandfather,' he muttered in his sleep, 'why did you lie to me?' and then, as he turned over in the earthy ground of the Deadlands, the cool chill of the night dragged him out of his dream with a sharp, shocking jolt.

Above, in the trees, the nightjars were making their familiar sound. Set against the alien backdrop of the other wildlife in the Deadlands, there was something reassuring about hearing a bird call he was used to. But the sound of his grandfather's voice had unsettled him, reminding him of the terrible things he had heard about the Deadlands, the lies that had kept him from asking the right questions.

'Everything about life before was complex,' his grandfather had said. 'Too complex and terrible to understand.'

'Was there anything good?'

'Nothing at all.'

The old man had spun tales like silk about the evils of sweatshops, weapons of mass destruction, terrifying religions, complex derivatives markets, Christian pie-eating contests, conspiracy theories, death hop-scotch, fizzy acid sweets, never-ending jigsaw puzzles, mobile phones that burned the brain, beauty pageants that you had to change your face for, unicycles and pension plans. Everything that was bad and evil about the old world. Everything that was untrue.

'My father, the man whose name you have, was called Richard Carter Warren. His parents deserted him as the Storms came in the fractured remains of a city. He raided food stores called supermarkets as the rain fell, diving into the cold grey depths of the rainwater in search of food in filthy cans that he could feast upon in the evenings. He was one of the lucky ones. He lived in a high tower above the city and was forced to watch as the world died. He lived there with his brother.'

'It's not *really* true though, is it, Grandfather?' Carter had asked, wide eyed and afraid.

'It is true,' the old man had replied. 'And I think it's safe to say that the Deadlands were and are never a place to be – even if you are one of these so-called Scouts. I can only hope lessons have been learned.'

'How did Richard Warren get here? How did he survive out there all alone in the Storms?'

'He was a survivor,' his grandfather had told him, 'just as you are. He said that not long after the waters dropped, he got sick with a fever and his brother left him there to die. Years later he woke up here in the Community. The Industry saved him. They saved us all.'

As he rubbed the crusty sleep from his eyes, the crispness of the edges of his dream evaporated and Carter was left alone in the darkness of the trees with the sound of his grandfather's words resonating inside his head. The bent-down grasses of the trail behind him had already begun to repair, springing back in the night blackness. He held on tightly to the bag, clasping the contents to his chest, feeling a strong resolve deep inside himself. The screen had said that Isabella was dead. But it had said that he was dead too. And that was a lie.

With no torch, only the pale moon to guide him, Carter felt his way through the trees, moving westwards towards the long road of the ridge. He couldn't risk going through the open valley to be confronted at night by the wolves, but wandering around in the forest at night seemed to offer little more comfort. Even though the sound of the nightjars was considerably better than the growling of the sharp-toothed pack, he needed to be high out of the reach of predators if he was to have even half a chance of making it through the night.

Shivering, he continued onwards until he stumbled upon a worn-out building with a flat porch roof that overhung a smashed-out room filled with empty shelves. Exhausted, he hauled himself onto the surface covered with soft leaves and bird droppings. High above the scratching on the ground, he curled foetal-like until the darkness pulled its arm around him. And, as it came, it dragged him into the depths of deep sleep, the rusty black scissors and book bag held tightly in his hands like talismans against the night.

When he opened his eyes, the sun had cast a leafy green light across the woodland and he was, to his own surprise, still alive and invigorated from the sleep. The first and only thought in his mind when he woke up was the Tower that he'd seen so many times across the Black River, from his nights on the hills with Isabella. It would be safely sheltered and high enough to get a view of all the surrounding area and he'd be able to defend himself against any wild animals that came. He'd be able to see what else was out there. And get a good view of the new Barricades. If he could find a way back in, he might be able to see if Isabella was still alive.

From the broad ledge of the roof he had fallen asleep on, he couldn't see above the canopy of trees but there was a smattering of clearings in the wood before the contours of the valley turned around the ridge, following the same S-shape of the river. He could just about make out the top of the tower to the south west of where he was, glinting dangerously in the sunlight. The track would guide him around the ridge and then back eastwards towards the tower. It would take him most of the day.

Carter lowered his body down onto the ground, his stomach rumbling furiously as he looked around for anything to eat. He snacked on the rest of the food he'd transferred from the book bag to his pockets and scanned the forest. There were bitter berries, purple-drop hangers and white nettle-ferns, and all sorts of grasses. He had to start thinking about something other than the synthetics he was used to. But even through his hunger, something inside him felt stronger than ever.

There would be no chicker out here. He plumped for some black berries filled with a dark red juice that trickled down his chin as he gorged himself on them. He'd tasted things that were marginally worse and, apart from a slight dizziness, they didn't seem to have made him feel any sicker than the pain in his arm. After he ate, he cleaned the wound in his shoulder with some damp leaves until it was free of blood. The puncture wasn't deep but the grey-blue cloud of a bruise had spread across his chest and down his arm. Gritting his teeth, he moved onwards.

By early afternoon, although he was sweating and tired, he'd made good progress. From the narrow ridge he could see down into the valley and across towards the Community. A worm-like Transporter snaked through from Proclamation Plaza until it disappeared, deep underground into the Catacombs. The flashing glitter of the Barricades in the warm orange sun blinded him if he looked directly into its glare but in the daylight, everything seemed terrifyingly normal; tiny ants of people moving slowly through the thin streets with a small gathering in Unity Square. He wondered if one of them was Lily.

He could see the vehicle park too and a cluster of wolves lounging in the sun in the open grassland. At the edge there was the small brick building that he and Lily had crouched together on as the rivulets of rain ran down their necks inside their clothes. Carter had been shielding her from the worst of it, protecting her with his body while he felt her lean against his shoulder – the same shoulder that now ached with the pain of the puncture wound she had given him.

Standing between him and the wolves was the Tower block. It loomed dark below him at the edge of the gorse-covered valley surrounded by a moat of undergrowth and bushes. He blinked in the sun. He would be there soon.

Far to the west, a mess of dark grey clouds plotted the late afternoon downpour in earnest. Carter accelerated his pace down the side of the ridge towards the Tower. He had between two and three hours to make it to shelter before the rain started. Keeping one eye on the occasional movement of the rats in the bushes, and the other on his intended destination, he moved quickly and carefully.

From the edge of the ridge, the Tower looked different than it had all those years ago when he had crouched in the ruins on the Blue Hills with Isabella. He'd imagined that beyond the Tower was blackness but the light from the sun no longer looked like it was being sucked into a vortex. At the lower levels, the light flowed through the Tower like water. All across the valley, between the trees, were smashed pieces of buildings and the old life.

By the time he reached the base of the ridge, a gentle flurry of rain had started and the Tower, nestled between the ridge and the river, almost seemed further away, like the trunk of a thick tree reaching up to the sky. Carter measured the distance and looked at the sky, silently picking up his pace despite the pain wracking his body. Within minutes he'd broken out into a sprint, crushing leaves and jumping over the moving creatures that darted out in front of him as he hurtled through their woodland. Luckily, they seemed more wary of him than he of them.

He had to hurry. There wasn't much time before the Storm hit.

Chapter Twenty-One

The Mission

Alice

By the end of the first week, forty of the Industry support team had arrived above ground. Although they popped out of the shaft green and bleary-eyed, they were fast, obedient and expertly trained, exponentially more effective than Grenville and Walford. They requested that Alice read them the opening pages of the manifesto, the rules and the plan in their two-hour readjustment break so that they could get straight to work. And they worked like machines, worked *with* machines, somehow reigniting the engines of some of the vehicles and using them to haul things from one end of the new community to the other.

'This is for construction purposes only,' said Alice firmly to the teams. 'Once we have established ourselves, there will be no more personal transport. These vehicles will be decommissioned and destroyed. Quinn is finalising the details for a public transport system that will span this area.'

Within three weeks, all the cars, trucks, waste metal and fencing that they had dredged from within the city had been piled up on the banks of the river creating a shiny, multicoloured barricade all around the edges. To the south-east, the support teams had set up recycling areas for the rest of the metal, foodstuffs and building materials.

'We link up the energy that's being used underground, generated from cell division,' said Quinn. 'It's the cleanest energy you can get and we've learned a lot from Drakewater regarding security. We can use some of the existing infrastructure for power distribution when the repairs are finished and then we'll have a full above-ground electrical supply.'

Alice looked at her face carefully.

'That's not a small job; I don't envy you. Do you think this is even a good idea, the right idea? When the power's back and everyone's above ground, how do we make sure we don't return to the mess we were in before?'

Quinn looked back at her screen.

'*We* don't,' she said. 'You do. You and Filip. And I don't envy you, either.'

Alice nodded and smiled.

'Touché,' she said. 'But it's what we all have to do.'

'Are you sure about this?' Filip's face was lined with dust from the inside of one of the houses in Drummond Row where Alice had insisted they meet in secret.

'I have to,' said Alice. 'I have to go there one last time to be sure, to stop the dreams and to finish this once and for all.' She took his hand and held it tightly to her face. 'How can I ask all of them to forget if I can't do this myself? I need to be at peace with this.'

Filip pulled her close.

'I'll come with you, but you have to promise me that we use the time out there beyond our barricade in the... what do you call it again?'

'The Deadlands.'

'We make our time in the Deadlands count. We make it worth-while. We use it to show people what the dangers are like out there so that they know what happened, so that they know what we did to this world and why it can never happen again. Agreed?'

Alice nodded her head.

'Agreed.'

Filip smiled and pulled Alice towards him, kissed the top of her head and headed towards the doorway.

'We'll go this afternoon. I'll get the equipment together and you brief Quinn on what needs to happen while we're gone. And Alice...' He turned before leaving the room and moved back towards her. Holding her head between his palms and kissed her again, this time intensely on the lips with a definite passion before disappearing from the room. He closed the door quietly and Alice looked at her own fingers, red-rimmed and bitten, and wondered whether, after all this time, she really was strong enough to be the person she needed to be.

The tunnel that looped under the river and into the south-west corner of the new community had been, before the Storms, a pedestrian subway. Tiny pieces of coloured mosaic tiles clung to the walls as if held in place by chewing gum. Alice had been through there many times on her own when she should have been at school but nobody ever caught her or told her mother, not even the man who played his guitar.

He was usually there with a dog that had a thin piece of rope around its neck. The dog would always whine if she'd stopped to watch. The two of them would sit in a dusty alcove set back into the wall of the tunnel that had a shelf at the back of it and a bricked-up doorway where the man kept his sleeping bag, a book and a sock full of money. There had been a mournful quality on the faces of both the man and the dog but, however much she'd petted the dog until his tail wagged in a sorrowful loop, it had been the man whom Alice had wanted to save the most. The dog, she thought, would be better off staying away from Prospect House.

'What is the point of that book?' Alice had asked the man one morning, wondering if he could even read. 'When do you get time to read it?'

The man had looked at her and smiled. 'It's a history of Ancient Rome,' he'd said. 'You don't read it; you absorb it.'

Alice hadn't been able to imagine that; that if she were only to have one book in the world, the Ancient Rome book would be it.

'Why do you keep your things on that shelf?'

'Because it's the safest place,' he'd said in return and had let her stroke the dog while he'd changed a string on his guitar. 'It's where nobody would think to look.'

Alice shivered as they neared the entrance to the tunnel. Inside it looked dark and terrifyingly eerie. As Filip shone a torch around the sides of the walls, eyelets of mosaic winked back at them as if complicit in their secret task.

'Is this it?' said Filip. 'Is this the right one?'

Alice looked at the inch-square tiles in their multicoloured alliance: scenes of a windmill, a beach, and children playing, all oblivious to the events that had chipped their hard surfaces and changed the world above them forever.

'Yes,' said Alice. 'This is it.'

The floor of the tunnel was layered with the same muck as the streets; paper, plastics and twigs that had been pushed to the sides as the water had subsided and eventually dried to form small dirty rivulets that left tramlines on the sides and in between the floor tiles. In one corner there was a doll, missing one arm, but still dressed in the remains of what would have been a light-pink cardigan, now dark brown with dried sludge.

'Are you sure you want to do this?' Filip held Alice's arm tightly.

'Yes,' said Alice and walked onwards, holding her torch out in front of her, casting a bright white flare through the darkness.

When they climbed the steps to the other side of the city, they were greeted with an explosion of wild colour. The stairwell led upwards to the pavement that had once run alongside the river. A path that was now covered over with trash and soil, thick with plants.

In the time since the water had subsided on the rich fertile ground on the other side of the river, fields of piercing blue flowers had dotted the wasteland like shrapnel. Poppies crowded across a new field that had been fertilised with the overspill of silt. The shops that had once lined the waterfront were destroyed, contents strewn over the length of the walkway, and further upriver, in the distance, Alice could make out the skeletal shape of the boat still wedged in between the buildings further upstream.

'Let's get away from here,' she said, pulling Filip into the littered side streets. 'I don't trust being near the river.'

They moved inland, following the trail of the streets past abandoned houses and stores, picking their way over hillocks of glass that had been smashed into needle-thin splinters, and the shattered bones of humans and animals lost in the Storms. In the debris they untangled individual tragedies. There was a kennel with the skeletal remains of a dog still chained inside, and a pram that had somehow become entangled in the shredded canopy of a shop and hung dolefully, swinging as the wind blew. And, more than once, they passed withered strings of bones that still hung from thick cords of rope attached to the highest parts of buildings like macabre flags, clad in the wasted rags they'd died in, except for their shoes, which lay scattered. In her mind, Alice could hear the delicate strains of the Bruch concerto and her heart felt heavy and desperately sad.

'Are you ready to start filming?' said Filip. 'We need to capture the danger and destruction out here.'

'Is it fair to show them this?'

'Is it fair *not* to? This is the best deterrent we have, but it will only work once we are established and we have something to compare it against. Our future generations deserve to know what destruction we created and the devastation it caused.'

Filip stepped sideways to avoid the partial skeleton of a horse, its legs boldly spread across the width of the pavement. The open skull was split into two pieces by half of a stone gargoyle that had fallen from the building above. The other half was still stuck there, grinning inanely as it gazed out across the river.

'You're right,' she said and they both switched on the cameras that were attached to the helmets of their suits. They squeezed hands tightly and Alice walked in front, scanning the devastation with the wide lens.

'My name is Alice Davenport,' she started, 'and this is the Deadlands.'

The journey to Prospect House took them just over two hours and in that time they had to stop filming on three occasions.

'Some of this stuff is just too horrific,' breathed Filip. They sat and held each other close in the dark alleys where skeletons had gathered in corners, some whole but most in parts. Through the labyrinthine streets they paused to peer into the darkness of the water-damaged shop fronts and cold, empty offices. An undertaker's shop devoid of coffins sat with its lonely sole headstone still attached to the wall. There was still the faint smell of chemicals mixed with salt and wild garlic that hung with lavish intent in the air.

'The coffins probably sailed off down the river with the bodies still in them,' said Filip. Alice shook her head. 'Burial at sea,' she replied, and in the ugliness, they both found something small to laugh about. They sat there in the macabre gloominess holding hands until they both knew it was time to move on.

While Alice had been prepared for the destruction of the city and having to confront everything that had ever meant anything to her, what she was not ready to face were the rats. With thick, hairy bodies the size of small dogs, they skittered amongst the ruins, flicking their tails and baring creamy stained teeth set in wide, red-rimmed mouths. Both Alice and Filip screamed when the first set came towards them and ran through the water-torn backstreets to a building with stairs steady enough to climb.

Behind them came the wolves, one pack tearing through the streets in rapid succession, snapping hungry mouths and baying like demented lunatics, clawing at the doors of shops and leaping through half-broken windows after their prey. Alice and Filip watched them from a third-floor roof, hidden out of sight but shooting at them with loud snaps of pistol fire that were enough to make them retreat momentarily back to the edges of the city streets.

'Where do you think they came from? They're not indigenous.' said Filip.

'Maybe from the other side of Drakewater. Maybe they escaped from a zoo – who knows what else is out there?'

'They came at around this time before, when…' Filip couldn't bring himself to say Jonah's name, but they both knew what he meant.

It took them three hours to reach the higher ground on the other side of the city. Although the graffiti on the walls had crumbled to a pale wash of colour and some buildings had drifted into mounds of dust, the district felt familiar to Alice. Familiar, but not in a good way. Not in the same way that her nostalgia for the house in the country warmed her soul with memories. This was a sour recognition of a life that she had been more than happy to leave behind. Eventually, they came to the end of the last house in the row, and from behind the backdrop, the tall square building loomed up in front of them.

They had arrived at Prospect House.

The cheap yellow grass that had once covered the local authority's offering of a park opposite the block of flats was now a luscious green, reminiscent of a meadow. Most of the rubbish had naturally cleared to the sides of the park and heaped into piles. A smattering of white and yellow flowers poked through the long grass that buzzed with midges and butterflies that flapped lazy wings in the bright sunlight. A solitary car lay upside down and sat in the middle of the grass, rusted and worn with brambles crawling out of the windows and over the roof, smashed headlamps looking out across the view. It had the feel of a modern art sculpture park.

When the calm, almost peaceful air had settled over them, they followed the weedy path to the entrance of the flats. Bees hummed excitedly around a bush, heady with flowers, reminding Alice of a summer afternoon she'd spent cutting back the trees in the garden with her father before things had changed.

'What do you want to be when you grow up, Alice?' he'd said to her, kind fingers caked in thick black earth.

'I want to be an explorer, Daddy!'

Alice had then run into the bee-filled bushes covered in thorns, pulling them apart with tiny hands. Her father had spent hours with her that afternoon pulling out the splinters of bramble and treating the stings with antiseptic cream. Between the whimpering cries, Alice repeated the same seven words over and over.

'I still want to be an explorer.'

'And I still do,' she whispered to herself now, and Filip squeezed her hand.

As they climbed the stairs, the musty smell of piss and decay was strong – but not as overpowering, Alice thought, as when she'd lived there.

'There'll be a blockage between the eighth and ninth floors that we're going to need to move,' she said.

'That's not a problem.'

Filip switched off their cameras. He kissed her softly on the forehead. 'Are you sure you want to do this?'

'Of course I'm sure,' she said. 'I have to.'

When they reached the eighth floor, the stairway was clear all the way up to the roof. The sideboards and tables that Hutchinson had used to barricade the way were gone with the only reminder being thin slivers of wood that had been well-trodden into the stairs.

Alice looked at Filip.

'Something's wrong,' she said. 'This isn't how I left it.'

They edged along the balcony until they reached the door marked 59 and pushed it aside gingerly. Inside the flat were the remnants of her previous life: the pictures, the furniture, her books and clothes. But the rough boards she had stuffed over the balcony windows had been replaced with smart, clean window guards on one side, the black, rusty scissors had been carefully placed on the mantelpiece and, most shockingly, the body of Hutchinson had gone.

'Someone has been here,' said Alice slowly. And repeated: 'This isn't how I left it.' She drew her gun from her belt and held it firm in her hand.

'Hutchinson?' whispered Filip. 'How could he still be alive after all this time?'

'He can't be,' said Alice. 'I killed him.' She picked up the orangey-black scissors that still held the traces of the burnt ochre colour of blood. 'With these.' Filip took the scissors and stuffed them into his backpack. A ring of charred stones and half-burned wood-sticks filled one corner and smoke stains crept up the edge of the wallpaper.

'We have what we came for; now let's go,' he said, pulling at her arm. But Alice walked into the kitchen and ran her finger down the tiles that had pictures of drab flowers and ugly, sad birds.

'This isn't like the other places we've passed through,' she said. 'It's clean.' She opened the kitchen cupboard. It was half-full of dried goods and cans. A bowl of water stood on the counter top.

'There's somebody living here,' she said. 'What if... what if... he's not dead?'

Alice felt an ice-chill down her back. Killing him once had been horrific enough. Having to do it a second time might prove to be more difficult. They both looked towards the hallway and up the stairs.

'Or what if your mother came home?'

Alice's fingers were trembling as she pulled the gun out in front of her. At the top of the stairs, she and Filip stood alongside each other and inched across the landing in absolute silence. The door to her room was ajar and as soon as they peered through the crack, it was obvious that it was empty. Alice nodded towards her mother's room. Her mother's den.

From the window outside, the sound of gulls floated in, muted against the closed door of Alice's mother's room but enough to jolt them both in momentary shock. They crept along the corridor and Alice held her ear to the warped wooden door. She beckoned Filip with her finger. Through the inch-thick reproduction wood came the sound she was least expecting – a heavy, regular elephantine snore.

Alice felt her heart sink. She shouldn't have hoped. She should never, not even for one second, have believed in hope.

Her mother would never, ever have come back for her.

'Who are you?' Filip had one hand on the boy's shoulder, pinning him to the bed while Alice pointed her gun directly at his temple. His bloodshot eyes opened slowly and a trickle of froth dripped from his mouth onto the bedspread.

'I'm sick,' he said. 'Help me.' Alice kept the gun pointed squarely between the boy's eyes. For a split second she thought it might have been Jonah, that he might have, somehow come back to her. But when her eyes focused again she could see that the boy looked around eighteen, possibly older. A thin fuzz of whisker covered his upper lip and chin and his hair was long and lank, gathered around his neck in matted curls. That would have made him twelve, maybe thirteen at the time of the Storms.

'How long have you been out here?'

Filip pulled back the covers; the boy was shivering with fever, his hands wrapped around his own body were clammy and warm. The room smelled of sickness, Alice thought, like the inside of a hospital. She lowered the gun and reached into her backpack and pulled out some pills, stuffing them into the boy's mouth and washing them down with the water they had brought with them. He coughed and then spluttered but didn't bring the tablets back up. Alice hoped they might do some good. He was a little pale and clammy but, when she checked, he didn't seem to have any injuries and his heartbeat was strong.

'Are you really here? Is this another dream?' He smiled weakly.

'You just have a fever,' she said, hoping she was right. 'You'll be fine in a few days.'

Filip looked at the boy and then across at Alice.

'We can't take him,' he said. 'What if he has something serious and infects the others?'

Alice rubbed her fingers across the furrow of her temple.

'But we can't leave him,' she said. 'He looks like he has the flu.'

She turned her attention to the boy. 'Have you been sick?'

He shook his head. 'My body aches,' he said weakly. 'I just don't think I can get up.'

She put her hand on his forehead. 'He has a temperature but he doesn't have a rash,' she said to Filip finally. 'We need to take him.'

'I'm not sure…' started Filip, his face mapped with concern but Alice interrupted him.

'He comes with us – but we'll need to take him straight back to the infirmary in the Ship. Get him looked after properly.'

'Are you absolutely sure that's the right thing to do?'

'It's the only thing to do. He might not survive out here without help.' She pulled the sheets and bedspread back over him and trickled a little more water down his throat. He gulped it slowly then dropped his head back onto the pillow.

'How long do you think he's been there?' asked Filip in disbelief.

Alice shook her head. 'No idea,' she said. 'But I think he must have come here after the water subsided.' She looked around the room. 'There's no way he'd have been able to survive in here. Maybe he made it to higher ground before the Storms?'

Filip picked at the wallpaper and pulled off a strip. 'Even if he did, without the Industry it must have been almost impossible. Food, shelter, clothing – almost everything has been destroyed. It's... unbelievable.'

Alice nodded and eyed the space she'd once called home. The garish interior was ugly and seemed dated way beyond its time. After five years in the clean sleekness of the Ship, it looked bawdy and cheap.

'I don't know how he did it. But it seems that he did. He's thin and undernourished but alive.' She pulled the covers closely around the boy and tucked them underneath him so that he was cocooned tightly. With a corner of the sheet, she wiped the thin layer of sweat from his face and he made a tiny motion of thanks with his head.

'Who are you?' she whispered, touching him gently on the side of the cheek. 'Tell us who you are.'

The boy opened his eyes so that a tiny crack of white was visible. 'My name is Richard Carter Warren,' he managed and promptly drifted back off to sleep.

In the living room, Alice picked through the remains of her belongings and found some paper and a pencil. Filip watched as she scribbled furiously then folded the paper and placed it on the mantelpiece. When she had finished she felt a calm wave wash over her. If Richard survived the Storms, then someone else could have. And now, she had said all she needed to say. For the first time in a long time, she felt like she could breathe all the way out.

Everything else she piled into the fireplace and set it alight. All except a rough wooden trap that leant against the wall.

'He ate the birds,' Alice mouthed quietly while she and Filip, warming their hands on the glowing embers, watched the sun disappear behind the horizon.

'We'll leave at dawn,' she said with defined finality. 'That way we should make it through the city safely and through the tunnel by mid-morning.'

Filip nodded as she ran her finger along the blade of the scissors.

'What will you do with those?'

'They're the last thing that reminds me of here. I'm going to put them where they'll never be found.'

When the first shards of light filtered through the window coverings, they slunk from the flat. Filip made a stretcher for Richard – a bed sheet doubled over and tied tightly to a pair of broom handles – but for the majority of the journey they didn't need it. The boy stumbled between the two of them, carried by their fervent intention to get back to the community they were creating, back to their home.

At the busker's alcove in the tunnel, Alice wrapped up the scissors in a fragment of cloth and placed them onto the ledge at the back with the possessions of the busker who had long since disappeared. Alice wondered if he'd been in the tunnel until the last moment, swept away by the tidal wave of water. Richard looked confusedly between Filip and Alice, rubbed his forehead, but said nothing.

'When we get back to the others, I want you to arrange for this tunnel to be sealed at both ends,' said Alice. 'Tight. Impenetrable. Unbreakable. I want us sealed off from the outside to keep us safe from everything that's out there. From both ends and with hard trophene. I want this place never to be found.'

Filip nodded in agreement and put his arm back around Richard.

Alice paused for a moment and looked back into the darkness. She knew sacrifices had already been made – and many more would follow before their new life could begin. Her heart ached for Jonah but she knew he would not be the only casualty as they continued to build their new world. Things would be different now, thought Alice, but some of the terrible sacrifices would be worth it.

Then, together, the three of them stumbled in perfect silence past the bricked-up alcoves and mosaics towards the pale circle of light at the other end of the tunnel.

Chapter Twenty-Two

The Note

Carter

In the thick grass that surrounded the tall, faded building, there was no shortage of insects that hissed and clicked, picking at Carter's skin through his shredded shirt. The dark grey cloud had crept its way across the sky throughout the afternoon and was now plump and ugly, positioned directly above him, waiting to release the remains of its cargo across the ruins of the city. Survival was the most important thing now. He pushed thoughts of Isabella to the back of his mind, He couldn't bear to believe she was dead.

He made it inside before the first of the rains came – up the inky dark stairs and through the innards of the tower block. As the rain started to fall across the city, he pushed open the smashed remains of the doors to each of the flats, exhausted. Each was empty, desolate and ruined, with everything broken – until he came to the one at the end. Apart from some dust, the door that stood slightly ajar was pristine and the number 59 on the door was almost shiny.

The flat was nothing like the house in the Deadlands that he had been into with Lily. There was no water damage and it smelt surprisingly cool and fresh. A few feathers floated from corner to corner and some insects crept across the floor but, all in all, it was remarkably clean and tidy. There were a pile of books at one side of the room and some blankets wrapped tightly in plastic on a rester. Carter walked towards the large doors that led out onto a balcony overlooking the city. Someone had boarded them up in part and covered the rest with clear plastic. There was something calm about the room, something different.

In a corner stood a box with EMERGENCY RATIONS, written in thick red letters across the top. It looked solid and full. Using a knife from the kitchen, he prised it open and inside there were cartons with pictures of food on them. He chose the SUPER LONG LASTING STEW NEW VARIETY and pulled the ring on the can.

It tasted sour and made him feel sick. But it was vaguely edible and better than nothing. The next one, FISH COCKTAIL, was less appealing and, as he swigged it back from the can, he retched violently and threw the can into the dirty, brown sink. The sharp clank sounded throughout the whole of the apartment, and upstairs there was the dull flutter of movement.

Back through the kitchen door Carter looked up the stairs and tested his weight against the first two.

'Hello?' he called tentatively, but there was no answer. On the wall leading up the stairs, there was the crinkled paper of an old, battered map with the word GONE scrawled across the middle. He traced his finger around the edges of the landmasses. In the unfamiliar world in which he now found himself, a map was just what he needed. Then there was the scratching, moving sound again. He looked up and down the stairs.

Tiny paw prints pattered the edges of the stairs on top of heavy boot marks that had once trod straight up the middle. Carter lifted his leg slowly and set it down on the next stair. The wood creaked like an aching bone. He took the next stair slowly. As he made it to the top, the shuffling started again.

'Hello?' he said, his voice sounding hollow. 'Hello!' His heart beat faster as the noise became louder. Then he saw it. As the rat-like creature with a billowing tail came racing down the landing, past him and down the stairs, Carter screamed. The animal, too, let out a terrified yelp as it slipped out of the door and bounded out of the flats. Carter watched it as it went, his legs shaking and the relief leaving his body in a half-guffaw.

He climbed up the last step and moved loudly along the corridor to wake any other creatures that might be hiding or sleeping. There were no people here; they had long gone. Upstairs, the rooms were less well kept but each had a clean rester and in each one was a pack of clothes in a plastic coverlet. Carter pulled open the pack and, inside, there was a shirt that was in slightly better condition than the one he was wearing and a pair of jeans that didn't need a belt. He put them on and felt the fresh softness of something old and something new wash over him.

He wrapped his arms around himself and thought of his parents, desperate to make a new life for everyone, sacrificing themselves for a new Community. He still couldn't decide whether he admired them or hated them but, more than anything else, he wished they were with him now. Them and Isabella. Somehow he would get back to her; he would make the change he had promised. He made his way downstairs and gently pulled the map off the wall; from this height, he might be able to work out where he was. He'd known the tower was a good choice.

As he crossed the room towards the balcony, he found the note still propped up against the wall on the mantelpiece. The paper had yellowed with age as well as much folding and unfolding. But in the last rays of the day, he could still pick out the words slowly as they slipped from the page.

If you are reading this, then you will have survived the Storms that raged for over five years and destroyed much of what was real to people. Who knows what stories you have heard or how long after I have written this letter you will find it, but I can guarantee you that whatever we create in the future will be by careful design. This letter is our legacy – what we leave to you by way of you knowing we were here. But do not follow us, do not come for us. Our community is designed for peace, sustainability and freedom.

We will likely have already closed our borders and have the technology to create whatever it is that we need. We do not need the old world and its old ways and, in time, we will have erased much, if not all that remained before.

We are creating a paradigm shift, changing what it is to live in a world where materiality and complexity no longer define who we are and what we want for the world around us. We are the change we want to be.

You cannot be with us, but do not be against us. Create a world for yourself that you are proud to be a part of and that enables you to be the person you want to be. It will not be easy, but believe me when I tell you that after what I have been through, nothing is impossible.

Some notes for survival:

Beware of the wolves – they seem to come mostly in the afternoons or whenever they are hungry.

The river is poisoned – do not try to cross it or attempt to swim in it. If you do, you will die.

There are plants you can eat; they exist in the woods and the forests but be careful.

Take rainwater from the roof – even the rainfall has a pattern. If you observe it for long enough, you will create a pattern for yourself. Choose well; live well.

And finally, this is for my mother – should you ever come back to look for me, you should know that I went to a better place. My life without you has been more than it could have been with you – I knew that then, and I know that now.

Also know that I am safe, and with or without you – I always was. This is just the start of things.

Alice Lisle Davenport

P.S. Please do not remove or destroy this note.

At the bottom, three more words had been scrawled in a completely different script. The writing was fresher, less faded.

Go to the balcony

Carter looked at the words for a long, long time before he put the note back on the mantelpiece and picked up the map. Twice more he picked up the note and put it back before he had memorised every word; every word that had been written by Alice Davenport herself. Alice, the original Scout from the countless films of those initial days above ground, where the Scouts and the First Gens had built a new future for everyone. This is where it had all started.

He opened up the door out onto the balcony to taste the sweetness and relief of fresh air. The rain was still light and slow but there was a swirl of dark cloud that blotted out the brightness of the sun, and a gloomy shadow that heralded the start of another big downpour. In the distance, Carter could just make out the shapes of tall buildings and the dark outline of a giant wheel. And, although it wasn't in view, out across the floodplain and past the river, the late afternoon lights of Unity Square twinkling back at him would shine oblivious and blur with the rain.

There was no going back now, without a plan and without a purpose. But he would find one and create a place that he could bring Ariel to eventually – although he had no idea how. His heart ached at the thought of the Community and of Isabella; she would have loved the new world. But he would do what his parents would have wanted. He would rest and wait until he had a plan of clear direction. There would be more places like the farmhouse he and Lily had visited where there would be books to learn from and a way to survive. And he would make sure everyone knew about the Industry. And Isabella might even be alive, deep down in the Catacombs. He would find out. He would find a way, and he would save her.

The faint line of the horizon marked the difference between land and sky. He pulled out the map and rested it on the railing, looking at the shapes of the landmass against the skyline. It was then he realised that the underside of the map was different, hand-drawn, notated with references, and snaking across the middle was the thick loop of the Black River. In the far corner was the Community, its sketched features all crossed out with scratchy red colouring. Across where the Community lay on the map, someone had written: DANGER – KEEP OUT.

Spreading out into the Deadlands, the map was marked with tiny crosses and clusters of squares that looked like they might be buildings. Carter felt his mouth open wide: the map had been drawn after the Community had been established. He cast his eyes from the map across the edges of the brittle landscape and traced the horizon with his finger. He would follow the markings and use the direction of the sun to find them.

It was only then that he noticed how the thick piles of stones in the undergrowth below the balcony were arranged. Not randomly, but in a very distinct pattern.

There were patches – faint and less bright patches where only thin, raised amounts of tangle had grown over the stones that were embossed with green. The stones were set in straight lines and curves that spelled out three words that made his hands tremble as the final rays of the pale sun shone across the derelict Deadlands. He put down the map and looked again at the ground as he read the stone words embedded in the grass over and over. His heart beat faster as the words rose up to meet him.

THERE ARE OTHERS

A Letter From Ceri

Hey there,

Thank you very much for reading *The Rising Storm*. I hope you enjoyed finding out what happens at the end of the world. But what happens after the end of the end? You'll have to wait and find out.

The other two books in the trilogy will be coming very soon. If you'd like me to drop you an email when the next book is released, you can sign up here:

www.cerialowe.com/email

If you love Alice and Carter the way I do, it would be great if you would consider writing a review and telling other people – especially which bits really resonated with you and what you really liked. It's so important to get your feedback so that the people of the Community have a voice. It's what they need, right?

Don't worry; I won't share your email address with anyone – I'll just use it to keep you up to date with anything related to the Industry.

And if you want to find out more about me, you can also visit my website or follow me on Facebook or Twitter.

I look forward to hearing from you!

Ceri

@cerilowepetrask

cerialowe

www.cerialowe.com

Acknowledgements

This book has been some time in the making, which makes thanking the many people who have contributed and supported me take longer than it should. But I'll give it a shot.

Firstly, my coaches Lucy Pearce, Michael Druce and Annie Grove-White for giving me the confidence to start this at the outset. My initial readers, Dorota Filipowicz, Bobbie Allen and Kerry-anne & Nancy Mendoza, for their encouragement and inspiration; Iseult Murphy for her excellent, ongoing ideas and diligent editing; and Hannah Quinn, for her overwhelming love and support, re-reads and for not ever letting me give up. My family: for my dad, John Lowe, and especially my grandmother, Elvira Lowe, for believing in me – I still think of you every day. And special thanks to Kristina Kunsteinaite. For Formentera, which has always been there and always will be – especially Can Gavinu where the first page of the first draft of the first chapter of this book was written. And then, thanks to those who've been there in the final stages, giving me encouragement and understanding: my forever friends – Becky, Jayne, Jill, Sarah, Janine and Claire, my creative writing groups, my Twitter and Facebook friends and followers. And most especially to Lara for knowing I could do this – and to Barney and Pablo for the constant distractions.

Huge thanks to my editors Hannah Todd and Ellen Gleeson, and publisher Oliver Rhodes and his amazing team at Bookouture for their excellent interventions and support. But also for believing in Carter and Alice and what they have to say about the world today – and in the future. For those I know and love, this is for you; you inspire me. But more than anyone, this book is for my sister, Sally Andrews, who reminds me every single day what it means to be strong and independent and to always make life worth living – whatever the circumstances.

'Conventional names define a person's past: ancestry, ethnicity, nationality, religion. I am not who I was ten years ago and certainly not who I will be in twenty years… The name 2030 reflects my conviction that the years around 2030 will be a magical time. In 2030 we will be ageless and everyone will have an excellent chance to live forever. 2030 is a dream and a goal.'

— FM-2030, transhumanist philosopher and futurist